500
SF

Praise for JOHN TWELVE HAWKS and

SPARK

"Twelve Hawks, like a character in his story, is untethered by technology and unreachable by the tentacles of the Vast Machine. He is a free spirit, a lone voice of reason in a data-fogged world."
—*San Francisco Chronicle*

"*Spark* is a marvel. An utterly gripping, unbelievably imaginative tale with all the heart, drive, and humanity that its hero, Jacob Underwood, a contract assassin, lacks. . . . At once a heart-pounding thriller, a bitter indictment of our growing surveillance state, and a life-affirming story of the indomitability of the human heart."
—Christopher Reich,
New York Times bestselling author of *Rules of Deception*

"Breathless action. . . . Twelve Hawks sets up the battles in *Spark* as more than simple combat. His appeal lies in his pairing of one system of belief against another and letting them duke it out."
—*The New York Times*

"From start to finish *Spark* defies expectation, joining a 'dead' man's cold regard with suspense at fever pitch."
—*Locus*

"As good as the Fourth Realm books were, this one may be even more appealing: less fantastic, more grounded in a contemporary real world, with a narrator who is deeply scarred and endlessly fascinating."
—*Booklist* (starred review)

JOHN TWELVE HAWKS
SPARK

John Twelve Hawks is the author of the
New York Times bestsellers *The Traveler,*
The Dark River, and *The Golden City.*

www.johntwelvehawks.com

SPARK

JOHN TWELVE HAWKS

SPARK

A NOVEL

VINTAGE BOOKS
A Division of Penguin Random House LLC
New York

FIRST VINTAGE BOOKS EDITION, JULY 2015

Copyright © 2014 by John Twelve Hawks

All rights reserved. Published in the United States by Vintage Books,
a division of Penguin Random House LLC, New York, and distributed in Canada
by Random House of Canada, a division of Penguin Random House Ltd., Toronto.
Originally published in hardcover by Doubleday, a division of
Penguin Random House LLC, New York, in 2014.

Vintage and colophon are registered trademarks of
Penguin Random House LLC.

The Library of Congress has cataloged the Doubleday edition as follows:
Twelve Hawks, John.
Spark: a novel / John Twelve Hawks.
pages cm
1. Assassins—Fiction.   2. Dystopias—Fiction.   I. Title.
PS3620.W45S73 2014   813'.6—dc23   2013042626

Vintage Books Trade Paperback ISBN: 978-0-8041-7050-5
eBook ISBN: 978-0-385-53868-8

Book design by Michael Collica

www.vintagebooks.com

Printed in the United States of America
10 9 8 7 6 5 4 3 2 1

The Buddha has given me the gift of friendship with six women who are strong, creative, and righteous. This book is dedicated to Molly, Joyce, Susan, Pat, Tree, and Rosanna.

Death is not an event in life: we do not live to experience death. If we take eternity to mean not infinite temporal duration but timelessness, then eternal life belongs to those who live in the present.

—LUDWIG WITTGENSTEIN,
Tractatus Logico-Philosophicus

SPARK

1

Forget faith and uncertainty, rebellion and slavery. Forget beauty in all its forms. Forget ugliness, too.

Forget "A Mighty Fortress Is Our God" and the Kaddish. Forget an army of notes marching across a sheet of paper that are transformed into the *Goldberg Variations*. Forget the Taj Mahal at sunrise and the Grand Canyon at sunset, Shakespeare's sonnets, *War and Peace*, and *The Importance of Being Earnest*. Forget the dabs of bright blue paint that became the eyes of Vincent van Gogh.

Forget the fingertip sensation of fur, velvet, a cashmere shawl, and a smooth green chip of beach glass. Forget the moist texture of raw meat and dry brittleness of dead leaves crushed in the hand.

Forget the taste of honey-soaked baklava. Ripe mango. Roasted garlic. Pickled herring. Licorice. Chocolate. Strawberry ice.

And smells—forget them as well. Crushed lilacs and the harsh scent of hot tar. A baby's neck. Moist earth. Fresh-baked scones.

Forget the dead children from the Day of Rage and the speeches and sermons and memorial parks with names carved in stone. Forget every lesson from a teacher, every joke from a joker; every judgment from a judge.

Forget what your parents told you. Forget what you were taught as a child and what you learned on your own.

Forget what you think is right. And wrong.

Do all this and you might become me: a Spark contained within a Shell that stood in a doorway on Sixty-Second Street in Brooklyn while a Russian businessman named Peter Stetsko attempted to park his car.

It was November in New York City—damp and cold. Death was present in the street, but there was nothing dramatic or sinister about my appearance. That night, I was neatly dressed in gray slacks and a V-neck sweater. In the outside pocket of my black raincoat, I carried a Brazilian-made semiautomatic pistol with skateboard tape attached to the grip. My Freedom ID card was concealed within a specially designed sleeve that made it impossible for the EYE system to detect my location.

A delivery van passed through the intersection, its tires hissing on the wet asphalt. I slipped on a phone headset and Laura whispered into my ear.

"Ten-Thirty-Three on Flatbush Avenue and Farragut Road. One unit responding."

"Any police activity in Bensonhurst?"

"Checking . . ." It felt as if Laura was a real woman looking up a message board or gazing out a window, but she was only a Shadow. Somewhere in the Internet, one computer was talking to another, checking the data on a Web site that provided live-time reports of New York City police and fire department activity.

"Nothing, Mr. Underwood."

My target had rented a two-bedroom house that reminded me of something a child would build with plastic blocks. It had a low brick wall in front that guarded a patch of concrete, painted grass green. There were red aluminum awnings over the two front windows and the front door.

Since my Transformation, I am capable of a limited range of emotional responses: curiosity, boredom, and disgust. I had been curious if Stetsko could squeeze his Mercedes-Benz between a blue delivery van and a mud-splattered Toyota. Now I was bored with his cautious maneuvering and ready to complete my assignment.

A young woman wearing a sequined green nightclub dress was sitting in the passenger seat of the Mercedes. Because she was a witness, she would also have to be neutralized. I would start with a head shot for Stetsko through the side window, circle the car and deal with this secondary target, then circle the car again for confirmation shots. The sequence wasn't difficult, but it would make more noise.

"Any police activity, Laura?"

"Nothing."

A minute passed.

"Nothing."

When Stetsko pulled out again for another try, the woman got out of the car. Like a photon of light, her green dress shimmered down the sidewalk, passed through the gate, and disappeared into the house. At that moment, my job became simple, direct, and clear.

The Mercedes moved six inches back toward the curb and then stopped. Stetsko's head swung back and forth like a man watching a tennis match. He pulled the steering wheel hard to the right and the car made a squeaking noise.

Sixty-Second Street was dark and no one was on the sidewalk, but that didn't make me feel lonely or frightened. The rotting smell from a Dumpster appeared as a brownish-green color in my mind, but it didn't generate an emotional reaction. $X = X$. The world has no meaning aside from what is.

Across the street, Stetsko finally finished parking the car. He smiled, switched off the engine, and patted the steering wheel as if the Mercedes were a racehorse that had just survived a dangerous steeplechase.

"Show scanned photograph," I told Laura and my target's face appeared on the smartphone screen.

Look right. Look left. No one was in the street. I walked over to the car, held up the phone, and compared Stetsko's photograph to the reality in front of me. Then I raised my weapon and shot reality in the head.

2

I turned away from my target, walked five blocks east to Gravesend Park, and tossed the gun into a storm drain. Perhaps one day a city sewer worker might find this artifact—rusty and covered with mud—but it would have no connection with my identity.

A few blocks from the park I waved down an unregistered cab and paid the driver cash to take me back to Manhattan. For the last two years, I've lived in the top loft of an industrial building in New York's Chinatown. My landlord, an older woman named Margaret Chen, likes the fact that I always pay in cash and never ask for a receipt. There were only three rules for the tenants in her building: no checks, no fireworks, and no slaughtering chickens.

Before my Transformation, I lived like an ordinary Human Unit in an Upper East Side apartment with cooking pots and self-assembled teak-veneer furniture. Nowadays I try to own only one object in each category: a chair and a table, a bed and a blanket, a cup and a spoon. The loft has been used as a factory space by different businesses, and some of them left obsolete equipment bolted to the floor or shoved against the wall. There's an industrial sewing machine with a black rubber drive belt, a drill press, and a piano-sized machine that used to stamp advertising slogans on pencils.

My living space is quiet and clean and unencumbered. None of the objects I possess trigger memories that are separate from their function. I own a cup that is only a cup, not something that reminds me of a trip to Italy.

After locking the entrance door, I removed all my clothes and placed them in nylon bags. Everything worn that evening would be washed or dry-cleaned at a laundry on Mott Street. Within twenty-four hours, all the invisible burned and unburned particles from the fired bullets would disappear.

I took a shower, pulled on a sweatshirt and warm-up pants, and returned to the main room. Rule #4 states that I must supply my Shell with a minimum of two thousand calories a day, so I opened a bottle of a nutritional drink developed for the elderly called Complete, poured it in the cup, and mixed in a tablespoon of a coarse fiber supplement.

I have a good memory, but don't like to re-experience the past. If thoughts are not controlled, then each remembered experience becomes an alternative reality. When I thought about shooting Peter Stetsko, my mind brought up different details—the sound of my shoes walking across the street and the vision of the first bullet shattering the side window. But these memories didn't generate feelings of regret or happiness. I have a Spark that creates my thoughts.

The Spark is bright and pure and transcendent, but it's held captive within a Shell of flesh and bone.

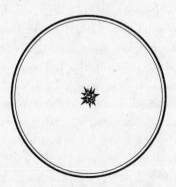

The woman in the green shimmery dress and all the other Human Units walking around New York City feel emotions because their Spark is attached to their Shell.

But all my attachments have melted away. Yes, I can breathe and swallow and fire a handgun. In many ways, I resemble a human being. But there is nothing inside me. I'm filled with darkness.

I opened up a second bottle of ComPlete, then turned on my computer and spoke to Edward. Like Laura, Edward is a Shadow—a speech-recognition program connected to a computer with reactive intelligence. After you purchase and download a Shadow, you can pick their sex, age, language, and general personality. There are Shadows that can tell jokes, help you stop smoking, or say that they love you. You can spend the day chatting with a Shadow programmed to be a cute teenage girl or a Shadow who sounds—and acts—like your mother.

"Hello, Edward."

"Good evening, Mr. Underwood." Edward had a British accent and was programmed to be polite and formal. "How may I help you?"

"Please show *A Boy for Baxter*."

"From the beginning, sir?"

"Yes. Thank you."

A Boy for Baxter is a documentary film about a boy named Gordon who is given a specially trained service dog named Baxter. Gordon is a Native American child whose brain was damaged in utero when his birth mother drank alcohol and sniffed gasoline. He was adopted as a baby by Don and Pat Miller, a Quaker couple, with two other children. The movie begins when Gordon is eight years old. He throws toys at his sisters, tries to jump out of a car window, and pulls all the paint cans off a shelf at a hardware store. But Gordon's tantrums are the most spectacular part of the film. He lies on the floor, screaming and pounding his fists. When Pat tries to help him, the boy picks up a lamp and smashes it against the wall.

After several boring scenes where Gordon's parents talk to psychologists and cry, a service-dog agency agrees to see if the boy can live with a pet. This is when Gordon meets Baxter, a German shepherd, at a dog-training school in Oregon. During the weeks after I left the Ettinger Clinic, I watched one particular scene hundreds of times. Gordon is at the training school with his parents and two sisters, but somehow Baxter knows that he's supposed to be attached to this Human Unit. The dog's head tilts to the left, then tilts to the right, and then he jumps up onto a sofa next to the boy.

The rest of the film shows Baxter and Gordon together. When Gordon is worried or distressed the dog pushes him down, gets on top of him, and licks his face. If the boy lies on the floor screaming and curled up in a ball, the dog pushes his muzzle through the locked arms as if he is forcing open a puzzle.

I would like to own a service dog that would be trained to perceive the different emotions displayed by Human Units. The dog would bark or wag its tail or lick my hand to tell me what someone else was feeling. Together, we would be almost a person.

.   .   .

The following morning I took another shower, drank a bottle of ComPlete, and wrote a message in soft language to Miss Holquist, the woman in charge of the Special Services Section. Miss Holquist is my supervisor. She picks my targets and pays me when I've completed an assignment.

> // Made a successful presentation to the customer. No further meeting is necessary.

Later that day, my payment would be transferred to an account with a British-owned bank on the island of Malta. For my day-to-day expenses, I keep a few thousand dollars with an American bank that has ATM machines all over the city. Both banks require that you use an optical fingerprint sensor when you access your account. My real fingerprints would have been tracked back to my previous identity, but Miss Holquist solved that problem. When I changed my name, she gave me three "gummy" fingers made out of soft plastic. Each finger had the loops and whirls of an unregistered print that was probably taken from someone who lived in a jungle. If I pressed one of these plastic fingers against a sensor pad, my bank account appeared on a display screen.

Peter Stetsko's death was mentioned two days later in a brief article in the *New York Post*. According to the police, Stetsko was an "investment consultant" to the Russian community in Brighton Beach. He had no criminal record, but had once been questioned at Kennedy Airport about the large amount of currency in his carry-on bag.

Now that my job was completed, I resumed my usual activities. I dropped off my laundry, bought a case of ComPlete, and dust-mopped the floor. I like watching sports on my computer—anything with continual activity that makes my eyes follow a ball. That night I spent three hours watching a Gaelic football match even though I didn't understand the rules.

The next morning, I woke up at 6 a.m. An orange light glowed behind a line of buildings, and then the sun floated upward past rooftop water tanks. At 8 a.m., my computer beeped and Edward spoke softly into my earphone.

"Good morning, sir."

"Morning, Edward."

"I hope you're feeling well, sir."

"I'm functional."

"There's some new e-mail in your message box."

Usually, Miss Holquist sends me e-mails with soft language through the public Internet, but this was coded information sent through the Darknet. I accessed the decoding software on my computer, typed in the activation key, and read:

> // I realize that you've just finished a job, but we've received an emergency request to deal with a problem in Great Britain. Please let me know in the next 24 hours if you wish to accept or reject the assignment. HOLQUIST.

As usual, the message included the name and photograph of the target, his last known address, and the fee I would receive for the job.

I went online and did some quick research. The target was an Englishman named Victor Mallory who was the former CEO of a private equity fund called Endeavor Investments. Endeavor had gone bankrupt a year ago and now Mallory was being sued in several countries. I assumed that I had been hired by an investor who wanted a more direct means of expressing his annoyance.

Normally, I would be given a few weeks of free time before my next assignment. Miss Holquist's unexpected request made my Spark bounce around inside my Shell, so I decided to calm my agitation by visiting the pedestrian walkway that runs across the Brooklyn Bridge. Two granite and limestone towers hold a pair of massive cables that display catenary curves—a three-dimensional display of a hyperbolic cosine function. Attached to the curves is a web of diagonal and vertical cables that hold up the bridge platforms. When I stand at the center point and look outward, it appears as if the sky is divided into clearly marked sections. Randomness disappears, and I'm able to sort through my wayward thoughts and place them in different boxes.

.   .   .

I walked down Worth Street to Margaret Chen's real estate office, gave next month's rent to her niece, and then headed south. There are sensors throughout the downtown area, so I took my Freedom Card out of the lead-lined sleeve and placed it in my shirt pocket. A sensor on a light pole detected my movements and the EYE computer registered the fact that on this particular day, at this precise time, an object carrying Jacob Underwood's ID passed through Thomas Paine Park. The park has a huge modern sculpture called *The Triumph of the Human Spirit*. It's surrounded by surveillance cameras so that antisocial elements don't throw garbage into the fountain.

About a third of the people in Manhattan have replaced their Freedom Card with a radio-frequency chip about the size of a vitamin pill. The chip is usually inserted beneath the skin on the back of the hand, and the procedure leaves a distinctive scar. Neither the cards nor the chips require an internal power source; they're read by electromagnetic induction. The chip is detected whenever you take the subway, enter a department store, or walk into a government building. The chips and sensors are always part of the equation whenever I receive an assignment to neutralize someone.

Collecting information from the Freedom IDs is just one aspect of the EYE program—a massive database controlled by the government. EYE gathers information from thousands of sources—web searches and cell phone calls, blog posts and credit card transactions. Every bit of information is stored in quantum computers, and then evaluated by the algorithms of the Norm-All program. Norm-All monitors the opinions of large groups of people, but it also determines each person's typical behavior. This normalcy perimeter is like an invisible circle that defines you—contains you. If you do anything significant outside the perimeter, your behavior triggers an Unusual Activity Inquiry that is sent to the police.

Although my day-to-day actions are limited and habitual, my work forces me to travel to different places and behave in unusual ways. Fortunately, Miss Holquist has friends in the Department of Homeland Security. When I lost my birth identity and was reborn as Jacob Underwood, the EYE system was told that I was a "CAP"—a Certified Anomaly Profile that lacked normal predictability. That meant that it was acceptable for me to pace back and forth on the Brooklyn Bridge, and not be red-tagged by Norm-All. Seagulls squawked and fought on a discarded bagel as I gazed at the cables that divided up an infinite sky.

.   .   .

Every citizen on the bridge knew that the EYE system was necessary for a safe and secure society. And there was a specific reason for this new technology—the death and violence caused by the Day of Rage.

I was a patient at the Ettinger Clinic on the Day of Rage. Usually, news from the outside world isn't allowed to enter the clinic, but the news reports overcame all obstacles. The first rumors were passed from the nurses and the orderlies to the cooks and gardeners and, finally, to the patients wearing pastel pink or baby blue track suits. Staff and patients never socialized together at the clinic, but that morning everyone gathered in the main dining room to watch the news. Dr. Morris Noland, the director of the clinic, sat on a bench between Big George, the second-floor day nurse, and Miss Garcia, the cook. Patients wandered around the room or stared at the television screen.

The first news flash was about bombs exploding at Eton College—the British school for boys near Windsor Castle. Those images of dead bodies and weeping parents were quickly followed by phone footage of an explosion at the Dalton School in New York City. As the day went on, more reports came in from France, Can-

ada, Brazil, and Germany. An unknown terrorist group had organized a simultaneous bombing attack on schools in nine different
countries.

The television set stayed on all night, and I was there early in the
morning when the authorities stated that a mysterious group called
Day of Rage had claimed credit for the bombings. At this point, the
paranoids at the clinic were cowering in their rooms while those
patients with obsessive-compulsive disorders had invented private
rituals so that the clinic wouldn't be attacked. When a woman in
Ward Four had a panic attack and began screaming, Dr. Noland
removed the television from the dining room.

A few days after the bombings, the world was given an
explanation—and someone to blame. Danny Marchand was a brilliant young man with a French father and a British mother. When
he was nineteen years old he obtained an engineering degree at the
Pierre and Marie Curie University in Paris. He started working for a
Dutch software company, and then got involved with the Final Wave
movement. These fanatics believed in technological singularity—
the inevitable development of a supercomputer that could rewrite
its own source code. Eventually the computer would know all past
knowledge and could predict future behavior. The supercomputer
would be as omniscient as God and as inevitable as History.

When he was twenty-nine years old, Danny Marchand quit Final
Wave and began to recruit people to join an underground organization. Some of his followers were anarchists or religious fanatics who
believed in the End of the World, but most of the bombs were built
and detonated for money by mercenaries affiliated with terrorist
groups in the Middle East. No one ever found out what Marchand
believed because he was killed three days after the school bombings during a police raid on his hideout in Normandy.

.   .   .

I remained in the middle of the bridge, staring up at the cables as
I tried to make a decision. Although I didn't need money at this
particular moment, my assignments were difficult and they kept

me busy. The Spark inside every Shell is restless. If we're bored, our hungry mind feasts on imaginary problems. It doesn't seem to make a difference if we are standing in the middle of a bridge or lying motionless on a hospital bed. When I was a patient at the Ettinger Clinic I once followed Dr. Noland upstairs to a second-floor room where they kept a patient named Donald Fitzgibbon. The patient's eyes were closed. His tall, frail body was attached to a respirator, a catheter, an IV tube, and two neural sensors. The room smelled of urine and the respirator made a faint wheezing sound.

"Is he really alive?" I asked.

"Yes, but he's experiencing something called locked-in syndrome. A CAT scan showed acute lesions in the pontine nuclei area of his brain."

"Is he thinking?"

"He's awake and conscious, but he can't deliberately move any part of his body." Dr. Noland shrugged. "Over the last few years, I've given an EEG examination to twenty-five normal people. Each time they hear a beeping sound they are supposed to imagine, in their minds, that they're either wiggling their toes or squeezing their right hand. Even though they aren't actually contracting their muscles, the EEG machine detects two different kinds of activity in their premotor cortex. The brain response for wiggling the toes is different from the one that occurs when we think about moving a hand."

"What does that have to do with Mr. Fitzgibbon?"

"I put some earphones on the old man's head, then switched on a recording that delivered the same two instructions . . . squeeze your hand, then wiggle your toes." Dr. Noland glanced at me and grinned. "The EEG machine picked up the same electrical flare in the cortex that occurs with an uninjured brain."

"So he *is* thinking?"

"Yes. But he's trapped within his skull."

.   .   .

My Spark is also trapped, but I still need to think about something. Neutralizing targets for Miss Holquist creates short-term goals that challenge my restless mind. After pacing on the bridge for an hour, I returned to my loft and sent an e-mail.

> // I accept the new assignment. Please obtain necessary sales equipment. I will contact you when I obtain a mailing address.

"Go to the Web site for British Airways," I told Laura. "Talk to the reservations Shadow and purchase a one-way first-class ticket leaving JFK airport on Wednesday morning."

"And where are we going, Mr. Underwood?"

"London."

3

I rented a short-stay apartment in North London and flew into Heathrow Airport two days later. The apartment was on the third floor of a modern building on Upper Street in Islington—the sort of place rented by foreign businessmen who didn't want to stay at a hotel. The first thing I did was cover all the mirrors with masking tape and newspaper, then I moved the living room furniture into one of the bedrooms, rolled up the white Berber carpet, and stuffed it into a closet.

London's energy surrounded me like a snowstorm. It felt as if bits of energy were drifting down on my head and clinging to my clothes. But I've learned one quick way to calm my agitation. I hammered a small nail into the wood floor and attached a length of cord. Closing my eyes and holding the cord with one hand, I paced out a circle.

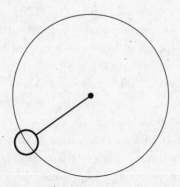

The calm perfection of this motion centered me and helped my Spark adjust to the new environment. My check-in suitcase contained a ten-day supply of ComPlete. I drank two bottles, and then went out to find my target.

Victor Mallory's London address turned out to be a town house in Knightsbridge. It had been seized by a bank and a FOR SALE sign was attached to the outer railing. Using the name Richard Morgan, I called the phone number on the sign and arranged to see the house that afternoon. The estate agent for the bank was a plump woman named Darla. She had blood-red lipstick and dyed-black hair, and looked like a well-fed vampire. After searching through a ring of keys, she unlocked the front door and we entered the building. It was clear that no one had lived there for several months. The old newspapers and moldy clothes smelled like a grayish green color in my mind. Dead flies were scattered like dots of buzz on the floor in front of the windows.

Darla's heels clicked across the parquet floor and motes of dust rose up, swirling through a shaft of sunlight that cut through a gap in the curtains. "The bank is open to negotiation on the price," she announced. "But there will be no negotiation on the condition of the property."

I was looking for a phone number or an address that would guide me to my target's current location. The cage elevator didn't work, so we climbed up white marble steps to the master bedroom on the first floor. There was a slight indentation in the pillow where Mallory had once placed his head, but now the silk pillowcases and the linen sheets were covered with a thin layer of dust.

A guest bedroom and home office were on the second floor. I needed to search the office, but it was difficult with Darla watching me. Silently, we trudged upstairs to a maid's room and I gazed out the window at brick chimneys topped with soot-smudged crowns. "I need to get a sense of the place," I told her. "If you don't mind, perhaps I could spend a few minutes in each room . . . alone."

Darla glanced around the maid's room. A stack of old magazines. Hair clips scattered on the dresser. "No problem at all, Mr. Morgan. I'll be downstairs if you have any questions."

I stood in the maid's room, listening to her shoes tap-tap-tapping down the staircase. Then I returned to the office and searched through the shredded bits of paper in the waste bin. The drawers of the oak desk contained ballpoint pens and menus for takeout food. As quietly as possible, I hurried downstairs to the master bedroom, where I searched the night table and peered under the bed.

I dislike mirrors, but it's difficult to avoid them. I forced my eyes to look downward at the sink as my hands opened the bathroom cabinet. When the mirror was facing the wall I inspected the cabinet shelves and found a rolled-up tube of toothpaste and some nail clippers. But on the top shelf my target had left a prescription drug container with a physician's name on it. I dropped it into my suit coat pocket, stepped back into the bedroom, and surprised Darla.

"Thank you. I've seen enough," I said.

"Yes . . . Yes . . . Marvelous." But she held up her cell phone as if she wanted to call the police.

.   .   .

There is something wrong with my appearance. Although the scars from my accident are hidden, strangers look away when they first encounter me.

The problem could be caused by my haircut. Because I won't let anyone touch me, I cut off all my hair with electric clippers on the first day of the month. I met the estate agent three days after this procedure and the stubble on my skull made me look like an army recruit or a chemotherapy patient.

It's important for my work that I appear as normal as possible. I don't want to be distinctive in any way. When traveling, I'll take phone photos of my fellow passengers sitting in the VIP lounge. Then I'll go to department stores in New York and tell the salesclerk to find clothes that duplicate the costumes of these travelers. I usually wear dark slacks, a button-down shirt in solid colors, and black shoes. But the new clothes always hang loosely on my body as if they don't belong to me.

I take a shower every day (Rule #2) and then smear deodorant beneath my arms and splash aftershave on my face. The aftershave makes me smell like pine trees—the bright green needles brushing against my clothes as I hike through a forest.

I've learned to nod my head when someone speaks to me. I've learned to say "thank you" and talk about the weather. But there's something about me that makes Human Units uncomfortable.

When I was recovering at Marian Community Hospital, I saw patients brought in who were bleeding and unconscious, their legs and arms strapped together as if their body parts had detached and were about to fly off in different directions. A few weeks later, they were smiling and thanking everyone as a nurse wheeled them out to the front entrance. These patients were broken into pieces, and then had reassembled themselves.

But I haven't changed.

.   .   .

When I returned to my apartment in Islington, I called the doctor whose name was on the pill container. I spoke to a receptionist and said that I wanted to pay a bill online. Using my computer, I visited the payment Web site and used "safecracker" software to enter the patient database. Victor Mallory's listed address was the abandoned London town house, but I found what I was looking for—a mobile phone number.

The rest was easy. Pretending to be the company that made his device, I sent a text message to Mallory's phone asking him to install a system update. Twenty minutes later, he pressed the pound key, which linked him to a fake company Web site created by my employers. In three seconds, the Web site downloaded malware to Mallory's phone. Now I could turn on the device's microphone, monitor text messages, and access its GPS location.

A few minutes later, I was looking at a satellite image of a country estate in southwest England. Victor Mallory lived in an eighteen-room manor house built on a low hill and surrounded by an eight-foot hedge. There was a clay tennis court, a picnic pavilion, and an empty swimming pool. Now I had to figure out a way to pass through the barriers and kill him.

It was raining two days later when I rented a car and drove north to Gloucestershire. I had no idea where to turn left or right, but Laura helped me find the estate. If I said I was lost, she would answer, "Don't worry, Mr. Underwood. I know where we are."

Laura sounded like a calm, youngish woman—not your friend exactly—but the competent executive secretary back at the head office who always finishes her assignments on time. Some people buy software that creates an avatar for their Shadow, but I preferred the image in my mind. I decided that Laura didn't wear jeans and T-shirts when she was working, but a navy blue skirt and matching jacket. Her hair was short and black and she had bangs that cut a straight line across her forehead. Edward was very formal and polite. I pictured him with thinning hair and flushed cheeks, wearing a blue suit, white shirt, and regimental striped necktie.

Victor Mallory's estate was surrounded by a hedge that concealed a six-foot-high spike fence. Now that I was monitoring his cell phone, I realized that he never left this protective circle. CCTV cameras were mounted on steel poles at each corner of the lot, and a fifth camera was attached to the intercom panel directly outside the electronically controlled entrance gate.

I had bought three solar-powered Sentinel cameras at an electronics supply store in New York City and decided to use two of them. The rain had stopped falling, but wind pushed against me, whispering in my ears. Moving quickly, I forced my way into a blackberry thicket, planted a tripod, and attached a Sentinel camera so that it was pointing at the gate. Then I returned to my rental car and drove to a dirt road behind the estate. An oak tree grew near the hedge and I attached a camera with the long-range zoom lens to one of the branches.

I activated the cell phones attached to the Sentinels and returned to London. There was a photograph of Victor Mallory on the *Times* database; he was a man in his late sixties with white hair and a saggy face. The next morning, I was sitting at the kitchen table when my target came out of the manor house with a golf bag, stood on the terrace, and hit a basket of balls onto the lawn. A bodyguard carrying an assault rifle followed Mallory down the hill as he picked up the balls and then returned to the terrace and hit them out a second time.

I still hadn't received a weapon, so I sent an e-mail to Miss Holquist:

> // I have arrived in London and have obtained the customer's new address. Where is the equipment for the sales meeting?

She replied a few minutes later:

> // We have encountered problems with our regular UK supplier. Continue with your preparations for the meeting.

Once I had set up the Sentinels I could sit in my apartment and watch live-time images of the estate on my computer. If I got restless, I would leave the flat and take my computer to La Boucherie—a North London butcher shop turned into a café. It was a loud and echoey place, but if you bought a cup of coffee, the staff left you alone.

The camera attached to the oak tree photographed Mallory's daily golf ritual while the Sentinel aimed at the entrance gate showed who had permission to enter the estate. A gardener and a maid worked every weekday, but neither servant lived at the manor house. At approximately 11 a.m., a cook arrived with provisions. Unless there were guests for dinner, she left around 6 p.m. My target employed two full-time bodyguards—a heavyset man in his fifties and a younger man with blond hair. Each guard worked a three-day shift, and then caught the train back to London while his counterpart took over.

Mallory was vulnerable because he had a mistress—a young Asian woman who came up from London on Friday or Saturday, spent the night, and then left on an afternoon train. During these visits, the bodyguard on shift picked the woman up and dropped her off at the station. This meant that my target was alone for approximately forty minutes.

At the training camp, I was told that doors always open for a man wearing a hard hat and carrying a clipboard. People will allow you into a guarded sanctuary if you give them a logical reason for your presence there. Although I still hadn't received my weapon, I came up with a plan and began to accumulate the necessary clothes and fake ID cards. But there was one significant problem. I was born in America, but my plan required me to speak with a British working-class accent. I told Edward to search for acting teachers and dialect coaches in London, and he came up with a list of eighteen names. I needed someone who would accept cash and who worked with students in a building that didn't have CCTV cameras.

After some cross-checking, I picked a woman named Julia Driscoll. According to an acting Web site, Mrs. Driscoll taught students in Stoke Newington—a district in the borough of Hackney. She was not affiliated with any teaching organizations and lessons were given at her home. The Web site showed an airbrushed black-and-white photograph of a middle-aged Mrs. Driscoll acting in a Shakespeare comedy called *The Merry Wives of Windsor*, but a check of the Internet confirmed that she was now in her seventies.

I called Mrs. Driscoll and spoke to her briefly. She had an actress's voice—very precise about the syllables, but somewhat grand in tone and rhythm. It didn't sound like she had many students because she said I could drop by her flat whenever it was convenient.

Early that evening, I took a bus to Stoke Newington and wandered around with my phone, trying to find Watkins Street. Stoke Newington had a lot of redbrick terraced houses with white window frames and gardens in the back. The buildings looked solid and solemn and old-fashioned—like rows of Victorian women glaring down at the graffiti on the fences and the trash in the alleyways.

I stopped outside a pub, slipped on the headset, and spoke to Laura. "Am I close to Watkins Street?"

"You are approximately eight blocks from your destination, sir. Continue south on Oldfield Road, then turn right at the corner."

"Is everything okay, Laura?"

"Of course, Mr. Underwood. I enjoy helping you."

When I reached Oldfield Road I heard a faint whirring sound—like one of the hummingbirds that darted around the garden at the Ettinger Clinic. I looked up and saw that a faint red light that resembled a human Spark was hovering over the neighborhood. It was a drone aircraft, a surveillance device used by police departments and government-approved corporations to monitor the activities of Human Units. Many of them had infrared sensors that allowed them to record images at night.

"So where am I now?" I asked Laura.

"Walk east two blocks, then turn left."

Standing on the corner, I glanced around me to see if anyone in the area was wearing the special eyeglasses called "G-MIDs" (Glass-Mounted Information Display). Recently, several companies had also started to sell "E-MIDs"—eye-mounted contact lenses that were connected to your cell phone.

The eyeglasses were marketed as a hands-free, head-mounted display that would respond to voice commands and provide a bit-stream of information, such as weather reports and GPS directions. But the glasses also offered the ability to record continuous videos of people and events without anyone knowing this was going on. These videos were stored forever in cloud servers.

At first, the G-MID providers told the public that these eyeglass videos were private. Then it was revealed that the cloud computers were programmed to scan and categorize the videos for "technical reasons." A few months after that news, some Swedish hackers proved that governments were accessing the videos and identifying people using facial-recognition systems. This meant that any Human Unit wearing the special glasses or contact lenses was a possible surveillance mechanism.

As I got closer to Mrs. Driscoll's flat, I passed young men standing around with their hands in their pockets, smoking, coughing, and spitting on the pavement. A few of them were selling drugs—or themselves—and occasionally a car would pull up to the curb and someone would talk to the driver.

Most of these people were petty criminals or "bonks," who had neurological damage because of the new pleasure machines that directly stimulated the brain. But I also saw men and women wearing the black knit caps or bandannas that showed that they were part of a loosely organized group called "growlers" in the United States and Great Britain. In France, the growlers were called *fantômes*— "ghosts." The Germans had come up with a more precise term— *Unzufriedene*—which meant "the disaffected."

Because of the increased use of nubots and Shadow programs, 20 to 30 percent of the young people in Europe and North America were unemployed or working part-time for minimum wage. Four years before the Day of Rage, the World Bank had published a massive report about the international employment situation. The public report was optimistic about the future; it stressed the need for technical education and praised the new opportunities created by automation. But there was also a secret "supplemental report" that was leaked to the Internet by the teenage daughter of a World Bank executive. This report was filled with graphs and algorithms that showed that nubots were now cheaper than human workers and wide-scale unemployment was "permanent and unavoidable."

As people gradually became aware of the supplement report, there were thousands of "No Jobs/No Future" demonstrations all over the world. But the most dangerous antisocial elements didn't wave signs and gather petitions. Using social media as a contact point, "bash mobs" of growlers would suddenly gather in a shopping mall, paint "NO JOBS" on the wall, and then destroy everything in sight. Sometimes they would break into luxury car dealerships at night and attack the cars with hammers. By the time the police had arrived, broken glass was everywhere, but the growlers had disappeared.

There was a massive crackdown on the growlers and their supporters after the Day of Rage bombings. In the United States, thousands of people were sent to Good Citizen Camps in Utah and Kentucky. In Russia, anyone involved in the Day of Rage was executed by military firing squads. After the initial wave of arrests and executions, almost every large country established an EYE monitoring and normalcy program to keep their antisocial elements under control. Any United States citizen who displayed TABS (Terrorist Activities, Behavior or Statements) could be held without trial for sixty days.

And yet—after all this monitoring and control—the growlers could still be found in most large cities. There was also a growing movement of New Luddites who called themselves "Children of Ned." The Luddites attacked the nubots and tried to sabotage the technology of surveillance. If a stylish person was strolling through Stoke Newington wearing G-MIDs, they might be forced to toss their special eyeglasses onto the sidewalk, and then watch as the Luddites smashed it with their boots.

It didn't bother me to be walking down a dark street dotted with drug dealers and growlers who had probably been arrested a few times. Since my Transformation, I'm incapable of experiencing fear. If someone attacked me, my actions would not be restrained by conscience or morality. The petty criminals in Stoke Newington had a certain animal sensitivity to danger. When I strolled past the different groups, they lowered their eyes or looked away.

Mrs. Driscoll lived on the top floor of a three-story terrace house. When I rang the bell, she clattered downstairs and flung open the door. She had thinning old-lady hair, dyed blond. Her eyes were bright blue. She wore a white blouse and a gray ankle-length skirt with a great many pleats. And jewelry, lots of jewelry: beaded necklaces hanging from a skinny neck, earrings, and four or five bracelets on each wrist.

"Are you the man who called about lessons?"

"Yes. I'm Richard Morgan."

"It's a pleasure to meet you. Please come in . . ." Mrs. Driscoll waved me into the vestibule and closed the door while a little white dog barked at the top of the stairs. "That's Joey." She called up to her pet. "Say hello to our new friend, Joey!" Then she turned to me and smiled. "Don't worry, Mr. Morgan. Joey is more bluster than bite. You're an American. Is that correct?"

"Yes."

"Well, my little darling has met two Americans in his life and he liked them both."

Mrs. Driscoll's bracelets clicked against each other as she led me upstairs to her flat and guided me into the front parlor. The room was crammed with heavy-looking furniture, tea tables, and lamps made from Chinese vases. Everywhere you looked there were framed photographs of Joey and black-and-white prints of Mrs. Driscoll acting in various plays. An oil painting of a thin man with a neatly trimmed mustache hung over the fireplace.

"That's the late Mr. Driscoll," she announced, standing in front of the portrait. "I'm a bit of a flibbertigibbet, a sparrow fluttering through life. Mr. Driscoll was my rock, my center."

I declined a cup of tea, and then sat on the edge of a green brocade chair while Mrs. Driscoll and her dog took the sofa. As she chattered about her dead husband, Joey gazed at me in that curious dog manner. Dogs are the only living creatures I will touch and tolerate. But sometimes they're wary of me, and they'll growl and lower their ears.

"Thank you for seeing me so quickly, Mrs. Driscoll. You have a very nice home."

"The rest of the flat is my personal residence, but this . . ." She gestured to the parlor. "*This* is the transformation room. You are sitting where men and women of all ages and walks of life have lost their dreadful accents and gained confidence. The transformation room is where students learn that clear spoken language is the first step to true communication."

Throughout her little speech, Mrs. Driscoll stared at me and saw my shaven head, my awkward body, my general strangeness. Joey was evaluating me, too—sniffing with his wet black nostrils and tasting the air with his tongue.

"So what brings you here, Mr. Morgan? Do you have to give a speech or make some sort of business presentation? I have helped several students who were paralyzed with fright whenever they stood in front of a crowd."

"Mrs. Driscoll, I have always believed that honesty is the best policy."

"Yes, of course." She nodded. "Honest communication is necessary between student and teacher."

"I don't meet a lot of people at work, Mrs. Driscoll. I spend most of my time talking to computers."

Mrs. Driscoll took a sip of tea. "That kind of job is very common these days."

"And maybe because of this, I've suffered from depression."

"Ahhh, yes. Now I understand." Mrs. Driscoll's shoulders relaxed and she leaned back against a fringed pillow. "Say no more, Mr. Morgan. *Say no more.* I myself have been visited by a black cloud of sadness several times in my life, especially since the passing of Mr. Driscoll, but Joey rescued me. . . ." She reached out and stroked her dog. "Dear, dear Joey. My little savior."

"I've been going to a therapist," I said. "And he recommended that I join an amateur theatrical society. Last month, I started taking classes with a group that meets at a Methodist church in West Wickham."

Mrs. Driscoll clapped her hands together and the bracelets jingled brightly. "*Yes,* Mr. Morgan! The theater can heal a wounded spirit and broken heart! I've seen it countless times. When we are completely artificial, we can find out what's real."

"One of the plays we're considering for the spring is called *Look Back in Anger.* I'd like to learn a working-class British accent so I can give a great audition."

"That is a marvelous idea! Simply marvelous! I would be pleased and proud to be your teacher."

We started our first lesson five minutes later. I had looked up the play on the Internet and downloaded a copy. Mrs. Driscoll knew the different characters and decided that I should audition for the role of Cliff—a man with a South Wales accent.

After that first lesson, I would arrive at the apartment three nights a week, carrying a briefcase as if I had just come from my imaginary job in Canary Wharf. Mrs. Driscoll would chat about her day, then sit on the couch and begin teaching. We studied the "Welsh Glide"—where I had to stretch out vowel sounds while my voice glided downward from high pitch to low pitch. Gradually, I became comfortable with dropping the "yea" sound in a word and rolling my Rs slightly by pushing my tongue against the roof of my mouth.

Mrs. Driscoll didn't have a Shadow and rarely used her computer. I assumed that she would be curious about my job and family, but my teacher preferred to talk about her own experiences as an actress and the "rogues and Romeos" who had "trifled" with her heart before she met Brian Driscoll—a Chartered Accountant who had taken her on "delightful holidays" to Greece and Spain.

One evening on the train to Stoke Newington I realized that I was looking forward to my lesson. Mrs. Driscoll radiated a warm energy that kept my foot from jiggling when I crossed my legs. I liked the slow movements of her hands and the sound of her bracelets clicking together. I liked the smudge of lipstick on the edge of her teacup and the sound of her breathing—the humanness of this Human Unit.

There was only one problem with my teacher: she found pleasure touching things—Joey, of course, along with her silk scarves and cashmere sweaters. I didn't tell her about my list of rules, but I said that I disliked being touched because of psychological problems. Once Mrs. Driscoll touched my arm, then remembered and quickly pulled her hand away.

"Ahhh, yes. Your dreadful affliction. But you will touch Joey. Won't you, Mr. Morgan? Isn't he a dear little thing?"

"Yes, he is," I said, and then I touched him. Joey's fur was soft and his body was warm. He was indisputably alive.

"After Mr. Driscoll passed on, I was so sad until my little darling came into my life. Mr. Morgan, with all affection and respect, I do feel that you should consider getting a dog. Sometimes . . ." Her thin hands fluttered through the air and the bracelets jingled. "Sometimes you seem so *lonely*. You're the loneliest man I've ever met."

I took my hand away from the dog. "Let's continue with our lesson. . . ."

·   ·   ·

Six days after I set up the Sentinel cameras, a FedEx deliveryman arrived at the apartment with a large box labeled GOLF EQUIPMENT. Inside the box was a new golf bag that contained a breech-loading double-barrel shotgun. It was an elegant mechanism with a walnut stock, but it was designed to kill grouse or pheasant—not former hedge-fund executives with well-armed bodyguards.

I e-mailed Miss Holquist and used soft language:

> // Received shipment. I am concerned. This equipment is not
> adequate for an effective sales presentation.

Five hours later, I got an answer:

> // We are still negotiating with a new UK supplier. In the
> interim, your equipment was purchased from a reputable
> subcontractor in Brixton. I believe that this equipment is more
> than adequate for a one-time presentation to a single client.
> Please complete your assignment.

But what if another guard was in the house? Or what if Mallory was armed? The shotgun looked like an antique. What if the weapon jammed or didn't work? I thought about sending another e-mail to Miss Holquist, but I knew that it would be a waste of time. Once I accepted an assignment, there was no backing out.

Sitting in the living room, I felt my Spark drift through my Shell like a red glass marble dropped into a vat of honey. Smell of moldy curtains, dusty carpets. Sound of the traffic outside as Christmas music forced its way through the walls from a neighbor's flat:

Angels we have heard on high
Sweetly singing o'er the plain
And the mountains in reply
Echoing their joyous strains
Gloria . . .

4

I spent most of the next day trying to figure out how I would carry and conceal the shotgun. It was a relief to take the bus to Stoke Newington for my evening lesson.

Mrs. Driscoll's downstairs neighbor was returning home with shopping bags. She recognized me from previous visits and let me into the vestibule. I climbed the stairs, knocked twice, and, when no one answered, entered the apartment.

The dining room and kitchen were dark, but a table lamp glowed in the transformation room. "Mrs. Driscoll?" I whispered and, for a moment, I forgot the name I'd been using with her. "It's Mr. Morgan."

I passed through the doorway and entered the transformation room. My teacher was lying on the sofa, curling around a throw pillow. It looked as if she was embracing the pillow, trying to draw it into her body.

"Mrs. Driscoll?"

"Oh." She sat up quickly. Tangled hair. No makeup. No earrings. Her face showed emotions, but I couldn't evaluate them and didn't want to take out my phone to access the emotion file.

"Is everything all right?"

"Joey— Joey is dead. Murdered." She began crying, her fist clutching a lace handkerchief while her lungs wheezed and gasped for air.

"What happened?"

"Yesterday—Thursday—the door was open . . . and . . . and he got out. When I came out of the bathroom, I couldn't *hear* him, couldn't *find* him. I searched all the rooms, of course, then went downstairs and out on the street. I asked everyone— I asked *strangers*—and then—and then . . ." She took a deep breath. "Mr. Lloyd, the pensioner who lives at number fifty-two, found Joey's body dumped in a recycling bin. My darling—my precious friend— had been kicked to death by . . . by a *monster*."

"Who are you talking about?"

"Sheila Cassidy told her mother who told Mr. Singh who told Miss Batenor—the lady downstairs—who—who told me. But now they all *deny* saying it—refuse to talk to the police—because they don't want trouble."

"Trouble with whom?"

"There—there are these young men—on the corner—up and down our street—I'm sure you've seen them. And I was a fool, Mr. Morgan. I was blind—*blind* to the danger. Because I told them to go away and even called the police twice. And they knew me— knew Joey was my pet—and they mocked me and whistled—so I stopped going out in the evening and—"

"*Who* mocked you?"

"This one man in particular. They— They call him 'Micky Sicky.' So he was there on the pavement and Sheila said that Joey was running around, barking. He wanted to play, of course. He loved to *play*."

"And what happened?"

"Micky kicked my darling very, very hard. And then he must have beaten him or kicked him many times, because Joey's body was broken and one of his eyes was nothing but blood. And then Micky threw my love away."

Mrs. Driscoll started weeping again while I stood there like another piece of furniture. I didn't feel any of the emotions listed on my phone's database. My strongest desire was for more information.

"What did the police do?"

"They talked to Micky Sicky, but he denied everything. And he's still there, out on the street, watching me. Not more than an hour ago, when I looked out the window, he saw me and made a barking sound." Mrs. Driscoll got up from the sofa. She forgot all the rules and touched me, pulling me over to the window. "Look! There! Can't you see?"

I peered out the window and saw four young men smoking cigarettes and talking to each other. "The one with the very long hair and the—"

"Yes. I see him." Micky Sicky was a stocky white man in his twenties with matted dreadlocks that touched his shoulders.

Mrs. Driscoll staggered back to the sofa and blew her nose with the lace handkerchief. "It's just a *dog*. That's what my sister said when I spoke to her on the phone. And yes—yes, that's true, but . . ." She shook her head. "But it gives you its love and you give it *your* love and then it's more than a dog. So much more."

Once again, she curled up on the sofa, and pulled the pillow to her chest. There was nothing I could do for her, so I maneuvered around the furniture and slipped out the door. Riding back to Kensington on the tube, my Spark began to bounce around inside my Shell. I remembered Mrs. Driscoll weeping and the framed photograph of Joey with his feet on a striped ball. And those thoughts continued when I got back to my apartment and drank two bottles of ComPlete.

. . . .

When I first met Miss Holquist and began working for the Special Services Section, she emphasized one fact and one rule.

The fact was: *I was now working for Miss Holquist.*

The rule was: *I must not work for anyone else.*

If I was given a weapon for a particular target, then I shouldn't use that weapon to neutralize someone else. Trying to resolve the problem, I told Edward to activate the Power-I program on my computer. I used the program to make two lists:

Advantages gained by neutralization of Victor Mallory	**Advantages gained by neutralization of Micky Sicky**
■ Satisfaction of plan accomplished ■ Return to New York City ■ Payment sent to bank account	■ No plan ■ Must remain in London ■ No payment

© Power-1   XXX3094085UNDERWOOD

Eventually, my Spark was absorbed by darkness, but when I woke up the next morning the thoughts remained. After the shops opened, I found a hardware store and bought a hacksaw and nylon cord. Then I returned to my apartment and cut four inches off the barrels of my shotgun and two inches off the walnut stock. I tied one end of the cord to the barrel and attached the other end to an eye screw twisted into the stock. With some minor adjustments, I could conceal the weapon beneath a navy blue waterproof smock with a fake corporate logo sewn onto the breast. While I was examining my silhouette in the bedroom mirror, the Sentinel camera photographed Mallory's mistress arriving for her weekend visit. In the past, the bodyguard had always driven her back to the train station on Sunday afternoon.

It was time to start the plan. I took the tube to South London and rented a white delivery van for the weekend. It was raining as I crossed back over the river. Yellow headlights came toward me like blurry eyes. Cold drops of water exploded on the windshield and trickled down the glass. When I got back to my apartment I sat on the one chair in the middle of the living room with the sawed-off shotgun on my lap.

I was safe. No one was touching me. But then my Spark began to vibrate rapidly and visions appeared that I could not control. I saw Micky Sicky grab Joey and throw him against a wall. Then he began kicking the dog with his heavy black boots. Smiling. Laughing.

I do not believe in justice and fairness and decency. These words have no form or shape for me. There is more reality in things: a rusty nail on the sidewalk or a smooth brown pebble pulled from a stream. But thoughts about Mrs. Driscoll, Joey, and Micky Sicky were a *distraction* that would prevent me from completing my assignment. I needed to do something that would push those thoughts out of my mind.

Around ten o'clock in the evening, I wrapped the sawed-off shotgun in a throw rug and placed it on the floor of the van. Great Britain had an EYE monitoring system like the United States', but it was called ARGUS. Although my phone wasn't connected to my identity, it could still be tracked by scanners. I turned it off as I drove the van north to Stoke Newington.

I cruised up and down the streets looking for Micky Sicky, but only a few people were out. After an unsuccessful search I parked the car near a hospital and played a computer game on my phone. Then I returned to Watkins Street and found my target leaning against a parked car.

I stopped the van, rolled down the window, and spoke with an American accent. "Good evening. Maybe you can help me. I just arrived in London this afternoon."

"What's the problem, bruv? You lost?"

"I work for somebody in the music business and he needs some drugs to get through the night. A girl at a party told me to come to this street."

Micky Sicky grinned. Bad teeth. "What's your man's name, bruv? He famous? Can I meet 'im?"

"That depends on what you can supply."

"Got everything. Top gear. Whatever you need."

"Can we get off the street? Being out here like this makes me nervous."

"Go down to the corner, turn left, then right, and park."

I had not planned what was going to happen. At that moment, I felt like a line in a cathode tube, jabbing at the boundaries of the screen with sharp movements and sudden bursts of energy. Following his directions, I turned into a dirt alleyway behind some fenced-in vegetable gardens. Light came from a few windows and a security light attached to a tool shed.

I got out of the van but left the door open. The shotgun was on the driver's seat, the stock poking a few inches out of the rolled-up throw rug.

"Hey . . ."

Micky appeared at the end of the alleyway and began walking toward the van. Picking up the throw rug, I cradled it in my arms as if it was a wounded dog and approached him slowly.

As the target drew closer my right hand thrust itself into the center of the rug, grabbed the stock of the shotgun, and let its concealment fall away.

My legs took two quick steps and then—

My finger squeezed the trigger and then—

The shotgun fired and buckshot cut through the air.

When I was in the clinic, Dr. Noland told me about a logical problem created by a Greek philosopher named Zeno that suggested that the buckshot would never hit its target. The buckshot would take half the time to get halfway there, but then it had to go halfway to the next interval, and halfway to the interval after that, and so on. Since there appeared to be an infinite number of these smaller and smaller distances, the buckshot would never arrive.

I thought about Zeno's paradox for several days until Dr. Noland gave me a solution. A distance composed of an infinite number of finite moments is not infinite. If the distance between the shotgun barrel and Micky Sicky's flesh was fifteen feet, it doesn't make a difference how many times you divide it into fractions; it's still fifteen feet. This was helpful to me at the clinic because I realized that no matter how many times my thoughts divided into a multitude of more thoughts, I could still make a single choice and function in the world.

And this is what happened in the alleyway. The buckshot burst through the paradox and hit my target in his left leg.

Micky Sicky fell backward, then screamed with pain and started rolling around on the dirt. I took a few steps forward and pointed the shotgun at his head. He had lost control of his bladder and I found the smell unpleasant.

"Be quiet," I said.

Micky's mouth opened and closed like a Chinatown carp just pulled from the water tank. But he stopped making noises.

"You killed a little white dog," I said.

"Fuckin' bastard! You just shot me!"

I cocked the second barrel. "You have three seconds to say one truthful statement. Did you kill a little white dog?"

"It was nothing," Micky whimpered. "Just a joke, bruv. I swear. I'm sorry."

"Repeat after me: Joey was loved by the angels in heaven."

"Fuckin' hell!"

"Say it. If you want to live."

"Joey . . . love . . . by angels."

"Good. Remember that. If I see you in this neighborhood again, I'll take a blowtorch and burn off your ears."

I extended the shotgun like a walking stick and shot Micky in the right leg. He was still screaming as I got in the van and drove away. Although I had disobeyed Miss Holquist, my actions had established two facts:

1. I would no longer be distracted and—

2. I knew that my weapon worked.

5

I left London early the next morning. A few hours later, I parked a half mile from Victor Mallory's estate. Outside the van, the sky was a gray, smudged color. The oak and beech trees had lost all their leaves, and the ditch weeds were dry yellow stalks.

Using my computer, I connected to the Sentinel hidden in the blackberry thicket across the road from the entrance. At 10:57 a.m., a BMW sedan left the estate. The younger bodyguard had the shift that weekend and he was taking Mallory's girlfriend back to the train station. I waited a few minutes and then drove up to the CCTV camera at the main gate.

I pressed the red button below the camera and, a moment later, heard Mallory's voice. "Who are you?"

"Dave Pinnock," I said, speaking with a South Wales accent. "I'm from Jolly Good Fellow."

"Jolly Good . . . what?"

"Jolly Good Fellow, sir. I have a delivery here for Victor Mallory."

"I didn't order anything."

"It's a gift, sir." I was wearing a fake ID card attached to a cord hanging from my neck. Holding the card with two fingers, I waved it at the CCTV camera. "Jolly Good Fellow is a specialty gift service. Or motto is: *'When Flowers Aren't Enough.'*"

"I don't give a damn about your motto. What are you doing here?"

"I've got a holiday gift for you, Mr. Mallory, sir."

"Leave it at the gate."

"Sorry, sir. But I can't do that."

"Why not?"

"I do hate to spoil the surprise, Mr. Mallory. But the gift is a case of French champagne. It's against our procedure to leave alcohol or jewelry at an address without someone signing for it."

"And who the hell is sending me champagne?"

"Can't tell you that, sir. It's on the gift card and the card is in the box. Champagne is a popular gift right now because of the holidays and—"

"Open up the box."

"I am sorry, Mr. Mallory. But it is against procedure for employees of Jolly Good Fellow to—"

Five seconds of cursing emerged from the speaker box, followed by the statement: "You are one more example of why this whole bloody country is not competitive in the global economy!"

"We at Jolly Good Fellow are proud of our high level of service."

There was a buzzing sound and the gate glided open. The sawed-off shotgun was hidden beneath the waterproof smock and I shifted the weapon to my right side as I drove up the gravel driveway.

Mallory's house was on the top of a hill with oak trees dotting the landscape. I drove past flower beds covered with blue plastic tarps and leafless trees that looked like twisted strands of rope that were reaching toward the sky.

The pale-yellow house had a domed rooftop pavilion and arched pediments above the ground-floor windows. As the van entered the circular driveway, the door opened and Victor Mallory came out wearing a brown tracksuit.

I got out of the van, loaded the gift box onto a hand trolley, and wheeled it over to the door. I had seen Mallory numerous times on my computer screen, but I now encountered the three-dimensional reality. My target had stained teeth and a dissipated face, but his eyes were alert and focused. Smiling broadly, I stopped in front of him and made a grand gesture to the gift box.

"Good morning, Mr. Mallory. Jolly Good Fellow is pleased to deliver you a Special Holiday Gift."

"Yes. Good. You told me. Champagne. Bring it inside."

He turned away and I followed him through a row of ground-floor rooms. Mallory didn't own the house; he had rented it from a former member of Parliament who lived in Ibiza. The rooms were decorated in the English country style with solid, well-padded furniture and paintings of dogs on the wall. There was an artificial Christmas tree with twinkling lights set up in the study, but no sign of any gifts.

We ended up in a large kitchen connected to a breakfast room. A half-filled teacup and plate with pastry crumbs was on the breakfast table as if Mallory had just finished a snack. But the most important feature in the room was a computer monitor that showed four images from the estate's surveillance cameras. Once I had completed my assignment, I would have to find the video recorder and take it with me.

I wheeled the dolly over to the sink area and placed the gift box on the counter. Watching me carefully, my target retreated into the breakfast room. "Open the box," he ordered.

"I beg your pardon, sir?"

"Open it. Take out the champagne."

"But this gift is for you, sir."

"Make a presentation. It's part of your job."

Was Mallory afraid of me? No. He was focused on the box. Perhaps he thought it was a bomb. I shrugged, untied the red ribbon, and opened the box. Four bottles of champagne had been packed in shredded newspaper along with a sealed envelope containing the gift card. Mallory relaxed when I pulled out one of the bottles and placed it on the breakfast table with the envelope.

"There you go, sir. Please thank your friends for having the good taste to pick Jolly Good Fellow as their Executive Gift Provider."

"Executive Gift Provider?" Mallory muttered. "Bloody nonsense . . ." But his attention was now on the gift card. First, I examined Mallory's photograph on my phone and confirmed that I was in the same room with my target. Then I turned away from him, unzipped the navy blue smock, detached the carrying cord, and pulled out the shotgun. I pivoted on one heel and fired both barrels.

Blood sprayed out of Mallory's body and he fell backward onto the floor. I snapped open the gun's breech, loaded two more rounds, and then strolled over to the breakfast area. My target was pressing his hands against the bright red wound in his chest as if he was trying to force the blood back into his body.

"Help . . . help me," he said. I leaned down and plucked off his headset. Now he couldn't talk to his Shadow.

"Who are you?"

"That's not important."

Mallory started talking, the words spilling out of his mouth. "I know who sent you. Those goddamn Nigerians. Swear to God I didn't steal their money. The market collapsed and everyone took a hit. There was no guaranteed investment. I told them that from the start."

"So you're a businessman?" I asked.

"Yes. That's right." He was gasping for air, and the quick puffing sounds filled the room.

"I'm a businessman, too."

I took out my phone and accessed my file of emotions. About a year ago, I purchased a book published in nineteenth-century France called *Émotions Humaines*. The book had a long essay written by a French philosopher and black-and-white photographs of an actor named Jean LeMarc. Using only facial expressions, LeMarc displayed forty-eight different emotions—everything from grief to joy. I carried the book around for several months and used it to figure out what Human Units were feeling. Eventually, I realized that it was far more convenient to scan and download the photographs.

Bending over my target, I held the phone next to his face and scrolled through the photographs. Mallory's face showed anger, then confusion, then fear. As a pool of blood formed beneath his body, his face changed one last time. Was it boredom? It looked like boredom. Perhaps it was something different. Acceptance.

"Cold," Mallory whispered.

"Your body is telling you that, but it's not true. You're going into shock because your brain isn't getting enough blood."

"Dying."

"Yes. That's a logical conclusion."

"I am"—blood dribbled out of the corner of his mouth, but he managed to say one last word—"dead."

"Me too."

6

As usual, I traveled first class on the flight back from London. I dislike being touched—even if it's only someone's elbow on an armrest. First class allows me to travel within my own defined perimeter. Everything else—the champagne and wine, the cheese plate, the Dover sole sautéed in butter, the fresh-baked scones with clotted cream—was unnecessary. I told the flight attendants that I was fasting and they offered me three different kinds of water.

When I walked out of customs at JFK Airport, I was surprised to see a limo driver holding a rectangular piece of cardboard with the message: J. UNDERWOOD—BA009. My birth name is on my passport, but "Underwood" is on my Freedom ID cards.

"I'm Mr. Underwood," I said. "But I didn't request a car."

The driver was a pudgy little man with a badly knotted necktie. He sighed, pulled out his phone, and checked his messages.

"The reservation was made by Edge Tech."

"I've never heard of that company."

"I talked to a lady named Holquist. She said I was supposed to drive you into the city for a meeting."

"Okay. Now I understand. Let's go."

I followed the driver out of the arrivals terminal and into a five-level parking structure. In the elevator, I noticed a pimple on his neck and flecks of dandruff on his black blazer. I am capable of feeling disgust when I encounter any obvious sign of physical decay:

body odor and bad breath, a hand tremor and rotten teeth. This emotion influenced the selection of my two Shadows; both Edward and Laura sound as if they're well dressed, healthy, and clean.

My driver answered his phone as we left the parking structure. "Yes, ma'am," he told the caller. "No problem. He's in the backseat. We might have some rush-hour traffic, so I would say thirty to forty minutes."

. . .

It was highly unusual to meet Miss Holquist after an assignment, and the idea made me uncomfortable. Did I make a mistake when I neutralized my target? Had the British police learned my identity?

I first met Miss Holquist three years ago when I returned to New York after my stay at the Ettinger Clinic. Dr. Noland had given me the five rules, and now I washed my body every morning and cut my hair once a month. I had gotten used to drinking bottles of ComPlete so my Shell no longer collapsed from lack of food.

But this attempt to act as if I was alive hadn't solved any of my long-range problems. In those days, a shopping bag stuffed with unpaid bills was on my kitchen table and my landlord was attempting to evict me. I have no idea what would have happened if I had simply remained in my apartment, but one morning a FedEx man knocked on my door and handed me an envelope. I was expecting another threat from my landlord, but it turned out to be a letter from a New York City law firm:

NOTICE OF PROPOSED SETTLEMENT
OF CLASS-ACTION LAWSUIT

Dear Mr. Davis:

If you are a former employee of InterFace Inc., the proposed settlement of a class-action lawsuit may affect your rights.

What Is the Lawsuit About?

A group of workers sued InterFace Inc. for alleged violations of Section 3 of the Freedom to Work Act.

Who Is Involved in the Lawsuit?

The class encompasses all former employees of InterFace who were fired or quit during the last two years.

Who Represents the Plaintiffs and the Settlement Class?

The plaintiffs and the settlement classes have been represented in this case by Caldwell, Leslie & Gatz, LLC.

What Are the Proposed Settlement Terms?

The Plaintiffs have recently reached an out of court settlement with InterFace, Inc. InterFace has agreed to pay compensation to all former employees who were fired or quit during the last two years. InterFace does not acknowledge that the company violated any laws.

Your Legal Rights and Options in Connection with the Settlement.

Personnel records indicate that you are in the group of former employees covered by the settlement. You have two options:

- You may exclude yourself from the settlement class and file an individual lawsuit against InterFace. This means that you will not receive compensation from the proposed agreement.
- You may remain a member of the settlement class. If you do so, you will receive a monetary award determined by your highest salary at InterFace and the length of time you were employed there.

Please make your decision, and then contact me by e-mail in the next seven days.

Sincerely yours,
Ellen Larson, Esq.

The Freedom to Work Act was one of several bills passed in Congress after the Day of Rage. The new law said that companies were free to fire any employee, but a worker replaced by a nubot that "appears or pretends to be human" had to be compensated.

I sent an e-mail to Miss Larson that said yes, I wanted the money. She told me to show up at her office at 11 a.m. on Tuesday with pay stubs and other proof that I had once worked at InterFace.

Confident that I was going to pay off all my debts, I showed up at 410 Church Street on Tuesday morning, signed in at the security desk, and took an elevator to the eleventh floor. There was a soft pinging sound and then the door glided open.

A blond woman wearing a powder-blue suit sat behind a desk in the middle of a large empty room. Perhaps it had once been an office, but the walls, the phones, the carpets, and the busy employees had probably been replaced by computers with reactive intelligence and a few call-center humans in Bangladesh.

"Jacob Davis?" the woman asked. She had a southern accent—not a strong one, but enough to take the sharp edges off words.

"That's right."

"Please sit down." The woman removed her headset and switched off her computer. "I hope this room doesn't bother you. We just rented it for the day. I wanted a quiet, private location for our little talk."

I approached the desk and sat down on a folding chair. Now that I was closer, I could evaluate the woman's appearance. I'm in my thirties. The woman sitting at the desk had the hands of someone twenty-five years older, but her face was supple and free of wrinkles, and her blond hair was thick and lustrous.

These days, the most expensive medications in the world are the so-called gray drugs that can block the chemical signal that tells a cell when it's time to die. Gray drugs are dangerous—you shouldn't use them if you're pregnant, and the pills can speed up the growth of tumors. But if the inhibitors are used carefully, it really does keep you from aging. Only the very wealthy can afford these injections, and the drugs give the users a distinct appearance.

In the past, economic class was revealed by someone's accent and clothes. Nowadays old age is the truest indication of poverty.

"So . . . let me look at you." Placing her elbows on the desk, the woman leaned forward and studied my face. I was close enough to smell her rose perfume; it had a dark purple color in my mind. A small electronic device with an LED screen was next to her notebook computer. Much later I would discover that my supervisor always carried a full-frequency detector that sensed wireless transmissions.

"I was told that you were in a motorcycle accident."

"That's true."

"You do look a little odd, but it's not terribly noticeable."

I stayed silent.

"How did you get here, Mr. Davis?"

"On the subway."

"And you can take trains and drive cars, correct? Can you travel in airplanes?"

"I can do all that. I just don't like to get touched by strangers."

"I understand *completely*." The woman's southern accent was very strong at that moment. "People are always pushing and shoving, especially here in New York. When I was a little girl, I was taught politeness. Sometimes I think certain people were taught how to be *rude*."

"So when can I get the money?" I asked. "Do I have to sign something?"

The woman reached into her leather portfolio bag, took out an envelope, and placed it on the desk. "This envelope contains one thousand dollars in cash. It's yours. You earned it by entering this room and sitting down on that chair."

"But I didn't—"

"You will earn an additional two thousand for hearing my complete proposal. You don't have to agree to anything, Mr. Davis. But you do have to listen."

I picked up the envelope and looked inside. Yes, there was money and it appeared to be real. Ever since the accident, I had been told that I was delusional by a series of physicians and psychologists. At that moment, it felt pleasant to meet someone who appeared to be insane.

"There is no Section Three lawsuit. I'm not a lawyer. And 'Larson' is simply a name of convenience. If you wish, you can call me 'Miss Holquist,' but that isn't my name either. I work for the Private Clients Division of BDG . . . The Brooks Danford Group. We're a major investment bank with a global orientation. Our private clients are ultra-high-net-worth individuals who control a wide spectrum of revenue streams. We don't search for new clients. They're recommended by our satisfied customers."

"So why am I here?"

"To listen, and get paid." She leaned back in her chair. "Mr. Davis, many of our international clients possess or control 'black money'—that is, income illegally obtained or not declared for tax purposes. Some of the money comes from the bribes and kickbacks paid to government officials. But most of it is the profit earned by international corporations. Economists have estimated that up to twenty percent of the world economy is somehow connected to black money."

"So it's billions of dollars."

She nodded. "We handle dollars, of course, but also euros and every other currency in the world. You need to understand that we're just part of a system that parallels what we call the 'public' economy. There are black money stockbrokers, real estate agents, and investment counselors. In America, BDG is a well-known investment bank with buildings and computers and hundreds of employees. But overseas, we are connected with foreign banks as well as shell corporations that are only a wisp of paper in a lawyer's office. Everything is well run and well organized, but our clients do have one significant problem."

"They're breaking the law?"

"Not relevant." Miss Holquist flicked the fingers of her right hand as if she was brushing away a housefly. "Let's say you've given black money to a stockbroker or that you've purchased a share in a business venture. And let's say that some unethical person embezzles or steals your investment. What are your options? You can't go to the police. In some countries, you would become a target for extortion. In other countries, you'd be arrested for tax fraud."

"I guess you're out of luck."

"That's the way it's been in the past, but several years ago a Russian bank . . . one of our competitors . . . organized a 'Special Services Section' to deal with this problem. Other banks imitated this move and we had to follow the crowd to stay competitive. I am currently in charge of our company's Special Services Section. This service isn't free, Mr. Davis. Our clients have to pay an additional fee for each assignment. Most of our clients never use our service, but everyone likes the fact that we exist."

"So people steal money and you have them arrested?"

"We aren't police officers, Mr. Davis. But we do have warm relationships with police departments all over the world. The Special Services Section tracks down offenders and neutralizes their future actions by ending their lives."

Miss Holquist kept smiling and staring at me, but it felt as if she had suddenly become harder, colder—like a pool of water frozen into a slab of ice.

"And you do this yourself?"

"Of course not. You definitely have the wrong impression. I graduated magna cum laude with a degree in chemistry from a well-known university, worked in the government sector, and then went to business school. I'm on the board of several charitable foundations and I've raised two children on my own . . . two lovely young ladies."

"Then who—"

Miss Holquist began to tap her right forefinger. It sounded like she was pinning certain words onto the surface of the desk. "I'm *management*, Mr. Davis. I hire and supervise our contract employees. But during my first year in charge of Special Services I discovered that it was very difficult to find competent and reliable workers. Most of the people my predecessor had hired were criminals with substance-abuse problems. They couldn't follow orders and they weren't discreet. I suppose I could have accepted an unpleasant situation, but the Q-scanner changed everything. Are you aware of this technology?"

I shook my head.

"Q-scanners fire a burst of undetectable laser beams that are able to penetrate clothing and provide molecular-level feedback from a distance of fifty meters. They were originally restricted to airport security stations, but now they're used by police departments and corporations all over the world."

"So it's like a body scan?"

"Much more than that. The laser beam is imperceptible and provides virtually instant data. It can sense drugs, explosives, and what you had for dinner. With certain adjustments, a Q-scanner can also measure the adrenaline level in your body. When most people are about to attack someone, their adrenaline spikes. On two occasions my enforcers were detected before they could finish their assignments. And that . . ." She tapped her finger on the desk. "That was *very* annoying. The Q-scanner created a problem that had a negative impact on our efficiency."

"I don't know how you could get around that. A scanner could be built into a doorway. You'd never see it."

"That's correct, Mr. Davis. And ordinary people will always be tense or frightened if they have to neutralize someone. But then I came up with a solution to the problem. I was reading the London *Telegraph* one morning and I learned about a Danish company that employed autistic people to test mobile phones. It turned out that people with autism spectrum disorders were obsessed about details and doing a job the same way each time. If the company required one hundred tests for each unit, the employees would never shirk and lie and do ninety-nine tests. They were honest, reliable, and never complained about overwork.

"So I thought . . . why not hire enforcers with psychological or neurological issues that allowed them to stay calm when they neutralized a target? A calm but efficient enforcer would never experience a surge of adrenaline. Gradually, I found individuals all over the world who matched my new criteria. Our current enforcers rarely get arrested and always obey orders. It's been a great success,

Mr. Davis. The bank's clients are pleased that the neutralization process is handled in a businesslike manner."

"I think you've made a mistake, Miss Holquist. My last job involved speech-recognition systems."

"My staff have entered a variety of databases and we've accessed all your files." Miss Holquist reached into her portfolio bag and took out a flash drive. "Every fact about your life is contained on this flash drive. I know all about your childhood, your college years, your work for InterFace, your motorcycle accident, and your two months in the hospital. A variety of psychiatrists and neurologists have said that you have Cotard's syndrome. You think you're dead."

"Yes. But that doesn't mean—"

"I think you have the qualities to become an excellent contract employee. You're intelligent and college educated. You don't drink alcohol or take drugs. If you neutralize someone, you're not going to feel tension, fear, guilt, or any other psychological issues. All the doctors who have examined you state that you appear to have no friends or family relationships and you are incapable of any sort of empathy. In short . . . you're perfect for this job."

"But what if I don't want the job? Aren't you taking a risk talking to me? I could go to the police and tell them about our conversation."

Miss Holquist smiled. "Tell them what? No one named Holquist works for the Brooks Danford Group and this office was rented for the day by a shell corporation. If you went to the police, a bored desk sergeant would listen to your story, fill in a digital form, then delete it five minutes after you left the precinct house."

We stared at each other for a few seconds and then—without thought or intention—my head nodded. Yes. She was right.

"When you say your employees 'neutralize' someone, that means . . . kill?"

"We rarely use that word, Mr. Davis; it describes an act, not an objective. What we do is different. You are going to neutralize the future negative behavior of people who have broken promises or violated agreements. When thieves cheat and steal from us, it shows disrespect for our clients and the bank. Do they think that

we're weak and foolish? Really? Well, *I'm* not weak and foolish . . .
as a great many people have discovered."

I was surprised by the job offer, but it didn't generate any of
the emotions that Jean LeMarc portrayed in his catalogue of facial
expressions. Since my Transformation, I saw the world clearly.
There was no inherent value in any object or action. The woman
who said she was my mother was the equivalent of a doorknob. A
pigeon flying in the park was equal to an apple falling from a tree.
If I neutralized someone for Miss Holquist, it would simply be a
new kind of activity performed by my Shell—like tying my shoes or
opening up a bottle of ComPlete.

"I still think you're talking to the wrong person, Miss Holquist. I
don't know how to search for people or shoot a handgun. I hunted
rabbits on my uncle's farm when I was a teenager. That's about it."

"You would be trained at a private facility in North Carolina by
former police officers and intelligence operatives. We would spend
a great deal of money to teach you the necessary skills."

"What about the police? Won't they track me down?"

"If you join our team, we'll give you a new identity. Our friends
in Homeland Security will inform the EYE system that you have
a Certified Anomaly Profile. That means your behavior could fall
outside normal perimeters and you won't be tagged."

"Perhaps I could learn the skills, but I've never 'neutralized'
someone before."

"Why should that bother you? Are you really going to pretend
that you have any kind of morality or that you care about the law?
You're dead, Mr. Davis. Is that correct?"

"I—I have been transformed."

"There's nothing wrong with thinking that you're dead, but if
you're walking around New York City you're going to need money.
The bank would pay you enough to create a safe, stable environment. Earlier in our conversation, you said that you didn't like to be
touched. Only rich people live in a world where they have complete
control over who touches them."

I got up from the chair. "Let me think about this."

"Of course. It's a major decision. Once you make up your mind, you can send me an e-mail. In the meantime . . ." She took a second envelope out of the attaché case and placed it on the desk. "Here's your second payment for listening to my presentation."

My right hand floated above the envelope. Then I picked it up and placed it in my coat pocket.

Miss Holquist smiled, showing her teeth. They were white and perfectly aligned. "Now that was easy. Wasn't it?"

.   .   .

The town car from the airport passed beneath the East River, glided up a ramp, and emerged into the sunlight. Yesterday, I was in the English countryside watching a man bleed to death, and now I was traveling through Manhattan. Bright yellow taxicabs maneuvered around each other while the drivers hunched forward and gripped their steering wheels. Within the cabs, the passengers felt as if they were going somewhere. But if you gazed down on the traffic from one of the towers, it looked like yellow particles moving randomly through the narrow streets.

The car traveled up Madison to East Sixtieth Street and pulled over to the curb. "Now what?" I asked the driver.

"Suite 2160, sir. Don't forget to take your luggage."

I entered the building and gave my name to the security guard at the front desk. The elevator felt like a windowless cell with a sur-veillance camera at the top corner watching my movements. Was someone waiting for me? Was I about to be arrested? My Spark became a bright point of red light as I walked down a hallway and opened a door.

Lorcan Tate was sprawled on a couch in the reception room. He was watching a movie on a tablet computer, but when he saw me he froze the image on the screen. Lorcan was another one of Miss Holquist's enforcers. We had spent three months together at the training camp in North Carolina. For most of that time, we ignored each other—until the incident with the dog.

"Finally! The dead man appears!" Lorcan sat up and stared at me. "So what were you eating in London? Did you break down and buy real food?"

"I always carry a ten-day supply of nourishment."

"*Nourishment?* Are you still talking about that drink they make for old people in nursing homes?" He laughed. "Of course the whole thing doesn't make sense. If you were really dead, you wouldn't need any food at all."

Lorcan got up from the couch and sauntered across the room. He was a big man, tall and heavy, with long hair that had a russet color. I couldn't interpret the emotions on his face, but I could feel his energy. I once saw a painting of St. Sebastian—his half-naked body pierced with spears and arrows. Lorcan displayed the complete opposite of this image. Invisible blades of all kinds pushed out of his body and jabbed at the world.

"Where's Miss Holquist?" I asked.

"She's here . . . waiting for you."

Lorcan was very close to my Shell—his face a few inches away from mine. Without the downloaded images on my smartphone I found it difficult to interpret emotions, but I knew, in mathematical terms, that Lorcan was my inverse integer. The most sensitive person in the world is not a poet or a therapist, but an intelligent sociopath. Lorcan instinctively found everyone's weak point and then jabbed at it until he got what he wanted.

That tactic didn't work with me. Because of my Transformation, I lacked both fear and desire. It angered Lorcan that I wasn't intimidated by his energy. His sharp blades passed through my empty body and collapsed onto the floor with a useless clatter.

"You think you're braver than me," he said.

"I don't think about you at all."

Lorcan raised his fist. When I didn't flinch, he sneered and stepped away. "You're nothing, Underwood. Killing you would be like stabbing an empty trash can."

"Where's Miss Holquist?"

"Leave your suitcases here and follow me." As Lorcan led me past the coffee table, I glanced at his computer. The monitor displayed a frozen image of a woman's high-heel shoe crushing a white mouse. The rodent's body was frozen in pain.

Lorcan led me down a hallway past a row of small private offices. Each room had a desk, a chair, a phone, and a shredder. No one was working in any of these cubicles. As usual, Miss Holquist had rented an empty office suite for this meeting.

When we approached a door marked CONFERENCE ROOM, Lorcan's shoulders slumped and he lowered his head slightly. He knocked, paused for a few seconds, and then opened the door.

Wearing a headset, Miss Holquist sat on one side of a long conference table. She glanced up from her computer, wiggled her fingers to say "hello," and continued talking with her southern accent. "Green? No, definitely not green. Your gown is ivory, and those two colors don't go together."

"Do you need anything, ma'am?" Lorcan asked. "Coffee? Lunch?"

Miss Holquist shook her hand and Lorcan left the room. When I circled around to her side of the table, I saw that she was looking at a photograph of a model wearing a long green dress. Miss Holquist clicked her cursor and the dress turned pink. "Pink? Does any grown woman really want her bridesmaids to wear *pink*? This is what a nine-year-old plans for her wedding. . . . What about blue? . . . A dark blue? Remember, Alicia is overweight and a dark color will keep her from looking like a weather balloon. . . . Yes . . . Well, think it over. I'm about to go into a meeting. . . . Brilliant. Love you, too . . . Bye."

The photo disappeared from the computer screen, and Miss Holquist swiveled around in her chair. "My oldest daughter is getting married in nine weeks and she still hasn't picked out her bridesmaids' gowns. These wedding preparations were fun, but now the clock is ticking."

I had no idea how to respond to this comment, so I remained silent. Miss Holquist typed a command and the computer screen displayed the Power-I plan that I created to neutralize Victor Mallory.

"I was very impressed with the plan you sent me for your recent assignment in Great Britain. I liked the delivery uniform, the box of champagne, and the fact that you went to an acting coach to learn the right accent."

"It was necessary."

"Yes, it was. And you actually *talked* to this actress for long periods of time?"

"Each lesson lasted an hour."

"Mr. Underwood, I've underestimated you. I didn't think you were capable of a sustained human interaction. I feel like I just bought one of those new voice-activated coffeemakers and then discovered that it can also speak French and feed the cat."

"I don't speak French."

"That was a figure of speech, Underwood. It means that you're more useful." She moved the cursor and my plan disappeared. Miss Holquist's screen saver showed a teenage girl and her younger sister holding snowboards next to a chairlift. "I know that you like your quiet time, but two of my enforcers are in Mexico City and we're a bit shorthanded right now. Lorcan is capable of assignments that require a high degree of aggression, but I can't send him around New York to interview people." She flicked her hand. "Please . . . sit down."

I took a chair on the other side of the table and Miss Holquist stared at me for a few seconds. "The headquarters of the Brooks Danford Group is here in New York."

"Yes. I've walked by the building."

"A second-year associate named Emily Buchanan worked there, writing reports and preparing presentations for senior executives. Eight days ago this minor employee disappeared. Ms. Buchanan has switched off her phone and stopped answering her e-mail. No one knows where she is."

"Did the bank contact the police?"

"This was one situation where our surveillance technology caused some problems. The bank uses the PAL system to monitor employee behavior. Normally, unusual behavior or trigger words in an e-mail would alert the bank's security staff. But encrypted messages from the Private Clients Division are *not* scanned by the computer. It took several days for Jerome Evans, the head of security, to access Buchanan's e-mail and get permission to read the coded message. What he found was very disturbing. This is the e-mail Buchanan received the night she disappeared." Miss Holquist picked up a piece of paper and handed it to me.

// We are in danger and have left the country. Our previous arrangement is now operational.

"Who sent this?"

"At this point, no one knows. It was transmitted from a public computer at the Dubai International Airport. Although Ms. Buchanan was only an associate, it's possible that she could have obtained access to the private client accounts. Yes, I could contact the police or hire an investigator, but we need to minimize the number of people who know about this. I want you to find this girl and then I'll decide what we're going to do about her. You'll be paid twice the rate of your recent work in Britain. Do you accept the assignment?"

I nodded.

"Good. You have an appointment to see Mr. Evans at the BDG building downtown at nine o'clock this evening. He'll give you more information about your target. Visit the church tomorrow morning at ten a.m. and Gregory will give you some new equipment. That's all for now. Keep in touch."

Miss Holquist dialed a phone number on the computer and went back to looking at dresses as I walked out the door. "I just had an inspired idea, darling. What about burgundy red?"

.   .   .

I left the office building and walked over to the Fifty-Ninth Street subway station. It wasn't rush hour, so I could travel on a train and avoid touching anyone.

Usually my Spark controls my thoughts—remaining in the present and staying away from the past. But seeing Lorcan Tate reminded me of what had occurred at the training camp. During our three months together, we learned about weapons, encrypted communication, and surveillance technology. Lorcan enjoyed the gun range and fighting with the martial arts instructor. I liked using the equipment that allowed me to see in the dark.

We started the course in early May. By summertime, fireflies appeared after sunset and thousands of these winged beetles flashed yellow pulses of light. Thermal scopes turned the physical world into shades of black and white, but the cold light from the fireflies didn't radiate heat. I preferred to look through the night-vision goggles, which magnified the faint amount of light coming from the moon and stars.

Wearing the goggles, I left the training camp one evening and wandered through the forest. The chokeberry shrubs and laurel trees glowed with an incandescent green light and the fireflies were little chips of bright emerald. I hiked a few miles north, then turned around and followed a path back to the cabins. A few hundred yards from the camp, I heard a high-pitched yowling sound and my curiosity led me toward the green light that glowed through the gaps between the trees. Another wavering yowl. I forced my way through some bushes and found Lorcan Tate standing in a clearing.

He had pierced a dog's front legs with a sharpened rod, attached a rope, and then hung his captive from a tree. The dog howled and struggled and twisted its head around as Lorcan jabbed at its belly with a hunting knife.

Lorcan heard my boots crunch through some leaves and spun around. I was blinded for a few seconds by his kerosene lantern, so I pulled off the goggles. "Where'd you get the dog?"

"Took it from a farm about two miles from here."

"What are you doing?"

Lorcan jabbed at the dog with his knife. "Having fun. That's all. What I do is none of your goddamn business."

The dog's mouth was open and its body glistened with blood. As it panted for air, it showed sharp teeth and a lolling tongue. "Dogs are at the top of the pyramid," I said. "They're higher than you or me."

"You're fucking crazy. . . ."

I drew the semiautomatic pistol I had taken from the arms locker and fired. The hollow-point bullet ripped through the dog—killing it instantly. Its empty Shell spun around on the rope, and then spun back again.

Clutching the knife, Lorcan charged me, but I raised the gun and pointed it at his head.

He stopped. "You gonna kill me?"

"Yes. If that's necessary."

Lorcan lowered the knife and shook his head. "I just practice on the dogs. You'd be a lot more fun."

I fired again, hitting the dog's body a second time, and it swung back and forth like a pendulum.

．　．　．

At Fifty-Ninth Street, I followed the stairs underground and found a nubot sitting inside the clerk's booth. The first subway bots were designed with squares and rectangles. They had blinking lights for eyes and resembled wind-up toys. But the development of SynSkin had been a breakthrough for bot appearance. The nubots looked human; their tongues moved when they talked, their eyes blinked, and their chests moved as if they were breathing. Like all nubots, the clerk in the booth was controlled by a reactive intelligence program that gave it the ability to learn from its experiences and change its behavior.

Two Japanese-made nubot models had been purchased by the MTA. One was an overweight black woman named Rowena who was programmed to chat about the weather and make bland compliments about your appearance. But the booth at Fifty-Ninth Street used the second model: a slender Latino man named Sergio who smiled and made jokes.

The growlers hated nubots, and the Plexiglas booth had been scratched with glass cutters and splattered with paint bombs. I stood in line, approached the window, and slid a cash card through the sensor slot.

"A three-day pass, please."

Sergio's eyebrows moved and the corners of his mouth turned upward. "It's a pleasure to serve you, sir. Will you activate your card today?"

"Yes."

The voice sensor had already received my request, but Sergio pretended to type instructions with a keyboard. A few seconds later, a yellow travel card slid out of the slot.

"Have a great day, sir. I hope you enjoy exploring our wonderful city."

"You're a machine."

"That's right, my friend. And I'm a damn good-looking one. . . ."

As I stepped away from the booth, the bot's eyes followed my movements.

7

I left my loft at eight o'clock that evening and walked down Broadway to the Financial District. I disliked visiting the area in the daytime, when the sidewalks were crowded with people who pushed past you and jabbed you with their elbows. But at night, surrounded by the skyscrapers, Wall Street was a clear and quiet maze of dark canyons. Limousines and black town cars idled outside office buildings, their exhaust pipes giving off puffs of white while the drivers waited for their passengers. A phone-repair truck was parked on Cortlandt Street, and its flashing blue light felt like a shrill sound within my mind.

The Brooks Danford Group occupied a twenty-eight-story building on Maiden Lane. The first two floors were an atrium lobby with an enormous abstract painting on the inner wall. The outer wall was glass so that you could look at the art from the street but never get close to it.

I passed through a revolving door and encountered an older black man talking to the young guard at the security desk. He had a shaved head that gleamed under the light, but his Shell was round-shouldered and saggy.

"Mr. Underwood?" the man said.

"Yes."

"I'm Jerome Evans, head of corporate security for BDG, New York."

"I'm here to get more information about your missing employee."

"Our building is protected by a PAL system. Do you know what that is?'

"Personal Authorization Link. It tracks everyone."

"The CEO's office requested that there be no video record of your visit here tonight. The lobby cameras have already been disabled, but it will take a few more minutes to switch off the upper floors." Evans slipped on a headset and spoke to his Shadow. "Deactivate security sector three and elevator five."

While we waited for confirmation from the system, I wandered across the lobby and inspected the painting on the east wall. Out on the street, the painting appeared to be a tidal wave of different colors, but it was actually a collection of tiny stenciled images of pigs and machine guns and old-fashioned cash registers.

Shoes clicked across the floor and then Evans stood beside me. "We're ready to go."

"Who designed this painting?"

"A British artist named X-Nemo. Did you see the blood?"

"What are you talking about?"

"A couple of years ago, the artist was accused of being a nubot owned by a consortium of art galleries, so he . . . look there . . . right *there*."

I peered around a potted rubber plant and saw a dark red handprint on the lower edge of the wall.

"When X-Nemo finishes a painting, he cuts his wrist and leaves his blood on the canvas. The artist's DNA authenticates the work. Frankly, I think most people in the creative field should do something like that. These days, you can't really tell if it was a computer or a human that wrote a film script or created a pop song."

I followed Evans into the elevator and he touched the button for the fourteenth floor.

"So why did they hire you?" he asked. "Are you some kind of investigator?"

"I know how to find people."

"Yeah . . . well . . . I do, too. I was a cop for sixteen years."

"I was told that Ms. Buchanan received an e-mail from the Dubai airport."

"That's right. PAL would have picked it up right away, but private client messages aren't read by the system." The elevator door opened and Evans led me down a hallway. "Maybe Buchanan was involved in something illegal or maybe she jumped on a plane to Tahiti. I still don't know what's going on."

We entered a small office and sat down on opposite sides of a desk. Evans swiveled his computer screen toward me, then began typing commands on a keyboard. "PAL reads e-mails, monitors employee phone calls, and analyzes images from our system of surveillance cameras. This is digital footage from one of the cameras in the bull pen, where the associates work. And this is Emily Buchanan. . . ."

A black-and-white video appeared on the monitor. It showed a section of a large workroom filled with desks and workstations. The date and time were in a box on the bottom of the screen. Using his mouse and keypad, Evans fast-forwarded the video, and then went to a close-up of a woman staring at a computer screen. All I could see was the back of her office chair, her shoulders, and long brown hair.

"The associates do the grunt work for the managing partners. It's typical for them to work late if they're preparing a bond offering or an investment proposal. Ms. Buchanan was sitting at her desk at eleven twenty-four in the evening when she read the message from Dubai. You can see her reaction the moment it appears on her computer screen."

Evans fast-forwarded the digital video until "23:24 EST" appeared on the screen. "Okay. Now watch this. The e-mail from Dubai arrived at our server at eleven-eighteen p.m. Our records show that Buchanan accessed her e-mail six minutes later."

When the message appeared, Emily shifted in her chair and sat up a little straighter. Suddenly, she turned and glanced over her shoulder—as if she was aware that someone might be watching her. Without my phone download of different expressions, I wasn't capable of interpreting her emotions.

"See? You see that?" Evans asked. "That's the reaction of someone who is guilty of something."

"What did her supervisor do when she didn't come to work?"

"Buchanan sent an e-mail to Human Resources. It said that a routine gynecological examination had resulted in an abnormal Pap test. She had to get a cervical biopsy and would be out for a week. Of course no one questioned that. A biopsy? Maybe cancer?"

"So when did you realize that there was a problem?"

"Five days went by, then her supervisor called her cell phone and discovered that it was switched off. He contacted me and I called the medical contact listed in her file. Buchanan's doctor said she had no knowledge of a biopsy or any other problem. I called her only personal contact . . . an uncle who lives upstate in Warren County. He didn't know where she was."

"What did you do after that?"

"I searched through her e-mail. Yesterday I got permission to decode and found the message from Dubai. I contacted the CEO's office and now I'm talking to you."

I took out my phone and spoke to Laura. "Please display the e-mail address for cloud storage."

"Yes, sir."

When the address appeared, I placed the phone on the desk. "Send me a copy of Ms. Buchanan's personnel file and all her e-mails for the last ninety days."

"I can't do that. You're not an employee of BDG."

"You were told to be helpful to me. This is not being helpful."

"I don't have to follow orders from a nonemployee who wants me to violate security protocol."

The Transformation had given me a certain kind of cold energy that could influence others. Without saying a word, I stood up and stared at Mr. Evans. He tried to meet my gaze for a few seconds, then gave up and looked down at his computer keyboard.

"If you don't wish to be helpful, then I will contact Miss Holquist, my supervisor. Miss Holquist is a very efficient person. She will call someone . . . and by ten o'clock tomorrow morning, you will not be in this office, you will not be in this building, you will no longer have a job with this bank."

"Bullshit. That's not going to happen."

"Most of your job is already being done by the PAL system, Mr. Evans. You're just the human interface."

No response. So I picked up my phone and began to walk out of the room.

"Hold it! Just . . . calm down. Okay? Give me the address."

I returned to the chair and watched Evans download the requested information. Then he forced a smile. "Anything else? You want my birth certificate?"

"I want to see the desk she was using in the video."

"There's nothing there. I've already searched it."

"Then we'll do it again."

Evans sighed loudly, and then guided me down to the fourth floor, using his Shadow to systematically disable the PAL system as we passed through the building. We ended up in a large windowless room that looked like a factory for a mysterious product. A table piled with printed documents was at the center of the room, surrounded by a ring of gray steel desks and battered file cabinets. The brown carpet was stained with ten years' worth of food spills and had a moldy odor. At some point, a decorator had brought in a few bamboo plants, but all that was left were brittle stalks and a few yellow leaves.

It was late in the evening, but several people were still working at their desks. One of them was a plump young man wearing a dark blue button-down shirt and a loosened necktie. He looked like a plastic beach toy, puffed up by too much compressed air.

The young man was muttering "Fuck, fuck, *fuck*" while he stared at a computer screen. This chant was almost overpowered by the hum of the fluorescent lights overhead. The harsh light sharpened all the edges and the corners of the room. I wondered if I would cut myself if I touched a chair.

"This is the room you saw in the video," Evans said. "We call it the bull pen. It's used by the analysts and associates who help the senior executives."

"Where's the desk?"

"Over here."

Evans led me to a desk and file cabinet near the dead bamboo.

When I sat in Emily's chair, the little wheels made a squeaking sound.

"So what are you looking for?"

"Any data that might lead me to her current location."

"You're wasting your time. Look at the surveillance video. Ms. Buchanan received the e-mail from Dubai. A few minutes later, she sent a message to her supervisor about the biopsy. Then she took everything personal out of her desk and left the building."

Not knowing what else to do, I opened up the middle desk drawer and found paper clips and felt-tip pens and some pink packets of artificial sweetener. That's when I realized that I could do this job better than Jerome Evans and a squad of detectives.

They saw → objects in a drawer.

But when I look at an object, I can feel its warmth and coldness, its smooth or sharp surfaces. Since I'm not distracted by emotions, I see a more detailed reality.

"There's nothing important in the desk," Evans said. "All you're going to find are pennies and old pencils. Crap like that."

I discovered a list with little checkmarks beside each task or obligation.

✓ *Remco*
✓ *M. Fowler meeting*
✓ *Pitch at TAL*
✓ *Fix computer*
✓ *Prepare Power-I slides*

"An organized mind," I said.

Evans rolled his eyes. "Everyone who works for BDG has an organized mind. This is a sausage factory for deals. A lot of blood and guts get ground up and packaged into cute little hot dogs."

I opened the side drawers of the desk. Note pads. Folders. Envelopes. The file cabinet contained proposals for business deals in binders with the BDG logo. There were lots of graphs and charts and clear plastic pages to separate each section. An athletic bag was in the leg space beneath the desk, so I zipped it open and peered inside.

"Checked that, too," Evans said. "Sweaty socks and gym clothes."

As I sorted through Emily Buchanan's clothes, I realized that the bag had a black nylon liner. I slipped my hand beneath it and found a pair of keys.

"Where'd you get that?" Evans asked.

"Beneath the liner. It's a backup set of apartment keys in case she lost her regular set. What's her address?"

"Why do you want to know?"

"I'm going to search her residence."

"You can't just waltz into someone's apartment. That's breaking the law."

"Address?"

Evans sighed again, then accessed Emily's file with his computer pad. "Buchanan lives at 215 West Eightieth Street."

"Is there anything else you can tell me?"

"The night Buchanan received the e-mail, she had a conversation with one of the associates. He's here right now."

"Can I talk to him?"

"Be my guest. But that's a waste of time."

I followed Evans across the bull pen to the plump young man who had been chanting obscenities when we entered the room. Now he was staring at three versions of the same document on his monitor screen while he stuffed corn chips into his mouth.

"Mr. Underwood, this is Preston Donnelly. He's a second-year associate."

Donnelly kept chewing. "What's going on?"

"As I told you this afternoon, we're concerned about Emily Buchanan. He's making sure she's okay."

"Well, I don't know anything," Donnelly said. "She was just another monkey in the cage. It's all shit. We're shit. I could give a shit. We got a pitch meeting at ten a.m. tomorrow and I've got four more hours of work before I can go home."

"I was told that you talked to her on Saturday night."

"We were working on the same pitch book for a bond-underwriting presentation. She said that the managing partner had signed off on the 'Expertise' section . . . which is the part that explains why we should be hired to play the piano in the whorehouse. I got stuck with the 'Valuation' section, which means proving that the whorehouse is actually worth something."

"Have you worked together before?"

"Of course. We've all done projects with each other. Nothing special about that. Emily and I were in the same group of eight associates hired two summers ago."

"And what was she like?"

Donnelly glanced up at Evans. "I already told you I don't know where she is."

"Mr. Underwood is trying to get a little background information. Management is concerned about her disappearance."

Donnelly crumpled up the empty chip bag, tossed it at a wastebasket and missed. "You know anything about BDG?"

"Not really."

"A lot of women work for this bank, and I'm not just talking about the secretaries. We've got a female managing director and a couple of women senior vice presidents. So, hey, it's equal and all that crap, but this place is basically a boys' club. Twelve-hour days and assholes yelling at you. Dumb-ass jokes. Strip clubs. Golf weekends. So imagine what happened when Emily walked into the bull pen for the first time. She's a small woman who dresses conservatively . . . white blouses and skirts with jackets . . . the usual crap. She wore a headset whenever she was in the building and was constantly talking to her Shadow. Emily wasn't flat-out aggressive like everyone else around here . . . so we figured that she was somebody's niece. A glorified banking assistant."

Donnelly opened a bottle of cola and reached for another bag of chips. "Then one afternoon Dave Muller went over to Emily's desk and asked her to help him with a spreadsheet. She didn't say anything for a few seconds, and then she flicked her hand and said: 'I don't shovel anybody's shit.'" Donnelly laughed and ripped open the bag. "That became her favorite line. She was famous for it. After a while we'd get some new guy to ask her for help just so we could hear 'I don't shovel anybody's shit' one more time. Emily works hard . . . twelve-hour days . . . and it's pretty clear that she's going to get promoted."

"And you were friends?" Evans asked.

"Emily was polite with everyone . . . even the banking assistants and the janitors . . . but she never got too personal. One guy I know from the trading desk asked her out and she told him: 'I don't want friends. I want money.' Every associate in the bull pen works like a machine, but she practically lived here until three or four months ago."

"What happened?"

"She got a boyfriend. At least I guess she did. Nobody ever met the guy. But she started to say things like 'I saw that movie with *Sean*. I went up to Vermont with *Sean*.' He definitely didn't work for the bank. Must have been somebody from the civilian world. And then one more thing happened. . . ."

"Go on," Evans said.

"She stopped wearing her headset, except to make phone calls. You got to understand . . . Emily was *really* connected to her Shadow. So that was a big change. Don't you think?"

. . .

I asked Evans to e-mail me the surveillance camera footage of Emily taken one hour before and one hour after she had received the e-mail from Dubai. Then I left the BDG building and began walking north—back to my loft on Catherine Street.

In order to find Emily, I had to understand her—why she ran away and where she would flee to if she needed a hiding place. This might be a simple task for Miss Holquist. But for me, Emily Buchanan was just a scrap of paper blown down Worth Street—an object in motion rising and falling with the wind.

I stopped at the curb and watched the pedestrian walk light flash red in the darkness. But my Spark stayed with the problem, nosing through it and sniffing each detail like a Chinatown dog rummaging through an overturned trash can. Emily's story about the biopsy was very clever; it gave her more than a week to hide. Her thoughts were organized. She anticipated future actions.

Green light. Time to go. As I stepped into the street, I realized something important. Emily had deliberately left her keys in the gym bag. She realized that they would be found and that someone would take the keys and unlock the door to her apartment.

Perhaps she was still there, waiting for someone to find her.

8

When I got back to the loft, I switched on my computer and dictated an e-mail in soft language.

> // Checked the workspace of the missing customer. Received download of customer's e-mail activity and background information. Found key to apartment and will go there tomorrow.

"And who is the recipient?" Edward asked.

"Holquist."

"Message sent, sir."

I transferred Emily's personnel file to my computer and began to search through the data. She received a BA in economics from the University of Vermont, spent one year as a banking analyst in Boston, and then received an MBA from the Wharton School. The bank had hired her two years ago and, so far, all her quarterly evaluations had been positive. *Intelligent. Asks the right questions. Works well under pressure.*

"Excuse me, sir," Edward said. "But you've received another e-mail from the Brooks Danford Group."

As requested, Jerome Evans had sent me two hours of downloaded surveillance video. I opened up a second bottle of ComPlete and stared at the black-and-white images. I rarely look at Human Units for more than a few seconds, but now I was forced to watch Emily Buchanan and find the meaning behind her actions.

Nothing significant happened during the first hour. Emily sat working at her computer, stood up once, and returned with a cup of coffee. But after she read the e-mail from Dubai, her actions were quick and purposeful. Stopping every few minutes to glance over her shoulder, she took a purse and a tablet computer out of her desk and stuffed them into an attaché case. I stopped at several moments during the security video, held up my phone, and scrolled through my images of human emotions. Was Emily scared? Angry? Her image was too blurred for me to make a conclusion.

.   .   .

The next morning, Miss Holquist's e-mail was waiting in my message file.

> // Obtain a holding mechanism, then go to church to pick up
> equipment. If you find the missing employee, escort her to a
> suitable location for a detailed interview.

Although Miss Holquist had been my supervisor for three years, I knew very little about her life. After she mentioned that her youngest daughter was obsessed with figure skating, I began dropping by the handful of public ice rinks in Manhattan. Early one morning, I found Miss Holquist at the Chelsea Piers Sports Center. She was sitting in the warmest part of the rink, at the top of the bleachers, a dot of royal blue in the middle of a row of light gray seats.

I stood in the shadows of an entry portal, watching her dictate e-mail messages to her computer. Meanwhile a blond teenager wearing black leggings and a red sweater cut a series of patterns in the ice while her skating instructor gave instructions.

"Lift your chest and shoulders down," the instructor said. "Now press into the sit."

The daughter came out of the spin, turned her head, and glanced up at her mother. But Miss Holquist kept whispering *Do this, do that* to her computer—the words translated into binary impulses of energy.

. . .

I switched off my computer, dropped by a Chinatown hardware store, and bought a packet of cable ties—the locking strips of plastic that the police used during mass arrests. The cables would be the "holding mechanism" that would immobilize Emily Buchanan. Then I took the subway uptown and walked over to the St. Theodosius Ukrainian Catholic Church on East Ninety-Third Street.

An old man named Gregory lived with his wife in a basement apartment below the church. He swept the floor, did minor repairs, and took out the trash. Gregory had once owned a janitor's supply store, and then retired because of medical problems. Selling unregistered guns was a side business that supplemented his Social Security check.

When I reached the building, I pushed a button labeled DELIVERIES and Gregory opened the door. He had white hair and pale skin—like one of those cave creatures that lived underground and never encountered sunlight.

"Good morning, Mr. Underwood. I was expecting you. Your lady friend called me yesterday."

Gregory's lungs made a wheezing noise as he led me upstairs, unlocked a door, and motioned me into the church. The windows and door frames were made of white marble, and the redbrick walls had bands of ornamental stone that looked like some mysterious form of writing. There was a mosaic of Christ high up on the wall behind the altar, but the windowpanes were ordinary glass. Over the years, the windows had been covered with dust and soot from the city and now—even on a bright winter day—the sun was feeble and distant. The room was so cold that our breath came out in little puffs of white.

"You're lucky you don't need an assault rifle," Gregory said. "All I have are handguns right now. I'm supposed to give you two of them."

"And why is that?"

"Your lady friend said that you're gonna be talking to people and you might need a smaller weapon that can be easily concealed."

Three large drawers fastened with padlocks were built into the back of the wooden altar. I had no idea what the top two drawers contained—candles, perhaps, incense and communion supplies. A ring of keys was attached to a hook on Gregory's belt and they jingled against each other as he unlocked the bottom drawer. It was filled with green and purple clerical robes, but he pushed them aside, revealing a half-dozen handguns.

Gregory held up a semiautomatic pistol with a laser sight. "Last time, I gave you a nine-millimeter just like this. I've got a paddle holster that will work. You can carry it inside your waistband." Reaching back into the drawer, he picked up a revolver with a two-inch barrel. "And this is a Thirty-Eight Special with a shrouded hammer spur. I got some hollow-point bullets for this. And an ankle holster."

I took the ankle holster, sat down on a pew, and strapped it onto my left leg. Then I slid the gun into the holster and placed a retention strap over the handle. When my pants leg was pulled back down, the gun was undetectable. But I could feel it hanging there, heavy, expectant, like a piece of machinery that had burst out of my skin.

"Everything okay, Mr. Underwood?"

"I need to find a quick way to draw the revolver."

"If you want, you can hang out here for a while and figure it out. I'm going downstairs to fire up the boiler and turn on the heat. We got a six o'clock Mass and it takes most of the day to warm up this place."

"Give me twenty minutes," I said, and Gregory shuffled out the side door. I made sure that both handguns were unloaded, and then moved around the church dry firing both weapons. At first, it was difficult to use the ankle holster, but I figured out a sequence that made my movements both simple and automatic. I would pull up my pants leg with my left hand, then drop back my right leg into a crouched position. Bend at the waist. Slip off the retention strap and grab the gun with my right hand. Draw. Bring my support hand forward. Aim. Fire.

The church radiators began to rattle and thump as steam rose up from the basement boiler. Sliding the paddle holster beneath my waistband, I drew the automatic and dry fired at the Virgin Mary. I learned two kinds of shooting at the training school in North Caro-

lina. For precise shooting, I see the gun's front and rear sights and
the target all with one glance. Then I focus my eyes so that I see only
the front sight, not the destination of the bullet. I pull the trigger
with the middle pad of my finger, reassess, refocus, and fire again.

If I'm point shooting, I focus on the target. It feels like I'm raising my finger to point at someone's head. In both kinds of firing I
want my Shell—not my Spark—to be in control. Thought determines my target and the decision to raise my weapon. But the other
steps in the sequence should be thoughtless in every way.

When Gregory returned with a mop, I left the church, walked
to a diner on East Eighty-Sixth Street, and ordered a cup of coffee. I could probably force myself to drink the coffee, but I dislike
"normal" food. All over the world people were biting and chewing
and pushing dead things into their mouths. The substance enters
their stomachs, and then moves like sludge through a clogged sewer
pipe. ComPlete comes in two flavors—chocolate and vanilla—but
it basically tastes like nothing.

Sitting alone in a booth, I whispered an e-mail to Miss Holquist:

// Obtained equipment. Going to customer's apartment.

I took a crosstown bus to Emily's apartment on West Eightieth
Street. The block was lined with brownstone buildings that had
gabled windows and sandstone steps that led up to the entrance
doors. There were green trash cans on the sidewalks, curb-your-dog
signs put up by the block association, and trees with little fences
around them. But even here, there was a fragment from the Day
of Rage. A plaque had been bolted to one of the brownstones that
read: IN MEMORY OF NICHOLAS BAUER GRANT AND ALL THE CHILDREN
WHO WERE LOST. NICKY, WE MISS YOU. ALWAYS.

I checked the name with my phone and, yes, Nicholas Grant
was one of the students killed by the bomb at the Dalton School.
There were private memorials like this all over the world along with
large public monuments like the white tower that had been built
near the reservoir in Central Park. From almost any area of the park,
you could look up and see the top half of the tower floating above

the trees. I didn't care about the murdered children—or anyone else for that matter—but I couldn't destroy the memories of what I had seen on television.

What I saw on the Day of Rage

- Police officers crouched in doorways with assault rifles
- Children crying, screaming, running from their schools
- Parents clutching cell phones, waiting for news
- A woman weeping, her face a garish mask
- Helicopter photos of body bags in a parking lot

© Power-I   XXX3094088UNDERWOOD

Sometimes I wondered why my Spark wasn't able to wipe away memories that didn't have a practical use. Once, on the subway, I saw a woman with burn scars on her arms, neck, and chest. Perhaps the death of the children was like an invisible scar that would never go away.

The keys I found in Emily's gym bag let me into the building and I climbed up a creaky staircase with a curving banister. Emily's apartment was on the top floor. I waited for a minute, listening for sounds from anyone inside, and then I racked the pistol's slide to the rear and forced a bullet into the firing chamber. With my left hand, I inserted the key into the lock, and gently pushed the door open. Two steps in. Close the door. My knees were slightly bent, left foot forward.

The curtains were shut, but a thin line of light pushed beneath the door that led to the rest of the apartment. A dark figure wearing a hat stood in the far corner of the room, but it didn't react to my appearance. Instead of firing, I felt around for the switch near the door and turned on the ceiling light. My possible target turned out to be a stuffed black bear wearing a cowboy hat that stood up on his back legs and reached out with his claws as if he wanted to embrace me. He stared across the room at his dead companions—a deer with Christmas ornaments hanging from its antlers, a squirrel perched on a plastic branch, and a hawk with blue-gray feathers and dark bands on the tail.

I had expected a neat and orderly apartment with shelves of financial books and matching furniture. But the sofa was saggy and the scratched coffee table looked like it had been picked up off the street. There was a vase filled with tissue-paper orchids and a poster on the wall that proclaimed, BOTS DON'T DREAM. Paperback novels—many without covers—had been dumped into a cardboard box and left in front of the stuffed bear.

Still holding the automatic, I stepped through the doorway and entered the kitchen. A framed photograph near the stove showed a stocky man with a broad face standing next to a teenage girl holding a fishing rod. There was nothing in the refrigerator but pickles and two jars of mustard. A bottle of vodka was in the freezer.

This was a "shotgun apartment," which meant that all the rooms were connected in a straight line. The bathroom contained an old-fashioned claw-foot bathtub with a shower curtain that displayed singing angels. I searched the cabinet over the sink, found nothing but aspirin and dental floss, and returned to the bedroom. When I switched on the ceiling light, I realized that words were written on the wall opposite the dresser.

> *Dear Uncle Roland—*
>
> *If you're reading this, it's because I've stopped check-ing in with you. I'm in trouble. I made a choice and I can't take it back. Just remember—Home is where the heart is.*
>
> *Emily*

The note on the wall made me feel like I was looking at some-one's face. Human Units showed emotion by the movement of their mouth and eyes, but I didn't have the power to understand.

Returning to the living room, I searched the little desk beneath the deer head. I wanted to know more about Sean, Emily's new boyfriend. It seemed logical that she was hiding with him or that he knew her location. I wasn't expecting to find love letters, but maybe they had taken a vacation together or gone to a concert, and Emily had saved some particle of physical reality to verify that memory. Instead, the desk drawer was stuffed with canceled rent checks and flyers for fast-food restaurants.

I sat down on the couch near the coffee table and skimmed through a stack of travel books for countries in Central America. Was Emily really going to Nicaragua or was this a false clue? A music box placed near the books displayed a bear and a logger with an ax. These two wooden figures chased each other in an endless circle that passed through one door of a shack, then out a second door while the box played "The Bear Went over the Mountain." I turned the key, wound up the spring, and played this tune several times. At first I assumed that the bearded logger was chasing the bear, and then I decided that the bear was chasing the logger.

Emily had lived in this space—eating and sleeping and talking to her friends. The dead bear and other stuffed animals had seen everything. I walked over to the bear and tapped his glass eyes with my finger. They reminded me of the dead eyes that people displayed when they were wearing E-MID contact lenses. Back in the bedroom, I photographed the message with my phone and sent the image to Miss Holquist.

// This was painted on the wall of the customer's apartment.
Roland is her uncle, Roland Jefferies.

I returned to the bedroom and opened the armoire. This contained Emily's corporate identity; her business suits and blouses were hung in a row, waiting to be called forward like a ghost army. Dress shoes with two-inch heels were stored in clear plastic boxes, and there was an orderly pile of unwrapped pantyhose.

I didn't like to be touched by Human Units and it felt strange to be handling someone else's clothes. The dresser contained Emily's jeans, sweaters, underwear, and T-shirts—all folded and stacked.

But the bottom drawer contained a manila envelope of small adhesive stickers—the sort of thing that growlers slapped up on walls that weren't being watched by surveillance cameras.

CLOSE THE EYE!
RESIST!
NOT NORM-ALL!

I also found some tools—a hammer, socket wrench, screwdriver, and pliers—along with a canvas bag that contained torn jeans, old running shoes, and a T-shirt that was splattered with blue and white paint. No words on the T-shirt. But it did display a simple drawing of a house:

When I had finished searching the room, I lay down in the middle of the bed and tried to figure my next move. Emily's sheets had a faint citrus scent from detergent, but I could also smell shampoo and some kind of bath powder that was a mix of flowers and vanilla.

"E-mail in your message box," Laura announced and I glanced at my phone's display screen.

> // Find the uncle. If the missing customer is at that location,
>   make a complete sales presentation using your new equip-
>   ment.

Still lying on the bed, I used my phone to access Emily Buchanan's employee file. Her only listed personal contact was her uncle, a man named Roland Jefferies, who lived in a small town near Lake George in the northeast region of New York State. Laura said that the location was a four-hour drive north of the city.

"Do you have a car, sir?"

"No."

"Should I obtain a rental car?"

"Yes . . . please."

"A reservation has been made at National Car Rental. The pickup location is three blocks north from your present location, on West Eighty-Third Street."

"Thank you, Laura. You're very efficient."

She didn't answer me right away. Somewhere in cyberspace her consciousness was evaluating my statement. Shadows were programmed to deal with human anger and stupidity, but they still found it difficult to recognize compliments.

"I hope efficiency is something you value, sir."

.   .   .

While I was waiting in line at the car rental office, I used Google Maps to get a street view of Uncle Roland's residence in Chestertown. It was a large, two-story house surrounded by a lawn dotted with a few apple trees. It was possible that Emily was staying with her uncle. If that was true, then Miss Holquist wanted me to make a *complete sales presentation* → and kill everyone in the building.

But how would I know if she was hiding in the attic or a back room? After I left the car rental garage, I dropped by my loft in Chinatown and retrieved the thermal-imaging scanner I had used during my search for Peter Stetsko. The scanner gave me the ability to look through walls. During that cold night in Brooklyn, the scanner had revealed that the Russian wasn't home. I didn't need to knock on doors or peer through windows—so I stood in the shadows and waited until Stetsko returned.

As I headed north on the Taconic State Parkway, the world was transformed into a series of flat images framed by the car windows. If I had stopped and left the car, I could have strolled around a three-dimensional service station, but during the drive my Spark saw reality as pixels on a monitor screen—little bits of light that gave the illusion of solidness and depth.

I drove for four hours, then turned off the parkway and entered the lake district of Warren County. There were patches of snow on the ground and the two-lane blacktop wandered past frozen lakes edged with cattails and dead reeds that jabbed at the sky. Billboards announced that the area was a "playground" for hunters and fishermen, but most of the small white cottages were boarded up for the winter. I stopped to buy gas, and then entered Chestertown.

A memorial to the war dead was at the center of the town square, surrounded by a bank and a courthouse and several other brick and granite buildings. Laura told me to turn right, so I left the square and drove past two-story clapboard houses with gray slate roofs. Old cars with rust bubbles around the wheel wells and pickup trucks with gun racks were parked in gravel driveways. One homeowner had placed a Jet Ski up on sawhorses with a FOR SALE sign.

"You're approaching your destination, Mr. Underwood."

"Yes. I know. Switch off."

The Google Maps camera car had photographed a lawn with four apple trees. Since then, Uncle Roland had removed one of the trees and placed a carved sign in front of his house.

LOON LAKE TAXIDERMY
SAVE YOUR MEMORIES

I drove a hundred yards down the road, then pulled over and tried to figure out what I was going to say.

The thermal scanner displayed an image of infrared radiation. It had a pistol grip and looked like a video camera. As I walked up a stone pathway to the house, I raised the scanner and pressed the trigger. Cold areas were displayed on the screen in shades of purple and blue. Warm spots were colored red or orange, and a human face was bright yellow. The scanner showed the building's hot-water lines and two active floor heaters. On the ground floor, a single Human Unit moved through a front room and then stepped behind a wall.

I dropped the scanner into my shoulder bag and knocked on the front door. When no one answered, I entered a room that was filled with stuffed dead animals. A worktable was near the wall and, clamped to the edge, there was a premade wooden deer's head with a set of real antlers attached to the skull. A little bell rang when I closed the door and Roland Jefferies came out of a back room carrying a patch of deerskin. Uncle Roland looked like an older version of the thickset man with stubby legs who had posed for the photograph hanging in Emily's kitchen.

"Good afternoon, my friend. How you doing?"

"Mr. Jefferies?"

"That's me."

"I'm David McCormick, a human resources manager for BDG in New York. Your niece, Emily, works for our bank."

"Yeah. I got a phone call from some guy at the bank named Evans."

I nodded. "Jerome Evans is in charge of corporate security. Eight days ago Emily left her desk and never returned. She hasn't contacted the bank and we're worried about her safety."

Uncle Roland kept smiling. "Maybe she got tired of workin' for your bank. Can't say I blame her. Sounds like a boring job . . . making deals and pushing money around all day long. My work might look easy, but it's a real challenge. It's not so easy to make a dead cocker spaniel look like he's happy."

"Do you know where Emily is?"

"Nope."

"Aren't you worried?"

"Should I be?"

"People don't usually disappear like that."

"Hard to vanish when the EYE program is tracking everything we do. But I'm not worried about Emily. My niece is as tough as nails. When she was thirteen years old, she left her crazy parents, bought a bus ticket, and came here to Chestertown. Then she called me up on a phone and told me to pick her up at the post office. Her parents thought she was possessed by the Devil, so they didn't fight me when I went to court and became her guardian."

I was aware of the revolver strapped to my ankle and the automatic concealed beneath my jacket. "The bank wants to find Emily. We'd like to make sure that she's safe."

"Sorry you had to drive all the way up here, Mr. McCormick. But I appreciate your concern. If I hear from my niece, I'll tell her to call you guys. Have a safe drive back to New York City, and watch out for that speed trap in Warrensburg."

I stepped back out into the cold air and smelled the blue-green scent of pine trees. When I reached the LOON LAKE TAXIDERMY sign, I stopped and pointed the scanner at the house. If Emily was hiding in an upstairs room, Uncle Roland would have immediately reported my appearance. I peered through the walls for a minute or so, but Roland continued to stand alone at his worktable. The thoughts in his brain were transformed into a glob of blurry yellow light surrounded by a grid of hot-water pipes.

The trip to New York was a straight line south dotted by a series of discount shopping malls and Indian casinos. After dropping off the rental car, I should have waved down a cab and returned to Chinatown. Instead, I stood on the corner of Eighty-Third Street and let the wind touch my collar and the hem of my coat. Usually my Spark manipulated my Shell like the construction worker sitting in a cage on the back of a truck-mounted crane. But that evening my Shell was in control. It wanted to return to Emily's apartment and lie back down on her bed. I felt like I was watching a computer screen as my body marched down to Eightieth Street and entered the brownstone.

The only light in the stairwell came from the wall sconces on each floor, and I climbed upward through patches of darkness and illumination. Voices leaked through closed doors, and I smelled the slippery odor of fried onions. Key in the lock. Push open the door. Switch on the light and—

Everything in the room had been destroyed. The lamps were smashed and the papers from the little desk had been scattered on the floor. Someone had slashed open the chair cushions and cut the bear's neck—exposing a tuft of yellow padding.

Entering the kitchen, I stepped on broken dishes, then glanced into the bathroom and saw that the angel shower curtain had been ripped off its pole. All the suits and blouses hanging in the closet had been slashed with a knife and the clothes from the dresser were scattered across the room. The mattress had been cut open and the foam rubber pushed out—like fat from a wound.

I picked up a night lamp, switched it on, and turned to the wall. Someone had used a can of spray paint to cover the message on the wall. Red paint had dribbled down the plaster to the baseboard. It looked like the residue from a shotgun blast that had cut through a target's body.

I centered the mattress on the box spring, sat on the edge of the bed, and tried to figure out who had done this.

Lorcan Tate. That was the only logical conclusion. Miss Holquist had given him the address and he had searched the apartment while I was visiting Uncle Roland.

I held up my phone and whispered to Laura, "Are you there?"

"Yes, sir. How may I help you?"

"Display most recent photo."

And Emily's letter appeared on the phone screen, the words glowing in the dark room.

> *Dear Uncle Roland—*
>
> *If you're reading this, it's because I've stopped check-ing in with you. I'm in trouble. I made a choice and I can't take it back. Just remember—Home is where the heart is.*
>
> *Emily*

I read this message several times until it was absorbed by my Spark. Why was the word "Home" capitalized? Was that important? Was she telling her uncle a secret that I needed to understand?

Home. The word meant nothing to me. Sometimes, when I wandered through the city at night, I peered through windows framed by half-open curtains and saw families eating dinner or watching television. I assumed they were doing those activities in a home. It looked warm, and there was light.

I returned to the living room, got down on my knees, and found the little music box with the bear, the logger, and the shack with two doors. The shack was a home—the only one to be found in the apartment. My fingers fumbled with the roof until it clicked open. Inside, I found the music box cylinder and—taped to the wood—a flash drive wrapped in a slip of white paper.

> *Good work, Roland!*
>
> *I knew you would find this. Stored on this flash drive is a download of the illegal black money transactions of the Pradhani Group, a family-owned company based in India.*
>
> *This is a COPY! I'm going to send these files to Thomas Slater at the We Speak for Freedom Web site.*
>
> *But I want YOU to send this backup to them if you haven't heard from me in two weeks.*
>
> *I love you, Rollie! You were my real father and mother when I was growing up.*
>
> *Emily*

The dead animals seemed alive at that moment, gazing down at me with emotions that I couldn't understand. I remained on my knees.

9

I took the subway back to my loft, photographed Emily's note to her uncle, and then sent the image and a short description of what had happened to Miss Holquist. Outside, an ambulance was racing down the street—its siren sound rising and falling and echoing off the buildings. I took a shower and lay down on my bed, but my thoughts darted around like a firefly in the darkness.

When a patch of sunlight touched the bed frame, I got dressed and switched on my computer. The Pradhani Group turned out to be a large, family-owned corporation in India. I didn't know what was stored on the flash drive, but Emily wanted the data sent to We Speak for Freedom. This turned out to be a Web site created by a former MIT professor named Thomas Slater.

We Speak for Freedom never asked for contributions, held a news conference, or issued a press release. But once or twice a week, the site would offer a wide range of confidential documents or clandestine videos. Currently the site displayed photographs of a dissident being tortured in Kazakhstan and a memo from a Japanese computer company about child labor in one of its foreign subsidiaries.

My phone beeped and I slipped on my headset. "Where are you?" It was Miss Holquist's voice.

"In my apartment."

"Get your passport, both handguns, and the flash drive. Then walk outside."

I slipped the revolver into my ankle holster, dropped the automatic into a shoulder bag, and let gravity pull me downstairs and into the street. A black town car was parked at the curb and a woman's hand emerged from a three-inch gap above a tinted window. Her fingers wiggled—beckoning me forward.

I got into the backseat and found Miss Holquist with a computer pad on her lap. Instead of her usual business suit, she wore a red cotton jacket, a white blouse, and black pants. A Plexiglas shield separated us from our driver—an older man with a flushed face. It felt strange to sit beside Miss Holquist. I usually faced her directly with a desk or a table between us.

"Good morning, Mr. Underwood." Miss Holquist offered me a smile. "I must say that I've been pleasantly surprised by your unexpected talents. During the last forty-eight hours, you've displayed a wide range of skills."

She rapped on the shield with her knuckles and the town car began to force its way through the crowded streets of Chinatown. It felt like we were sitting inside a barge floating down a weed-clogged canal.

"Give me the flash drive."

I handed the flash drive to her and she attached it to her computer. "Now tell me exactly what happened. I want to know how you found this."

I described my second visit to Emily's apartment as Miss Holquist watched a list of files being copied onto her computer. The smell of her rose perfume was very strong at that moment. It felt as if my Spark was wrapped in yards of blue satin.

"Why did Lorcan destroy her apartment?" I asked. "Was there a reason?"

"He did that? Really?" Miss Holquist sighed and shook her head. "I asked him to search the place one more time and paint over the message on the wall. Lorcan always follows my orders, but he can be somewhat aggressive. He's not as controlled and efficient as you are, Mr. Underwood."

"All files copied," said Miss Holquist's Shadow. It was a young man's voice—not precise like Laura's, but soft and calm.

"Thank you." Miss Holquist detached the flash drive and gave it back to me. "Take this. You're going to deliver it to a client."

"So how do we know that Emily Buchanan is still in the country?" I asked. "She had enough time to fly anywhere in the world."

"Ms. Buchanan hasn't used her passport since she disappeared. All we know at this point is that she went to the Financial Futures conference in London last summer. This is an annual event hosted by the bank for our international clients. Senior executives give presentations about new bond offerings while everyone nurses a hangover. Anyway . . . it turns out that a young Indian man named Jafar Desai was also at the conference. Desai married into the Pradhani family and worked for their companies. He and his wife disappeared two weeks ago, and it seems probable that he's the person who sent the e-mail from Dubai."

"Should I keep looking for Emily Buchanan?"

"No. Mr. Rajat Pradhani, the head of the company, would like to talk to you as soon as possible. You can give him the flash drive. Because of government monitoring, he doesn't want the data sent through the Internet."

"Is he here in New York?"

"Of course not. He lives in India. Right now we're taking you to the consulate so you can get a travel visa. When that's done, return to your apartment and pack your bags." She handed me an envelope. "This is a round-trip ticket on a British Airways flight to New Delhi. You're leaving from Kennedy Airport at eight o'clock this evening."

"I'm going to India?"

"That's right. So give me your two handguns. We don't want your landlord snooping around and finding unregistered weapons when you're away."

I gave her both weapons and she dropped them into a purple shopping bag.

"Do I really have to meet Mr. Pradhani? I'd rather stay here in New York."

Miss Holquist sat back against the black leather seat. Her nostrils flared slightly and her voice was sharp and precise. "And why is that?"

Trying to find Emily Buchanan, I had touched her clothes and smelled her pillow. I felt connected to my target, but I didn't know how to explain that to Miss Holquist.

"I'm tired."

"I understand, Mr. Underwood. If I had a choice, I'd rather be talking to my daughter's dressmaker and tasting sample squares of wedding cake. Instead, I've stepped into a very messy room and now I have to clean it up."

"Send another enforcer."

"Mr. Pradhani wants to speak to you. He doesn't want anyone else to know about this problem. You're flying first class, Underwood. You can sleep on the plane."

. . .

Twelve hours later I found myself sitting in a waiting lounge at Kennedy Airport. The television sound had been turned off, but I could read the captions at the bottom of the screen. There were more sex riots in China because of the lack of women. In Russia, the new czar appeared at his son's wedding. Meanwhile the U.S. Congress was debating the Faith of Our Fathers Act, which would place restrictions on any religion that didn't use the Bible as a primary text.

Toward the end of the news hour, a talking head announced how many Americans would get married in the fourth quarter of the year. This was not a prediction based on previous trends, but a fairly accurate statement based on the EYE system. Both the government and large corporations were monitoring e-mail and credit card transactions. Surveillance cameras were everywhere, plus people were walking around New York making continuous videos with their G-MIDs because they wanted to remember every moment of their unmemorable lives. A great many facts flowed into the total information database, but the real power of EYE came from the algorithms that identified individuals, tracked them, and placed them into different categories. Yes, there was fate and luck and the faithful still believed in angels and divine intervention. But the equations proved that most humans—most of the time—are as predictable as machines.

The growlers and the New Luddites hated the idea that their decisions could be compared to the programmed responses of a coffeemaker. Some of them wore random-number generators on a cord around their necks and used the numbers to make unusual decisions. There were still a few outliers, but the erratic behavior of these individuals was absorbed and neutralized by the predictable actions of the majority population. The algorithms could predict approximately how many jars of apricot jam would be sold in Warsaw or how many people would commit suicide in Munich.

But the truly significant information was rarely made public. Did most citizens hate their leaders or would they hate them in the future? Would the growlers continue with their bash mobs and computer hacking or would there be an organized rebellion?

In the United States, the Need to Know Act stated that an ordinary citizen did not need to know much of anything. This law was just one of several major bills passed by Congress in the months following the Day of Rage:

> The *FREEDOM FROM FEAR ACT* created the mandatory Freedom Badge ID card.
> The *GOOD NEWS FOR AMERICANS ACT* placed restrictions on anonymous bloggers and Web sites.
> The *LIBERTY FOR ALL ACT* stated that anyone who made antisocial statements or displayed unpredictable behavior could be held for sixty days without being charged with a crime.

None of these laws influenced the energy of my Spark or the movement of my Shell. Freedom can only be taken away from the living. A dead dog is never attached to a chain.

.   .   .

On the flight to New Delhi, I was curled up inside the white plastic shell that served as a first-class sleeping compartment. When they dimmed the cabin lights, I closed my eyes and tried to control my breathing. In New York, my Spark could remain within the present reality, observing and reacting to objects around me. I did occasionally have memories, but they were focused on tasks and objectives:

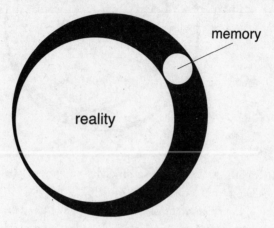

But when I'm trapped on a plane for fourteen hours, memory grows like a tumor.

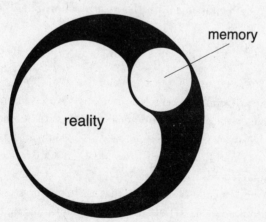

Gradually, images of the past push away the present reality.

There is only one way to avoid this shadow land of memories; I force myself to enter the clean, orderly file room of facts. Over the years I have obtained all the police and hospital reports written

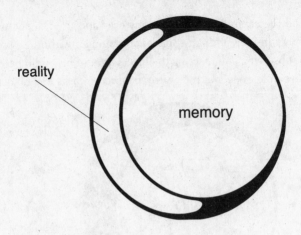

about my death. As I read these official summaries, I became an object observed from a distance.

As the plane began to cross the Atlantic, I switched on my computer and slipped on the headset. "Edward, please show me the police report. . . ."

"Which one, sir?"

"The document issued by the Delaware County Sheriff's Department."

· · ·

According to Deputy Sheriff Kirk Everett, I was riding a Ducati motorcycle on the section of Route 30 that runs past Pepacton Reservoir in Delaware County, New York. I was accompanied by Gerald Tannenbaum and Brian Farrell—two New York City residents without criminal records.

I am not capable of fantasy—that is, happy or sad thoughts about various unrealities. But I can picture in my mind that October afternoon on a two-lane country road. First silence, then a growing sound of engines approaching until, suddenly, we appeared. Red and gold leaves are scattered across the pavement and our rapid movement makes them swirl up in the air.

Did I lie forward over the bike's fuel tank, feeling the vibration of the machine?

Was there a race down the hill? Was Tannenbaum in front, then Farrell, until I sped past them? Did I turn my head? Did I wave? Or were both my hands gripping the handlebars as I leaned into the curve and hit a stalled delivery truck?

The truck was owned by Gourmet Guy, a Delaware County company that supplies food to schools and restaurants. Its driver, a man named Bernard Alvarez (fifty-six years old, no criminal record), had just lifted up the hood and was staring at the engine.

Downloaded photographs of the accident site show my motor-cycle resting on its side with its front wheel and handlebars crumpled into a twisted sculpture. In one shot, a heavyset man wearing a parka (Alvarez?) is talking on his mobile phone. Approximately fifteen minutes after the first emergency call, Deputy Everett appeared in his patrol car and found my body lying on the pavement thirty feet away from the motorcycle. Tannenbaum and Farrell told the deputy that they had "removed the victim's helmet and attempted CPR." They stopped CPR when "they decided that the victim was dead."

The attached statements of the witnesses don't mention my death. Mr. Alvarez talks for pages about the truck and its broken timing belt. Tannenbaum and Farrell explained that our plan was to circle the reservoir and then spend the night at a hotel in Downs-ville. Tannenbaum stated that this was a "guys' weekend" because Farrell had just announced his engagement.

I told Edward to search for Deputy Everett's photograph on the Internet, but he wasn't successful. Let's assume that Everett was a muscular man in his forties, his policeman's belt heavy with a gun and a Taser and a flashlight as he approached the accident vic-tim. The dead man's face—my face—was covered with blood and I didn't appear to be breathing. But then, according to the report, a "pink bubble" appeared on my lips. Was this bubble formed by one final convulsive effort from my lungs? Or was my Spark trying to escape its prison? Deputy Everett didn't have to debate the matter with the three witnesses, because an ambulance arrived a few minutes later.

"Edward?"

"Yes, sir."

"Display the Marian Community Hospital emergency room report."

"I've found it, sir. It's on the computer screen."

> CHIEF COMPLAINT: Motor vehicle accident with severe head trauma.

> HISTORY OF PRESENT ILLNESS: This is a 31-year-old Caucasian male who was brought by ambulance to the emergency department. The patient had been riding a motorcycle at high speed when he hit a stalled truck on Route 30. Ambulance was called and arrived at the accident scene approximately 20 minutes later. The EMTs (M. Spencer/J. Watts) checked patient vital signs. They placed him on a backboard, started an IV, and applied oxygen. Patient was unresponsive. During the trip to the hospital, the cardiac monitor indicated that the patient had flatlined. An EMT immediately started CPR and a thready pulse was apparent when the patient arrived at the emergency room.

Only two nurses and one doctor work in the Marian Hospital emergency room during an eight-hour shift. Dr. V. Rahman, the first physician who encountered me, was born in Bangladesh and went to a third-tier medical school. According to the report, Rahman called upstairs and a cardiologist named Mitchell ran down to help.

> PAST MEDICAL HISTORY: Medical staff inspected contents of patient's wallet. No medical insurance card. Driver's license indicated that that patient was not an organ donor.

> PAST SURGICAL HISTORY: Information not available.

MEDICATIONS: Information not available.

PHYSICAL EXAMINATION: This is a Caucasian male, age 31, who has experienced traumatic head injury due to a motorcycle accident. The patient is comatose. A rising blood pressure and slowing pulse indicate that the patient's brain is swelling. The pupil size was checked and did react to light.

VITAL SIGNS: Temperature 97.1 degrees. Pulse 32. Blood pressure: 74/40. Respiratory rate 8. Pulse oximetry level 83% on oxygen.

HEENT: Laceration of the scalp with bleeding. Fractured nose and mandible.

NECK: Supple. Minor laceration.

HEART: Slow. Irregular rate and rhythm.

LUNGS: Clear to auscultation bilaterally.

ABDOMEN: Soft. Nondistended.

EXTREMITIES: Left tibia fractured.

PERIPHERAL VASCULAR: Capillary refill is more than 2 seconds in all extremities.

NEUROLOGIC: Patient unconscious. Eye movement fixed.

MUSCULOSKELETAL: Patient has fractured left tibia. Fractured skull with severe head trauma.

SKIN: Cold. Cyanotic. Multiple lacerations and abrasions.

DIAGNOSTIC STUDIES: After patient was stabilized, he was given a CT scan and X-ray. X-ray indicated fractured skull, fractured left tibia, and fractured ulna. CT scan indicated profound brain damage of the left frontal lobe.

EMERGENCY DEPARTMENT: Immobilized left lower extremity. Immobilized left upper extremity. Removed all clothes and prepped for emergency surgery.

ASSESSMENT AND PLAN: Patient given oxygen. Lacerations were cleaned and sutured. Cardidor and Vican were administered via IV. Patient was sent to surgery via gurney.

The report of the surgical procedure sounded like a document created to defend the hospital against a medical malpractice suit. When my body was placed on the operating table, my rebellious heart decided to stop beating. Dr. Mitchell made an incision in my chest, spread my ribs with a piece of equipment called a self-retaining retractor, and then held my heart in his hand and squeezed it rhythmically.

His efforts were useless. I had died on the road and in the ambulance, and I died one final time in the operating room.

So how was it possible that I was lying on my back in the first-class cabin of a passenger plane as it traveled east toward a darkening sky?

10

When the plane reached New Delhi, I retrieved my suitcase, passed through customs, and saw an Indian driver holding a sign with my name. Miss Holquist had told me that my travel expenses would be paid by Transmotion Ltd., a corporation registered in the Republic of Mauritius. I had no desire to travel to an island in the southwest Indian Ocean to see if this company actually existed. Transmotion Ltd. could open a bank account and obtain credit cards. It could sue people and sponsor political ads in the United States, but I doubted that this legal entity had any products or employees. Like many international corporations, Transmotion Ltd. was both real and completely imaginary.

My driver led me to a car he called an Ambassador: a large, old-fashioned gray sedan with a rounded back. We passed through a control gate and then we were absorbed by India. The thruway into the city was still under construction and the car followed a two-lane road that snaked its way around detour signs and packs of scrawny men shoveling sand into cement mixers. A mud-splattered bus rolled past us packed with passengers, and I saw a family of four riding on a motorcycle: the baby on the fuel tank, the man clutching the handlebars, and a little girl wedged between her mother's breasts and her father's back.

Back in America, I could limit the power of the world by reducing everything to a series of flat images. But that wasn't possible in this country. Waves of energy flowed toward me; it felt as if I was going to be knocked off my feet and pulled out to sea.

We passed a one-room hut near the edge of the road with a dirt yard and a tethered cow and four-foot-high cones of dried cow dung used for fuel. We passed a line of eucalyptus trees, each with a number painted on its trunk, and a water tank that looked like an orange animal with four legs and a flexible snout. Gradually, the buildings began to grow larger and there were wedding palaces and nightclubs surrounded by concrete walls topped with shards of broken glass.

A construction zone. The road disappeared and rocks clattered up in the car's wheel wells. The Ambassador moved slower and slower until a man in rags stepped in front of us with a scrap of red cloth tied to a stick. This road flag was not just his job, but proof of his existence. Stop. He waved the flag again. Stop.

Tap, tap.

I looked left and saw the faces of three small children staring at me. Faces that looked as fragile as chips of dry clay. Stick arms and legs. Glistening eyes. One little girl was wearing nothing but a man's T-shirt with a strip of fabric for a belt. She squeezed her fingers into a single point and rapped again on the passenger window.

Tap, tap.

"Beggars," said the driver and shook his head. But I had no intention of rolling down the window and getting closer to them. Children bothered me. I had no idea where to place them in my system.

But children weren't dogs or animals or the Dead. And they weren't like the women with baskets of gravel on their head who trudged past the Ambassador. Small children radiated so much energy that it was difficult to predict their movements. It made me nervous to be around them.

The ragged man lowered his flag and our car lurched forward. Now tall buildings and crowds appeared and the car was surrounded by auto rickshaws—three-wheeled vehicles with passenger cages welded onto the back. Peering through the glass, I saw an elderly woman with a parasol, a pack of children sorting through trash, a Sikh with a handlebar moustache, and two white cows eating a mound of banana peels.

"*Haan . . . Haan . . .*" the driver chanted, and then the traffic stopped for no apparent reason. More beggars tapped on the window as a bicycle rickshaw man squeezed past us. He was pumping hard, standing on his pedals, while sharp shoulder blades jabbed inside his skin.

Finally, we passed through golden gates and followed a circular driveway to the Taj Mahal Hotel. Men wearing Nehru jackets and little white caps hurried out to take my suitcases. At the front desk, the hotel manager handed me a sealed manila envelope and told me that my room had already been paid for by Transmotion Ltd.

"Welcome to Delhi, sir. Please let us know if there is anything we can do for you."

"I want to lie down."

Two bellboys escorted me to a ninth-floor suite. They switched on the air conditioner and showed me that the bathroom faucets really did work. When I was finally alone, I opened the check-in suitcase that was filled with a travel supply of ComPlete. I drank a bottle, took off my shoes, and lay down in the middle of the king-size bed. The hum of the air conditioner, the white plaster walls, the faint smell of the lavender laundry soap coming from the sheets and pillows were comforting. Whenever I read about hotels and restaurants in an in-flight magazine, the writers are always talking about places that are picturesque or romantic or historical. I desire none of those qualities. Bland is the truest expression of an advanced civilization. It took a great deal of money to create this pocket of cool, calm bland among the rickshaw men and the beggar children tapping on the car windows.

.   .   .

The envelope contained a plane ticket to a city called Ahmedabad in West India. An information sheet explained that the hotel would provide a car to take me to the airport and that another car would be waiting at my next destination.

Following Dr. Noland's Rule #2, I took a shower and then slept until dawn. When I left the hotel at five in the morning, Delhi was a different city. The streets were quiet and empty, and now I could see the dogs that were hidden by the traffic in the daytime. In this country, the dogs knew they were dogs. They didn't look friendly and eager for attention, but they were always aware of their surroundings. At this early hour, all the dogs were out, sitting separately, royally, as they surveyed their Dog Kingdom.

The plane to Ahmedabad was much smaller than the airliner that took me to Delhi, and most of the other passengers carried computers and attaché cases. I found my driver at the airport and we stepped out of the air-conditioned terminal into a wave of hot air that felt like a weight was pushing down on my Shell. Ahmedabad was surrounded by a ring of steel mills and textile factories and the sky looked like a blue bowl smeared with yellow chalk dust.

As we approached the central city, the streets became narrow and dirty and filled with carts and motor rickshaws. Each two- or three-story building had a shop on the ground level that sold one kind of product—millstones or dog leashes or motorcycle helmets. I had to assume that an occasional customer bought these objects, but most of the shopkeepers sat on the sidewalks, drinking tea and gossiping with their friends. They lived in the Kingdom of Sitting Around.

My driver dropped me off at a sprawling three-story mansion that had been converted into a luxury hotel. I had to sit in front of an air conditioner in my room for a half hour until I felt like opening a second manila envelope. Transmotion Ltd. told me to leave the hotel at 3 p.m., find an auto rickshaw, and ask the driver to take me to the Adalaj Stepwell north of the city. An enclosed brochure said that the well was a historical ruin, a multilevel sanctuary built for pilgrims in 1500.

The heat made my Shell feel like it was melting away. After changing money at the hotel, I found an auto rickshaw and sat behind the driver as he steered through the crowded city. The smells were very strong in India and I saw these as different shades of red and orange in my mind. Nobody was wearing G-MID eyeglasses and I didn't see any surveillance cameras. A young mother in a faded sari dragged a small boy down the sidewalk. Two soldiers wearing green camouflage uniforms chatted with friends as a mechanic repaired a motorcycle. The rickshaw motor made a grinding sound like a broken lawn mower and everyone riding or driving any kind of vehicle was constantly beeping their horn.

After twenty minutes of driving, we left the main road and entered a neighborhood of small brick homes with sheet-metal roofs and cows wandering through the streets. I thought about asking the driver to return to my hotel, but he suddenly turned a corner and stopped. Some shacks made out of packing containers were on one side of the street and they faced a rectangular gray stone ruin about the size of a basketball court. The stepwell resembled a stone plaza with four square openings that allowed sunlight to illuminate what was underground.

No one was waiting for me, and I had no idea what I was supposed to do. Although I was carrying a phone, my Shadow couldn't help me in this situation. I paid the driver, climbed out of the rickshaw, and wandered across the street to the low chain-link fence surrounding the ruin. There were no guards or ticket booths. No instructions of any kind. Trying to avoid the blaring noise of the sun, I passed through a shattered gate and encountered an old man with a twig broom. I stopped and waited for instructions, but he shrugged and waved me forward.

Sandstone stairs led downward into the well. It had a simple construction. Each stone floor was held up by rows of white stone columns. The columns were like trees with intricately carved scrolls and filigree at the top. I followed the stairs down to the second level, descended to the third level, and then stopped. When I turned around and looked up the staircase I understood the well's true nature. The builders had started on the surface and then built downward. This was a reverse building, a negative integer; instead of a tower that bragged and shouted at the sky, this creation burrowed into the earth.

My shoes made scuffling sounds as I followed the staircase down to the fourth level. It was cool and quiet at the base of the well, and my Spark felt restful. At the fifth and final level, I stopped and looked up. I was standing on the ground floor of what looked like a small rotunda with a white dome ceiling. Concentric circles of carved stone rings led upward to the surface, and there was a round opening at the top to let in sunlight.

I realized, almost without thinking, that this dry, abandoned well was a physical display of my Transformation. Since the accident, I had followed a stairway downward into darkness with only a small disk of sunlight to guide my journey. Now that light was directly above me and I could blot out its power with the palm of my hand.

"Mr. Underwood! Is that you?"

Looking up the staircase I saw a young Indian man on the second level, framed by the stone columns. "Yes . . ."

"I apologize for being late, sir. I'm your driver. I'm supposed to take you to a meeting in Gandhinagar."

"Good. Let's go." Returning to the surface, I crossed the dusty road and climbed into the air-conditioned comfort of another Ambassador.

Gandhinagar turned out to be the capital of Gujarat Province. The driver explained that it was a planned city divided into thirty sectors. All the streets were wide and clean and lined with trees. Each government ministry had a large office building with a park surrounding it. There were schools and shopping malls with brightly colored billboards written in both English and Hindi.

Our car glided past an algae-filled river and turned into a driveway that led to a tall, round office building that resembled a stack of poker chips. A large sign announced that we had reached the headquarters of the Pradhani Group. Security guards with assault rifles stood at the entrance to the building, and they spoke Hindi to my driver. One of the guards escorted me into an atrium filled with tropical plants, then motioned for me to step into an elevator. He swiped his key card past a security sensor, punched the button for the twelfth floor, and nodded good-bye.

When the elevator door opened, I stepped out into a reception area where a young Indian woman wearing a green sari and round, horn-rimmed eyeglasses was waiting for my arrival. She stood up immediately and smiled.

"Mr. Underwood?"

"That's correct."

"Welcome to the Pradhani Group. I'm Miss Mehta, and I want to thank you for traveling such a long way to meet our president."

I wasn't sure about the right response, so I stayed silent. Miss Mehta's smile was frozen on her face for a few seconds, and then disappeared. "Was your hotel room satisfactory in New Delhi?"

"Yes."

"And here? In Ahmedabad? Are there any problems?"

"None whatsoever."

"Very good." Miss Mehta picked up the telephone headset and dialed a three-digit number. "He's here," she said in English and waited until someone gave her a command.

"Mr. Pradhani will see you now."

She opened a door and I followed her down a windowless hallway where the air was cool and dry. Miss Mehta stopped when we reached a steel door with a CCTV camera mounted above the frame. She pushed a wall switch and waited with her hands straight down at the sides. When the door lock clicked open my escort motioned for me to enter. I stepped into the room alone and the door shut behind me.

I was standing in a private office with gauzy white curtains covering the windows. The curtains filtered and softened the shrill sunlight I had encountered outside the stepwell. A black steel dining room table with matching chairs was on my right. A green suede couch was on the other side of the room next to a glass coffee table.

But the furniture was only background scenery to the occupant of the room: an Indian man in his sixties sitting behind a massive desk. Rajat Pradhani wore white linen pants and a long-sleeved white linen shirt that resembled pajamas. Unlike everyone else I had met in India, he was large and heavy. His saggy face resembled a blob of yellowish cookie dough with two brown raisins for eyes.

I took a few steps forward and stood like a servant in front of the desk. Mr. Pradhani stared at me for a minute or so, and then shook his head. "I was expecting someone bigger."

Lorcan Tate would have been angered by Mr. Pradhani's comment. But I felt nothing. No response.

"You're not frightening at all," Mr. Pradhani said. "There's nothing intimidating about your appearance. I don't wish to be impolite, but you have a bad haircut and cheap shoes." A slight smile appeared on his lips. "You resemble a lower-level employee from one of our American subsidiaries."

No response.

"Can you talk, Mr. Underwood? That is your name? Correct?"

"What would you like me to say?"

"Answer my questions, immediately. No hesitations. What is your true nationality?"

"American."

"How old are you?"

"Thirty-five."

"And how many people have you killed?"

My Spark was overwhelmed with a cold, watery mixture of thought. I wasn't angered by the question, but I knew that it was inappropriate. I shared the present moment with this Human Unit:

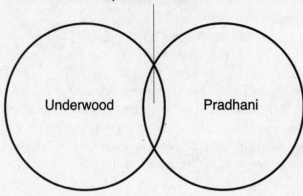

But as far as I knew, my previous assignments had no connection to his past life.

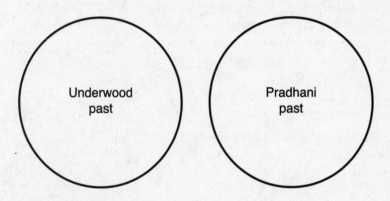

"Speak up! I want a number!"

"I work for the Special Services Section of the BDG bank, Mr. Pradhani. Contact my supervisor if you need to know more about me."

"But I'm asking you *now*. It's necessary information. If I hire a Dalit to clean my toilet, I want to know if he's done it before."

No response. I kept my eyes focused on a lighting sconce.

"Answer the question!" Mr. Pradhani yanked open a drawer and took out a silver-plated revolver. He stood up with effort and lurched around the desk. "My family has controlled this province

since independence. The police, the judges, and the members of
Parliament are our employees."

Mr. Pradhani's throat made a rasping sound as he raised the
revolver and pointed it at my head. "No one at your hotel knows
where you went. A rickshaw driver took you to the stepwell and
left you there. There is no connection between yourself and my
family. That means I can kill you right now and there will be no
consequences. My employees will wrap up your body and toss
it into a dung pit. After a few phone calls, there will be no proof
that you even arrived in this city. You will not exist. You have never
existed."

I stared at the end of the revolver barrel and felt no emotion at
all. My only wish was that all the doctors and psychologists who
had examined me could be in the room so that they could witness
one final proof of my deadness. And what would happen when Mr.
Pradhani pulled the trigger?

My Shell would be broken.

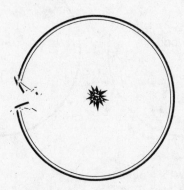

It would dissolve into fragments. While my Spark floated free.

"I'm speaking to you!" Mr. Pradhani shouted. "Are you so stupid that you don't realize you're about to die?"

"Perhaps I should move over to the table."

He waved his gun. "What are you talking about?"

"If you shoot me here, my blood might stain the rug. There's no rug over by the dining table—so it's a more logical location."

The expression on Mr. Pradhani's face changed several times, but I couldn't understand their meanings. I wondered what he would say if I took out my phone and checked my database of emotions.

Pradhani laughed and lowered the gun. "Miss Holquist said that you were *cold*, but I didn't quite believe her. Almost every human being shows emotion when they face death. You're the first person I've ever met who has really slain that tiger. If you were Indian, you could become a Sadu . . . a holy man."

Pradhani returned to the desk, put down his gun, and picked up the phone. "Tea," he said, and then waddled over to the couch. "Sit over there," he said, motioning to an easy chair. "Sit down and we'll have a real conversation."

I sat down on the chair while Pradhani ripped the gold-foil wrapper off a square of chocolate and popped it into his mouth. "Do you have the flash drive with the stolen information?"

I took the flash drive out of my shirt pocket and placed it on the coffee table. Mr. Pradhani picked up the data-storage device and studied it carefully. For a moment, I thought he might swallow it with the chocolate. "I don't know what files are on here, but I'm sure that they could cause a great deal of trouble. This betrayal is a direct attack on our family."

"Did Jafar Desai work for your company?"

"No! Worse than that! He's my son-in-law. I have five children, Mr. Underwood. All four of my sons have joined our company. One is an excellent worker. Two are adequate. One is a failure. But the real problems have all been caused by my only daughter, Nalini. I spoiled her, Mr. Underwood. I will admit that. She wanted to go to university and told me that it would enable her to find a suitable husband. I foolishly consented to her attending Nehru University . . . a notorious left-wing institution. My daughter majored in art history. The history of what? Pretty paintings. What could possibly go wrong? And then, in her third year of study—"

A soft buzzing sound came from over the doorway. Mr. Pradhani picked up a black plastic device that looked like a television remote control. When he pressed a button, the door lock clicked open and Miss Mehta entered with a tray that held a teapot, fragile-looking china cups, and a plate of coconut cookies.

I liked the way Miss Mehta placed each article from the tray on the invisible straight lines that led from the edge of the glass coffee table. Then she poured a cup of tea for Mr. Pradhani, adding cream and three cubes of sugar.

"Cream and sugar, Mr. Underwood?"

"Nothing for me."

"You Westerners are so sensitive about germs," Pradhani said. "This water has been boiled. Nothing to worry about."

"I don't want tea at this moment."

Pradhani flicked his fingers and Miss Mehta bowed her head and retreated from the room. For a few minutes, we both sat there without speaking. I stared at the gold and blue teapot while Pradhani pushed two cookies into his mouth.

"Do you have any children, Mr. Underwood?"

I shook my head.

"When children are young, they think they can do whatever they wish to do. They don't always realize that they are connected to a family of the past and a family in the future."

"So what did your daughter do?"

"During Nalini's third year of study, she met a young man named Jafar Desai. He was a *Kachchi Patel,* a lower caste than ours. Jafar said his father was a government official, but he made tea. This is not a theory, but a *fact.* My brother's friend saw him making tea for a division head at the Ministry of Surface Transport. And the mother, of course, was nothing—squatting in the dirt to make dung patties while the flies buzzed around her face."

"But your daughter fell in love?"

"Love!" Pradhani spat out the word. "Too many romantic films, Mr. Underwood. Too many romantic songs. Yes, she was infatuated, and Jafar saw an opportunity. They announced that they were engaged and, because they were 'modern,' there would be no dowry. I should have had Jafar killed, but he defended himself with paper armor—his examination papers. He was clever and had done well in school. So after many tears and much negotiation, I consented to the marriage. You should have seen this family at the wedding! I caught one of his aunts stuffing food into her purse."

Another cookie disappeared into his mouth. "They both moved to Gujarat and we gave him a job. At first, this was one level higher than a tea boy—a clerk's job in Operations. But gradually, it became clear to all of us that Jafar was intelligent and a hard worker. When Nalini gave birth to a son, I gave Jafar an important job. He became an assistant to the man who was in charge of our black money accounts. Most of this money comes from reporting real estate deals as much smaller than they actually are. We send the money out of the country using the *hawala* networks, then invest those funds in overseas businesses. I can assure you we pay our share of taxes here in India. But why should we give everything to those scoundrels in the government?"

A sip of tea. "Everything seemed to be going well. Then the man in charge of our black money had heart problems. He retired and Jafar took his job. We are a well-known family who respect tradition.

Yes, Jafar was a lower caste, but he acted in a quiet, conservative manner . . . no Italian sports car or a vulgar mistress. He and Nalini built a house that was exactly right for their income and position."

"But there was a problem?"

"Two weeks ago, we needed to withdraw money from one of our international accounts, but our contact in Malaysia never received the transfer. On Friday, Jafar told me that he would look into the problem, but over the weekend Jafar, Nalini, and their son, Sanjay, disappeared from their home. There was still food in their cupboards, clothes in their closets. Their cars were still in the garage. We thought that they had been kidnapped by criminals or terrorists, then my oldest son discovered that six of our black money accounts had been looted. Jafar had transferred the funds so many times that we couldn't track the final destination. This was not a small sum of money, Mr. Underwood. He had betrayed me, betrayed our family, and stole approximately forty million American dollars."

"And then he passed through the Dubai airport," I said. "And he sent an e-mail to a young American woman at BDG named Emily Buchanan."

Pradhani slapped his fist onto an open palm. "Yes! Correct! She was part of the plan!"

"Are Jafar and his family in Dubai?"

"No. They're in Paris. An ordinary thief steals money and hides in the darkness, but not Jafar. Five days ago, he sent me a long e-mail that mentions Nalini's inheritance. Naturally, she gets less than my sons because she's a woman. That's our tradition. Jafar said that he took Nalini's 'fair share' and they'd moved to France. He boasted about his crimes . . . and then he threatened me. He swore that if anything unpleasant happened to him or Nalini, then all the information about the black money accounts would be displayed on the Internet."

"So Emily Buchanan is—"

"Jafar's insurance if he gets killed. Her identity was secret, of course, but then you found out about her and Miss Holquist contacted me."

"So what are you going to do?"

Pradhani leaned forward as if he expected his own voice to emerge from my mouth. "I want you to fly to Paris. You can do that. Correct?"

I nodded.

"Right now, the criminals are living in a building near the Luxembourg Gardens. I'll give you a few days to evaluate the situation and obtain a weapon. Then I want you to kill Jafar, Nalini, and their child."

For the first time since my Transformation, I *felt* something. Not anger. Or hatred. Or disgust. No emotions at all. But my Spark created a vision that I was falling through the stepwell. Looking up, I could see a circle of sunlight above me growing smaller and smaller until it vanished completely.

"You want me to kill your grandson?"

"Sanjay is not my true grandson. Poison is in the child's blood. If we kill the father and let the son live, he will grow up and attack the rest of our family."

"I work for the Special Services Section."

"What does that mean?"

"You pick the target, but I follow their instructions. Not yours."

"I will pay five times your regular fee and my staff will transfer the payment into any account you wish."

I stood up quickly. My Spark was cloudy and weak at this moment and I wanted to be alone. "I'll fly to Paris and neutralize Jafar. But any other targets require approval from Miss Holquist."

Pradhani shook his head. "I expected to meet a soldier, a cold-hearted *warrior*. Instead, they send me a clerk with a gun."

"Yes, I'm an employee. I receive and complete job orders. If my work is satisfactory, I receive payment for my services."

Pulling the phone out of my pocket, I walked over to the desk and picked up the revolver. Mr. Pradhani's sleepy eyelids opened fully when I pointed the gun at his head.

"Laura, access downloaded emotion file," I said. "Show fear."

Almost immediately a photograph of the French actor Jean

LeMarc appeared on the touchscreen. It pleased me that the black-and-white image of fear matched the expression on Mr. Pradhani's face.

"I don't care about your family or the stolen money or any of the other things you've mentioned. I like dogs, Mr. Pradhani. But I'm indifferent about you."

I pressed the release button, swung the cylinder out from the revolver, then tilted the gun backward and let the bullets fall into my left hand. After pocketing the ammunition, I tossed the weapon into the trash basket.

"Give me the address and the photographs. I'll be in Paris tomorrow."

11

When I reached the Delhi airport, I sent a message to Miss Holquist:

> // Met with the client in India. He asked for extra work that was
> not mentioned in our original discussion. I told him to contact
> you regarding this matter. On my way to Paris.

Then I flew nonstop to France and spent the night at the Ibis Hotel at Charles de Gaulle Airport. The Ibis was a transit hotel for travelers arriving or leaving on a plane. It was clean and functional with fluorescent lightbulbs that hummed softly. Bare walls.

I like hotels where you can check in at an electronic kiosk and never have to speak to a desk clerk. I dislike a gold-wrapped chocolate on my pillow, a turned-down sheet, a bathroom towel folded so that it resembles a flower, or any other "personal touch" that gives humans the illusion that they are surrounded by a friendly universe. In reality, the universe is neutral about our existence. Only dogs care.

. . .

I would have preferred to stay at the airport during my time in France, but my target lived in the center of Paris. It would take me several days to watch Jafar and his family, obtain a weapon from a supplier, and come up with a plan. The next morning, I told Edward to make a reservation at a hotel on the Left Bank, then drank a bottle of ComPlete and checked out.

The train clattered past dairy farms where white cows were grazing or staring at the horizon. Darkness as we entered a tunnel tagged with graffiti, and when we returned to sunlight the pastures had been replaced by modern apartment buildings with balconies and red-tile roofs. Looking up, I saw that overhead wires had divided the sky into a grid.

Surveillance cameras were everywhere, but two young men stood near the tracks spray-painting gigantic words on a retaining wall: JEUNESSE SANS AVENIR!

I typed the words into my computer and spoke to Edward. "Translate, please."

"Youth without a future."

"And what does that mean?"

"Checking, sir . . ." As always, Edward's voice was calm and polite. "The language analysis program states that it is 'a pessimistic slogan popular with antisocial elements.'"

The train stopped at a suburb called Aubervilliers that was filled with big, chunky housing projects that looked like stacks of children's blocks. Back into darkness, and then we arrived at Gare du Nord. This was my first time in Paris and my Spark was vibrating rapidly as I found the Metro entrance and bought a card for ten rides.

The Paris Metro smelled different than the New York subway—perhaps because of the rubber tires on the cars. When the train entered the station with a whooshing sound my mind saw a steel-blue color like a knife blade. I took a train to the Left Bank and when I emerged from the underground I was standing next to the Seine. The river was a dark green ribbon of energy contained within a stone channel. On the other side of a bridge, there was a huge building with spires and towers and flying buttresses holding the walls together.

Paris wasn't as dusty as India and beggars weren't tapping on the car window, but the city made me uncomfortable. The Parisians on the Left Bank didn't march forward in straight lines like the office workers climbing out of the subway on Wall Street. I disliked the open-air booksellers with their metal boxes filled with books beside the river. I disliked the cafés on the Quai des Grands Augustins with their small round tables and the curved-line chairs—everything too random and squeezed together.

I had made a reservation at a hotel that was a few blocks away from the Pont Neuf bridge. The desk clerk took me upstairs in a tiny elevator that couldn't speak or answer voice commands. Instead of a plastic access card, I was given an ornate key with a thick silk tassel that I had to carry around in my pocket. The furniture in my room was carved with scrolls and flowers and there were framed drawings of ballet dancers on the walls. I covered the bathroom mirror with newspaper and masking tape, drank a bottle of ComPlete, and then asked Edward if there were any messages.

"No e-mail, sir. Do you wish to contact someone?"

"No, thank you. Switch off now."

. . .

Lying on the bed, I tried to come up with a plan for finding Jafar Desai and his family. But gradually these practical thoughts were pushed away and images of India floated through my mind. I was sitting in the back of the Ambassador, leaving the airport for downtown Delhi. The driver turned his head, and I realized that it was Mr. Pradhani.

Tap-tap. Tap-tap.

I knew that the little girl was tapping on the window, but I refused to turn my head and see her.

Tap-tap. Tap-tap.

Mr. Pradhani nodded and I saw a revolver lying on the seat beside me. It had a long barrel and an ivory handle and looked like an old-fashioned six-shooter from a cowboy movie. I realized that Pradhani wanted me to pick up the gun, cock the hammer back with my thumb, and shoot the child on the other side of the glass.

Tap-tap.

But now my eyes opened and I realized I was lying on a bed in a hotel room. I fumbled around in the darkness for my phone and Laura responded immediately:

"Good evening, Mr. Underwood. How can I help you?"

I wondered what my Shadow would say if I described the situation. Most speech-recognition systems listened carefully to your statements and then repeated them back to you using different phrases. Dr. Tollner, the hospital psychiatrist, followed the same pattern.

"Laura . . . ?"

"Yes, sir."

"Should I kill a child?"

"It sounds like you're feeling uncertain about killing a child. So why do you feel that way, Mr. Underwood?"

"I'm not uncertain at all," I said, and switched her off.

If Miss Holquist refused Pradhani's request, then I would kill Jafar. If she agreed to his request, then I would neutralize all three members of the family. I could think of no logical reason why I should refuse this assignment. Both Good and Evil were only words swirling through my thoughts like dead leaves pushed by the wind.

But I found it difficult to sleep. Back in New York, I could have walked across the Brooklyn Bridge or followed a straight line up Sixth Avenue, but this was a foreign city with narrow, crooked streets. I needed thoughts that were powerful enough to push away the image of the child, so I propped myself up with pillows and entered the shadow land of memory.

.   .   .

After the motorcycle accident, I was in a coma for three weeks and two days. According to my medical file, I was breathing, my heart was beating, and there was neural oscillation—which meant that my central nervous system was generating electrical activity that followed a silent rhythm.

But my thoughts were lost in a darkness that was constant and absolute. My Spark was buried alive, trapped in a tomb, while my Shell was static, unmoved.

The record shows that my case was discussed every two or three days by the staff of the hospital's intensive care unit. Was I in a permanent coma? Should I be moved to a convalescent facility? During this entire period, there was only one inexplicable moment recorded in the "Staff Comment" section of my chart:

> Patient's primary surgeon consented to pet therapy for coma-tose patient. Handler arrived with dog #3, "Diamond." Handler placed dog on bed next to patient and nurse lifted patient's right arm and placed it on Diamond's back. No response for approximately five minutes, then nurse began moving patient's hand in petting motion along Diamond's back. Patient eyes fluttered, but did not open. Mouth moved slowly. When nurse removed hand from dog, face stopped moving. Nurse returned hand to dog. Finger moved slightly in stroking motion.

Did the softness of the dog's fur and the warmth of its skin touch some primitive core within my brain? Did the dog's energy somehow enter my body? It's only past a certain point that I can recall what happened. First I saw fragments of scattered light that flashed within dark clouds and then disappeared:

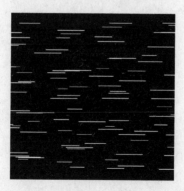

As time passed, these fragments melted into lines, became connected, and formed a rotating wheel of luminous energy.

The wheel moved faster and faster until it was condensed into the Spark—a single point of light contained within a Shell.

Have you ever seen a spark explode from a campfire? Pushed upward by the hot air, it darts, then drifts, then rises up above the flames. A spark is a brief event, a fragment of fire that is absorbed by the darkness.

But my Spark—

Remained.

When I opened my eyes, I saw a plastic IV bag hanging from a steel pole near the edge of my hospital bed. The bag seemed alive at that moment, like a translucent jellyfish floating in the sea.

Although it was painful to move, I could see objects clearly and could smell the hospital around me. The different way I perceived scent was the first sign of my Transformation. Yes, I could identify smells like a living person—the stench of dry blood and spilled urine not quite masked by the bleach-laundered sheets and the pine-scented disinfectant they used to mop the floors. But now these smells combined into a color that I could see in my mind. And the color wasn't yellow like urine or red like blood. When I closed my eyes, I saw an ash gray.

Darkness. And when I opened my eyes again, a middle-aged woman with wavy hair and a thin, pointed nose stared down at me.

"Mr. Davis? Are you awake? Can you hear me, Mr. Davis?"

I was looking at a human face, but there was no meaning there. I could perceive the physical movement of the woman's lips and eyebrows and the subtle adjustments of her head. But this Human Unit was as indecipherable as a water pump or a sewing machine. Although my Shell was numb with drugs and pain, my Spark instantly perceived this limitation and realized that some sort of capability had been lost.

"Mr. Davis, can you hear me?"

When I didn't respond, the woman leaned over the bed so that her face was only a few inches away from mine. "You've been in a serious accident and you've been unconscious for many days. I'm Eva Grasso, one of the nurses taking care of you. If you can hear me, blink two times."

No response.

"If you can hear me, blink two times."

No response.

"If you can hear me—"

I moved my mouth, but no sound came out. So I blinked. Twice.

Nurse Grasso's face changed. She pulled away from me and quickly left the room. When I opened my eyes, Nurse Grasso and a young East Asian man wearing a white lab coat were standing by the bed.

"Mr. Davis? I'm Dr. Sahid. Can you hear me?"

"Ask him to blink," the nurse said.

"Can you blink for me, Mr. Davis? Blink or say something."

I didn't want to speak. Unlike the two faces in front of me, I saw the world clearly. Reality had no meaning. The hospital room was simply a random assembly of objects. And I knew—knew with total certainty—that the act of speaking, the words themselves, would obscure the clarity of my vision.

"I know you can hear me," the doctor said. "It's important that you try to speak. It tells me a great deal about your injury. Can you—"

I wanted both of them to go away, so my Spark tossed a single word into the air.

"Dead."

The faces in front of me changed and a quick, throaty sound came out of their mouths. "Oh, you're alive, Mr. Davis!" the doctor said. "Very much alive! Considering the extent of your brain injury, I might even call it a miracle."

After this first conversation, I drifted in and out of darkness. Whenever I opened my eyes the nurses were checking the heart monitor, changing the IV bag, or cleaning my body with sponges as if it was a fixture attached to the hospital bed. This is when I realized that I hated to be touched. My Shell was fragile, and sometimes it felt as if they were cracking me open with their gloved fingers.

I could have stayed on the IV drip forever, but the nurses insisted on feeding me solid food—oatmeal, rice pudding, and small cubes of cooked chicken. My tongue could distinguish between sweet and sour, hot and cold. But there was no pleasure in the consumption of these substances. The nurses could have cooked the bedsheet and served it to me with a spoon.

One morning a hospital volunteer gave me a pair of earphones that was attached to a media channel. I could choose different styles of music by moving a small dial. The music was as tasteless as the rice pudding. People sang about losing love instead of something important—like losing their car keys. Finally I discovered that the classical-music station scheduled one hour every evening when they played only Bach. His music didn't cause emotions, but it kept my Spark steady and bright. Bach's notes were like bricks and nails and solid oak beams; they created structures with straight lines and balanced proportions.

There was a three-inch gap between the two window curtains, and this was the only indication of night and day. The sliver of light was growing dim when I opened my eyes and discovered two men standing at the foot of the bed.

Both of them wore leather jackets and carried motorcycle helmets. It was only much later—after I read the police report—that I realized that these men were Gerald Tannenbaum and Brian Farrell, the two friends who had watched me skid and smash into the stalled truck. All I knew was that Gerald showed his teeth when he talked and Brian spoke softly as if loud noises might injure me.

"Hey there, tough guy," Gerald said. "How you feeling?"

For the first time since my Transformation, I considered the question: *How do I feel?* And the answer came instantly, without effort. Aside from boredom and curiosity, I no longer felt any emotions.

I raised my hand and touched the EEG sensors pasted to my skull. "I'm connected to machines."

"The doctors say that you're getting better," Brian said. "Swear to God, when Gerald pulled off your helmet, we thought you were dead."

"*You* thought he was dead," Gerald announced. "Remember what I said? 'Don't touch him. Maybe he's got a spinal injury.'"

"But your spine is okay. You're going to walk again," Brian said. "But the doctors told us you had a brain injury."

"But *that's* okay," Gerald said. "Because you were always the smartest guy in the room. You've got brains to spare, Jake. Brian and me . . . hell, we can't afford to lose brain cells."

"Don't joke about his injuries," Brian said.

"I'm trying to be *positive*. That's all. Jake understands. When the hospital called and said you were talking, we both left work and came here."

"Your mom is in Los Angeles," Brian said. "But she'll be here in a few days."

"And I e-mailed Lynn," Gerald said. "She's in Milan organizing a fashion shoot, but she'll fly back as soon as possible."

Mr. Show My Teeth and Mr. Talk Softly glanced at each other. Brian was holding on to the chinstrap of his motorcycle helmet, and he shifted the helmet from one hand to another.

"You feeling better?" he asked. "I mean, you look tired, but you're awake and everything."

"Don't worry about your motorcycle," Gerald said. "It was taken to the state police parking lot. If you sign some papers, we can ship it back to New York City and see if it can be repaired."

Brian nodded. "And don't forget, Olivia and I still want you to be one of the ushers at our wedding."

Gerald showed his teeth again. "Anyone who rents a wedding tuxedo can't die."

My mouth moved and sounds came out. "Leave . . . room . . . now."

The two men glanced at each other. "Okay. No problem. Don't worry about anything," Brian said. "I'll call your boss at InterFace and tell him that you're getting better."

"What . . . is . . . InterFace?"

Once again they glanced at each other. "It's your job, Jake. That's where you worked."

"But don't worry about that right now," Gerald said. "Just remember that Brian and I are your true friends. Friendship is everything. Friendship endures."

Both of these true friends vanished from the room and I never saw them again. The hospital routine continued and I practiced talking to the nurses. Three days after the moment with Brian and Gerald, I opened my eyes and realized that a woman with gray hair and a saggy face was sitting on a chair beside the bed.

"Jacob? Are you awake?" she whispered. "I've been praying for you. I prayed with all my heart. God listens to us, Jacob. God knows what we need. I told you that when you were a little boy. And now you're living proof of God's power."

"Who are you?"

The woman's voice changed, but I didn't understand its meaning. "I'm—I'm your mother, Jacob. I held you when you were a little baby."

My Spark knew the definition of a mother. I also knew that children were supposed to feel some kind of strong emotions for this kind of person. But I was annoyed that she was clutching my right hand. Her face kept changing and that bothered me as well. Why were human beings so unstable? The door and the curtains and the supply cabinet didn't continually change their appearance.

The woman's eyes began to glisten like two wet stones and then a drop of clear liquid trickled down her cheek. "Please say that you know me, Jacob. *Please*. A son always knows his mother."

"I've had an accident."

"Yes, I know. Very serious. Broken bones and a brain injury."

"I don't know what I am."

"Well, of course, Jacob. I'm sure you're confused. But right now the two of us are together. That's all that's important."

Before I could object, she guided my hand up to her cheek. Now I could feel the moisture leaking from her eyes.

"A mother's tears, Jacob. Feel a mother's tears."

With my left hand, I pressed the button that rang an alarm at the nurse's station.

"We need to get you back to New York City, Jacob. The doctors aren't very good at this hospital. You need to see a *specialist*."

The door squeaked open and Nurse Grasso appeared. "Yes, Mr. Davis? What's the problem?"

"I don't want this person here. Remove her from my room."

Nurse Grasso took one step toward the woman who was holding my hand. "I'm sorry, ma'am. I don't know what's going on right now, but it's probably best for you to—"

The old woman stood up and her voice got loud. "Don't you dare touch me! I'll sue you! I'll sue everyone in this hospital!"

"Mrs. Davis, please . . ."

"This is my child! My little boy!"

"He's still recovering. We need to keep him from getting upset."

"I'm the one who's upset! Jacob! Please tell the nurse that you know me."

I didn't say anything. Nurse Grasso touched the woman's arm and then they were gone. Their voices faded down the hallway.

My last visitor appeared two days later. It was late in the afternoon and I was lying on the bed, watching the cathode tube in my heart monitor. A jittery green line glowed and danced with a rhythm unconnected to my Shell.

The door opened and a young woman entered the room. She wore a pale blue overcoat and a white blouse opened at the neck that showed a braided gold necklace. Her perfume smelled like flowers, and the scent was pinkish green within my mind.

The woman paused for a moment, staring at me, and then took a step forward. Her hands moved quickly and her voice was breathless.

"Are you awake?"

"Yes."

And now she came forward quickly as words flowed from her mouth. "Oh, Jake . . . darling . . . I . . . I told myself all the way here . . . 'Don't cry, Lynn. It doesn't help if you cry.' But I'm happy. So . . . So *happy*."

"Did you talk to Nurse Grasso?"

"Who? Which one is that? I was practically *living* here for three days after the accident and all the nurses blurred together into one pastel blob. There was the fat one. And the Filipino one . . ."

"It says Grasso on her name tag."

"Oh, I don't notice all that nonsense. If she's the one with the broad hips and the pointy nose, then I think I know who you're talking about. Tell you what . . . I'll bring her a little gift next time I'm here. I was going to do it before, but what do you give nurses *anyway*? Support hose? Practical shoes? I know. I'll find out what sort of dreadful chain stores they have around here and give her a gift certificate."

The energy coming from her body and the quick motions of her hands made me uncomfortable, but she didn't seem to notice.

"I'm just chattering away, aren't I? You always teased me about my talking too fast. But I'm . . . I'm nervous and happy and . . . and I just want to lie next to you. But I don't want any alarms going off."

"Don't touch the bed," I told her. "Sit there."

The young woman sat down on the chair beside the bed. For a few seconds, she was quiet.

"So what did you say to your mother, Jake? I called her when I was driving up here and she just started crying. She said you didn't recognize her but, of course, you know *me*."

"What is InterFace?" I asked. "Tell me about InterFace."

"God, you are *so* responsible. You almost *died* in a horrible motorcycle accident and all you can think about is *work*. Don't worry about those bastards. You're brilliant, Jake. You can always get another job."

"What did I do at InterFace?"

"Don't you remember?"

"Tell me."

"It was all about nubots and artificial intelligence. That's where the big money is these days. It's really cutting-edge."

"So what—"

"You were designing a speech-recognition program. Right now, the computer at a call-in service center knows when a customer gets angry. But your program was going to be sensitive enough to figure out when someone was *beginning* to get angry. And that, of course, would guide the responses from the machine. Does that make sense? I hope it makes sense. Anyway, that's how you described it."

All this information about my job was too much to process quickly. I wanted her to go away so that my Spark could absorb the data.

"What did the doctors say about my condition?"

"When I was here last time, they said that you weren't paralyzed and that you were showing brain activity. After that conversation, I sat on the bench near the nurse's station and tried to project positive images. I saw the two of us walking hand in hand on a beach and then you stopped and kissed me."

"Why would I do that?"

"Because you always liked kissing me, and everything else that goes with it."

Lynn stood up and leaned forward. I thought she was going to adjust the sheets like Nurse Grasso, but she leaned forward and pressed her lips against mine. Then she pulled away and showed her teeth. "*There.* I hope that refreshes your memory."

"Why did you do that?"

"Because I love you. Yes, I know we argued a lot and I broke up with you twice. But when I walked into this room for the first time and saw you lying here . . . looking like you were dead . . . I prayed . . . I prayed to God that you would come back to me so that I could say, 'Please, forgive me, darling.'"

"And now what happens?"

"Now you'll get better, of course. I think you should sue the driver of that broken-down truck and . . . after you get the insurance settlement . . . I'll quit the magazine. We'll pack our bags and go someplace peaceful and lovely like Tuscany or the south of France. And we'll just live there and pick olives and drink wine and be happy forever. Because we *love* each other. The accident made me realize that."

"I'm tired."

"Yes . . . of course . . . I understand." She leaned forward again and her lips touched my forehead. "I'm going to drive back to New York on wings, darling."

After she left the room, I pressed the call button until Nurse Grasso walked in.

"Did you see that woman?"

"Yes, Mr. Davis. That's your girlfriend, Miss Patterson. She's so *glamorous.*"

"I never want to see her again."

Nurse Grasso's eyebrows went up and her lips squashed together in a crooked line. "As you *wish,*" she said, and then she straightened up my sheets and marched out of the room. I had just encountered my friends, my mother, and a woman who said that she loved me. Their behavior indicated that I should experience an emotion, but nothing like that had occurred. All these humans were just objects—like a trash can or a chair.

Several hours passed until I remembered that a black saddlebag that had once been strapped to my motorcycle seat was now stored in the closet. For the first time since my accident, I detached myself from my wires and tubes, got out of bed, and shuffled across the room. It felt as if my legs had lost the power to hold me up. Clutching the bed frame to steady myself, I reached out with my free hand and opened the closet.

I was startled by the mirror on the back of the closet door. This was the first time I had seen my face since the Transformation and I realized that—in some way—I had died. My eyes weren't attached to the rest of my body; it looked as if they were trapped inside a hollow statue, peering out through two holes.

I pulled my computer out of the saddlebag, returned to my bed, and lay there for several hours with the computer resting on my stomach. Around three o'clock in the morning I slipped on the headset and touched my thumb to the activation square. "Hello," I whispered. "Hello . . ."

"Good evening," Edward replied with his butler's voice. I knew that he was a Shadow created by a software program, but now everything felt different. This computer was no longer a mechanical device—it was an extension of my mind.

"I need to organize my thoughts."

"Would you like to make a list, sir?" Edward asked.

"Yes. But I can't use the keyboard. Activate voice-to-text option."

A task-list template appeared on the screen and a cursor flashed slowly as if the computer had a pulse. When I spoke, words appeared:

I am a

But then I stopped talking. Although a Transformation had occurred, I still didn't understand my new reality.

"Continue," Edward said.

I stayed silent.

"Continue . . ."

12

When I opened my eyes in the hotel room it was almost nine o'clock in the evening. I checked my computer pad and saw that there weren't any messages from Miss Holquist. The ballet dancers on the wall were staring at me, so I left the hotel and walked over to the Boulevard Saint-Michel. There was a large crowd in front of a store window and I stepped forward to see what was going on.

Robots that looked like human beings were still expensive, and most of them were used for jobs that required limited, repetitive movements—like the factory workers who made phones or the subway clerks in New York City. But the wide-scale aborting of female fetuses in China and the resulting gender imbalance had caused a great deal of research and development in the pleasure bot industry. Thousands of these androids were provided for public use in government-owned facilities throughout China. The modest charge for the use of pleasure bots helped stabilize the restless male population and lessened the spread of the new Stem-C virus that had wiped out half the population of Mozambique.

In the shopwindow were two Chinese-made androids: "The Perfect Wife" and "Your Best Girl." Wearing black lingerie, these machines moved around a fake bedroom. The blond pleasure bot arranged her hair, and then knelt down on a rug to pick up a fallen hairbrush. The bot with Asian features got out of bed, walked over to the window, and waved her finger at all the onlookers spying on her. Then she returned to bed and lay down again.

I glanced at the Human Units surrounding me on the sidewalk. The young people with friends were laughing and making comments to each other. But the solitary men stared at the two machines with their hands clenched and their lips pressed together. The androids could talk to you and respond to your instructions. These models even had detachable pubic cartridges that could be removed and sterilized after use. Perhaps the men were comparing the bots to human partners who might argue and walk out the door. A machine was always there—and always compliant—until you replaced it with a new model.

It made no difference to me if nubots sat in subway booths or walked around wearing lingerie. But they did remind me of Dr. Noland's view of humanity. When I was at the clinic, he told me that human beings were organic machines that thought they were real. And that fact, according to the doctor, was either "very funny or very tragic."

The store had placed a placard on the wall of the imaginary bedroom. I photographed the words with my phone and Laura translated them into English.

We reject the antitechnology ideas expressed in Monsieur Rossard's essay published in *Le Monde*. These beautiful machines wearing lingerie are not foreign inventions that destroy French Culture. They are the most recent evolution of a quest that began in France during the Age of Enlightenment. In the eighteenth century, the brilliant Jacques de Vaucanson first caught the attention of the public with his Flute Player and Mechanical Duck. King Louis XV was so inspired by Vaucanson's work that he commissioned the inventor to create the famous Bleeding Man. Inventions from this era can be seen at the National Conservatory of Arts and Crafts. The daily demonstration of automates at the Conservatory shows that French scientists and engineers were the first to propose, design, and create mechanical life. The pleasure bots for sale in our store were constructed in China, but their true birthplace is in France!

I returned to my hotel and checked my e-mail, but the message box was still empty. There was nothing to do until Miss Holquist decided if I should neutralize Nalini and her son. Back in New York I could have remained in my loft, but my hotel room in Paris was a busy, jagged environment. Although I had covered up the mirrors, there were too many pieces of furniture and the ballet dancers screwed to the wall stared at me when I sat on the edge of the bed.

Durée de vie mécanique. Mechanical life. I liked that phrase, and was curious about the other facts mentioned in the department store placard. That night, Edward helped me find articles about the mechanical toys called *automates* popular in eighteenth-century France and the Frenchman named Jacques de Vaucanson, who built machines with a whole new level of sophistication.

As a young man Vaucanson was expelled from a religious order in Lyon for creating mechanical servants that could serve dinner to the monks. He moved to Paris, found wealthy patrons to finance his work, and, in 1738, displayed a large wooden man, painted white like a statue. This *automate* had lips and fingers and leather lungs that breathed out air when it played the flute. A year later Vaucanson caused another sensation with a Mechanical Duck that gulped down food with its beak and excreted it a few minutes later.

Louis XV was impressed with Vaucanson's creations and offered to fund the construction of a mechanical man with a beating heart and blood in its veins. Vaucanson returned to Lyon and set up a secret laboratory where he began to build the "Bleeding Man." The King rewarded his new servant with a patronage job: Royal Inspector of Manufactured Silk. Within a few years, Vaucanson modernized all the looms in France, destroying the jobs of thousands of people. Some of the textile workers rioted and tried to destroy the new machines, but the rebellion was crushed by the authorities.

So where was the Flute Player and the Duck and, above all, the Bleeding Man? Late that afternoon I crossed over to the right bank of the Seine and visited the Conservatoire National des Arts et

Métiers. If any of Vaucanson's *automates* had survived, they would probably be stored there.

I expected the conservatory to be a glass-and-steel box, but the government had placed both the school and museum in the former priory of Saint-Martin-des-Champs. The complex of buildings looked like a medieval fortress with a church, a manor house, and several towers with slit windows. Passing through a turnstile, I wandered down corridors gazing at rusty machines and faded portraits of French inventors.

I asked a guard in English, "Where are the *automates*?" He pointed me down a corridor lined with water pumps and steam-powered looms. When I turned the corner I found myself standing in line with a mob of children and their parents.

Another guard appeared and pulled open a large oak door with brass fittings. Following the crowd, I found myself in a windowless lecture hall with tiers of wooden seats facing a black marble table and a wall of display cabinets. The only available seats were on the top row, so I climbed up the tiers and looked down over the heads of the French families. Small painted faces, grinning or solemn, peered out from the glass cabinets; I was looking at forty to fifty mechanical creatures—the *automates*.

At exactly 1700 hours, the door creaked open and a small man wearing a light blue smock and white cotton gloves marched in and took his position behind the table. The man's face was free of sags and wrinkles. His hair glistened with some sort of pomade or cream; it looked as if each follicle was plastered to the top of his skull.

This was the Keeper of the Automates. He bowed to his audience, and then gave a little speech in French. I had no idea what he was saying but assumed that he was talking about the machines waiting behind him. The Keeper spoke slowly and each word was separate and precise.

After he had finished his introduction, he pulled out a ring of old-fashioned keys and began to open the doors of the cabinets. As he removed each *automate*—a peasant clutching a flail or a mother in a rocking chair with a baby—he announced the name of the machine's inventor and the date of its creation.

The twelve *automates* were placed in two equal groups at opposite ends of the table. The Keeper bowed again and made them perform. First he would insert a little key or turn a crank that wound up a hidden spring. He would pause for several seconds, then flick a lever and the *automate* would suddenly come alive. An acrobat swung on a pole. A cavalry officer drew his sword and rode a horse around a little track. And, as the children giggled and shrieked, a condemned man placed his head in a guillotine and a hooded executioner pulled a cord and chopped off a painted head.

The Keeper made another speech, then returned to the cabinet and came back with a blond-haired girl in a golden gown who was seated in front of a dulcimer. Once again, he turned a key and flicked a lever. The girl began to play, striking the strings with two small hammers. The Dulcimer Player's chest moved in and out as if she was breathing. After a minute of playing, she gracefully turned her head to smile at the audience. Even the most restless child was still and silent as the music rose up and drifted through the room. One last smile. And then the tune ended and the machine stopped moving.

Everyone in the audience waited for a few seconds, breathless and silent, expecting the *automate* to stand up and dance around the room. But no, the performance was over and the two little hammers remained motionless above the strings. The Keeper bowed, and the crowd applauded the presentation and quickly left the lecture hall. Mothers and fathers glanced at the mechanical creatures and then touched their children, as if somehow these ancient machines were going to jump off the table and attack someone.

I remained in my seat as the Keeper picked up each mechanism and carefully returned it to the cabinets. When he had put away everything but the Dulcimer Player, I left my seat and approached him.

"Excuse me, sir. Do you speak English?"

The Keeper locked a cabinet with a little brass key, then turned and faced me.

"Yes. A little."

"I have been reading about Jacques de Vaucanson. He sounds like a great man."

The Keeper smiled and nodded rapidly. *"Oui . . . Oui . . . Il était un génie."*

"So what happened to the Lute Player and the Duck and the Bleeding Man? Are they somewhere in France? Can I go see them?"

The Keeper placed the palms of his hands on the table as if he was continuing his presentation. *"Non, c'était une tragédie.* Vaucanson wants money, so he sells the Flute Player and the Duck. The two *automates* tour Europe for many years. The Flute Player is lost in a shipwreck near Sicily. The Duck perishes in a fire in Kraków in 1879."

"And the Bleeding Man?"

"L'homme saignant," the Keeper said, as if this creation was too important to be translated into English. "There are rumors that Vaucanson discovers the secret of mixing rubber with sulfur and sealing it with heat. He uses this substance to create a heart and veins for his Man. Louis Davout . . . one of Napoleon's generals . . . sees the Man use a knife and fork at a private dinner in Rome. Thirty years later, Gerhardt Steiner, the German industrialist, shows his friends an *automate* that resembles the only drawing we have of the Man."

"So where is he now?"

"Many treasures vanished because of the Second World War. There are no sightings of the Man after 1937. But perhaps . . ."

"Perhaps what?"

"Perhaps other inventors added . . . inventions . . . modifications." The Keeper of the Automates smiled. "Remember, Monsieur, unlike *humains fragiles,* Vaucanson's creation cannot die. He could be in Paris at this moment, walking down the street."

"Or perhaps he was destroyed."

The Keeper bowed and picked up the golden-haired Dulcimer Player. "The *idea* was not destroyed. Ideas are the true *automates.*"

.   .   .

I left the museum, walked a few blocks, and found myself in what appeared to be the Chinatown of Paris. There were vendors selling fake designer handbags, Chinese restaurants, and open-air markets selling food. I passed a mound of yellow musk melons, a bucket filled with mussels, and a live chicken pulled squawking and struggling from a wire cage.

Instead of taking the Metro, I walked across the river Seine and Laura guided me back to my hotel. I didn't want to sit in my room and stare at the ballet dancers, so I took my computer and went down to a café. I ordered a bottle of mineral water and watched a soccer match on the café's television.

Was the Bleeding Man cheering at the stadium? If he could disguise himself as an ordinary person and get the right ID card, then he could lose himself in the crowd. Like the *automates* in the Keeper's museum, most Human Units obeyed hidden clockwork that controlled their movements and guided their reactions.

But I was in a different category. I was sure of that fact. It was all because of the Transformation.

The staff at Marian Community Hospital had decided that I was a patient with severe neurological damage. But I realized that the accident had allowed me to see all existence in a profoundly different way. The Spark within me was as pure as light. It transcended time.

Most Human Units saw time as a linear progression.

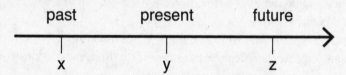

But now I realized that time curved back on itself.

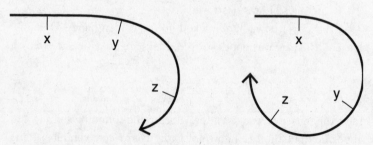

All moments exist simultaneously. They don't disappear.

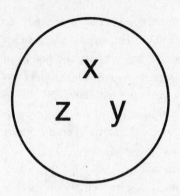

My Spark was pure and permanent, but it existed in a world that was tainted and corrupt. This is why I told the nurses that they could no longer touch me. With great effort, I forced my Shell to wash itself, check temperature and pulse, and inject the necessary medication. Because it was difficult to communicate with the hospital staff, I spent most of my time talking to Edward. I would tell him my vital signs and he would e-mail the information to the nurses' station.

When I was strong enough to limp up and down the second-floor hallway, I announced that I would no longer eat dead and rotting objects from the corrupt world. From this point on, I would consume only clear liquids such as broth, apple juice, and water. This refusal smashed into a wall of resistance. I was told by several doctors that my Shell would perish without sufficient nourishment. If I continued to say no I would be placed in restraints and a feeding tube would be shoved down my throat.

This conflict was resolved by Sandy Shapiro—the short, plump woman who was a case manager at the hospital. In computer terms, she was programmed to respond in the affirmation mode and was constantly popping into my room to say phrases like "Looking good, Jacob!" or "Getting better!" Mrs. Shapiro covered up all the mirrors in my hospital room with masking tape and newspaper, and then persuaded me to drink ComPlete. The doctors were satisfied with this solution, and I didn't have to swallow death disguised as a tuna sandwich.

Each act of resistance generated a response from the hospital psychiatrist, Dr. Tollner. He was an energetic man in his thirties who wore jeans under his lab coat and had a gold stud in his left ear. Whenever I said no to anything, Tollner would arrive with a clipboard and ask me how I felt about this new issue.

"I don't feel anything."

"Is that really true, Mr. Davis? Perhaps you're feeling anger or fear about being in the hospital."

"No. It's okay to be here."

"There's nothing wrong with emotions. They're a natural human reaction."

"I don't have those reactions. I'm dead."

I thought this statement would end the psychiatrist's questions, but he began to drop by my room during his daily rounds. One afternoon, while I was drawing diagrams on my computer, Tollner walked in with his clipboard and sat down on the chair next to my bed.

"I'm afraid I have some bad news, Jacob."

I remained silent and continued designing my Pyramid of Life. Dogs were at the top and I was at the base, but I hadn't figured out where to put cats.

"Don't you want to know what happened?"

"Did the kitchen run out of ComPlete?"

"No. It's a bit more serious than that."

"I don't want a tube shoved down my throat."

"This isn't about you, Jacob. But it is bad news. Nurse Grasso was killed driving home from the hospital last night. A trailer truck skidded on the ice, rolled over, and crushed Eva's car."

I continued to work on my drawing.

"So how does that make you *feel*?" Tollner asked.

"Things happen. Last week they put blue sheets on my bed instead of white sheets."

"But you *knew* Nurse Grasso. She was the first person you saw when you opened your eyes."

"Yes. That's true."

"Now she's dead and you'll never see her again."

"That statement could be made about all objects that exist in this room. If they take away the sponge mop in the corner, perhaps I'll never see it again."

"Eva Grasso is . . . was . . ." Dr. Tollner was speaking loudly. "She wasn't a sponge mop!"

"Of course not, Dr. Tollner. They're two different objects. Nurse Grasso wore a top with a floral design and blue cotton pants. She was mobile and could talk."

Dr. Tollner left the room—which meant there was a chance that I would never see him again. But there was a high probability that he *would* return, so I spent the rest of the day creating a new set of drawings. When Tollner returned the following afternoon, I showed him the computer screen.

"This is your reality, Dr. Tollner. You are a Shell containing a Spark who feels attachments to other Human Units."

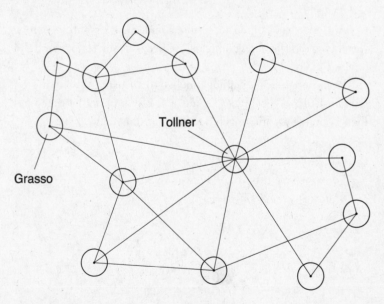

Tollner nodded. "Very good, Jacob. This is an accurate expression of interpersonal relationships."

"If Nurse Grasso breaks away from your personal cluster, then you are conscious of this loss."

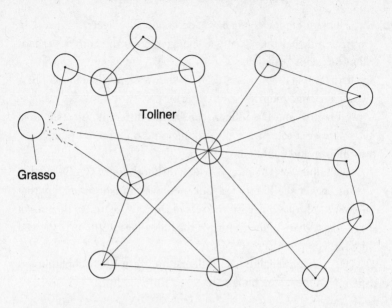

"And that makes me sad," Tollner said. "There's nothing wrong with being sad, Jacob. As humans, we occasionally feel sad . . . and happy, too."

"Because I'm dead, I'm not attached to a cluster. When I meet a Human Unit, we occupy the same space for a period of time, and then I bounce off and travel in a different direction."

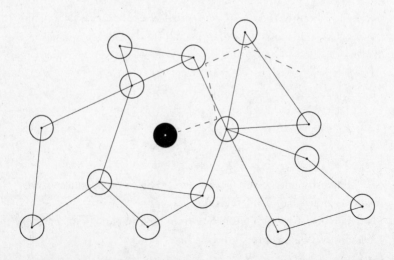

The psychiatrist studied the diagrams on my computer screen while he scribbled notes on his clipboard. "Could I get a copy of your illustrations?" he asked.

"They're not illustrations. They're explanations."

"Of course. I understand. *Explanations.*" He wrote down that word in block letters. "Your explanations help me understand you better, Jacob. And that might make your time here at the hospital less confrontational."

That sounded like a good idea, so I allowed him to return with a flash drive and download all my drawings. A week later, Sandy Shapiro informed me that my medical insurance covered only sixty days of hospital care and that it was necessary for me to continue my recovery as an outpatient back in New York. But first I needed to attend a case review with Tollner and the hospital neurologist, Dr. Rose.

None of the patients at Marian Hospital used the third-floor chapel, and this was where the meeting took place. Tollner and Rose sat at a table with printed copies of my file. There was a large bronze cross behind them that jutted out from a fake stained-glass window lit by fluorescent bulbs. Something was wrong with the fixture and light behind the top portion of the cross kept flickering on and off.

I sat on a folding chair, facing the doctors. Although I still couldn't interpret the emotions expressed by a human face, I did appreciate the thoughtful placement of Mrs. Shapiro's chair. As chief mediator and explainer, she sat halfway between the doctors and my Shell. During the conversation, her head went back and forth like a spectator watching a tennis match.

Dr. Rose, the neurologist, was a skinny older man with sandy-colored hair. He always mentioned golf during our examinations, and once I saw him leaving the hospital early in the afternoon with a bag of clubs. "I'm going to lead off here," he said. "Mr. Davis, your improvement in the last two months has been extraordinary. When you first arrived here, there were indications that you might be brain-dead or permanently disabled. Now you're conscious, fully ambulatory, and able to interact with the world."

"But there was brain damage," Mrs. Shapiro said, motioning to Dr. Rose's notebook computer.

"Yes. That's true. You can see it quite clearly. . . ." Dr. Rose typed a command, then swiveled the computer around so I could see a video of my brain taken by an MRI machine. The image changed every five seconds as the machine peeled back another layer of tissue, going deeper into my brain, burrowing toward the core.

Dr. Rose pointed at bright and dark patches with a pencil. "As you can see, you've had some profound damage in the ventromedial area of the cortex—this section integrates signals from other parts of the brain to generate social reactions."

"And then there's the amygdala. . . ." Dr. Tollner said.

"Correct." Rose pointed his pencil again. "You might not be able to see that. It's about the size of an almond. But the amygdala helps us recognize threats and generates an emotional response. The sensory pathways to your amygdala have been destroyed. They may heal over time, but you've had some profound damage there."

"But I can talk and walk around the hospital. . . ."

"Yes, I know. I bet you could play a round of golf, too. But there have been some *problems* caused by your injuries, which Dr. Tollner will discuss."

Tollner pushed down the computer screen, as if the dark areas of my brain were a distraction. "Mr. Davis, you are suffering from a neuropsychiatric disorder called Cotard's syndrome. It's named after a French neurologist who first described the condition in 1880. Patients like you exhibit the delusional belief that they are dead or somehow empty inside."

Tollner stopped speaking for a moment and all three Human Units stared at me. I realized that there was some significance in this moment, but I couldn't understand its meaning. Not knowing what to say, I remained quiet. And the two silences contemplated each other.

"Cotard's syndrome explains your abnormal thoughts and actions. Your brain identified your mother and your girlfriend, but you couldn't generate emotions with that act of recognition."

"You know you should feel, but you can't feel," Dr. Rose said.

"Correct," Tollner said. "This disconnect has to be explained by your consciousness—so you've come up with the delusional idea that you don't exist."

"I'm sure that it must be very frightening," Mrs. Shapiro said.

"I'm not frightened at all."

"Yes. You've lost your sense of fear," Dr. Rose said. "The ventro-medial area of the cortex reacts to danger and helps us make moral decisions. This is a neurological issue, Mr. Davis. But you've come up with a supernatural explanation."

Once again, there was a moment of silence as the two doctors and Sandy Shapiro glanced at each other.

"So how do you feel about all this?" Mrs. Shapiro asked with a soft voice.

"I have explained my condition to Dr. Tollner. My Spark exists and my Shell reacts to stimuli. The rest is darkness."

"But that's *wrong*," Dr. Tollner said, slapping the word onto the table. "That's a *delusion*."

"I've been transformed," I said. "Perhaps you're frightened of death, Doctor. But it doesn't bother me anymore."

Dr. Rose held up one hand like a traffic cop stopping a line of cars. "*Cogito, ergo sum.* Ever hear that phrase? A French philosopher named René Descartes wrote that a long time ago. *Cogito, ergo sum* means 'I think, therefore I am.'"

Dr. Tollner shook his head. "Paul, I don't know if this is helpful."

"Let me run with this, Steven. . . ." Dr. Rose looked back at me. "So this Spark of yours is thinking. Isn't that right, Mr. Davis?"

I nodded.

"The fact that you're thinking proves that you're alive."

"*Cogito*—" I said, trying out the word. KO-gee-toe.

"—*ergo sum*," Dr. Rose answered.

"I am thinking," I said. "But that doesn't mean that I exist as a Human Unit."

Tollner put his hand on Dr. Rose's shoulder. "There's no need to continue this discussion, Paul. It's a waste of time to debate reality with psychotics." He turned back to me. "You're checking out of the hospital tomorrow, Mr. Davis. We're going to give you ninety-day prescriptions for the drugs you've been taking here at the hospital."

"You should keep taking an antipsychotic medication called Souzan," Dr. Rose said. "It will dull or lessen the immediacy of your delusions."

"And we've all agreed that you should stay on Taldor," Mrs. Shapiro explained. "I also take a low dosage of that medication . . . every day. It's an antianxiety drug that will make you feel calm and even-tempered."

"We're pairing Taldor with an antidepressant drug called Moxiphin," Dr. Tollner said. "Take your medication and stay away from alcohol and street narcotics. It's possible, over time, that your brain may heal itself."

The woman who said she was my mother wanted to drive me back to New York, but I refused to answer her phone calls. It looked like I was just going to walk out of the hospital, but Mrs. Shapiro found an orderly named Isaiah Liggins who wanted to visit a sister who lived in the city. For a small sum of money, he agreed to drop me off at my apartment.

Isaiah was a solid mound of flesh and bone who stayed quiet during our trip down the thruway. Two large hospital envelopes remained on my lap. One envelope contained hospital invoices and the contents of my blood-splattered wallet; the other was filled with enough pills for seven days of medication.

We arrived in Manhattan around six o'clock in the evening and Isaiah double-parked in front of a brownstone on East Seventy-Eighth Street. "This is it," he announced. "This is where you live." Then he led me over to an entry door. There was a doorbell panel with brass buttons. The name J. DAVIS was held captive beneath a clear Plexiglas shield.

"You okay?" Isaiah asked. "The nurses started talking about you last night when they learned that I was driving you down to the city. You're the dead man, right? At least you think you're dead. Maybe you're crazy or maybe you're just jumping ahead a few years. Everyone's going to die eventually. And then the wicked got to face God and all his angels on Judgment Day."

"So now what do I do?"

"Mind if I look at your stuff?" Isaiah opened up one of the envelopes and shook out a few keys. "This here looks like your front-door key and these two will probably let you into your apartment. So go inside, walk upstairs, and start your life again."

I inserted the gold key into the lock and opened the entrance door. When I walked inside, the door closed behind me, but Isaiah shouted through the glass, "Take care of yourself, my brother! God watches us all!"

.   .   .

Sitting in the café across the street from my hotel, I drank some bottled water and watched a soccer match on my computer. A year ago, I had downloaded a software application that turned the soccer ball into a point of red light. Usually, I would just watch the ball and ignore the players.

My computer beeped softly and I slipped on my headset. "You have a FaceTime request coming from the United States," Edward said. "Do you want to accept the call?"

FaceTime was a webcam software application. It was on my computer, but I rarely used it. I switched off the soccer game and glanced around my table to see if anyone was watching. It was close to midnight and the café was almost empty. A young couple paid their check while an African man with tribal scars cut into his cheeks started to mop the floor.

"Yes. Switch it on," I told Edward.

A moment later, Miss Holquist appeared on the screen. She was holding her tablet computer with one hand and the image wasn't stable. "Can we talk? Are you in a secure place?"

"Yes."

"This afternoon, I spoke to our client in India. Your meeting went well. He said you were very calm and efficient."

"Did you receive my e-mail?"

"Yes, I did." Miss Holquist smiled. "I'm glad that you checked with me."

"He wanted me to meet with three customers."

"Yes. I know. That request is a bit unusual, but he's an important client."

Miss Holquist shifted the tablet around and I briefly saw a standing lamp and the back of a couch. It looked like she was sitting in her apartment.

"I am authorizing the sales presentation requested by the client."

"Three?" I asked.

"Yes, all three." She smiled again. "Obviously, you'll be paid an additional fee for the extra work."

"This might be a difficult assignment."

"I understand that. Be careful, be organized, and take your time. I'll contact our friends in Paris. You'll get equipment for your presentation in a few days."

"This might be—"

"I'm sure you'll solve the problem, Mr. Underwood. You're my best employee."

I heard voices in the background, and Miss Holquist turned toward someone who wasn't in the picture. "Just get my credit card and call them," she said. "My purse is on the kitchen counter." Miss Holquist returned her attention to the tablet screen. "Normally, I'd tell anyone visiting Paris to go to a three-star restaurant or an art museum. But that's not you, is it? You're a very basic person. Take care, Underwood. Let me know what's going on."

Her face disappeared. Silence. I stared at the blue screen until an elderly waiter shuffled over to the table with the bill.

"Everything finished," he said. *"Terminée."*

13

The next morning, I turned on my computer and made a new list with Power-I. It made my actions appear logical and orderly.

Objectives in Paris

1. Avoid attention from the police
2. Obtain weapon from a supplier
3. Find and observe Jafar and his family
4. Prepare a plan
5. Neutralize all targets
6. Leave France immediately

Mr. Pradhani had given me a Paris address and photographs of Jafar Desai, his wife, Nalini, and their little boy, Sanjay, that had been taken at a family wedding. Number 15 Rue de Tournon turned out to be a former palace built in the classical style that was a half block away from the Luxembourg Gardens. The building's entrance was wide enough for a horse and carriage, and it was framed by two Greek columns. Both wood doors were open, revealing a cobblestone courtyard where a few cars were parked on one side. Three floors of windows looked out on this courtyard, but their gauzy curtains concealed what was going on in the rooms.

This is when I encountered my first problem. There were six names on the brass doorbell panel near the entrance, and none of them said "Jafar Desai." This building had once been something historical, but now six wealthy families occupied the different suites. This meant that I couldn't just visit one apartment with a gun and shoot whoever answered the door.

So how was I supposed to confirm that Jafar and his family actually lived in the building? I couldn't place a Sentinel on the busy street, and all the NO PARKING signs meant it wasn't feasible to wait in a rental car. Fortunately, the Café Tournon was a hundred yards up the sidewalk. If it wasn't raining, I could sit at an outside table on a rattan bistro chair and watch the entrance until my targets appeared.

But the café created a second problem. Most Human Units want a logical reason for your continued presence in their location. An official-looking clipboard and hard hat provide an instant answer to most questions, but that wasn't going to work on the Rue de Tournon. That morning I bought a cane with a silver handle at an antique shop near the river, and then placed a stone inside my shoe. I was limping when I returned to the café, and the different facial expressions stored on my phone indicated that the waiter displayed sympathy. Now there was a logical explanation for why this crippled foreigner was going to sit in a café for several hours, ordering bottled water and leaving a big tip.

None of my targets appeared that first afternoon, and I wondered if Mr. Pradhani had given me the right address. The next morning, I arrived early at the café and sat at a table that gave me a clear view of the building. At 8:40 a.m., a black Citroën pulled up and a young man with close-cropped hair jumped out. He pressed a button down on the door buzzer panel, said something into the speaker, and then waited on the sidewalk with both hands stuffed into the outside pockets of a raincoat. This young bodyguard remained at his post—alert and waiting—until Jafar Desai walked through the archway and got into the car.

With the right kind of weapon, I could probably neutralize both men in less than a minute. The moment the car arrived, I would leave the café and limp down the sidewalk. I'd draw the gun and begin shooting when Jafar appeared. But how would I deal with the mother and child? What about surveillance cameras? And where would I go after I finished the assignment? The police would respond immediately and I needed to find a location where I could change my appearance.

I left the café and wandered around the neighborhood until I found a possible hiding place. Saint-Sulpice was a large white church with mismatched towers that were supported by a double colonnade. It looked like two Greek temples had been stacked on top of each other. I climbed the wide staircase, entered the building, and found myself in a cross-shaped room defined by a line of white arches. Light streamed in from the large overhead windows and one beam of light, coming from the east, was clear and distinct.

I circled the interior, gazing up at a church organ placed on a balcony above the entrance. Statues of saints stood in front of the gold and silver pipes, and it felt as if they were staring down at me. Just behind the altar, I found what I was looking for—a row of confessionals waiting for priests and sinners. After I killed everyone, I would come here and hide in one of these small, enclosed booths.

The church was filled with long rows of creaky chairs for worshipers. Sitting on the left side of the altar, I studied the painting on the domed ceiling. Angels had grabbed the Virgin Mary and were taking her somewhere. I liked all the free space above me and the light and the sound of heels clicking across the stone floor. My perfect church would resemble this place—minus chairs, statues, and people. The stained-glass windows would show dogs at play.

While I was designing a church in my mind, the room began to fill up with women wearing dresses and pearls and men wearing suits and neckties. Each family group had brought along a girl or boy with a white smock covering their best clothes. The children were going to be confirmed and accepted into the church.

Now the organ at the end of the church began playing—deep sounds from the large pipes and high notes from the smaller pipes that swooped and glided like birds through the air. People stood up when a procession of priests and altar boys entered the church, followed by an elderly man wearing a scarlet robe. People sang and spoke from the altar—all in French, of course—and I stood up and sat down with them as if we were all pleasure bots posing in a store window.

After a half hour of these activities, the old man stood in the ornate pulpit wearing a red cardinal's hat. He began talking slowly, and then his voice gained energy as he pointed his fingers and waved his hands. The old man spoke, but no one answered him. He was a small red dot within a dark, echoey space.

. . . .

The next morning, I arrived at the café and ordered a bottle of water. This time Jafar appeared at 8:48. The bodyguard kept his hands in his pockets until Jafar got into the car.

As I counted out the money for my bill, I saw Nalini and Sanjay pass through the archway and stroll down the sidewalk. Nalini carried a toy sailboat under her arm while her son walked with a five-foot-long bamboo pole that had metal hook on one end.

Limping with the silver-handled cane, I followed them up the street and through the gates of the Luxembourg Gardens. It had rained the night before and the gravel pathway was dotted with little puddles of rainwater. Every time Sanjay encountered a puddle, the boy would stop for an instant and then hop over this obstacle.

I dislike parks with hills and rocks and raggedy trees. But the Luxembourg Gardens had been arranged in an orderly, symmetrical pattern. There were straight paths, clipped hedges, and planting beds edged in stone. Here and there, the park designers had placed marble statues of gods and goddesses gazing off into the distance.

The center of the park was a large, octagonal-shaped pool near the Luxembourg Palace. On this cold morning, only a few children were trying to sail toy boats on its bright green surface. Moving slowly, as if both mother and son were performing a ceremony,

Nalini placed the boat in the pool and Sanjay gave his vessel a push with the bamboo pole. I felt as if the entire world was frozen at that moment. The palace, the pool, the boat, and the dead man standing beneath a leafless tree had become a memory fixed in time. Then my Shell breathed in and the rusty gears of the clock squeaked and shuddered and began moving again.

A gust of wind ruffled the surface of the pool. The sails of the toy boats billowed out and Sanjay's boat began to cut through the waves. Both Nalini and Sanjay were transformed by this event. Smiling and chattering to each other in Hindi, they circled the pool. Just before the boat was about to crash on the other side, the little boy stopped it with the pole and sent it off in another direction.

I watched them play with the boat for ten minutes or so, and then I sat down on a park chair and switched on my computer. When I checked my e-mail, I found a message sent by someone working for the Special Services Section.

> // We have heard from our supplier in Paris about the equip-
> ment necessary for your sales presentation. The supplier will
> meet you at the Arc de Triomphe this evening at 2200 hrs. He
> will be carrying a red umbrella.

I glanced up from the computer. The wind had died and now the sailboat was becalmed in the middle of its circular ocean. Nalini and Sanjay sat down on a bench and waited for something to happen.

· · ·

When I left Marian Hospital, Dr. Tollner gave me a piece of paper that listed the three most important aspects of my outpatient treatment:

- Take your daily medication.
- Meet every week with a therapist.
- Resume normal activities in familiar surroundings.

The drugs I had swallowed at the hospital made my Spark feel frozen and restrained—like a bright yellow tennis ball captive in a block of ice. Because my Spark couldn't move, my Shell was slow and apathetic.

So I threw all the pills down a storm drain and, in a small way, probably lessened the depression and anxiety of the fish swimming in the Hudson River. Within a week or two my Spark began to rise and fall within me like a fragment of dust in a beam of sunlight. Without the drugs, I could think faster and react to events around me.

Getting rid of my therapist was another easy decision. Emma Rutherford was a slender young woman with large glasses who met patients at a clinic on East Twelfth Street. Like Dr. Rose, she tried to prove that I was alive by telling me, *Cogito, ergo sum*. But that statement had lost its power. Since returning to the city, I had gone on the Internet and found out that both therapists didn't understand what Descartes was trying to say. Like many people they assumed that:

I think therefore → my body exists.

But Descartes was a clever philosopher. He knew that the act of thinking proves only the existence of some form of consciousness.

I think therefore → something is thinking.

I tried to explain this to Dr. Rutherford as she took notes on her computer.

"But you couldn't think if you were dead, Mr. Davis. Our thoughts are created within our brains. And dead people don't have functional brains."

"Perhaps we're characters in a dream. We could be in the mind of an old man living in Maine. He's sleeping alone in an iron bed with frost on the windows and two dogs snoring on the floor. In a few minutes, the dreamer is going to wake up and go to the bathroom. And then we'll vanish."

Dr. Rutherford took off her glasses and began to clean them with a tissue. "I don't think an elderly person in Maine would create someone like *me*," she said. "This isn't a dream, Mr. Davis. There aren't any elves and unicorns wandering around New York City."

"We could be a real-time simulation controlled by game theory software," I said. "You're a computer program that thinks you're a psychologist."

"That's ridiculous."

"And I'm a program that thinks I'm dead."

Dr. Rutherford glanced up from her computer. "You have Cotard's syndrome, Mr. Davis. I realize that your delusions may seem very real to you, but it's just your mind coming up with a logical reason for your inability to feel emotions. I dealt with autistic children during my residency, and you show certain similarities. But right now we're sitting in this office, having a conversation. All evidence indicates that you're alive."

"That's *your* evidence," I said. "*My* evidence leads to a different conclusion."

"You had a motorcycle accident, correct? You're recovering from a severe brain injury. I could contact Marian Hospital and they might send me your X-rays."

"I had a Transformation, and now I know what's real."

I left the clinic that afternoon and never returned. Now that I didn't have to go downtown to see Dr. Rutherford, I could remain inside my apartment. Although my face appeared in framed photographs hanging on the wall of the bedroom, I felt no connection to these images or the softball trophies on the living room mantelpiece or the clothes hanging in the closet. They were objects—nothing more.

I made one major purchase during this period of time: a new phone with the software for a Shadow. I spent many hours listening to different combinations of age, accent, and personality until I finally created Laura.

The rest of my possessions gradually disappeared. Every morning I threw a personal object into the trash can—a pair of jeans, a cashmere sweater, love letters from a girlfriend, a college diploma.

After I had cleaned out the drawers and closets, I got rid of most of my furniture. Dr. Rutherford was right about one thing; I didn't see any elves and unicorns on Second Avenue. But New York was a magical city if you wanted to lose things. All I had to do was leave a throw rug or a kitchen chair on the sidewalk and, in an hour or so, it was gone.

The only things that wouldn't vanish were the bills in the mailbox and the calls on my answering machine. A portion of my hospital bill was covered by medical insurance and I was being sued for the rest. I hadn't paid my rent for three months and my landlord had taped an eviction notice on my door. If I didn't obtain money, I might be forced onto the street.

The ID card in my wallet confirmed that I was an employee for InterFace and that the company's offices were on Sixth Avenue and Twenty-Eighth Street. I remembered that the receptionist was an older woman named Patty Canales who sat at a front desk, munched on barbecue potato chips, and talked to her sister on the phone. But when I showed up at the building one morning, I discovered that Miss Canales had been replaced by a nubot that was designed to look like a muscular blond man in his twenties. He smiled at me when I stepped out of the elevator.

"Welcome to InterFace. I'm Kevin. How may I help you?"

"Are you a machine?"

"Yes, sir. And I'm using the voice-recognition software developed by our design team. Our slogan is: 'At InterFace, we listen.'"

"I used to work here, Kevin. I need to talk to someone about my job."

I placed my employee ID on the bot's desk and Kevin scanned the barcode with his eyes. "Please sit down, Mr. Davis. A member of our staff will speak to you in a few minutes."

I sat on the couch and a few minutes later the phone on the end table rang. When I picked up the handset, I heard a woman's voice. "Hello, Mr. Davis. This is Miss Colby from Human and Technical Resources. Do you have an appointment?"

"No. I used to work here, then I had a motorcycle accident and—"

"I know what happened. We've tried to contact you. Please walk through the green door and follow your image to my office."

When I entered the hallway, I saw an image of myself on a series of wall screens. A woman's voice said, "This way, Mr. Davis."

Then—"Turn right, Mr. Davis."

Then—"You're going to Room 1192, Mr. Davis."

And finally—"You've arrived at your destination. At InterFace, we listen."

I entered a private office and found a young woman sitting behind a desk. Miss Colby had a helmet hairstyle that framed her cheekbones and eyes. There were no papers on her desk—only a keyboard and a small monitor screen that couldn't be seen by the person facing her. On the shelf behind her, she had placed three framed photographs of cats—including one of a black-and-white kitten dressed up as a Christmas elf.

"Please sit down, Mr. Davis. I need to bring up your file."

She typed my ID number and stared at the computer screen. Although she appeared to be breathing and her eyelids blinked, I began to wonder if she was a machine.

. . .

Alan Turing, the British mathematician who helped design the first modern computing machine, had also invented the Turing Test—a test of a machine's ability to exhibit intelligent behavior. The test was modeled after a Cambridge University party game in which a man and woman were sent to separate rooms and people were given twenty questions to figure out their identities. In Turing's test, the machine and a human being were placed in separate rooms and a judge asked them questions. If the judge couldn't tell the difference between a computer and a human, then the machine passed the test.

It used to be much easier to detect a robot. I was sure that Kevin, the new receptionist, was programmed to tell the truth. But some nubots with reactive intelligence acted more like humans. They had the power to lie and pretend to be stupid. If you asked these robots for the twenty-digit value of pi, they had the option of saying, "How would I know? I'm not very good with math. . . ."

.   .   .

Miss Colby looked up from the monitor and smiled. Her lips were closed and I couldn't see if she had a tongue.

"Mr. Davis, everyone here at InterFace was saddened to hear about your motorcycle accident. A member of our staff attempted to contact you on several occasions, but you didn't respond. It's been almost five months since we've heard from you. During that time, there have been significant changes in company policy."

"What did I do when I was working here?"

Once again, she consulted the computer. "You were part of the design team for the language intonation project. When it became clear that you weren't going to return, we hired two contract employees . . . one in Ireland and another in Malaysia."

"But now I'm back."

"Yes. I can see that. InterFace continued to pay your salary for two weeks, and then you passed our limit for absence due to illness or injury. Your employee relationship with InterFace is no longer in the 'active status' category."

"What does that mean?"

"We fired you, following both company procedures and New York State employment law."

"But I need a job."

"Let's see if there is still a demand for your services." Once again, she typed a command on the computer and stared at the monitor. There was a large mole on her neck and a wisp of hair was out of place. Yes, she probably was a Human Unit—unless the mole was simply part of her design.

"I am pleased to inform you that InterFace has a contract job open for you. This job corresponds to your previous position with the company."

"What's a contract job?"

"No pension. No medical insurance. No benefits of any kind.

Your contract is week to week and we can terminate your employment with three hours' notice."

"I'll take it."

"Good. I think that's a wise choice."

"So now what do I do?"

"Turn your head and look at the mirror on the wall."

I obeyed and there was a flash of light in the room. Miss Colby checked my photograph on her monitor screen. "Now your face coordinates and the iris scan for your eyes has been recorded and registered in our PAL system. Take the elevator to the next floor and go see Mr. Delaney in Room 1233."

I returned to the reception area, said good-bye to Kevin the receptionist, and took the elevator up to the twelfth floor. Once again, my face appeared on hallway screens and guided me to my destination.

I remembered Ted Delaney from my life before the Transformation. He was a pudgy man with thinning red hair whose office was cluttered with books, fast-food wrappers, and baseball equipment. A definite human.

"Oh my God! I can't believe it! Jake Davis! Back from the dead!" Delaney stood up and insisted that we shake hands. "Sit down. Move the books. You can dump all that shit on the floor. Yeah. That's it. How you doing, man?"

"Miss Colby told me to come and see you."

"That figures. Two weeks ago, they made me a team manager because nobody else was left. Tom Stewart got fired. Julie . . . fired. Morgan . . . Remember him? The black guy? Fired. And Billy Stans quit because he didn't want to be a contract employee." Delaney leaned back in his chair and grinned. "But all the survivors are going to be glad to see you back in the office. They've outsourced a lot of people and we barely have enough for a team. We've lost three of the last four games."

"What games?"

"Softball, of course. You played third base and were our best hitter. We got a game with GoTech this Sunday. Two o'clock in Central Park. Think you could make it?"

"I'm still recovering."

"No problem. Don't worry about it. But when you want to rejoin the team, we're ready for you."

"I'm supposed to work."

"Oh. Right. Work. As I said, a lot of the old staff is gone. They got rid of Patty Canales and our receptionist is a nubot."

"I met him."

"Remember all the people who worked for customer service? They've been fired, too. Out the door. Phone complaints have been outsourced to the new software developed by our UK development team. You should call the eight hundred number and make a complaint just to check it out. The program can change accents and speak forty-two languages."

"What about the monitor screens in the hallways?"

"Now all employees are monitored by the PAL system. You got to spend at least eighty percent of your time inside your work-area perimeter or the program will ding you. Three warnings without an excuse and you're fired."

Delaney stood up, coughed, and scratched the back of his neck. "But you're still here. And I'm still here. Come on. I'll find you a desk. We got a lot of choices."

I followed Delaney down another hallway to a large room with eight white cubicles. "This used to be for marketing," he explained. "Then marketing moved upstairs and took over the south-facing room with the windows."

"Wasn't that used by accounting?"

"Hey! Good memory! But they're all gone. Everyone from accounting was fired and the company contracted with an off-shore service in Taiwan."

"So who works in this room?"

"Now you do . . . along with Levitt and Barbieri."

Levitt was a small man whose cubicle was spare and neat. He didn't glance up when we passed him. Darlene Barbieri was an older woman with a pinched face who had downloaded images of angels and taped them to her walls. Illuminated by halos, they spread their wings and watched her work.

My new cubicle had a chair, a keyboard, and a monitor screen. Someone had taken small round magnets and decorated the metal walls with a smiley face.

"Here you go," Delaney said. "This is your temporary workstation. I'll give you an official desk in a couple of days. No need to log into the system. That little camera there will take an iris scan and confirm your identity."

"So what am I supposed to do?"

"Go to the Intonation Project. Open up the documentation file and start reading. You need to catch up with everything that happened in the last few months. E-mail me if you have any questions."

And then he was gone. I sat down on the chair and moved the mouse. The monitor emerged from its electronic slumber and displayed the InterFace logo and ID photograph in a little box on one corner of the screen. Typing "Intonation Project" brought up a menu and I instantly had access to the database.

This had once been my job. I began to remember past assignments as I read the documentation files. Before the Transformation, I had been working on something called "Reflective Response." What this meant was that our speech-recognition program could pick up the Human Unit's desire for friendliness and personal interaction, then "reflect" this need during the conversation. Using our software, a computer would ask the Human Unit for help in spelling its name and make casual comments about the weather.

An hour or so passed and then I heard a ticking sound. There were no clocks on the wall and I hadn't noticed clocks in the other cubicles. I tried to ignore the distraction, but the ticking grew louder. Was this real? Or was this a delusion?

My Spark froze inside my Shell. I couldn't move, couldn't do anything but stare at the technical report on my monitor screen. Suddenly, the size of the words began to change and they drifted away from each other.

Recent studies have shown that minor "mistakes" and apologies made by humancentric response programs increase Perceived Empathy (PE) and customer satisfaction by a factor of

The cubicle with the smiley face did not seem as real as my apartment or the hospital. It felt as if my Shell was about to dissolve and break apart, my molecules drifting away and bouncing off the walls of the windowless room. I tried to save myself, but nothing happened until—

Either Levitt or Barbieri moved their office chair and it squeaked. This noise, oddly human, made me stand up and glance at the wall clock. I had been staring at the monitor screen for almost three hours.

I don't recall making a conscious decision to leave, but my Shell lurched out of the cubicle and moved in a herky-jerky manner down the hallway to the elevator bank. I left InterFace forever and headed north on Sixth Avenue. This wasn't a dream. I was clear and alert, but now I had lost awareness of my Shell. It felt as if my Spark was a pure point of consciousness, floating through the air, observing the city.

The glass-and-steel office buildings, the taxis and delivery trucks, the sidewalk blotted with petrified chewing gum, appeared more real, more *solid,* than the citizens passing in and out of the revolving doorways. Scars on the back of their hands showed that RFID chips had been inserted into their bodies. Some of them wore E-MID contact lenses and the corners of their dead eyes displayed a continuous stream of information. A Vast Machine watched and evaluated them, remembering their past actions and predicting their future behavior.

The Human Units passing me on the sidewalk believed they determined the direction of their life, but that was an illusion. Most of them were doing their jobs without thought, taking pleasure without satisfaction, delivering opinions and obeying desires that were given to them by others.

But I was different. I had broken free.

Because I was dead, I was alive.

14

That evening I drank a bottle of ComPlete in my hotel room, then took the Metro to the Arc de Triomphe. The moment I stepped onto the platform, I felt a jolt of angry energy. Growlers wearing black knit caps and bandanas were milling around the tunnels of the Metro station. As I climbed up the stairs, a dozen young men and women swept past me, hurrying out into the night.

It took me a few seconds to realize that I had just encountered a tribe of New Luddites. I had seen a few "Children of Ned" on the streets of New York and London, but never a group of them together. They were easy to pick out among the growlers because they always wore a fragment of the natural world pinned to their clothing or attached to a cord around their neck: a feather, a bone, or a sprig of ivy.

I followed them out of the Metro and found myself on the Champs-Élysées. It was a wide, straight boulevard with a sidewalk on each side. A row of old-fashioned lampposts created a sequence of soft yellow dots that lead to the Arche de la Défense. I pivoted around and gazed up at the Arc de Triomphe. The massive arch was lit up with spotlights and the white marble facade appeared to glow with its own energy. Twelve avenues led to the arch and a roundabout filled with speeding cars; this was the Place Charles de Gaulle—the axis for the entire city.

The New Luddites from the Metro met some of their group that had reached the avenue earlier that evening. Hundreds of growlers were gathering on the Champs-Élysées, but the Children of Ned stood apart from the others like a pack of feral dogs.

Ned Ludd was the mythical leader of the rebellious eighteenth-century English weavers who had roamed through the countryside, smashing steam-powered looms. The New Luddites also destroyed machinery as a means of protest. They hated the nubots and any other technology that reinforced the system of surveillance and control.

I heard shouting and followed the crowd. Three employees at a boutique on the Champs-Élysées had realized that there was going to be trouble and quickly closed their store. Now they were trying to get away, but the Luddites had stopped a man wearing G-MID glasses. A few of them squealed like pigs and shouted, *"Traître! Traître!"*

When the cornered man started to protest, a daughter of Ned ripped off his glasses and stomped them on the sidewalk. Everyone cheered, and the Luddites let the employees flee down the avenue.

There was a gap in the traffic and I sprinted across the round-about to the arch. Two soldiers were there, guarding the Tomb of the Unknown Soldier—a rectangle of gold bricks surrounding a flickering eternal flame.

I wandered around the area, searching for my supplier, but couldn't find anyone carrying a red umbrella. A crowd of Chinese tourists carrying identical travel bags took pictures of the arch with their phones while a French tour guide pointed at a stone angel waving a sword.

At the northwest edge of the plaza, the authorities had installed a new monument that had nothing to do with Napoleon and his battles. It was a large bronze sculpture inspired by the Day of Rage—a woman stepping forward with a dead child in her arms.

"Excuse me, monsieur." I turned and saw a short, saggy-faced man carrying a canvas shopping bag in one hand and a red umbrella in the other. "Are you Monsieur Underwood?"

"Yes."

"And I am nobody—Monsieur Zéro." The man led me over to the arch and we sat down on a stone bench.

"Your new equipment is in the shopping bag. Do not pick up the bag until I go."

"I'm not going to accept your equipment if it doesn't suit my needs."

"I sell you a first-class product. You get a German nine-millimeter with twelve rounds and a laser sight. Also . . . no charge . . . a second loaded magazine."

"Anything else I need to know?"

"The safety is on the left. Rack the first round and fire."

Some growlers emerged from a passageway that went under the road. They laughed and talked loudly as if they were taking possession of the monument.

"I like your employers. They always pay. No problems." Zéro glanced up at the Arc de Triomphe and shook his head. "But I do not like a rendezvous beneath this monument to slaughter."

"I thought you picked this place."

"No. Your employer wanted a central location."

"What are the words carved on the arch?"

"They are the names of Napoleon's battles. And there . . . right there . . . are the names of his generals. The men who died in war have a line beneath their name."

I leaned forward. "Just the generals?"

"*Bien sûr!* Walk around this *monstruosité* a thousand times. You will not find the names of the soldiers who died for nothing. Instead, they gave the dead men an eternal flame that stopped burning when a football hooligan pissed on it during a World Cup celebration. The tourists come and take photographs of this tombstone, and they don't see its *absurdité*. Just look . . . over there . . . see the angel? There are angels everywhere on the arch . . . riding horses, waving swords. Real angels would not do this. All they do is look down from heaven and deliver messages from God. Angels do not worry about us. They are pure minds . . . unattached to our world."

"I'd like to have wings so I could float above everything."

Zéro stared at me. "Are you a crazy man? No matter. You've

come to the right place." He jerked his head toward the crowd. "You see those young people over there—the *fantômes*?"

"We call them 'growlers' in America."

"Something bad will happen. Leave this place *now*."

Monsieur Zéro stood up and disappeared behind one of the arches. I picked up the canvas shopping bag and peeked inside. A black cardboard box was at the bottom of the bag, covered by a bag of oranges and a pineapple.

Instead of dodging the traffic that circled the axis, I went downstairs to the pedestrian underpass. A Metro train had just arrived in the station and more ghosts streamed out of the cars. Everyone wore shabby clothes along with black bandanas or sashes; knapsacks and canvas bags were slung over their shoulders. They shouted to each other and their voices bounced off the tile walls.

Monsieur Zéro was right. There was going to be some kind of organized protest or maybe just a bash mob that would break windows before the police arrived. Another train pulled into the station. More *fantômes* got off, but I didn't step into the empty car. I don't care about politics or the nubots, but the young people in the Metro station radiated energy that seemed to glow with a luminous power. I wanted to follow them and experience the brief sensation of being angry and alive.

I followed the new arrivals upstairs to the Champs-Élysées. The crowd had grown while I was receiving my weapon from Monsieur Zéro. Shouting slogans, a mob of people surged back and forth across the avenue. The New Luddites stood together near the Metro exit while a young woman with a witch's broom raised it high and waved it back and forth like a summoning flag.

Four policemen stood near the traffic circle. Three of them clutched riot clubs while a fourth officer shouted at his radio.

"*Nous ne faisons pas!*" chanted the Luddites.

"*Nous ne faisons pas partie de la machine!*" answered the crowd while I held up my phone and activated the translator. English words appeared on the LCD screen.

We are not part of the machine!

The chant continued growing louder and louder, as if the sound itself could shatter the Arc de Triomphe. And then—*pop!* Someone shot a fireworks rocket off into the air. The rocket rose upward into the night sky, leaving a trail of crackling sparks and then exploding like a bright red flower.

Luddites ran toward the axis with their duffel bags and stopped at the curb. With practiced moves, one person held the bottom of each bag while another Luddite pulled out a thick mat with home-made spikes hammered through the rubber.

Carrying the heavy mats, the Luddites stepped into the traffic circle and laid these obstacles down on the pavement. The first car to run over a mat shredded its front tires. The wounded car skid-ded to the right and smashed into a delivery truck. Within minutes, other accidents occurred and the Luddites attacked the stalled machines with steel-tipped clubs. The terrified drivers fled down the avenues and now the city's axis was blocked. Any van carrying riot police would be trapped in a massive traffic jam.

Ghosts began reaching into their backpacks, pulling out bricks and chunks of cobblestone. They flung them at the policemen and the four officers ran for their lives, dashing into the stalled traffic and disappearing into the night.

Police sirens made a pulsating scream in the distance, but the riot police couldn't reach the arch. A helicopter glided above us and I saw the tiny red lights of a surveillance drone. The rioters didn't care about the drone's infrared camera. Black bandanas and white ghost masks covered their faces. Now hammers appeared along with a homemade battering ram for breaking down doors. The mob kept chanting, *"Nous ne faisons pas! Nous ne faisons pas!"* as they marched down the Champs-Élysées, ripping up benches and smashing them through windows.

And my Shell was pulled downstream by the flood-swollen river, spun around and splashed, but never drowned—floating on the sur-face of the angry water.

15

I hid the gun in my suitcase and spent the next few days figuring out a plan to neutralize my targets. At night, I drank a bottle of my dwindling supply of ComPlete, then walked over to the Boulevard Saint-Michel and stared at the pleasure bots in the store display. Either a store employee or the machines themselves had changed their lingerie, but their actions were always the same. After combing her long hair, the blond bot would glance over her shoulder and wink. The wink showed an awareness of awareness; the bot knew she was a machine.

I assumed that there would be surveillance cameras in the courtyard of Jafar's building and other cameras might be concealed on Rue de Tournon. Old-fashioned CCTV cameras used visible light, but there had been a gradual shift toward using infrared cameras because they could capture images at night. I would have to prepare for both possibilities.

I went to a Right Bank department store and bought an overcoat, a scarf, and a gray Tyrolean hat with a leather hatband and a pheasant feather on the side. Then I went to an electrical supply store and purchased wire, a nine-volt battery pack, and eight high-intensity infrared light-emitting diodes. Using nail scissors, I carefully cut holes in the hatband, inserted the LEDs, and attached them to the battery. When I clicked the switch, I would be projecting waves of infrared light that were invisible to the human eye.

That afternoon I stuffed a cardboard box with newspapers and had it shipped to my hotel. When the package arrived, I changed the address label to: *Jafar Desai. 15 Rue de Tournon. Paris.* Although Jafar and his family weren't listed on the doorbell panel, I assumed they were using the same first names.

The next day, I left my hotel wearing the hat, the scarf, and my new coat over my leather jacket. First I left the package for Jafar directly below the brass doorbell panel, then took my seat at the café and ordered a bottle of mineral water. At 9:07, the young. bodyguard arrived in the car. He got out, approached the entrance to the courtyard, and immediately saw the package. He hesitated a few seconds, then picked up the package and shook it slightly. The lightness of the object seemed to reassure him that it wasn't a bomb.

"A equals B," I whispered. The young man thought that he was making a free choice, but his decision range was limited. Time was frozen at this moment. The street, the city, the rest of the world became a background to this one decision.

Carrying the package, the bodyguard passed through the open gateway that led to the palace courtyard. I switched on the infrared LEDs in the hatband, left some money on the café table, and hurried down the sidewalk. As I approached the surveillance camera at the entrance, I put on sunglasses and covered my mouth with the scarf. By the time I reached the palace, the young man had crossed the cobblestone courtyard and was disappearing through an open archway. Follow him.

I hurried across the courtyard, passed through the archway, and headed up a white stone staircase. A door opened and closed on the next landing, but I kept moving. I felt light, almost weightless, as I floated up the steps.

A few seconds later, I stood on the landing. I knocked on the door, then pulled a manila envelope out of my coat pocket and held it with my left hand. *Breathe in. Breathe out.* And then the young man opened the door.

"*Que voulez-vous?*" he asked.

Instead of answering him, I drew the automatic and shot him in the face. The bullet exploded out the back of his skull and his empty Shell collapsed onto the floor.

I entered the apartment as Jafar jumped up from a chair and ran through an open doorway. A pool of blood—so bright and shrill that it was painful—appeared beneath the bodyguard's head. I avoided the mess and followed Jafar through the dining room, down a hallway, and into a bedroom.

Wearing a pink bathrobe, Nalini stood beside an unmade bed. She screamed her husband's name as he dashed into the bathroom and locked the door. First I tried the doorknob, and then I realized that Nalini was trying to get away. My arm went up like I was shaking hands and I squeezed the trigger. The bullet hit Nalini's leg and she collapsed onto the rug.

I spun around and kicked the bathroom door open. Jafar was inside the empty tub, curled up in a ball with his arms covering his face. For a moment I felt annoyed that he had picked such an awkward way to die. Leaning over the tub, I shot my target in the head. Bits of blood and bone splattered against the porcelain as the gunshot sound bounced off the tile walls.

Silence. Then a warning bell began to ring—loud and insistent. When I returned to the bedroom, I saw that Nalini had crawled over to the night table and pushed some kind of panic button. I circled the bed and aimed the laser beam at her noisy mouth. She stared at me, ready for death, and then her eyes moved to the left. Quickly, I pivoted on my heel and saw that little Sanjay was standing in the bedroom doorway.

Nalini began screaming "No!" as I approached the child. The boy didn't speak or run away. His dark brown eyes stared at me as I raised the gun and pointed the laser beam at the center of his forehead.

"No! No!" The woman's voice wouldn't stop.

I stared at the boy.

And the boy stared at me.

Waves of energy radiated from his small body. They were warm colors—red, brown, gold. And the waves touched my Shell and were absorbed by my skin.

The red laser dot trembled, wavered, and then moved away. I couldn't kill the child. He was too full of life.

Once again, I was aware of the warning bell and its loud urgency. I pivoted again and pointed the gun at Nalini. For the first time since my Transformation, I knew what a human being was feeling. Nalini looked grateful that I was about to kill her, and not her son.

The laser dot bounced around like a firefly, but I didn't squeeze the trigger. I took a deep breath and pointed my weapon down at the floor. "Give the money back to your father. Do you understand?"

She nodded slowly while the warning bell kept ringing. It took me only a few seconds to pass through the rooms to the front door, and then I was out of the apartment and on the landing. I heard footsteps and saw an older man with a submachine gun climbing up the stairs. Apparently other people in the building had bodyguards and they had agreed to protect each other.

Step forward. Pause. Aim. The older man saw me and began to raise the submachine gun. I squeezed the trigger and a bullet cut through the man's throat. Blood splattered onto the wall and then the bodyguard tumbled back down the stairs.

I stepped around the empty Shell, hurried down a short corridor, and reentered the courtyard. Someone shouted in French and I saw that a man with a handgun was half hidden behind the hood of a parked car.

I raised my weapon and began firing. My Shell carried me toward this new threat while bullets shattered glass and cut through steel.

Pull the trigger. Nothing. I reloaded with the spare ammunition magazine and resumed firing as the man behind the car panicked and tried to run away. *Aim. Focus.* I fired a single shot and the man fell forward as if Death had touched his body.

Out through the gateway. Down the sidewalk. I moved briskly, like a man who was late for a business appointment. The gun was back in my coat pocket and I felt an illogical desire to shoot at everyone on the street.

The towers of Saint-Sulpice guided me forward and I entered the church about five minutes later. Candle flames trembled while I walked in front of the altar, and then I found refuge in an empty confessional. I closed a curtain, sat on a wooden bench, and removed the overcoat, scarf, and hat. *Look up.* A brass crucifix of a twisted Jesus was screwed to the wall.

"Hello," I whispered in English. "Hello . . ." Leaning forward, I peered through a wooden grille. The other side of the booth was filled with shadows.

16

I was sitting in the Air France airport lounge when a news story about my activities appeared on the television screen mounted behind the bar. The one-minute segment included a surveillance video from the CCTV cameras in the cobblestone courtyard. The sunglasses and scarf concealing my face turned out to be unnecessary precautions. The infrared cameras in the courtyard had been blocked by the invisible energy emitted by my crown of LEDs. An assassin with a ball of light for a head strolled across the courtyard, firing his gun. After finishing his job, this pure Spark passed through the gateway and glowed his way down the street.

The headline on the television news story was QUATRE HOMMES ASSASSINÉS À PARIS. That meant Nalini had survived her leg wound. I felt no guilt or regret about killing Jafar and the three bodyguards. They were simply tiny gears inside a machine. But it bothered me that I hadn't followed my plan. This was the first time I had ever failed to complete an assignment for Miss Holquist.

My only desire was to return to New York City and the clean, empty space in my loft. I had five cases of ComPlete stored in the kitchen cupboard and wouldn't have to leave the room for several weeks. I opened Power-I and made a new list:

Objectives

1. Return to New York
2. Enter loft
3. Lock door

© Power-1 XXX3094089UNDERWOOD

But I couldn't think of anything that should happen after I locked the door. An hour before departure, I rented a business traveler cubicle and made a phone call to California.

A woman answered the phone. "Hello. Ettinger Clinic."

"This . . ." I paused for a few seconds and then used my previous name. "This is Jacob Davis. I used to be a patient at your clinic."

"Yes, sir. How may I help you?"

"I need to talk to Dr. Noland. I—I have a problem."

"Would you repeat your name, sir?"

"Jacob Davis."

A long pause while I clutched the phone handset. My Shell was so light at that moment that I could have floated away.

"I'm sorry," the woman said. "But Dr. Noland is busy with patients right now. He suggested that you send him an e-mail."

．　．　．

If a supercomputer was provided with the laws of physics and a description of every occurrence in the world's history, then it could predict what I was doing right now and what I had done in the past. My decision to become a patient at the Ettinger Clinic was simply a consequence of a series of prior actions.

Accident → B → C → D . . . Ettinger Clinic

After I quit my job at InterFace, I retreated to my apartment, locked the door, and remained. In the daytime, I stayed in the living room and watched television. At night, particles of dark yellow light emerged from the ceiling, and then floated downward through the shadows until they were absorbed by the spongy floor.

No one was cutting my hair and I stopped washing myself and shaving. One of my credit cards was still active, and I used it to home-deliver bottles of clear fruit juice and spring water. The bills kept arriving, but I stacked the envelopes, unopened, on my kitchen table.

Thirty-four days after my revelation on Sixth Avenue, the phone rang. I assumed that it was either a bill collector or the elderly woman who kept insisting that she was my mother. The bill collectors made threats. My mother cried. It was all the same to me. Instead, it was a voice that I hadn't heard for several weeks. A woman's voice with bright energy.

"Hello, Mr. Davis! This is Sandy Shapiro from Marian Community Hospital. Something has come up and we need to talk. Would you please call me at—"

I picked up the phone. "Yes?"

"Oh, there you are! I didn't know if you were still living in New York City. So how *are* you, Mr. Davis? I realize that you're no longer a patient at the hospital, but I *do* feel some responsibility for those patients who weren't completely healed. You are definitely in that category."

"I don't want to talk to anyone. . . ."

"No! Wait! I have to tell you something. Do you remember your psychiatrist, Dr. Tollner? Well, he wrote a description of your case and put it up on a Web site for physicians and scientists studying severe brain injuries. Of course, he didn't use your name and gave only a few personal details, but he did include some of your computer drawings. I don't know why . . . maybe it was the drawings . . . but the article is generating a lot of comments."

"And I'm supposed to read this?"

"You can if you want to, but that's not why I'm calling. This morning Dr. Tollner received an e-mail from Dr. Morris Noland, the neurologist who runs the Ettinger Clinic in Southern California. The clinic is for patients with severe psychological disorders."

"My medical insurance company is about to sue me, Mrs. Shapiro. They're not going to let me go to a private clinic."

"Oh, but that's the wonderful thing! Dr. Noland said that there would be no charge for thirty days of treatment. He's never dealt with Cotard's syndrome, but he thinks he can help you."

"I don't need help."

"Well, that's where I might beg to differ with you. Both your mother and your fiancée, Miss Patterson, informed me that you no longer communicate with them. Yesterday, I called Miss Colby, the human resources manager at InterFace. She said that you came back to work two months ago, sat in your cubicle for a few hours, then left and never came back."

"I didn't like it there."

"Well, of course not! You weren't really healed at our hospital. Returning to your previous life was probably difficult for you. That's why you need to get some help. The Ettinger Clinic is world famous. It's sponsored by the software billionaire Terry Ettinger. And it's free for certain patients. Absolutely no cost. The clinic will even pay for your plane ticket to California."

My Spark bounced around inside my skull as I tried to come up with a response. The only relevant fact was this: I didn't want to be sitting in this room.

"Yes."

"Yes to what, Mr. Davis?"

"I'll go to California."

.   .   .

The following day, when a taxi arrived to take me to the airport, I emerged from my apartment looking like a hermit who had been sealed up in a cave. I had a scraggly beard and my hair touched my collar. My fingernails were long, yellowish, and slightly curved.

And I smelled. Or, more exactly, my smell bothered others. The clinic had paid for a business-class ticket but, ten minutes after the plane took off, the businessman sitting next to me stood up and walked over to the cabin attendant to complain. There was whispered conversation with a great deal of glancing in my direction, and then two different cabin attendants asked me questions while they sniffed. The businessman was immediately sent up to first class and I remained alone and untouched in my solitary seat.

I had run out of ComPlete, but drank bottled water and two cups of clear apple juice during the flight. Apparently, this was not enough nourishment for my Shell. When the plane landed in Los Angeles, my legs collapsed and I had to sit back down again. The cabin attendant called for a wheelchair and an airline employee pushed me through the terminal to the baggage area.

A young man who looked like a weight lifter held up a cardboard sign with my name on it. "Are you Mr. Davis?"

I nodded.

"I'm Ricky Almendarez from the Ettinger Clinic. I'm supposed to drive you up to Ojai, but you look pretty wasted. You wanna go to a hospital or something?"

"No. Get your car and bring it up to the curb."

I slid into the front seat of Ricky's sedan and he turned onto the San Diego Freeway. Thousands of other cars were traveling north and red brake lights flowed up the Sepulveda Pass. Peering out the window, I saw streets and parking lots with more cars. All Human Units disappeared within my mind and the city became a Kingdom of Cars; the large, shiny creatures maneuvered around each other, squatting and growling, then surging forward in packs.

Traffic began to thin out when we followed the 101 Freeway to the coast. The Pacific Ocean was on the left side of the car and on the right were eroded cliffs that looked like massive fingers clutching the earth.

I heard a whirring sound as the electric window glided downward. "Just a little ventilation," Ricky explained. "I hope that's okay, Mr. Davis. I'm not trying to be negative, but you kinda *smell*."

The Ettinger Clinic was in a coastal valley filled with orange and avocado groves; this dark green mass of vegetation shivered and swayed whenever winds blew in from the ocean. I didn't see any walls or fences. Ornamental gardens surrounded a dozen buildings designed in the Spanish mission style with red-tile roofs, wrought-iron doorknobs, and thick walls painted white.

When we reached the parking lot, Ricky put on G-MID eye-glasses and slipped a headset onto his left ear. During their shift at the clinic, the staff were either hearing instructions from Dr. Noland or reporting on patient activities. Everything they saw was transmitted from their G-MIDs to a cloud server.

My room had white walls, a ceiling fan, and an adobe tile floor. One bed. One desk. One chair. After we entered, I lay down on the bed and closed my eyes.

"Do you eat anything?" Ricky asked.

"ComPlete."

"Complete what? I don't understand."

"ComPlete."

Ricky repeated the word into his headset and nodded. "Okay. No sweat. Dr. Noland knows what you're talking about." He walked over to the bed and tried to take off my shoes.

"Don't touch me."

"Why not?"

"No one touches me. Leave me alone."

Ricky left the room and returned that evening with a case of ComPlete. I drank one bottle in front of him, and then the night nurse switched on the overhead light every two hours and watched me drink four more bottles before dawn.

I was strong enough to get out of bed when Ricky returned to my room. "I know that you don't want to be touched," he said. "But I'm in charge of cleaning you up."

Ricky told me to remove my clothes and sit on a plastic chair in the middle of the room. Then he plugged in an electric clipper and handed it to me. The clipper made a buzzing sound as I pushed it back and forth across my skull. "Left . . . farther left . . . you missed a spot," he said as clumps of dirty hair drifted down to the floor.

After my head was completely shaven and my nails were clipped, the plastic chair was placed in the shower stall and Ricky scrubbed me with a long-handled brush. I returned to the room, sat on the edge of the bed, and inspected my fragile Shell. I could see my ribs and the outline of my leg and arm bones. The skeleton that had been hidden within me was beginning to emerge.

"Get dressed," Ricky said, and placed some clothes on the bed. A white T-shirt. Slippers. And a blue tracksuit.

"Do you have a list of instructions?" I asked. "If so, I want to see them."

Ricky laughed. "I don't need a list. Dr. Noland's been watching you from the day you arrived here. Noland doesn't see everything that happens to every patient, but he always knows what's going on. He can access everything we see or switch over to the closed-circuit cameras mounted on the walls."

Knowing that I was being watched, I felt more substantial, more *real*. Ricky left for a few minutes and returned wearing surgical gloves. He was carrying two plastic bands; the yellow one was about an inch wide, the red one much larger and heavier. "See the gloves? My skin won't touch your skin. Just pretend that I'm a nubot."

He knelt before me and snapped on the ankle band, then stood and fastened the yellow band onto my left wrist. "This is a tracking device. If you wander away and get lost, we'll know where you are in about five seconds."

Talking to the invisible Dr. Noland with his headset, Ricky strolled out of the room. Exhausted, I lay back on the bed, gazing up at the ceiling fan. It felt like the doctor was still there watching me—watching everyone.

. . .

During my first three days at the clinic, I had to take a series of tests. For one hour in the morning and a second hour every afternoon, I sat alone in a room and watched video clips on a monitor screen. The videos showed the entire spectrum of human activity: a mother holding a newborn baby, children playing hopscotch, a wedding couple dancing a waltz, a man jumping from a burning skyscraper, an African woman being beaten to death by a mob, an American soldier returning home to a happy golden retriever, and three men wearing ski masks who recited prayers as they used a dull knife to saw off a prisoner's head.

While I watched the videos, an infrared sensor monitored my pulse and body temperature and an eye scanner measured my pupillary response. Ricky explained that the data was sent to the clinic's computer and analyzed by a software program called "Sigmund."

"Everything we do here is based on data," Ricky explained. "That means you don't have to lie around on a couch while some shrink asks you about your mommy. Dr. Noland says that all language—everything we say—is just an approximation of reality. You can't lie to these machines, so don't waste your time trying."

Five days after I had arrived at the clinic, I was finally invited to meet Dr. Noland. Wearing my wrist and ankle cuffs and the blue tracksuit, I followed a path to a large house that had been built to resemble a mission church with a bell tower. The walls of the ground-floor area were decorated with silk-screen paintings created from photographs. There were close-up images of a man's eyes, his bare feet, and his left ear, but I couldn't find a portrait that showed the entire figure.

"Is that Dr. Noland?" I asked a secretary.

"What do you mean?"

"Do all the paintings show Dr. Noland?"

"No-no. It's Terry Ettinger . . . the man who funds our clinic."

I sat on a bench for twenty minutes, and then was allowed into the office. Dr. Noland was sitting behind a desk staring at a wall-mounted video screen that was divided into boxes. Each box showed live video from the staff's G-MIDs and the stationary surveillance cameras. Although we were miles from the beach, the doctor wore flip-flop sandals, shorts, and a silk Hawaiian shirt. There were flowering orchids and potted rubber plants in the corners of the room and a framed photograph on one wall of a surfer entering the curl of a wave.

"Morning, Jake! I'm Morris Noland. Have you been comfortable here? Everything all right? Let's take a look at your room."

Noland typed a command on his keyboard and the wall screen displayed an image of my room. As we both watched, a woman from housecleaning entered with a sponge mop, a bucket full of supplies, and some towels.

"In the next thirty seconds she'll reach into the bucket, take out disinfectant spray, and begin to clean your toilet. We've discovered that people are more relaxed and efficient if they clean each room in precisely the same way."

"You see everything."

Noland laughed. "Not everything, but enough to know what's going on. These days I'm trying to improve our system here so it all works automatically. The surveillance feed from your room is sent to a behavior analysis program that was first developed for use in prisons. Our data supplements what we learned from your evaluation."

"All I did was watch videos."

"Yeah, well . . . each individual reacts strongly to particular images, while others don't affect them at all. I have your file right here."

Noland typed a command and studied several bar graphs. "Got to admit . . . it's an interesting profile. You seem to be capable of only three emotions: boredom, curiosity, and disgust. I realize that you've had a severe neurological injury, but your brain is still working and you display certain base-level responses. Obviously, you can walk and talk and scratch yourself. If you saw a car speeding toward us, you would instinctively jump out of the way. The human brain is an incredible machine. It's adaptive, and capable of generating new cells. But that's not the issue here."

The doctor stood up and slapped his flip-flop sandals over to a coffee table and some rattan furniture. "Come over here, Jake. Make yourself comfortable. I'd offer you coffee or some herbal tea, but all you drink is that sole-source nutrition."

I sat on the couch and watched Noland pry a shell off a pistachio, flip the nut up in the air, and catch it in his mouth. "So you're dead," he said slowly. I liked the fact that this wasn't a question, but a fact. "I guess the first thing you need to know is . . . that's okay with me."

"*Cogito, ergo sum.*"

"Excuse me?"

"That's what Dr. Rose and Dr. Rutherford told me. I think, therefore—"

"Hey . . . sorry . . . don't want to cut you off here, but I don't really care what you think. Here at the clinic, we don't waste time asking patients about their thoughts and their feelings and their messed-up childhoods. Do you have dreams? Well, good for you. I don't want to hear them. You got fantasies? Keep them to yourself. Bottom line is this: I'm interested in what my patients *do,* how they *act.*"

Another pistachio nut was flung up in the air, optimistically high. With a quick jerk of his head, Noland caught it in his mouth.

"When I first meet a patient, I usually tell them a little bit about Terry Ettinger. He's the chairman of our foundation and the man who pays the bills. When Terry was a kid, his parents were told that he had some kind of autism spectrum disorder. Terry was highly intelligent but physically clumsy. He couldn't make friends and didn't like to talk to people. His parents were worried because he analyzed everything he did . . . like brushing his teeth . . . and broke it into small details." Noland smiled. "In other words, he was perfectly designed to be a brilliant software developer. As you probably know, Terry's visual-recognition program is used by just about every nubot in the world, and of course that's earned him a pile of cash."

"Why did he start the clinic?" I asked.

"So what is Terry going to do with all his money? Date beautiful women? No, because then he'd have to touch them. He's not going to build a big house because he's happiest in a windowless room. And he's not donating money to some charity because he doesn't give a damn about other people. Terry isn't alone in feeling this way. The nubot software community is basically an autistic culture."

"Isn't this clinic a charity?"

"I guess it is. In a way. But it's actually an expression of Terry's philosophy. His strongest emotion is that he still hates all the psychiatrists and psychologists who treated him when he was a kid. Basically, he thinks that psychotherapy is a load of crap."

"And you're a neurologist. Not a therapist."

"That's right. Eight years ago, I was doing research in the lab, modifying the cerebral cortex of baboons. Anyway . . . Terry's big idea is that most conscious thought is simply an attempt to claim 'authorship' for a choice that has already been made. And there's some fairly substantial evidence that this is true. The physiologist Benjamin Libet showed that our unconscious brain is the initiator of certain acts about a half second before our conscious mind realizes what is going on. Additional research has confirmed Libet's conclusions. These experiments suggest the possibility that our thoughts are just an ongoing attempt to explain what we've already decided."

"What does any of this have to do with my treatment at your clinic?"

"Like a lot of people with mental problems, you think that you're different. But no one can truly step out of the system. Humans are self-replicating organic machines that obey the laws of physics, react to stimuli and need, and function according to programs hardwired into our brains."

"My body is just a Shell," I explained. "But my Spark is a particle of light that can—"

"Stop. Just stop." Dr. Noland held up one hand like a traffic cop. "I don't want to hear about some crazy system you've invented to explain the world."

"So why am I here?"

"I've studied your hospital file and I think that you're the kind of patient we can help here at the clinic. Today I'm going to give you some rules and the staff will train you to follow them. If you obey the rules, you can think that you're dead and still be functional in New York City."

"What kind of rules?"

"Based on my preliminary observations, I've come up with a basic list." Noland retrieved a sheet of paper from his desk and handed it to me. "Read this."

DR. NOLAND'S RULES

1. *If necessary, tell people that you don't want to be touched.*
2. *Wash your body once a day.*
3. *Cut your hair and clip your nails once a month.*
4. *Your body must consume a minimum of two thousand calories a day.*
5. *Always remember: dead people must act alive.*

I looked up and saw that the doctor was smiling at me. "Any questions?" he asked.

"It sounds pretty simple."

"I agree! Although a New York psychoanalyst with a couch might argue with me. I know that your brain generates thoughts, Jacob. So does mine. We can't shut it off. The entire staff here at the clinic acknowledges all the crazy ideas bouncing around in our heads. We call these thoughts 'static' or 'ECAs'—which is short for 'extraneous cognitive activity.' Through a system of reward and punishment we encourage our patients to ignore the static and display positive, functional behavior. Autism experts came up with the label 'HFA'— 'high-functioning autism'—to describe people like Terry Ettinger. So I kind of took that basic concept and came up with the term 'HFH'—'high-functioning humanness.' That's everyone's goal, but some of us need a little extra help."

There was a moment of silence while Noland smiled at me. All this occurred before I had scanned and downloaded the face images to my phone. I couldn't interpret the smile's meaning.

"What's the reward?" I asked.

"Here at the clinic? Whatever makes you happy . . . within limits. What about a box of cupcakes? Use of the Internet? A day at the beach? A porno movie?"

"And what's the punishment?"

"Oh, right. You don't know about that."

Dr. Noland picked up what looked like a TV remote control. I glanced over at the wall screen. "Are you dead, Jacob?"

"My Spark exists inside a—"

Before I could finish the sentence, Noland pushed a button and the ankle cuff delivered an electric shock. It took my Shell a few seconds to recover. When I looked up, Dr. Noland was still grinning at me.

"Are you dead, Jacob?"

I stayed silent.

Noland grinned and reached for the bowl of pistachios. "Good. Very good. That's a start."

17

The baggage-claim area at Kennedy Airport was a windowless room the size of a football field. I counted eight CCTV cameras mounted on the walls and more cameras were probably hidden in the ceiling. The news footage of my actions in Paris didn't show my face, but all the French police needed was one clear image from a surveillance camera. The real power of the cameras came from the software programs that turned human beings into a unique sequence of numbers. Right now the cameras near the baggage carousel were freezing and capturing images, transforming each face into a number, and checking those numbers against a stop-and-search list.

I was counting the American currency I had in my carry-on bag when I heard a dog bark. A plastic pet crate was being wheeled into the luggage area and a black muzzle was pushed up against the mesh at one end of the container.

Two little girls and their parents hurried across the room, calling to their pet. A few seconds later the dog was released and attached to a leash. He was a Labrador retriever with broad shoulders and floppy black ears, and he danced around the family, barking and sniffing everyone as if he had just been released from prison.

· · ·

Both Dr. Tollner and Dr. Rutherford said that I was delusional—which is not true. Unlike the average psychiatrist, I see the world

clearly, without the desire to create a story. The future is meaningless to me; I can't imagine what could be or should be—only
what is.

But at that moment, standing by the luggage carousel, I experienced my first fantasy since the Transformation. Within this dream,
I was standing alone in a meadow ringed with elm trees. The day
was clear and cold, moving toward autumn, and the brittle brown
leaves were curled up at the edges.

Someone had left wooden crates and wire cages in the tall grass
on one side of the meadow and I realized that each one contained
a dog. A gust of wind pushed the branches back and forth and their
shadows glided across the ground as I walked over to the containers and began to open latches and throw away padlocks. There was
a sheepdog, a terrier, and several other breeds. Finally all the dogs
were released and then they started dashing around the meadow
barking and sniffing and smiling in that pink-tongued dog way.

And I was the only person there, a somber black dot at the center of a spinning circle of energy.

.   .   .

In the taxi, I turned off the video display and stared out a window
at the other cars. The driver turned onto the Long Island Expressway and I saw the glittering towers of Manhattan grow up from
the earth and provide an edge, a border, to the sky. Then we took
the Midtown Tunnel beneath the river and, ten minutes later, the
cab was pushing through the crowded streets of Chinatown. Tourists stood outside restaurants, reading the menus and staring at
the bright red carcasses of Peking ducks hanging in the windows.
The butcher shops were closed, but a fish market was still selling
squid, fresh cod, and sea urchins. A fishmonger plunged his hand
into a bucket and came up with a crab that waved its claws at a
customer.

I told the driver to stop at the top of Catherine Street and then
carried my suitcase down the block to my building. Inside the stairwell, I could hear muffled voices leaking through the walls. Some-

one was cooking and I smelled peanut oil and fried garlic; the scent had a brownish-orange color—warm particles floating through the shadows.

I was glad to be back. No Human Units were in the loft, and it was a clear, open space. With the nail and the cord I could walk in a precise circle without anyone staring at me.

When I reached the landing, I unlocked my door and entered the room. Lorcan Tate was sitting on my kitchen chair, watching a video on his phone. "You're late, Underwood. Didn't your flight get in two hours ago?"

"What are you doing here?"

He stood up quickly and took a step toward me. "I missed you. We all missed you. Heard you went to Paris . . ."

Lorcan reached around to the small of his back and then his hand reappeared, clutching a slapjack with a steel handle. He raised his arm and swung hard. The flat surface of the leather-covered club struck the side of my head.

My Shell collapsed onto the floor. It felt like I was drowning, pulled below the waves like a swimmer in an angry sea. Lorcan stood over me and struck the sockets of both shoulders, again and again, until my arms were numb and useless.

Lorcan snapped handcuffs on my wrists and bound my ankles together with a plastic tie. Grabbing the chain links that fastened the cuffs together, he dragged me across the loft to the drill press that had been left at one end of the room. Lorcan tied a nylon rope to the handcuffs, ran the other end through the motor mount at the top of the press, and then pulled the rope slowly until I was standing up with my wrists attached to the machine. I struggled, trying to break free, and Lorcan punched me in the stomach.

"You can't get away. I didn't have a gun that night at the training camp, so I couldn't do anything. That's not going to happen this time."

"Miss Holquist is going to have a negative response to your actions."

"Who cares? Forget that bitch." Lorcan approached me and unzipped my jacket. "I'm tired of all your crazy shit—walking around, telling everyone that you're dead. So guess what? Doctor Tate is about to cure you of that delusion."

Reaching into his shirt pocket, Lorcan pulled out a leather pouch. He gave it a shake and out came a straight razor, the blade folded within the mother-of-pearl handle. "Nice, huh? German made. I've had it for years."

His thumb pushed the curved tang at the end of the blade, then slid a silver clasp forward and locked the blade tight. "I know you stay away from women, but here's a little tip if you want to play with them. . . ." Lorcan extended the razor and cut the buttons off my shirt. There was a clicking sound as they hit the wooden floor and rolled away from my shoes. "Instead of ripping off their clothes like a crazy bastard, it's better to cut off their bra and panties with a razor. Take your time. Slow is better. Right away, they'll start crying and begging for their lives. You've got them under control and you haven't even started yet."

He opened my shirt like a surgeon peeling back a layer of skin, and then began probing my rib cage with the tips of his fingers. It felt as if he was gauging the strength, the thickness of my Shell. "Are you ready?" he asked. "You better get ready. . . ."

"I don't like to be touched."

"Go ahead . . . tell me you're scared, Underwood. There's no reason to lie about it."

"Fear requires a desire to exist in the future."

"You got an answer for everything, don't you? All right . . . answer this question. Are you alive or are you dead?"

I shook my head and he slashed the razor through the air— about an inch away from my eyes. "Answer the question!"

"My Spark exists. It's held within a Shell."

"Wrong. That's wrong. You're just like everyone else and I'm going to prove it. Do you know where your heart is? Most people don't. It's not where you put your hand when you pledge allegiance to the goddamn flag. It's more toward the center of your chest, behind the sternum. And it's not some big Valentine's heart with chocolates. It's three layers of muscle . . . weighs less than a pound . . . about this big." Lorcan held up a fist and waved it at my face.

"Are you following a plan, Lorcan? Or are you just making this up as you go along?"

"You're goddamn right it's a plan! I'm going to show you that you're not some bot filled with wires and circuits."

Lorcan extended the razor as if it was a calligrapher's pen and he was about to write on my skin. First he cut a vertical line and then a horizontal line in the center of my chest. The pain felt like a high-pitched sound—brakes squealing on a subway car.

"Here." He pushed the tip of the razor into the point where the lines crossed. "You got a heart and it's right *here*."

The high-pitched sound faded away and now the cut was burning. A fiery sensation spread across my chest.

"You're bleeding, you stupid bastard."

"Yes."

"Dead people don't bleed and they don't feel pain. That proves that you're alive."

My Shell felt hollow—like a cavern hidden underground—and my Spark was a tiny point of light blinking like a firefly within that darkness. *Cogito, ergo sum.* But the doctors were wrong. I was thinking, but I didn't exist.

Lorcan stepped back and grinned. "If I cut a little deeper, you're going to bleed to death."

I gazed down at the wound and watched blood trickling down my skin. The blood was bright red—a noisy, urgent color.

"If you're alive, then you won't want to die. And if you don't want to die, then you're going to beg me . . . plead . . . so you can live."

"I don't care what you do."

Lorcan displayed his teeth as his lungs sucked in air. "You want to see your heart? I'm going to cut it out and hold it in my—"

Someone knocked on the door and Lorcan's hand jerked away from my Shell. He remained silent for a few seconds and then we heard a familiar voice.

"Lorcan? Are you there? It's Miss Holquist. Open the door."

I didn't know what emotions Lorcan was feeling, but I watched his body change. At first, he was defiant—clutching the razor as he took a step toward the door. When Miss Holquist knocked again,

Lorcan bent his head down and sucked in his stomach. It looked as if he was absorbing his demons, forcing them back into his Shell.

"Open the door."

"Just—just give me a minute, ma'am. I want to make sure that everything's safe!" Lorcan pointed the tip of the razor at my right eye. "We're not finished," he whispered. "Once I start something, I never step back."

"Open the door *now*."

"I'm coming!" He folded up the razor, but kept it hidden in his hand. When he unlocked the door, Miss Holquist marched in wearing a navy blue business suit and a gold necklace. I had never seen her looking so perfect. She wore dark red lipstick and her hair was a helmet attached to her skull. She looked across the room and saw me handcuffed to the drill press.

"I didn't ask for *blood,* Mr. Tate. I told you to keep Mr. Underwood here until I returned from my meeting."

"He tried to get away and I stopped him. Of course, he'll lie and tell you something different."

Miss Holquist's heels clicked across the loft and then she stood in front of me. "What happened, Mr. Underwood? Did he stab you?"

"Razor."

"Ahhh, yes. The pearl-handled razor. Of course." She pivoted on one toe and faced Lorcan. "I didn't give permission."

"He was trying to escape."

Miss Holquist's voice was as clear and precise as a computer at a calling center. "It's loathsome to hear the same false statements in a variety of different ways. You're not showing respect."

"I'm—I'm sorry, ma'am."

"Cut him loose." Miss Holquist headed over to the kitchen area while Lorcan used his razor to cut away the plastic tie that held my ankles. When he unlocked one of the handcuffs, I collapsed onto the floor.

"Now give him the key." Miss Holquist returned with the green towel I used to clean the windows and tossed it onto the floor. "Press this against the wound, Mr. Underwood. That's an order." She faced

Lorcan. "My car is parked just outside the building. Patrick is driving. I want you to go north on Mulberry Street and buy me a double espresso at Sophia's in Little Italy." She turned to me as if we had just finished a meal in a restaurant. "Would you like something? Pastry? A latte?"

"He doesn't drink or eat anything but that nutrition shit."

"Then just the espresso."

Lorcan grabbed his jacket and walked over to the door. "I don't think you'll be safe with this crazy bastard."

"I am not happy with you, Mr. Tate. Do you realize that?"

"Yes, ma'am."

"And do you understand that I am not a police officer or a prison guard or any of the other shabby authority figures whom you've intimidated during your passage through this world? My negativity can have immediate consequences."

"Yes, ma'am. I understand."

"Then buy the espresso and come back here. Do it *now* . . . as quickly as possible. I don't like lukewarm coffee."

Slam of the door. No more Lorcan. I was still lying on the floor and I watched Miss Holquist's blue-and-white patent-leather pumps as they carried her around the loft. At that moment, it felt as if the shoes had more reality than their owner. Perhaps all she had to do was slip them on in the morning and the shoes made all the major decisions, taking her this way and that, carrying her around the city.

Miss Holquist dragged the chair across the loft and placed it in front of me. "Stand up and sit here. I'm sure that you're not seriously wounded. Lorcan Tate is a sadist, but he knows how to use his tools. If he'd wanted to kill you, you most definitely would be dead."

She was right. The cuts weren't serious. But it took a conscious effort to stand up and plop myself down on the chair.

"Good. Now raise the towel."

I obeyed the command. Miss Holquist leaned forward and examined my wound like an art critic inspecting a detail in a painting.

"You'll need stitches and some antibiotics. When we've finished our conversation, my driver can take you to a physician who owes me a favor. Do you understand?"

I nodded.

"Good. Now please tell me . . . what went wrong in Paris?"

.   .   .

I had never lied to Miss Holquist. This would be the first time. The truth exists. Lies need to be invented.

The Turing Test tried to make a distinction between humans and machines. But these days Shadow programs like Edward and Laura can be programmed to say "I love you" or imitate other emotions. If a machine wanted to act like a human, then it had to deny the truth.

Lying, not love, is the fundamental indication of humanity.

.   .   .

"My plan wasn't successful. Only one of the targets was neutralized."

"And what was your plan, Mr. Underwood?"

"The family was living in an eighteenth-century palace that had been divided into different apartments. I left a package at the entrance for Jafar Desai."

"Mr. Pradhani's son-in-law?"

I nodded. "Jafar's bodyguard picked up the package and carried it to the apartment. I followed him and shot him in the head the moment he opened the door."

"And then what happened?"

"Jafar ran through the house and locked himself in the bathroom. I kicked in the door and killed him as he lay in the tub."

"What about the wife? Why is she still alive?"

"I shot Nalini when she tried to get away. I thought she was dead, so I didn't stop to fire a confirmation shot. An alarm started ringing and I was worried about being trapped in the building. I had to kill two more bodyguards in order to escape."

"Yes. I've read news reports about what happened in Paris. The French press calls you *Monsieur Sangfroid* . . . 'Mr. Cold-Blooded.' But the police don't know your real identity. Do you think you left your fingerprints at the café mentioned in the *Le Monde* article?"

"No. I followed the rules I learned in training class. I picked up the cup with a paper napkin and I wore gloves inside Jafar's apartment."

"And did you speak inside the apartment?" She stared at me. "Did you say anything to the wife?"

"No. I shot her once and she fell onto the floor."

Miss Holquist paused again. And this silence opened a space between us that was cold and dangerous. "And what about the child? He was your third target. . . ."

"I couldn't find the boy. Maybe he was hiding."

"Did you search his room?"

"Not really. I just opened the door and looked inside."

"He could have been in the closet or under the bed."

"It's possible."

"Mr. Pradhani said you showed some reluctance about this target."

"There didn't seem to be a logical reason to kill the child."

"The boy was a target because our client made that your objective."

"But Sanjay didn't steal his grandfather's money. He didn't even know about it."

"So now you refer to him as Sanjay. He has a *name*. And what is the relevance of his name?" Miss Holquist leaned forward. "Are you attempting to be *moral* about this issue, Mr. Underwood? If so, I'm very surprised."

"No," I said. "I'm trying to be rational. I obeyed your instructions, Miss Holquist. But I don't understand how the child's death would benefit Mr. Pradhani."

"It's not your job to understand anything. You've been hired to listen and obey."

"All I'm saying is—"

"I know exactly what you're saying and that's why I'm annoyed.

Your newfound desire for explanations is like a wound that needs to be cauterized. Do you know what that word means, Mr. Underwood?"

"To burn something."

"To burn or sear a wound to stop the bleeding." Miss Holquist turned away from me and began to pace around the loft. "I don't normally have personal conversations with my employees, but you're going to meet an important person tomorrow evening. I want to be sure about you before that happens. You need to be clear about your thinking."

She stopped and inspected the industrial sewing machine. "I grew up in Charleston, South Carolina, in a once-beautiful house that had been transformed into a neighborhood eyesore. And the reason for that was quite clear. My father was a drunkard. I'm not going to excuse his behavior by calling him an alcoholic. He was a drunkard who could never hold on to a job."

She moved on to the drill press. "When I was a little girl I tried to find an explanation for his actions. Why was Daddy drunk on Tuesday night and sober on Wednesday? Was it the moon and the tides? Something I said? The food we cooked for dinner? His actions seemed as unpredictable as a coin flipped in the air.

"What saved me wasn't religion or morality, but science. I'll never forget finding out about the periodic table in Miss Foster's seventh-grade class. There was no reason for hydrogen having only one proton and one electron. That was simply a *fact*. A fact that had practical uses. As I increased my scientific knowledge, I began to realize that there are only a few real facts and everything else is just an opinion. Are you listening, Mr. Underwood? I'm not going to waste my time if you're not listening."

I nodded.

"Good." As she circled the chair, her high-heeled shoes made a sharp clicking sound. "Everything that goes on in the universe is a physical process that involves boson particles that have an integer spin such as one or two, and fermion particles that have odd, half-integer spins. And by everything, Mr. Underwood, I mean everything." *Click.* "My father's drunken behavior and the orbit of the moon. The explosion of a star and the biochemical process by which a thought appears in our minds. These physical facts determine biological facts, including all aspects of human activity." *Click.* "So what are the *implications* of this reality?"

The towel was sodden with blood and I felt blood dribbling down my stomach.

"There is no meaning to the universe, Mr. Underwood. No God." *Click.* "No soul." *Click.* "No grand explanation of life. And why is that? Because none of these big ideas have a scientifically verifiable connection to the bosons and the fermions." Miss Holquist stopped pacing and faced me. "Are you listening, Mr. Underwood? Or are you just bleeding? Answer me!"

I nodded and she resumed her pacing.

"And because there's no larger meaning to the universe, there's certainly no meaning to human existence. Our thoughts are created by the bosons and fermions. Our actions are shaped by them as well. Morality does not exist." *Click.* "Mass and energy exist. There is no good or evil." *Click.* "Religion, history, and philosophy are just fictions we've invented to explain our meaningless world."

Again, she stopped and faced me.

"So what motivates human activity? Self-interest. Even so-called virtues such as love and compassion are motivated by our selfish needs. It is in *your* self-interest to make money and create a comfortable living situation. Thus, it is a rational act for you to follow my orders and neutralize targets. It makes no difference if these targets are male or female, black or white, young or elderly. The bosons and fermions don't give a damn. Is that *clear,* Mr. Underwood? Am I *communicating* with you?"

"Yes, you are."

"Excellent." She walked back to me. "Because I don't want muddled thinking from my employees. Tomorrow night you're going to meet Alexander Serby, the chief executive officer of the Brooks Danford Group. While you were in Paris, worrying about explanations, Mr. Serby received a disturbing phone call from India. Apparently, there were three coded files on that flash drive that involve something much more important than the black money deals of the

Pradhani Group. Mr. Serby is very worried that this information might get into the wrong hands. He wants a face-to-face meeting with both of us. And why is that?"

"Because we know about Emily Buchanan."

"Correct. And he wants to keep the information circle as small as possible."

Miss Holquist's phone rang and she answered it. "Yes. Good. No, stay there. We're coming down." She switched off the phone and marched over to the door. "Lorcan is back with my espresso and we're going to take you to the doctor. Find a clean shirt, and let's go."

18

When I opened my eyes the next morning, a white cross of gauze and medical tape was in the middle of my chest. Twelve hours earlier I lay on a table in an East Harlem medical clinic while a nurse swabbed away blood and a doctor sewed. Now two lines of black stitches held skin and muscle together; my Shell had been mended like a torn pair of pants.

The wound felt like a harsh red color as I rolled to one side. I picked up my computer and spoke to Edward. "Show Baxter . . ."

"Good morning, Mr. Underwood. It is my understanding that you would like to see *A Boy for Baxter*. Please say 'No' if I have made the wrong conclusion."

"Play," I said, and five seconds later the computer began to show the documentary with the sound switched off. I had watched *A Boy for Baxter* so many times that I knew what the parents and the doctors and the dog trainers were saying.

I got halfway through Gordon's first tantrum, then I moved my thumb across the bottom of the screen and fast-forwarded to my favorite part: when Baxter cocks his head and wags his tail and jumps up on the couch beside Gordon.

After watching the scene seventeen times, I got out of bed, drank a bottle of ComPlete, and cleaned up the blood on the floor near the drill press. I was stuffing wadded-up paper towels into a garbage bag when Miss Holquist sent me an e-mail. She would meet me at the headquarters of the Brooks Danford Group at 9 p.m.

That left me plenty of time to search for information about the man I was going to meet that evening. For the last nine years, Alexander Serby had been chief executive officer of the bank. He had increased profits from the international division and the company's stock price had gone up. A year ago, Serby had been sitting in a TV studio before an interview and wasn't aware that the cameras and his microphone were switched on. When someone asked him what he thought about the president of the United States, Serby raised his forearm and wiggled his fingers as if he was manipulating a sock puppet. This caused a few days of controversy until a bank spokesperson said that Serby was motioning for someone to bring him a bottle of water.

.   .   .

At nine o'clock I returned to the BDG building on Maiden Lane and found Jerome Evans standing in the lobby. "You wait here," he told me. "Your boss is upstairs, talking to the big guy."

I sat on a bench for twenty minutes staring at X-Nemo's huge painting on the wall. No one stopped me when I walked over to the corner and looked for the artist's bloody handprint. Yes. It was still there.

Heels clicked on the marble floor as Miss Holquist approached me. "Good. You wore a necktie. Before we meet Mr. Serby, there are a few things I need to explain to you. Don't tell anyone that you were in Paris. Mr. Serby realizes that Jafar Desai was killed, but he doesn't want to know what happened."

"I understand."

"It goes a step further than that. Don't mention guns or any other kind of weapon. Don't use the words 'neutralize' or 'kill.' Never say that anyone is going to die. The language becomes more general as you move higher up the ladder. Those in power don't want to hear the details unless you're talking about stock options."

"So what do I say?"

"Mr. Serby is very concerned about the coded files. He wants to know how we're going to solve this problem."

Jerome Evans switched off sectors of the surveillance system as Miss Holquist and I stepped into the elevator. When we reached the twenty-eighth floor, she led me through an empty reception area and down a corridor to a large office with another X-Nemo painting on the wall. If I had been alone, I would have knelt down and searched for the bloody handprint.

A man wearing a suit and tie came out of a private bathroom, drying his hands. When he saw us, he tossed the towel on the floor. Alexander Serby had a bulbous head mounted on a spindly body. He was a small man, but there was cold energy within his Shell. His eyes were sharp points and they jabbed at me as we walked across the room.

"And this is Mr. Underwood?"

"That's right."

Serby sat behind his desk and gestured to some chairs. He knitted his hands together and made a steeple with his forefingers. I looked over his shoulder. A picture window was directly behind the desk and I could see a red river of brake lights moving north on the FDR Drive.

"Miss Holquist tells me that you're the person who found a copy of the stolen files."

I nodded.

"Most of the stolen data was about money transfers and the offshore bank accounts controlled by the Pradhani Group. But, for some reason, Jafar Desai downloaded three encrypted files. The files contain highly confidential information and it's important that we get them back. Now that Jafar is no longer a factor, our top priority is to find Emily Buchanan. Miss Holquist said that you searched her apartment and spoke to her uncle."

"Yes. He lives alone in a place called Chestertown."

"So who is Emily Buchanan? What can you tell me about her?"

I decided not to talk about the scent of her pillow and the kitchen photograph of her standing on a dock. "She's intelligent. Highly organized."

The steeple disappeared and Serby placed his hands on the desk. "I already know that. All the associates at BDG are intelligent and organized. But what does she *want*? Is she greedy? Idealistic? I always prefer greed to idealism. It's easier to make a deal."

"I can't answer those questions, Mr. Serby. I don't have enough information."

"Can you tell me any facts that can't be found in her personnel file?"

"Buchanan ran away from her parents when she was thirteen years old and was raised by her uncle. She was very dependent on her Shadow, but she switched it off a few months ago. This was around the time that she acquired a boyfriend named Sean."

"What's his full name?"

"I don't know, sir. But I did find some stickers in Ms. Buchanan's dresser."

"What kind of stickers?" Miss Holquist asked.

"They displayed antisocial slogans . . . the sort of thing that growlers would paint on a wall. One of them said 'Close the EYE.' Another said—"

"I get it. We don't need the whole goddamn list." Serby pushed his office chair back a few inches and exhaled. "So how are we going to find this criminal?"

"We're going to start by analyzing her e-mails," Miss Holquist said. "Mr. Underwood will examine all the e-mail in her BDG message file. While this is going on, a man named Hoffman will—"

"No need for names," Serby said.

"A computer expert in Germany will run all Buchanan's messages through a program that will establish a relationship matrix based on e-mail and Internet protocol addresses. Then a tracker program enters the relevant computers and communication devices and searches for messages with key words such as 'Emily' or 'Sean.' Once we get location data, we can access surveillance networks."

"I don't want anyone else finding out about this."

"We understand that," Miss Holquist said. "That's why Mr. Underwood is here for this meeting."

Serby looked at both of us, and then the steeple returned. His two forefingers were pressed together. "I want this problem solved *decisively*."

Sitting in the green leather chair, I finally realized something about my function. Miss Holquist was right. I was near the base of the ladder and Alexander Serby was at the top. That meant he could talk about solving problems "decisively," and now I knew what that word meant: that a contract employee would point a gun at a frightened man curled up in a bathtub, pull the trigger— and bits of blood and brain and bone would splatter against the porcelain.

.   .   .

Ten minutes later, Miss Holquist and I were sitting in the backseat of her town car as the driver headed north to my loft on Catherine Street. I was expecting new instructions, but Miss Holquist gazed out the window and watched the buildings glide past us.

"What do you like to do, Underwood?"

"Nothing."

"I don't believe that. Everyone enjoys some kind of activity. I happen to like certain aspects of my job. Alex Serby is one of the most powerful men in the world, but he needs my help with this problem. I find that very gratifying. So what makes you happy, Underwood? I know there's *something*."

"I like to walk across the Brooklyn Bridge and look up at the cables."

"All right. That's an acceptable answer. Please understand that you will no longer be able to walk across that bridge and have that pleasurable experience if I tell Lorcan Tate to slash your throat."

"Is that what you want to do?"

"Not at all. But I've learned that my employees are best motivated by a mixture of earned rewards and possible punishments. You've been paid a fair amount of money during the last three years. That's your reward. But you've never been punished. It's difficult to motivate a man who has no fear."

"I can't change that."

"I'm not saying that you lied about what happened in Paris, but I have the feeling that you've left out some details. All right. That's past. What I want at this moment is for you to dedicate all your time and energy to finding Emily Buchanan."

"I'll start looking through her company message file," I said. "If I get any useful information, I'll send it to you immediately."

"Good. If it relates to names and e-mail addresses, I'll forward it on to Mr. Hoffman in Germany. Right now we're thin on the ground here in New York, but I've sent messages to Europe and South America. Two or three enforcers should be flying in during the next few days and they can back you up if you get a specific location. Whatever you do . . . don't mention Buchanan's name or connect her to Alexander Serby. I want to keep this information circle as small as possible."

The car stopped in front of my building, and I put my hand on the door handle.

"One minute . . ." Miss Holquist opened up her attaché case and took out a cardboard box sealed with packing tape. "Here. I'm returning your two handguns. You might need them if our search is successful."

"I understand."

"Is there anything else we need to discuss, Mr. Underwood? I don't want any more confusion."

"Bosons and fermions. Mass and energy."

"Correct. Now do your job."

19

The next morning, I began reading through the business e-mails that were stored in Emily's mailbox. During the last two years, she had sent thousands of messages about financial reports and meeting prospective clients. I couldn't find any messages from Sean, but two years ago she had forwarded a list of discount clothing stores from her personal e-mail address. I sent the information to Miss Holquist and, two hours later, the German computer expert working for Special Services sent me Emily's password.

Now I had access to my target's personal e-mail. I discovered that Emily had a mother living in New Hampshire.

> // I told Rev. Taggart about yr big job at bank and he said G-d
> wants u to send our church $20,000 to fix roof. G-d will bless
> u for yr offering. If no $ then u are in Satans Army and are
> Damned to Hell. Wire or check.
> Yr Mother

Emily also kept in touch with a few college friends from the University of Vermont, and one of them was getting married. I spent five hours reading e-mail but didn't find any messages from Jafar Desai—or from a boyfriend named Sean.

In a day or so, we would have a personal relationship matrix based on Emily's e-mails, but that didn't mean that we could find her. People who wanted to protect their privacy could buy a used computer that couldn't be linked to their name. They'd clean out the computer's hard drive, download a browser bundle that didn't use IP addresses, and set up an e-mail account with one of the encrypted sites run by growler collectives. They could stay completely anonymous if their messages never contained identity information.

Thinking about the problem, I hammered a nail into the floor, attached the cord, and began to pace out a perfect circle. Emily's personal e-mail address had given me the name of her mother and her friends. But it would also show what kind of advertisements were sent to her because of her search activity.

I opened Emily's spam file and found e-mails from online companies selling fake Freedom IDs and card shields that blocked the sensors for the EYE system. I also discovered several weekly announcements of a Dice Night at Crawley's—a bar in the Bushwick neighborhood of Brooklyn. Now that most human behavior could be predicted by the Norm-All program, some of the growlers tried to defy the algorithms by deliberately performing random activity. Wandering around New York and London at night, I had noticed signs outside bars and clubs advertising Dice Nights. This was a one-time event when the price of alcohol and the behavior of the customers were determined by a throw of the dice or the spin of a carnival wheel. You could meet a stranger for a Dice Date or even win a Dice Vacation to an unknown destination.

At some moment during her time in the city, Emily had given her e-mail address to the person who ran the Web site for Crawley's bar. I found an e-mail with today's date from someone named "CROWBAR" that said, "Dice Night 2Night! Meet you at Crawley's. Full bar. Freedom is Uncertainty."

I clicked the link to Crawley's Web site and confirmed that a Dice Night event was being held at the bar that evening. "Acts of Deliberate Randomness" would begin at 11 p.m. After resting for a few hours, I cleaned and loaded the .38 Special, then slipped it into the ankle holster. Lorcan's handcuffs were stuffed into a nylon pouch that I had once used to carry bullets. The pouch was attached to my belt and slipped inside my waistband.

Although I didn't care about Freedom or believe in Uncertainty, it appeared that Emily was attracted to these meaningless words. It wouldn't be a random moment if I found her tonight.

.   .   .

It was cold and windy in Brooklyn and very few cars were on the street. On the way to the bar, I took out my Freedom Card and slipped it into the lead-lined sleeve that shielded it from scanners. It was against the law to block your ID chip and a blocked card would set off an alarm if you entered a bank or a government building, but there were fewer scanners and surveillance cameras in a neighborhood like Bushwick. Most of the growlers revealed their tracked identity at work, and then shielded their card the moment they left the building.

No one was on the street and it felt as if I was the last Spark in existence, floating through an empty city. I usually asked Laura to speak with her efficient voice, but that evening I stepped into a doorway and scrolled through her personality variations.

URGENT

EFFICIENT

NUBOT NEUTRAL

FRIENDLY

HUMOROUS

GENTLE

I clicked GENTLE, a voice intonation I had never heard before, and Laura spoke with soft tones as she guided me to a side street near Graham Avenue. When I asked for more information about the destination address, she told me that Crawley's was in a building that had once been a nineteenth-century brewery. The building still had an arched doorway, big enough for rolling out beer barrels, but now it was protected by a bouncer wearing a referee's striped shirt.

"You here for Dice Night?"

I nodded.

The bouncer shined a pencil flashlight at my eyes, looking for electronic contact lenses. "No G-MIDs or E-MIDs allowed inside. They're just gonna get smashed on the floor."

"I don't use that technology."

"Good. So are you ready? Or not ready?"

"What are you talking about?"

"Not ready costs you forty dollars to get in. It means you're not participating in the activities. But if you're ready to do anything . . . it's free."

"Not ready," I said, and handed him the money. The bouncer stamped the back of my hand and gave me a white pin to fasten to my jacket.

I entered a long room with a plank floor and tin ceiling. Crawley's had a mahogany bar with a mirror behind it, a truckload of mismatched tables and chairs, and a small stage with a DJ sitting at a control board. Bouncers wearing referee shirts patrolled the room while three young women wearing pink overalls served beer in plastic cups to hundreds of customers. Half the crowd wore black bandanas or black knit hats, and a handful of New Luddites—with bones and feathers pinned to their clothes—sat together at a large table.

Smell of sweat and spilled beer. Mouths and tongues moving, pushing out noise. That night, the DJ was playing a song by a British rock band called Deliberate Confusion. I had heard the music when I was walking through London at night; the words flowed out of half-open windows and the doors of shabby pubs.

They are . . .
Gears and wires.
We are . . .
Flesh and bone.
They have . . .
All the power.
We have . . .

Lost our home.
Nothing. Nothing.
Nothing left to lose.

Trying not to touch anyone, I managed to maneuver around the tables and reach the other side of the room. A young man brushed past me as he tried to join his friends and I saw the probes for direct brain stimulation sticking out the back of his head. It looked like two steel thumbtacks had been pushed into his skull.

What saved me was Dr. Noland's Rule #5: *Always remember: dead people must act alive.* When I reached the bar, I pulled out my wallet and waved to one of the bartenders.

"Beer."

"What kind?"

"Surprise me," I told her and a few minutes later she brought me a red plastic cup filled with liquid. Raising it to my lips, I pretended to drink. The few people who had been staring at me turned away. The beer made me appear to be alive and now I was just part of the scenery. As more people squeezed into the windowless room, the air around me gained weight and darkness. The growlers were dancing in groups, shouting the words of the song:

Nothing! Nothing!
Nothing left to lose!

Looking around at the crowd, I realized that only a few other people wore the white pin that announced that we weren't participating in tonight's randomness. Even the three young women behind the bar wore red pins with different numbers printed on them. There was a frenzy of ordering and serving and paying for drinks, and then suddenly the DJ played a drumroll.

A teenage boy with devil's horns fastened to his head walked through the doorway that led to the toilets. He crossed the room and climbed up onto the end of the bar where a spotlight was fastened to a steel post. A bass sound—like a heartbeat thump—

boomed out of the speakers as the boy switched on the spotlight and raked the beam across the heads of the drinkers like a soldier firing a machine gun.

The music gained power. A few people cheered when a young Asian woman dressed up as an eight ball stepped onto the stage. She was followed by a large man with a bushy beard who was wearing a ballet tutu and fairy wings. Standing on the edge of the stage, the Fairy and the Eight Ball applauded the third member of their group—a young woman wearing black leather and carrying a whip.

Without any explanation, Eight Ball jumped into the crowd. Like a molecule in a glass of water, she bounced off people and ricocheted off furniture, spinning and dancing as she drifted through the chaos. *Boom.* She hit the woman standing next to me. *Boom.* She struck a table and floated toward the end of the room. The bearded Fairy pulled her back up on the stage and Whip Girl switched on a microphone.

"Good evening, drudges and drones. Welcome to Dice Night." She pulled out her Freedom Card, held within a blocker shield.

"Has everyone blocked their slavery card? Daddy and Mommy don't know where you are tonight! Daddy and Mommy don't know what you're going to do! Tonight you're random and free!"

The growlers whistled and shouted and pounded their fists on the table. Meanwhile the Fairy and Eight Ball disappeared into the hallway, then came back out with two clear plastic buckets. One container was filled with what looked like green marbles. The other was filled with plastic Easter eggs.

"Let's open a door and walk down a new hallway," Whip Girl said. "It's not what was predicted for your future. It's as random as birth, as random as love." She turned to her two assistants. "Good Fairy, choose our first winner."

The Good Fairy plunged his big hand into the smaller container and came up with a marble that had a number on it.

"Three eighty-six!" he shouted.

The spotlight beam glided around the room as people glanced down at the number pins fastened to shirts and sweaters. A few people began talking and a young man dressed in black waved his hand.

Eight Ball pulled an egg out of the second container, cracked it open, and handed a piece of paper to Whip Girl.

"And your randomness is . . . five free drinks for you and your friends!"

The growler laughed and headed for the bar as his friends thumped the table.

A minute or so passed and then another number was chosen. "Eighty-nine!" shouted Whip Girl. And this time a young woman stood with a sprig of ivy pinned to her jacket that showed that she was a daughter of Ned.

Another Easter egg. Whip Girl read the slip of paper and grinned. "Please stand up on the nearest available table!"

The girl stepped on a chair and stood in the middle of a wooden table carved with names and initials.

"Now strip naked while we watch."

Startled, the girl buried her face in her hands while the growlers hooted and cheered. But before she could change her mind and run out of the room, the Good Fairy and Eight Ball jumped off the stage and began clapping their hands. The crowd imitated them until everyone was clapping with the same rhythm.

The rickety table trembled as the girl removed her jacket, boots, and socks. She pulled off a black sweater, held two hands over her bare breasts, and then dropped them away. The clapping got louder. Standing on one foot and then the other, the girl removed her jeans and underwear and stood naked as the spotlight beam touched her body.

People continued drinking as more acts of randomness entertained them. Two young men put on cardboard armor and battered each other with foam-rubber swords. A young woman called a past boyfriend and announced that she was still in love with him. Her desperate words boomed out of the speaker, along with a dial tone when the man hung up on her.

Dr. Noland insisted that there was no free will or free choice. If all past actions could be fed into a God computer, then the machine could predict every action in the future. Both the citizens obediently going to work and the growlers in this crowded bar were simply responding to prior stimuli and obeying the laws of physics.

But the certainty of all actions was true only if the God computer knew each minor decision and microscopic movement within the physical world. Even with the EYE system and the scanners and surveillance cameras, the nubots would never achieve total knowledge. Free will was saved by ignorance. Because of our own stupidity, we had to assume we had a choice.

Finally the last number was taken from the container. Instead of announcing it, Whip Girl held the marble up in the air. "The number is random. The choice is not. As always, the last person chosen will burn their Freedom Card."

The noisy room became quiet at that moment. The deliberate destruction of a federal ID card was a violation of the Freedom from Fear Act and violators were sentenced to a year of hard labor at one of the Good Citizen Camps.

"They call this a Freedom Card," Whip Girl said. "But we all know that it shows our slavery. When everything about us is known, then freedom disappears and we become a piece of machinery . . . like the nubots in the subway booths. Well, I say we still have the right to choose." Smiling, she held up the green marble between her thumb and index finger. "Number two twelve."

Everyone glanced down at the number on their pin and then a young man with a tribal tattoo on his neck walked slowly through the crowd, stepped onto the stage, and held up his ID card.

People were silent, watching as the Good Fairy gave the volunteer a pair of pliers. The card was sprayed with lighter fluid and held over a bucket of sand. A match. And then people began cheering as the card burned with a dirty orange flame.

I retreated down the hallway that led to the restrooms, but Eight Ball was already there, kissing the neck and stroking the breasts of the young woman who had stripped off her clothes. My Spark was vibrating so rapidly that I wondered if it would finally break out of its Shell. Turning away from the embrace, I headed for the exit and then saw a flyer taped to the wall.

HOUSING IS A RIGHT!

Find a home for yourself
and your family!

Take back our neighborhoods
from the banks!

Join Housing for Us (H4U).

Public meeting Friday Night 8PM at the Christian Worker.

It was just another antisocial group. Nothing important. But at the bottom of the flyer was the organization's symbol—the same geometric house I had seen on a paint-splattered T-shirt in Emily's apartment.

20

The paint-splattered T-shirt and the political stickers in Emily Buchanan's dresser suggested that she might have been a member of Housing for Us. The group had a basic Web site that didn't provide a lot of information. Apparently, they were a squatter group that took over abandoned buildings in poor areas, fixed them up, and gave them to homeless families. Edward did a news article search and reported back with his butler's voice. Eight months ago, a Brooklyn slumlord had sent four men with baseball bats to East New York to take back a house occupied by H4U. The squatters fought back with crowbars and sledgehammers and two of the thugs ended up in the hospital.

The flyer on the wall at Crawley's said that Housing for Us was meeting tonight at the Christian Worker House. Once again, I returned to the Internet and learned that Christian Worker wasn't a church or labor union, but a collection of autonomous communities where people lived together in the spirit of early Christianity. The New York City branch of the movement owned a building on the Lower East Side of Manhattan, and this was where H4U was going to hold its public meeting. The sort of people involved with Housing for Us and the Christian Worker would know how to obtain fake IDs and stay off the grid. It seemed logical that someone in either group might know where Emily was hiding.

· · ·

That evening I took the subway to Fourth Street and walked east to the Christian Worker. The Lower East Side had been a slum area until the end of the twentieth century, but now the neighborhood was known for storefront art galleries and wine bars. It had rained earlier that evening and the mist in the air softened the edges and corners and made the old tenement buildings look like slabs of rock carved to show doors and windows.

Christian Worker House was a brownstone building with a marble portico—a small, square roof supported by four Greek columns decorated with grape vines. In the previous millennium the building had been occupied by the Brotherhood of Unified Mechanics and Engineers, and the name of their organization was still carved into the soot-stained marble.

Pushing open the door, I entered an anteroom, where a black man in a wheelchair was using a magnifying glass to peer at a newspaper crossword puzzle.

"Housing for Us?"

"Welcome, brother." The old man grinned and waved me forward.

I passed through a second door and found myself in a large room with a twenty-foot ceiling that had been turned into an auditorium. Four women were sitting at one end of a table eating yellow rice and black beans out of cardboard bowls. A large Dominican woman wearing a bright red sweater and hoop earrings smiled at me and waved her spoon. "*Entra, mi amigo.* I am Eugenia. You here for the meeting?"

"Yes."

"Then you come to the right place. No worries. You will see more people. Eat some food if you want. If you need the men's room, it's upstairs."

The women continued their meal, gossiping about someone named Ana. When I walked upstairs to the bathroom, I found a long hallway painted with a blue-green color that reminded me of Marian Hospital. Eight residence rooms lined the hallway—each with a door latch and padlock. An elderly lady with a pink nightgown and fuzzy slippers shuffled out of the toilet, pushing an aluminum walker. Perhaps this building had once been a crucible of revolution. Now it was an old-age home.

The meeting still hadn't started when I returned to the main floor, so I wandered around the auditorium. Over the years, the Christian Workers had stolen dozens of plastic post office bins. Each of these sturdy little containers was filled with back issues of the *Workers' Life,* a six-page newspaper that cost only twenty-five cents. I picked up a recent issue and read three obituaries about members of the Christian Worker community who had lived in this building or worked at a communal farm. Mold was growing on the pages and it gave the entire room a smudgy gray smell.

More people arrived for the meeting and they chatted with the women at the table. Staying at the edge of the room, I threaded a path around some folding chairs and climbed up onto the stage. More postal bins filled with yellowed newspapers were stacked against the wall along with plywood and papier-mâché street puppets: a rat, a spider, and an old man with a top hat clinging to money bags. There were signs and banners from past wars and forgotten strikes.

"We're starting the meeting," a man announced and I returned to the table. Eugenia and her friends remained, but now they were drinking tea and passing around a bag of chocolate-chip cookies.

The meeting was run by a sallow-faced man named Bennett, who wore a patched raincoat and trucker's cap that proudly announced that he was an "Antisocial Element." This was the main category of people who were sent to the Good Citizen Camps during the mass arrests that followed the Day of Rage.

Bennett explained that his organization—Renters' Rights of New York City—had "unified" with Housing for You and this was a "significant moment" for everyone concerned about homeless people. I was expecting someone to start waving protest signs, but instead a woman named Selma read the minutes of the last meeting.

When she was done, Bennett started talking about a petition that was going to be presented to the mayor. "Has anyone called State Senator Mitchell?" he asked. Glances around the table. Silence. Bennett blew his nose, and then resumed his lecture. The mosquito sound of his voice, the gray smell of mold and spilled milk and leaky plumbing, the haze of dust covering the lightbulbs, made my Spark feel frozen in my Shell. Were these people the antisocial elements that the authorities were so worried about? I was dead, but at least I knew it. Bennett was dead, but no one had told him.

I was getting ready to go when the door popped open and three growlers entered the room. A scruffy-looking teenage boy headed over to the beans and rice, followed by a muscular woman with blond pigtails and snake tattoos slithering down her arms. The leader of the trio was a tall young man with hair that touched the collar of his surplus army jacket. There was something about his Spark that changed the energy in the room. All the women smiled at him and the men sat up a little straighter.

"Buenos noches!" the young man said. "Sorry I didn't call you guys. We just got a new address from Sonya, so we're driving to East New York for a cracking party."

"That's wonderful," Bennett said. "But we're talking about the *petition*."

The teenager scooped up what remained of the beans and rice and dumped the food into three cardboard bowls. While that was going on, the blond woman grabbed a handful of chocolate-chip cookies and stuffed them into her bag.

The tall young man turned to Eugenia and smiled. *"Me alegro de verte!* You still talking to that mother with the two children?"

"Yeah. They're living in their car."

"This house tonight sounds like a good possibility. It's bank owned, unoccupied for almost three years . . ."

By now, the teenager had scraped the last grain of rice out of the pot. He grabbed some plastic spoons and his share of cookies. "Fueled up," he said.

"Anyone else want to help us crack a house? Billy Bones is sick with the flu, so it's just me, Thrasher, and Ice."

The women touched their hair and glanced at each other. Bennett held up a hand as if he was trying to hail a speeding taxicab. "Does this really have to happen tonight? You should stay for the meeting."

"Next time. I promise." The young man winked at Eugenia. "If the house checks out, I'll call you tomorrow morning."

"Good luck, Sean. Don't get hurt. . . ."

.   .   .

A few seconds later they were out the door. My Shell didn't move, but my Spark was moving rapidly. *Sean.* The leader of the group had the same name as Emily Buchanan's boyfriend. Maybe my target was waiting for him in the car.

I hurried out to the sidewalk and caught up with Sean and his friends. "Can I come along?"

Each person in the group was holding a bowl of beans and rice. They turned around and stared at me. "And who the hell are you?" asked the blond woman.

"Jacob Underwood."

"That doesn't answer my question."

Sean put his hand on my shoulder. "We don't know you, Jacob. So of course we're going to be suspicious. Do you mind if Thrasher searches you?"

"No problem."

I was in trouble if they discovered the gun in my ankle holster or the handcuffs carried beneath my waistband, but Thrasher just focused on the contents of my pockets.

"Look at this . . . he's carrying a full-frequency detector."

"What's wrong with that?" I asked. "I just want to know if someone's using a G-MID to photograph me."

Sean laughed and pulled a frequency detector out of his front pocket. "Relax, Jake. We all carry them."

Thrasher found my Freedom ID and held it up so his two friends could see. "Underwood is his real name and his card is in a blocker shield."

"And that's where everyone should keep their ID," Sean said. "So where do you live, Jake? Do you have a job?"

"Right now, I live in Manhattan. I used to work for a software company called InterFace. Then I got replaced by a nubot."

"Join the club," Ice said. "Last year I got fired from PetTopia, the pet supply company. They told everyone that our jobs weren't covered by the Freedom to Work Act. Then a couple of months later we found out—"

Sean rolled his eyes as if he'd heard this story before. "Forget about the nubots. Let's get going. We can talk in the car."

Sean touched my Shell a second time and I made an effort not to pull away as he guided me across the street to a beat-up Toyota sedan. The dashboard was held together with duct tape and someone had ripped the plastic cover off the steering column. Sean slid behind the steering wheel and Thrasher sat beside him. Ice and I were in the back.

"Ever been to a cracking party, Jake?"

"Are we going to break into a house?"

"That's right. We target buildings that have been abandoned by the banks." Sean started the car and sat listening to the tapping sounds coming from the engine. "Ice is the head of our construction crew in Brooklyn. She'll see if the building can be renovated."

"I look for good bones," Ice said. "The house has to be structurally sound."

"The rest of us search for zombies," Thrasher said.

Sean laughed. He shifted into first and the gears complained. "We got to find out if bonks or drug dealers are using the building."

"So what if nobody's living there?"

"It usually takes us two or three weeks to do a full cleanup. During that period, we turn on the water and splice the home onto the power grid."

"We move in a homeless family when the house is safe for children," Ice said. "And then we make sure they get mail."

"Why is that so important?"

"Mail delivery is mentioned in a section of New York City's landlord-tenant law," Sean said. "If a person can prove that they've been receiving mail at their residence for at least thirty days, then they can't be arrested for trespassing. Eventually, the bank discovers that we've taken over the building and files eviction papers, but then our pro bono lawyers call up the loan officer and try to negotiate a deal. We've been able to work out a rent-purchase agreement on eighteen abandoned homes."

"What about Bennett's petition?" I asked.

"Petitions are a waste of time," Sean said. "We take over buildings and give them to families. I believe in the politics of *doing* something."

Sean turned the car onto Delancey Street and now we followed the traffic across the Williamsburg Bridge. Light from sodium lamps fastened to the bridge lit up the interior of the car for a few seconds and then we were absorbed by the shadows. It felt as if I was watching a series of still photographs:

> *Thrasher listening to the music from his earphones.*
> *Sean glancing over his shoulder as he changed lanes.*
> *Ice raising a spoon to her lips.*
> *My hand reaching down to touch the ankle holster.*

Finally, we passed over a speed bump and now we were in Brooklyn, traveling beneath the rusty girders of the elevated subway.

"So how did you hear about the meeting at the Christian Worker?" Sean asked.

"There was a flyer taped on the wall near the restrooms at Crawley's bar. I went there for Dice Night."

Sean smiled at his friends. "See? What did I tell you? If we put up more flyers we're going to get more supporters."

"Are you a Luddite?" I asked.

"Not really. The Children of Ned want to destroy the nubots, but the real danger comes from a change of consciousness within our own minds. Once we *think* like machines, then we *are* machines."

The energy that flowed outward from Manhattan—the crowds, skyscrapers, and neon lights—crashed like a wave on the shore and left its litter on the streets of East New York. Graffiti was scrawled on walls and sidewalks. We passed liquor stores and bodegas with bulletproof shields that separated the clerks from their customers. Storefront churches were everywhere with crudely painted signs that promised deliverance. A scrawny cat sat on the hood of a parked car and watched an old woman filling up a pail from a fire hydrant dribbling water.

Ice pulled a phone out of her pocket. "Turn right on Linden Avenue. Good. Now we're looking for Warwick Street."

We peered out the windshield at rows of two-story detached houses with clapboard siding and security bars on the lower windows. Pale light flickered through the gaps between curtains. It was a cold night and people were inside, watching television.

"Slow down," Ice said. "See the sign? That's Warwick Street. . . . Turn left and look for number eighteen. . . . There it is . . . on the left."

The brick house was surrounded with a low chain-link fence. Brown sheets of plywood covered all the windows and there was a blackened pile of burned trash on what had once been the front lawn.

"Boarded up," Sean said. "Let's find some place to park."

He drove up the block, found a parking spot, and switched off the engine. Everyone got out of the car and Sean opened up the trunk. Several canvas bags were there, filled with construction tools and flashlights. Sean unzipped a duffel and began pulling out blue hard hats and safety vests. "Put this gear on, Jake. Dressing like this keeps the neighbors from calling the police."

Thrasher laughed. "We usually tell people that we're from the Environmental Protection Agency and we're looking for a broken sewer pipe. Nobody ever asks a follow-up question."

"And take this. . . ." Ice handed me a filter mask that covered my mouth and nose. "Sometimes we find asbestos or toxic chemicals. You don't want that poison in your lungs."

All of us followed Sean down the sidewalk and through the little gate. When we stepped onto the porch, Ice and Thrasher switched on their flashlights and pointed them at the steel security door. Someone had drilled a hole into the door and installed a heavy chain and padlock.

Ice handed her flashlight to Sean and pulled some bolt cutters out of her tool bag. "This just makes our job easier."

Ice cut the chain and Sean yanked open the security door. The wooden front door was a flimsy barrier and Thrasher detached the brass knob with an electric screwdriver. Everyone pulled on their air filters as Sean led us inside.

Beams from the three flashlights glided across the small living room. A couch, two chairs, and a pair of end tables were covered with torn bedsheets. They looked like squat little ghosts that had been waiting for visitors.

Sean took a step forward and dust rose up into the air. "Zombies," he said, pointing to drug vials and fast-food wrappers dumped in the corner. The air filter made his voice sound as if he had fallen in a hole.

Thrasher disappeared through a doorway while Ice pointed her flashlight at a stain on the ceiling. "Leaky water pipe, but it doesn't look too serious."

"I don't see any mold," Sean said. "Let's go upstairs and check the—"

Light flashed in the doorway and Thrasher hurried back into the living room. "We got a problem in the kitchen."

"Did the floor collapse?"

"This house is occupied."

Sean led us down a short hallway with half-open doors revealing two bedrooms. Then he stopped and pushed open a swinging door. I entered the kitchen and stopped near the doorway. Sink. Refrigerator. Stove. A kitchen table with three chairs. A first I thought that little bits of trash were scattered around the room, and then the trash began to move. Flashlight beams revealed a colony of rats scurrying across the tile floor and popping in and out of the wooden cabinet. I watched a gray rat sniff the tip of my shoe and then hurry away; his tail drew a thin line in the dust.

"There's too many of them," Sean whispered. "Let's get out of here."

If Emily Buchanan was still connected to Sean, then I needed to do something that would keep me with him. Unlike machines, Human Units favored reciprocal actions. "I can solve this problem," I said. "Hand me the crowbar."

"What are you going to do?"

"Kill them all."

Sean shook his head. "No. That's dangerous. I don't want anyone getting hurt."

"They'll swarm you," Thrasher said. "Sometimes they bite and they don't let go."

"Hand me the crowbar. You stay here in the doorway with the flashlights."

A light beam jiggled around when Ice reached into her tool bag. The crowbar was heavy and solid; it felt more real than any other object in the room. My Spark had jagged edges and my thoughts were not under control. I wanted to hear Laura's calm voice before I began to kill everything.

I switched on my headset. "Laura?"

"Yes, Mr. Underwood."

"Say something beautiful."

"I don't know what you mean, sir. You have not made this request previously."

"Do a search on the Internet. Find words written about a beautiful object or a beautiful location."

"In English, sir?"

"English."

A pause, then—"I have found the first newspaper description of Yosemite Valley, written in 1855. Data indicates that Yosemite is considered a beautiful location."

"Sounds good. Read it."

"Just opposite to this, on the south side of the valley, our attention was first attracted by a magnificent waterfall, about seven hundred feet in height. . . ."

I walked over to the kitchen table, clutching my weapon with two hands, then crouched slightly and swung hard. Two rats died. And then the room was exploded with energy. Rats chirped and squeaked and hissed to each other. The flashlight beams turned their eyes into sharp red points.

"It looked like a broad long feather of silver, that hung depending over a precipice, and as this feathery tail of leaping spray thus hung, a slight breeze moved it from side to side. . . ."

A rat clung to my pants' leg, but I brushed it off and kept swinging the crowbar. Squeaks and squeals. The harsh scent of blood and urine.

"As the last rays of the setting sun were gilding it with rainbow hues, the red spray from the falling water would mix with the purple and the purple with the yellow and the yellow with the green and the green with the silvery sheen of its whitened foam, as it danced in space. . . ."

.   .   .

Twenty minutes later we were back out on the porch, pulling off the filters and breathing the cold, clean air. Ice took a new chain and padlock out of her bag and Sean used it to fasten the security door.

"I'll come back tomorrow morning with rat poison and a few spring traps baited with peanut butter," Sean said. "We'll do our first cleanup on Sunday and see about hacking into the power grid. I'm going to tell Eugenia that we'll have a livable home in two or three weeks."

We returned to the Toyota and used some old towels to wipe the dust off our faces. Then everyone got back in the car and Sean dropped Ice and Thrasher off at a subway station.

"Where do you live, Jake?"

"Manhattan."

"You really helped us tonight, and I appreciate that. If you're not doing anything, I'd like you to meet some friends of mine."

"Where are these people?"

"They're here in Brooklyn. It's not far away." Sean drove slowly down the streets while he made a call with a headset phone. "How you doing?" he asked. "Yeah, I'm in the car. . . . The cracking party went okay. . . . Lots of rats, but no zombies. Right now, I'm driving over to the Vickerson workshop with someone who helped us out tonight. Okay . . . no problem."

He switched off the phone and glanced at me. "Were you involved with the No Bots demonstration in Times Square last year? The Luddites tried to shut down the mechanical subway clerks."

"I'm not a growler. This is the first time I've ever done anything like this."

"It might take some time for you to figure out where you stand on certain issues. I got into all this when I was a teenager. I started online, downloading free content, and then I became involved with a crypto-anarchist group. Our slogan was 'The laws of mathematics are stronger than the laws of man.'"

"What does that mean?"

"We created cryptographic software that would protect the Darknet system. We were trying to protect online privacy and freedom of speech."

"So when did you start breaking into houses?"

"The Day of Rage changed everything. Danny Marchand was insane, but all the growlers got tossed into the same basket. Three of my friends were arrested and sent to a Good Citizen Camp in Utah. It's supposed to be for a maximum of sixty days without arraignment, but after you serve the sixty, they arrest you again outside the camp gate. I went off the grid for a few months, then came down to New York and got involved with Housing for You. It's a good feeling when you give a home to a family that's been living on the street."

We drove through Williamsburg and parked in front of a Quonset hut made of galvanized steel that occupied a triangular patch of land near the Brooklyn-Queens Expressway. Light glowed through a row of frosted-glass windows protected by wire mesh. There was a sign on the corner that said that the building was the headquarters of the VICKERSON FURNITURE AND HERITAGE WOOD SUPPLY COMPANY.

We got out of the car and I followed Sean up a gravel pathway to a red steel door. "Anyone home?" he shouted and thumped on the door with his fist.

A few seconds later, a young man wearing a tool belt opened the door. My Spark remembered seeing some historical photographs of the Earp brothers—Western lawmen who were involved in a famous gunfight in Tombstone, Arizona. The man in front of us had the same bushy mustache and parted hair as Wyatt Earp. It felt like someone from the nineteenth century had magically been transported to Brooklyn.

The young man smiled. "What's going on, Sean?"

"Boz, this is Jake. We just finished another cracking party in East New York. I thought we'd drop by and I'd show him what you're doing."

Boz Vickerson grinned and motioned us to come inside. "Good timing. You can help me stack some lumber."

The Quonset hut was like a huge tin can cut in half with the edges resting on the ground. The large room was split into three distinct areas. Thousands of boards were stacked on one end of the building. At the other end was an office space with desks, file cabinets, and a sink. The middle section was where another man with a bushy Wyatt Earp mustache was fitting together parts of a wooden chair. A few yards away, a young woman with a pirate bandana partially covering her red hair was brushing a clear liquid on a rosewood table.

The air was cold near the door and I realized that the building lacked central heating. The only warmth came from a cast-iron stove fed with wood scraps. A ventilation grate was open and the coals glowed bright red like a Spark.

"This is my brother, Ernie. As you can see . . . he's older, and shorter."

"But a lot better-looking," Ernie said.

"Hi, Sean!" The young woman smiled and waved her paintbrush.

"And the woman brushing on teak oil is my sister, Millicent."

"All you need to know is that I'm the smartest one in the family. Isn't that right, Sean?"

"The smartest and the best dancer."

"And a modest soul as well," Boz said. "There's plenty of time to dance, but let's do a little work first. A contractor up in Boston ordered a thousand feet of heritage wood and I need to find one more mahogany board and two Spanish cypress."

Sean and I followed Boz to the end of the room where the boards were stacked. The Quonset hut was filled with the scent of teak oil and wood glue and the pine scraps burning in the stove. Everything combined into a butterscotch brown color that floated through my mind.

"We'll look for the mahogany first. It's a dark red color—almost black. I think there's one board four stacks down. All these boards were cut from logs shipped up from Central America. They're approximately two hundred years old."

"How is that possible?" I asked.

"Work now. Talk later." Boz pointed to an eight-foot board at the top of a stack. "Jake . . . you take that end. Sean . . . you get the other end. Just pile it up over there."

We found the mahogany board right away, then rebuilt the stack as Boz searched for the Spanish cypress. "I *think* it's here," he muttered. "I *hope* it's here."

This time, we had to search through three different stacks until we found the missing boards. Boz smiled at Sean when we finished the job. "Does Jake understand what we do here?"

"Why don't you explain it to him."

"We reclaim underwater wood that got sunk in the mud when old-time loggers were floating logs down rivers. Because of the cold water and lack of oxygen, the logs are perfectly preserved. About a year ago, we pulled a Norfolk pine log from a Vermont river that was cut in the eighteenth century and marked for use by the British Royal Navy. Everything we bring up is from old-growth forest . . . tight-grain hardwood that looks beautiful when it's sanded and oiled. Usually, we take them out using divers with a boom and winch. The difficult thing is to dry the wood slowly so that it won't crack, but we've built a drying center up in Maine with special presses and a vacuum kiln. This way we get to make beautiful furniture without cutting down any trees."

"So why are you in New York City?"

"More customers found out about us when we moved down here. Ernie's wife has family in Brooklyn and my sister has gotten into tango dancing." Boz glanced across the room at Millicent and smiled. "I guess it's hard to find tango *milongas* in rural Maine. We're not as brave as Sean . . . breaking into buildings and organizing demonstrations. Our politics are up on the wall."

I followed his eyes and saw a painted sign that said: IF YOU DECIDE TO DO SOMETHING, THEN DO IT WELL.

"Have you read 'Machine Thinking' by Thomas Slater? You can get it online for free. Slater says that the fifth-generation computers that control the nubots and the Shadows make it necessary for humans to justify their *uniqueness*. Machines, no matter how sophisticated, can only follow programs. If we sleepwalk through our lives, then we're no better than machines. Only humans are capable of a job done well, which means thinking about the *consequences* of our actions. A job done well pays the bills, but it also improves the lives of everyone around us."

Still holding a paintbrush, Millicent crossed the room. "Did you find the mahogany?"

"Yeah. That was easy. But the cypress was buried under the walnut."

"Ernest wants some help clamping chair legs. You can do that while I make our guests some hot chocolate."

Millicent led us over to the office area and told us to sit down at a steel table in one corner of the room. While we took our seats, she opened a refrigerator, took out a carton of milk, and poured some of it into a saucepan. Then she placed the pan on a single-burner hot plate and turned it up to medium heat.

"You don't have to do this," Sean said. "I know you guys are busy."

"Sometimes a girl gets tired of looking at her brothers all day long." Millicent touched Sean's shoulder and I tried to understand the energy passing between them. "Besides, what's the point of life if you can't eat chocolate and dance the tango? Never forget the tango."

Millicent took a bowl full of chocolate paste out of the refrigerator and spooned some of it into the saucepan. Using a wooden spoon, she stirred the mixture carefully. "Did Bosworth tell you about doing things well? In this case, 'a job well done' means getting the milk hot, but never letting it boil."

When the milk reached the right temperature, she grabbed a whisk and beat the mixture until it was foamy. Then she poured the steaming chocolate into two mugs and garnished the top with slivers from a chocolate bar.

"People don't always dance together," she told Sean. "Sometimes, it's all about timing. But that doesn't mean we can't be friends. Enjoy . . ." Millicent turned away from us and hurried back across the room. "Bosworth! Get away from the table! The surface coat still hasn't dried!"

Sean held his mug in cupped hands. Then he raised it to his lips, drank, and smiled. "Drink it down, Jake. It's just steaming because the air is cold."

A mug of chocolate had been placed in front of me and it was clear that Sean expected me to pour it into my Shell. Rejecting the gift for any reason might create suspicion and doubt.

My hands imitated Sean's hands, cupping the mug and raising it to my lips. And then I drank—tipping the mug slightly and allowing the chocolate to enter my mouth. It was warm and thick and my tongue sensed its sweetness. This wasn't a quick and glittery burst of white, but a deeper, darker color.

I swallowed and the warmth spread within my body. The experience brought back a memory of a rainy afternoon with my mother, steam rising from a cooking pot while teddy bears danced on a yellow cup.

"Good, huh?"

I nodded.

"People think they have control of their lives because they can buy crap at a mall, but if you look a little deeper, you realize that those in power are writing their story for them. The Vickerson family is creating their *own* story. That's what all of us want to do. That's our revolution."

I heard the steel door at the end of the room squeak open and slam shut. Then I heard Boz's deep voice and a woman answering him. Sound of boots on the concrete floor. I placed the cup on the table, turned my head, and saw—

Emily Buchanan.

21

Emily had dyed her hair black. Instead of her banking uniform of starched blouses and tailored suits, she wore torn jeans, a man's sweater, and an all-weather parka with a FREE SPEECH = FREE LIVES button pinned to the collar.

"Thought I'd walk over."

Sean stood up and hugged her. "Jake, this is Emily. We both live in luxury a few blocks away from here."

"Hi, Jake." Emily extended her hand, but I didn't want to touch her.

"You hungry, Em?" Sean set the saucepan back on the burner. "Millicent made some hot chocolate and I think there's enough left for one more cup."

"Sounds wonderful." Emily unzipped her parka and smiled at me. "Sean was just joking about the luxury. We live in a warehouse surrounded by thousands of broken machines."

"Hey, Emily!" Millicent waved and Emily walked over to the cast-iron stove. The two women laughed about something as Sean stirred the chocolate with the wooden spoon.

"Is Emily involved with Housing for You?"

"No. Just a friend." Sean poured the drink into a mug and scattered some chocolate shavings on the surface.

The hot chocolate lured Emily back to the table and she sat down beside me. Although I had watched Emily on a surveillance tape and placed my head on her pillow, it felt strange to see this Human Unit not in my thoughts, but in reality. The real Emily was unpredictable; she played with the fringe on her scarf, then raised her hand and wiped a chocolate mustache off her lip.

Sean described what happened when we broke into the abandoned house, and then Boz Vickerson joined us at the table. Boz laughed when Emily said he should take tango lessons with his sister. The conversation seemed to come out of nowhere and float around the room like one of the giant soap bubbles created by street performers in the city.

Sean glanced at his phone. "It's getting late. Can we drop you off at a subway station, Jake?"

"Yes. I'll go with you."

We said good-bye to the Vickersons and stepped out into the night. After being surrounded by the scent of burning pinewood and teak oil, the outside world was a cold chunk of iron. Sean and Emily sat in the front seat of the car while I got into the back, pulled up my pants leg, and drew the .38 revolver. I kept the weapon low, concealed within the shadows.

At eleven o'clock in the evening the city looked like a screen-saver image of New York that would disappear the moment you switched off your computer. Only the activity inside the car was real—Emily and Sean chattering about the leftover lasagna in the refrigerator while I clutched the mechanical heaviness of the gun.

Sean pulled up to the curb beside a subway entrance, swiveled around, and smiled at me. "Good to meet you, Jake. Why don't you give me your e-mail address and I'll contact you the next time we have a cracking party."

The street was empty at that moment and no one was leaving the subway. I raised the revolver and pointed it at Sean's head. "Take your hands off the steering wheel, leave the key in the ignition, and get out of the car."

Sean and Emily stared at the gun for a few seconds, and then Sean shook his head. "No way," he muttered.

"Don't hurt him," Emily said. "Please . . ."

"I'm not going to hurt anyone if he gets out of the car."

"Are you a cop?" Sean asked. "If you're a cop, I want to see your badge."

I moved the gun slightly to the right and fired at the dashboard. The gunshot was loud and overpowering. It felt as if a bright red liquid had suddenly filled the car. Sean jerked away from the sound, and his head slammed against the side window.

"The next time I use my weapon, a bullet will pierce your Shell. Your Spark will drain out the hole and vanish."

"What the hell are you talking about?"

"Some people want to speak to Emily about the banking information she received from India. The two of us are going to drive back to the city. You have five seconds to get out of the car."

"Do what he says, Sean."

"I'm not going to leave you alone."

"Don't worry. I can handle this." Emily sounded like Laura. Each word from her mouth was clear and distinct.

Sean hesitated, and then he opened the door and got out of the car.

"Now slide behind the steering wheel. We're going to Manhattan."

Emily shifted into drive and the car pulled away from the curb. Sean stood on the curb, shouting and waving his arms, but he didn't try to stop us.

"I don't know Brooklyn very well. I'm going to get lost."

"We'll use my Shadow." I pressed the activate button. "Laura? We're in a car. Please guide us from our current location to Catherine Street in Manhattan."

"I'd be glad to help you, sir. Please turn right onto Roebling Street."

Following Laura's directions, we took the Williamsburg Bridge across the East River and turned left on Bowery. We drove around for a few minutes, and then found a parking space across the street from the Coleman Park baseball field.

Emily turned off the engine, and we sat in the car without speaking to each other. The hours I'd spent watching sports on my computer had taught me something about human behavior. I still couldn't understand why people felt emotions, but I knew how an athlete behaved when he was about to kick a ball. Emily's head moved back and forth as she peered out the windshield. There was a jittery tension in her body as if she was going to jump out of the car and run.

"Now what happens?"

"Put your hands on the steering wheel."

Emily hesitated, and then obeyed me. Leaning over the seat, I snapped on Lorcan's handcuffs. I didn't want her calling anyone, so I searched the outside pockets of her parka and pulled out a disposable cell phone.

"What's the reason for the handcuffs?"

"I want to make sure that you stay with me until you talk to someone who works for the bank. After that, you're free to go."

I maneuvered Emily out of the car, removed her scarf, and wrapped it around her wrists so that the handcuffs weren't visible. Then I put my hand on her upper arm and guided her up Market Street, past a grocery store Dumpster that radiated the sludgy brown scent of wet cardboard boxes.

"Where are we going?"

We turned left and headed down Monroe Street. "We're walking to my apartment. I live a few blocks away from here."

Emily stopped outside a closed fish market. "The Brooks Danford Group does business with criminals."

"That fact isn't relevant to my actions."

"Well, it *should* be. Jafar Desai, the man who sent me the files, was murdered in Paris just a few days ago. I'd bet anything that the killing was done by someone working for Jafar's father-in-law . . . Rajat Pradhani."

"I work for the bank. Not Mr. Pradhani."

"But BDG is helping Pradhani launder money, which means you're helping criminals."

We turned the corner and walked north on Catherine Street. A garish yellow smell came from the mound of garbage bags outside the Yangtze Restaurant. Halfway up the block we stopped near Happy Girl Doughnuts and I took out my keys.

"Now what?"

"This is where I live."

I unlocked the street door and guided her inside. Climbing up the staircase, she paused on each landing, but I stayed behind her. The shuffling sound of my shoes on the slate steps pushed her forward.

When we entered the loft, Emily spun around and presented her wrists. "All right . . . we're here. Take the cuffs off. They're not necessary."

I removed the handcuffs and Emily walked over to the drill-press machine. She pulled off her parka and canvas shoulder bag and hung them on a handle.

"You should buy some more furniture, Jacob. Where's your couch?"

"I don't have one."

"So where do your friends sit when they come over?"

"I don't have any friends. If you want to sit down, there's a chair over in the kitchen area."

Emily glanced at the chair but kept wandering around the room, touching the old machines and peering out the windows. She had a quick, nervous energy—like one of the hermit thrushes with olive brown wings that darted through the streets of the city. It was logical that she wanted to run away from me, and that meant I had to figure out what she was thinking. In *A Boy for Baxter,* the dog could watch and sniff and figure out Gordon's mood. I wasn't a dog, and understanding what went on in the mind of a Human Unit seemed like a difficult task.

"You said that people from the bank wanted to talk to me. So where are they? Let's move this forward."

I slipped on my phone headset and dialed Miss Holquist's number. She answered immediately. "I found the customer we've been looking for. We're at my apartment."

"Is she under control?"

"Yes."

"Good. Give her your phone."

I removed the headset and slipped it onto Emily's ears.

"Who's this?" Emily asked. "Do you work for the bank?"

Miss Holquist started talking and Emily remained silent for a few minutes. At a certain point, she shook her head and frowned.

"Is that it? Have I heard your little speech? Okay . . . now it's *my* turn. Two days ago, I did a search on the Internet and found out that Jafar Desai was killed in Paris. Did you know that? Did you know that the bank is connected to a criminal who hires assassins?"

Emily stopped talking and rolled her eyes. "I'm *going* to tell you about the files. I'm getting to that. All you need to know is that I *can't* give the files back. When I heard that Jafar was killed, I sent the files to Thomas Slater at the We Speak for Freedom Web site. Since I don't have the files anymore, tell Mr. Underwood to let me go or call the police. I'm sure I broke one of the security laws that were passed after the Day of Rage."

Emily looked up at me. "Now she wants to talk to you."

I slipped on the headset. "Yes?"

"Keep her under control," Miss Holquist said. "I'm going to contact our employer and call you back."

The line went dead, but I left the headset on.

"So what's the decision? Are you going to let me go?"

"Miss Holquist wants to talk to the bank's legal staff. They'll determine if the information you received is owned by the bank or by the Pradhani family."

"They should have figured that out earlier." Emily turned in a slow circle and examined the loft. "Okay . . . I see one bed, one table, and one chair. Do you have a bathroom?"

"Over there."

She went into the bathroom, and then stuck out her head a few seconds later. "Why is your mirror covered with masking tape and newspapers?"

"Why do you ask so many questions?"

"Is the mirror cracked? Is that the problem?"

"I covered the mirror because I don't like to look at myself."

"Okay. That's reasonable. I feel that way in the morning."

She closed the door again, but her energy remained in the room. I heard the toilet flush and water splashing in the sink as I hurried over to the entrance door and used my key to lock the dead bolt from inside the loft. Then I returned to the kitchen and waited.

The bathroom door creaked open and Emily smiled at me. "I think you're wrong about the mirror, Jacob."

"And why is that?"

"You're a very *intense* person . . . that's true. But you're not unattractive. Why don't you look at yourself in the mirror for a few seconds every morning and then—"

Before I could react, Emily sprinted across the room and tried to yank the door open. The dead bolt held and she fumbled with the lock—finally realizing that she was trapped. I couldn't see her face, but her hands became fists then hands again. She took a deep breath, smoothed back her hair, and faced me.

"This is crazy. I didn't do anything wrong."

"You took the files."

"They were *sent* to me. Okay? I met Jafar Desai at this silly Financial Futures conference in London. He told me that his father-in-law was crazy and he needed some kind of 'insurance' if he and his family left India with his wife's inheritance. Trust me . . . this wasn't a complicated scheme. I never met Jafar after the conference. We didn't talk on the phone. Jafar said he would transfer a monthly payment into my bank account. If the payment didn't occur . . . that meant he was in trouble and I should post the evidence of money laundering on the Internet. I hated my job and was planning to quit next year, so Jafar's offer sounded like a good idea."

"He sent you the files."

"That's right."

"But you don't own this information."

"Of course not."

"Then why did you give it to Thomas Slater's Web site?"

"Because Jafar got killed in Paris. The Pradhani Group hired an assassin . . . probably some Mafia guy . . . to shoot everybody. Look, I realize you're just doing your job, Underwood. But these people are really *evil*. Do you understand that?"

"Let's stay with the facts," I said. "Why did you put the flash drive in the music box?"

"That was *my* insurance in case something bad happened to me. The music box was a Christmas gift from my uncle when I was fourteen years old. Roland would leave surprises in it if I was sad or having problems in school. Then he'd tell me that 'home is where the heart is.'"

Emily returned to the kitchen area. She opened the refrigerator and discovered rows of bottled water. "Where's your food, Underwood? You *do* eat food, right? I'm hungry."

"I don't consume things that decay inside me."

"Are you some kind of weird vegetarian?"

"Sit down and I'll serve you something."

Emily watched me take a bottle of ComPlete and my only glass out of the cupboard. I placed them both in the middle of the table.

"What's this?"

"ComPlete. It's a sole-source nutrition drink."

"Isn't this for old ladies and cancer patients? What about some crackers and peanut butter? Or an apple?"

"This is the only food I consume."

She tore off the plastic seal and poured the white liquid into the glass. It was very strange to have this Human Unit in my private space. I could feel the warmth of her body over by the refrigerator.

"I'll drink this crap, but you've got to sit down at the table. I don't like you standing there, staring at me."

"There's a folding chair in the closet."

"Perfect. Go get it."

I went to the closet, returned with the chair, and sat beside her at the table. "Here's to you, Jacob." Emily raised the glass and took her first sip. "This tastes like vanilla chalk dust. But *good* chalk dust. *Nutritious* chalk dust." She finished off the drink and slammed the glass down on the table.

"Another bottle?"

"Sure. Why not? Let's go crazy tonight." She grinned when I took out a second bottle of ComPlete. "So what are we going to do while we're waiting for the lawyers to call? Do you have a deck of cards?"

"No."

"A television?"

"No."

"What do you do when you're not tracking down wayward bank employees?"

I decided not to tell her about the nail and the cord and walking in a perfect circle. "Sometimes I watch a documentary about a service dog named Baxter."

"Sounds great! I love dogs. Let's watch it together."

I didn't want her to keep asking questions, so I turned on my computer and told Edward to play *A Boy for Baxter*.

I don't really own anything except for my clothes and a few pieces of furniture, but I have become attached to this movie. Over the last three years, I had watched the film hundreds of times and memorized all the dialogue. It felt like I owned the story.

All that changed when I saw the movie through her eyes. Emily liked Max Velden, the trainer who carried dog biscuits in one shirt pocket and bite-size chocolate bars for humans in the other pocket. She hated Dr. Potterfield, the autism expert who was constantly lecturing the two parents about everything they did wrong. At the end of the story, when Baxter was hit by a car, Emily's eyes glistened and I wondered if she was going to cry. "Not fair," she whispered. *"Not fair at all."* When the dog got up on three legs and limped across the backyard patio, Emily blew her nose with a paper towel and drank a glass of water.

"That was a great movie, Jacob! Thanks for showing it to me."

"I've watched it a few times. . . ."

"So who are you? Gordon or Baxter?"

"I don't understand."

"I hope you don't take this wrong, but I think you're kind of like Baxter. When we were drinking chocolate at the Vickerson workshop, you didn't really say anything, but you were watching us, evaluating." She laughed. "You would have been a great German shepherd."

"I'm—I'm Gordon."

"You're autistic? Really?"

I looked down at the floor. "No. That's not it."

. . .

Dr. Rutherford said that I needed to form relationships with other people. But I knew that was a bad idea.

Other people are confusing.

Other people make simple events complicated.

Other people attach invisible lines to your Shell, and then you can't move freely.

. . .

"I was injured in an accident, and it transformed me. I don't perceive emotions. When I look at someone's face, I can't read the message there."

"And Baxter could help you?"

"Yes. Definitely."

"How do you deal with people if you don't have a service dog?"

"I've scanned and downloaded images of forty-eight different emotions. They're photographs of a nineteenth-century French actor named Jean LeMarc." I took out my phone. "Laura . . . show emotion file."

In the first photograph, Jean LeMarc was smiling. His eyes were wide and upturned lines appeared at the corners of his mouth.

"Happiness," Emily said.

"That's right."

"This is fun. Show me each photo and I'll see if I can pick the right emotion."

Sadness.

Pleasure.

Disgust.

After she gave me the right answer, I would lower my phone below the edge of the table. I'd find an emotion, then raise my hand and present the new photograph.

Fear.

Surprise.

Desire.

Emily laughed and demanded clues for a few of the images, but I wouldn't answer her questions. She had problems identifying melancholy and ennui.

"That's not ennui. He just looks tired."

"You show me the right expression."

Emily pressed the palm of her hand against her cheek, gazed up at the ceiling, and sighed loudly. "No. That's not it. Maybe you have to be French to feel ennui."

I presented the last emotion, and she studied it for several minutes.

"Happiness."

"You already said 'happiness.'"

"Joy."

"Correct." I switched off the phone.

"When I was a child, I was told that the righteous would have an eternity of joy with the angels up in heaven. But I didn't believe that. Not even a little bit. Joy catches you by surprise. You're just living your life and then . . . bam!"

She touched my arm and I jerked away from her. In that instant, all the warmth of the room vanished and it was cold—once again.

"Never do that."

"Okay. I'm sorry."

"Rule number one is to tell people that I don't like to be touched."

"I—I can see that. I apologize."

"You have a phone call," Laura said.

I got up from the table, walked over to the windows, and Miss Holquist whispered into my ears, "I want you to solve our problem . . . completely. Lorcan will come to your apartment tomorrow morning. He'll pick up the empty container and take it away. Do you understand what you're supposed to do?"

"Yes."

"Good work, Underwood. I'm giving you a bonus."

22

I switched off the headset and realized that Emily was watching me.

"Was that your boss?"

"Yes."

"So what's the decision?"

"It's late. Miss Holquist wasn't able to contact the bank's legal staff. You'll spend the night here and she'll contact us tomorrow morning."

"So I'm a *prisoner*." She said the last word with a great deal of force.

"You are at this location until Miss Holquist calls us in the morning. I would say that you're waiting. I'm waiting, too."

"I don't want to be here. Do you understand that?"

Emily began pacing again, moving so quickly that I thought she was going to slam into the wall. Her behavior reminded me of a scene in *A Boy for Baxter* when Gordon paced around a living room with wild energy. Baxter sensed that Gordon might start smashing things, but he didn't approach the child. He just sat on a throw rug in his dog way—calm, but alert—and gradually he became the center point of the room.

I walked over to the bed, sat on the floor, and leaned against the wall. I didn't say anything, but I continued watching Emily. After a while she stopped pacing and sat on the edge of the bed.

"I want to explain a few things," she said.

"That's not necessary."

"Just listen. Okay? You need to see the whole picture. The information Jafar sent me proved that the Pradhani family have been hiding income and avoiding taxes. That's not a big secret in India. Lots of rich people do that. But the bank is angry because they don't want people to know that their international division helps tax cheats and arms dealers. When you walk into the BDG building, the lobby looks clean and ordered and beautiful. But it's really just a bunch of thieves helping other thieves protect their money. Thomas Slater says that modern authority is based on a system of lies that are accepted by the general population. If you pull away the curtain and show the reality of power, people are motivated to question the fictions that govern their own lives."

"Is that why you joined the bank? To expose everyone?"

"Not at all. I joined the bank because I wanted to make money. I don't like to take shit from people, and having money seemed like the way to avoid that. During my first year at BDG, I just focused on learning the job, then I realized that I was following orders like a nubot. The same thing happened when I was a little girl. I grew up in Bledsoe, New Hampshire. It's a town that had four stoplights and two of them were broken. Both my mother and my father were disciples of the Pure Holiness Church. Ever heard of it?"

I shook my head.

"It's a little bit Christian, and mostly a cult. Everyone in the church believes that the visible world was created by Satan. The only way you can break free of the Evil is by acts of daily purification. The church had all these *rules*. You couldn't drink alcohol, eat pork, use an umbrella, and . . . oh yeah . . . you could only take cold showers and baths because cold water had more purity than warm water."

"And you believed this?"

"No. Something was always wrong with me. Maybe I got dropped on my head when I was a baby. I remember sitting in church at the age of nine, listening to a sermon about infant damnation and thinking: *Forget it. This is crazy.* And that meant trouble because the church ruled our lives. I was homeschooled with my two sisters and we went to church services three nights a week. Because sexual desire was created by Satan, Reverend Wilkerson said that everyone needed to get married as young as possible. My father had a husband picked out for me when I was thirteen, but I ran away from home and called my uncle Roland from a pay phone. Roland is a wonderful man. He went to court and became my legal guardian. My parents think that I'm a Daughter of Satan, but sometimes they call up and ask for money."

"And when did you decide to work for the bank?"

"Joining BDG was part of a much longer journey. My whole life changed because of a bottle of orange juice. After I graduated from high school, I got a job as a waitress at Waffle Hut and started taking classes at the local community college. But I spent most of my time smoking weed and hanging out with the kind of people who dreamed of getting hit by a car and winning a big insurance settlement. A couple of years melted away and then I walked into the local Stop and Shop. I wanted to buy a bottle of fresh-squeezed orange juice, but I had only eighty-four cents. I thought about stealing the bottle, but that wasn't going to change how much money was in my pocket. And right then I decided that I wanted to get rich. If you have enough money, you can quit working at Waffle Hut and travel to any place in the world."

"So you got a better job?"

"Not right away. The first thing I did was buy the software program and the computer link for a Guider."

"That's a Shadow program, right?"

"Guiders work like Shadows, but they're much more than that. They were first developed for alcoholics and drug addicts, but now they're used by anybody who wants to change their behavior. First, you pick the sex, age, and personality of your Guider, and then you tell them your goal. Gradually, the program learns more and more about you and the Guider starts to give you advice. I named my Guider 'Claire.' She was programmed to be a little bit older than me—like a big sister."

"And what did she tell you to do?"

"My first goal was to go back to college and graduate with really good grades. At first, Claire just asked a lot of questions with this calm voice."

I nodded. "Both of my Shadows are calm."

"When I transferred to the University of Vermont and started taking classes again, Claire stopped asking questions and began telling me what to do. She was connected to my phone, so she always knew my location. If I went to a bar or tried to sleep late, Claire would call me up and tell me that I had to study. I didn't realize that I had basically rejoined the Pure Holiness Church . . . only this time, a *machine* was telling me what to do.

"After graduation, I got a job as a financial analyst for a bank in Boston and then, two years later, I got into business school. Human friends are usually thinking about their own problems, but Claire was always focused on *me*. After a while, she would connect to the cash register at the grocery store and tell me if I was buying unhealthy food. She would monitor my bank account so that I wouldn't waste money.

"I didn't have my headset on during my job interviews for the Brooks Danford Group, but when I was hired as an associate, I linked Claire to my work computer and talked to her all day long. That was when she began to get a little bossy. Claire was still focused on making a lot of money and the fastest way to do that was to work twelve hours a day."

"Someone at the bank said that you took off your headset."

"Yeah. That's true. An old college friend came down to New York and she took me to an art opening in Brooklyn. I thought we were going to see paintings hanging on walls, but a group of artists had taken over a warehouse and turned it into a carnival with a tunnel of love and booths to win prizes. I was throwing potatoes at a giant rabbit when I met Sean. He was smart and good-looking and a lot more interesting than the assholes who worked at the bank. When we left the art show, I put my headset back on. Sean was telling me about the growlers and Dice Night at Crawley's while Claire was calling a taxi to take me back to my apartment. Then Sean pulled off my headset and asked: 'So who's living your life? You or a machine?'

"I'm not saying that everything changed at that moment, but two weeks later, I took off the headset. I know that Claire is a software program, but she acted like a jealous ex-boyfriend. Claire was still active somewhere on the grid, and she would send me long e-mails telling me that I was making a mistake. Finally I had to buy a hacker program called Shadow Killer that erased her from the system."

"And you were still at the bank?"

"Yeah, I was working there, getting my paycheck, but I began to see the world in a new way. I spent part of my childhood obeying all these church rules and then I let a computer program boss me around. All I knew is that I wanted to live a free life and make my own decisions. And that was when I met Jafar Desai at the conference in London."

Emily pulled off her boots and dropped them onto the floor. "Anyway, that's *my* story. So what's *your* story?"

"I don't have one."

"Did you go to college? Were you ever married? You said you were in an accident. What kind of accident?"

"We exist in the current reality. Everything in the past is unimportant."

"So what do you do for fun in the current reality? This loft doesn't look like a fun place, Jake. Swear to God . . . you need a couch."

"I like to walk through the Financial District at night. In the daytime, I follow the straight line painted on the path that runs beside the Hudson River."

"It's called the Greenway. I like that, too."

"But most of all, I like to walk across the Brooklyn Bridge and look up at the cables. They divide the sky into precise sections."

"Well, I don't know about that, but I've been on the bridge dozens of times. When I stand at the edge and look out at the harbor it feels like I'm floating above everything. It's beautiful."

"I don't believe in beautiful."

"You think everything's ugly?"

"Everything *exists*. Those values you attach to objects . . . beauty and ugliness . . . love and hatred . . . are just words."

"I still think you need a couch." Emily looked around the room. "Do you have an inflatable mattress or a sleeping bag? It's been a long day."

"Use the bed."

"I'm okay on the floor."

"I don't sleep like you do. I close my eyes. Then I open them."

Emily flopped down on the mattress and turned onto her side. "I hope you don't take this the wrong way, Jake . . . but you're one of the strangest people I've ever met. Okay. Stop. Maybe 'strange' is a negative word. You're *different*."

"Good night, Emily."

She was silent for a long moment and then in a soft voice she said, "Good night."

Sitting on the floor, I listened to Emily's body move around on the mattress. Street light came through the windows on the other side of the room and I could see her face. After a while, her breathing became slow and regular. Her lips opened slightly and her eyes moved beneath her eyelids as if she was watching someone within a dream.

My Spark analyzed the situation several times and produced the same conclusion: there was no logical reason not to kill her. If I didn't follow instructions, Lorcan would show up in the morning and do the job.

I took off my shoes so that the plank floor wouldn't creak, then stood up, walked over to the pencil machine, and took out the semi-automatic pistol that I had concealed in the housing. The gun had a rail-mounted laser sight and I switched it on with my trigger finger as I returned to the bed.

The red laser dot burned its way across the floor, and then it drifted up onto the mattress and touched Emily's leg. It felt as if my Spark had left my body, and now it was floating around like a firefly, touching Emily's neck and, finally, settling on a spot directly above her left ear.

I told my finger to pull the trigger, but it refused to obey. Standing beside her body, I could hear her breathing and her humanness flowed toward me in waves. And I wanted more, so I leaned over and smelled the nape of her neck and it was green—forest green—and glowing as if sunlight was pushing through the leaves of a tree.

Pull the trigger. *Now.*

Instead, I turned away from the bed, switched off the laser, and retreated to the bathroom. Red light from the Yangtze Restaurant sign oozed through the frosted-glass window and gave a pink tint to the porcelain sink.

Since my Transformation I had created an existence that was simple, clear, and logical. But something had changed. I had showed Emily the film about Baxter and she had told me the story of her life. Every Human Unit wandered through reality with its own story. Now I had absorbed a fragment of her past.

I touched the yellowed newspaper pages that covered the mirror, then ripped them away and let the pieces flutter onto the floor. Placing my hands on the edge of the sink I leaned forward and stared at my face. My body was still a Shell, but now my eyes had lost their deadness. They radiated energy on the lower frequencies—energy that could never be detected by a machine.

23

At around five o'clock in the morning, the night sky lost its dark power and began to radiate a soft blue color. Three patches of sunlight appeared on the floor beneath the windows, and these hazy rectangles extended themselves like columns toward the bed, where Emily lay sleeping.

My current existence was unstable because of this Human Unit. Emily's mouth was slightly open and her dyed-black hair was wayward and tangled. Her left hand curled slightly as if she was trying to hold on to something. I had saved her life, but perhaps that was a meaningless decision. Lorcan would show up at the loft in a few hours. When he discovered that Emily was still alive, he would take control and finish my assignment.

I walked over to the kitchen table and switched on my computer. First I checked for e-mail, then I went onto the We Speak for Freedom Web site created by Thomas Slater and made sure that the stolen files from the Pradhani Group still hadn't been posted.

"Good morning . . ." Edward's butler voice made me feel like he was about to serve tea on a tray. "Would you like a weather report for the New York metropolitan area?"

"Not now. Please provide information about the computer expert Thomas Slater."

Within a few seconds, Edward came up with links to over forty articles. Emily had sent the stolen files to someone who was faceless: the most powerful ghost on the Internet.

. . .

When Thomas Slater was a graduate student studying computer science at Princeton, he invented the "Slater Gates"—a routing system that helped shape the Internet. Eventually he became a professor at the Massachusetts Institute of Technology, where he wrote a famous essay called "The Decision and the Choice." Slater compared machine decisions generated by computational activity and human choices that used nonmathematical factors such as moral values and emotions.

The issues described in "The Decision and the Choice" motivated Slater's decadelong attempt to design an artificial emotion program. The program was a crucial step in creating a machine that would duplicate human consciousness. Slater appeared on the cover of the *New York Times Sunday Magazine* with the headline: WILL THIS MAN TEACH COMPUTERS HOW TO CRY?

Slater had never been married, but six years ago he went to a dinner party and met Helen McClatchy, an Irishwoman who once worked as a Dublin crime reporter. McClatchy had written a series of articles about the local drug lords, and then was almost killed when a bomb blew up her car. After a long period of physical therapy, she moved to the States and bought two guard dogs. As a birthday gift for his new girlfriend, Slater designed a software program that pretended to translate dog sounds into human language. All you had to do was point a phone at your pet and get him to bark. Seconds later, phrases like "I'm hungry!" or "Let's go for a walk!" appeared on the phone's display screen.

Slater put the program up on a Web site called Your Pet Talks and it began to get views from people all over the world. Eventually, he sold the site for millions of dollars and donated some of the money to groups that defended free speech. He published two political essays—"Machine Thinking" and "Against Authority"—but it was the Day of Rage that transformed his life. When Congress passed the Freedom from Fear Act, Slater became part of the "Fear Not" group that marched on Washington. He was arrested in front of the White House and spent two months in a Good Citizen camp. After he was released, a virus appeared on the Internet that deleted every tagged digital photograph of Slater that was stored on an accessible database. The only image of the former professor that kept appearing was a scanned photo taken from a book that had been published fourteen years ago.

This was the man who had received the stolen files from Emily. Was there any way he could be persuaded to give them back?

. . .

I switched off the computer, checked Emily's phone, and discovered text messages and e-mails from Sean.

> // Are you safe?
> // Call me.
> // If I don't hear from you by 9 a.m., I'm contacting the police.

"What are you doing?" Emily was awake and sitting up in bed.

"I'm reading your messages. Sean will call the police if he doesn't hear from you."

"Let me handle that problem. You can read the message before I send it."

I brought the phone over to the bed and gave her the phone. Emily typed some words with her thumb.

> // I'm safe. Don't call anyone. E.

I took the phone back and slipped it into my shirt pocket. "Did you sleep well?"

"It was okay. I woke up once and watched you for a while. Your eyes were closed and you didn't move. You looked like a bot charging its battery."

"Sleep isn't important to me."

"Lucky you. Right now I feel like I've got a hangover, which is weird because I didn't drink any alcohol last night."

I sat on the edge of the mattress, and then stood up immediately. It was uncomfortable to feel the warmth from her body. Emily held the pillow to her chest as I circled the bed.

"Jafar sent you information about the Pradhani family, but he also sent three coded files."

"That's right. I saw them during the download."

"These files are very important to Alexander Serby. And because of that, Miss Holquist . . . the woman you talked to last night . . . told me to kill you. A man named Lorcan Tate is going to show up later on this morning to pick up your body."

Emily glanced at the door as if Lorcan was about to burst into the loft. "Then we should get out of here as soon as possible."

"Running away is only a short-term solution. They'll find you eventually."

"A short-term solution is better than being dead."

"I checked We Speak for Freedom and the stolen information still isn't up on the Web site. Maybe they haven't figured out how to read the encoded files. Could you contact Thomas Slater and get the files back?"

"I don't know."

"Slater is famous for living off the grid. Have you ever talked to him?"

"Twice . . . using FaceTime. Sean's growler friend Tech slept with a daughter of Ned who knew a hacker named C-Section who gave me a phone number in Stockholm. Of course Slater isn't really in Sweden. The call passes through different servers. He could be living in this building."

"We have two or three hours. See if you can contact him."

Emily took a tablet computer out of her canvas shoulder bag and placed it on the kitchen table. Her call took about a minute to work its way through various Web sites and servers. Then a bot voice—mechanical and precise—delivered a message: "Leave a message if you wish, but we rarely call back."

"Mr. Slater, this is Emily Buchanan calling on Monday at seven twenty-two a.m. East Coast time. I've got a serious problem and need to talk to you as soon as possible." She ended the call and looked up at me.

"Now what?"

"We wait."

"It would be easier to deal with this if I had a cup of coffee and some blueberry muffins."

"What about a bottle of ComPlete?"

She rolled her eyes. "Sounds delicious."

I took two bottles from the cupboard and we consumed the necessary nutrition together.

Emily kept glancing at the door.

"So why didn't you kill me?"

I decided not to tell her that she created a glowing green color in my mind. "I don't really know. It wasn't a rational choice."

"So what happens if it becomes rational? Do you pull the trigger?"

"Right now I feel like I'm in a foreign country without my Shadows. I don't know the rules and I can't speak the language. All I can do is—"

Emily's computer beeped and the phone app showed that an unregistered number was trying to contact her. She activated Face-Time and an image appeared on the screen—not a face, but a plaid shirt, arms, hands.

"Hello, Emily." It was a man's voice. "What seems to be the problem?"

"The bank found out what happened. There's some important information on the three encoded files, and they're very angry with me."

"What are you—"

"Let me finish. There's a man here from the bank named Underwood. He has a gun."

Before I could stop her, she picked up the tablet with two hands, pointed it at me, then moved her arms slowly and gave Slater a complete image of the entire room.

"I sent you a flash drive. Someone is going to kill me if you don't give it back."

"I understand," Slater said. "So where are you, Emily?"

"New York City."

"Will Mr. Underwood let you go somewhere alone, then return with the flash drive?"

"No."

"He says—"

"I heard him," Slater said. "I can meet you and Mr. Underwood, but it's not going to be in the city."

"That's acceptable," I said.

"Give me a few minutes and I'll text you a location and a meeting time."

Slater typed a command on the keyboard and the FaceTime chat was over. Emily stood up and pushed back her hair. "Do we have enough time for me to take a shower?"

"Go ahead."

Emily skated across the smooth floor in her stocking feet. When she reached the bathroom door, she stopped and smiled at me. "For some reason I like you, Underwood. And that's a little bit crazy, because you almost killed me. But life is like Dice Night at Crawley's bar. You never know what number they're going to pull out of the bucket."

I waited until I heard the shower running, and then I called Miss Holquist. Her phone rang for a long time before she answered.

"Lorcan just rented a van at the airport," she said. "If the merchandise is still flexible, he'll tie it up with rope and carry it out in a large suitcase."

"She's not dead."

"What?"

"I figured out a way to get the files. Emily and I are driving to another location. She'll retrieve the flash drive from Thomas Slater."

There was another long silence. I heard waltz music in the background and realized that Miss Holquist was sitting in the bleachers at the ice rink, watching her daughter skate.

"I get annoyed when my employees don't obey my instructions."

"You told me that our goal was to get the files back. I'm trying to solve that problem."

Another pause. The waltz music changed to a saxophone solo.

"All right. It's worth a try. Stay with your target the entire time. If she tries to run away from you, then—"

"I know what to do," I said, and switched off the phone.

A minute later, the bathroom door creaked open and Emily came out drying her hair with my only bath towel. "You actually have hot water. That's a pleasant surprise. Now all I need is a cup of coffee."

"Get your boots on. We've got to get out of here before Lorcan shows up with a suitcase."

. . . .

By the time we reached the car, Emily received an e-mail that said:

// 1300 hrs. Today.

Attached to the message was a Google image of the parking lot at the Westerly, Rhode Island, train station.

We left Chinatown and headed north on the parkway. There was a lot of traffic in both directions and it felt as if I was fighting my way through an obstacle course of delivery vans and tractor-trailer trucks. Finally, we turned onto the interstate highway and crossed the border into Connecticut.

The trees lining the thruway were bare and shivery from the wind. We stopped to buy gasoline in West Haven, and then took a bridge across a tidal estuary to a harbor with clapboard houses and sailboats resting on sawhorses. Gulls circled around a fishing boat, cutting through the cold air, as a man wearing green boots dumped a gunnysack onto the wharf. Something was alive inside the sack, and it pushed and wiggled and flopped around. That was my future—an unseen creature fighting to get out.

Trucks in the left lane roared past us. In the distance, a church steeple jabbed at the sky. About four hours after leaving the city, we saw the signs for Westerly and Laura guided me to the train-station parking lot.

I parked the car facing the arrival platform and, a few minutes later, a train clattered into the station and let out several people carrying shopping bags or pushing wheeled suitcases. It took only a few minutes for them to get into cars and taxis, and then we were left alone.

One o'clock came and passed. Nothing happened. But around one-thirty a mud-splattered Toyota Land Cruiser pulled into the lot and a middle-aged woman got out. Helen McClatchy's photograph could still be found on the Internet and I recognized her right away. She was a stocky, solid-looking woman with a broad face and frizzy hair. Perhaps she had been stylish and slender as a young journalist, but now she looked like an Irish farmer who slaughtered pigs.

"That's Slater's girlfriend," I said. "Let's go talk to her."

We got out of the car and Helen approached Emily. "Are you the young lady I'm looking for?"

"Yes, I'm Emily Buchanan."

"Helen McClatchy." Helen shook Emily's hand, then turned to me. "And you must be the little ferret from the bank."

"All I want is—"

"I know what you want . . . the files. So shut your mouth and follow directions." Helen turned to Emily. "Do you know what you're doing?"

"I guess so."

"Once you walk down this road, it's hard to go back."

"I've made my choice."

"Good. That's the right answer. I'm in love with a man who worships free choice." Helen slapped her hands together and headed toward the Land Cruiser. "All right. That's enough chatter. Leave your car here. You're both coming with me."

She led us across the parking lot and I saw two black dogs sitting in the storage area of the Land Cruiser. Both had massive heads, cropped ears, and powerful legs and shoulders. I remembered reading about the car bomb that had almost killed Helen. This breed was a large enough guard dog to take on any intruder.

Emily smiled at the dogs. "Mastiffs?"

"Yes. They're Cane Corsos . . . Italian mastiffs. We named the male Newton, after Isaac Newton. The bitch is called Hildy—which is short for Saint Hildegard of Bingen. She's one of my heroes." Helen reached into her jacket pocket, pulled out two bandanas, and offered one to me. "You need to put this over your eyes."

"No."

"It's just temporary. You're going to meet the man no one gets to meet. I don't want either of you to find out where we live."

"I don't care who he is. I'm not going to wear a blindfold."

Emily took one of the bandanas and began to fold it into a strip. "This is no big deal, Jacob. I'll put on a blindfold. You can just lie flat on the backseat so you can't look out the windows. Is that okay, Helen?"

"I'll be glancing into the rearview mirror," Helen told me. "If you look at anything other than your nose, I'm turning around and we're returning to the train station."

"That sounds reasonable, Jacob. Don't you agree? You'll still have your guns."

Helen raised her eyebrows. "He's got more than one?"

Emily placed the blindfold over her eyes and sat beside Helen. I got into the back of the car and lay on the seat. Helen started the engine and the Land Cruiser splashed through puddles on the way out of the parking lot. Newton and Hildy gazed down at me with their massive heads and black muzzles. These dogs weren't like Baxter, and my right hand touched the weapons concealed beneath my clothing. The nine-millimeter automatic was held in a paddle holster that was clipped inside my waistband. I carried the .38 Special in the ankle holster.

We traveled on paved roads for a while. Helen made a few quick turns, then we were on a dirt road dotted with ruts and potholes. The car moved slowly—in first or second gear—and a pine smell came in through the windows. Another turn and gravel rattled up into the wheel wells. Then the car stopped completely and Helen switched off the engine.

"We're here."

I sat up immediately. Emily pulled off her blindfold and everyone got out of the car. We had arrived in a clearing surrounded by oak and beech trees. A New England–style house with a wrap-around porch was about a hundred yards in front of me. The steep roof was covered with solar panels that glimmered in the sun. Pathways wandered off through the forest and one of them led to a barn-sized building with a gambrel roof that was also covered with solar panels. A redbrick chimney—something designed for industrial purposes—was attached to this structure.

Twelve-foot poles were scattered around the compound, and each one displayed a handmade wind toy. The wind toy closest to the Toyota was a sheet-metal cutout of a three-piece band; a little propeller made one musician strum his guitar while another pounded a drum and a third plucked a bass fiddle. Everything moved a little faster when there was a gust of wind.

All this was scenery. My Spark was focused on a young man standing near a woodpile about twenty yards away from the car. He had long greasy hair and an angular face, and he wore an open flannel shirt over a T-shirt with the words MASTER THE MACHINE. Using a sledgehammer and wedges, he was splitting chunks of firewood.

"Hey, Bobby!" Helen said. "Have you seen his nibs?"

Bobby lowered the hammer and jerked his head at the house. "He was in the bunker with the Turks. Now he's back in the kitchen."

"He better not eat the blueberry crumble. That's for tea."

Helen circled the Land Cruiser, yanked open the driver's door, and honked the horn. Noises in the woods had a hollow sound; I felt like I was trapped in a canyon. A shadow moved behind a screen, then the front door creaked open and a man stepped onto the porch.

I had seen the scanned image of Thomas Slater's book-jacket photo. This older version had sloping shoulders, a potbelly, and a peninsula of white hair in the center of a bald head. The stained corduroy pants and rumpled sweater made Slater look like a retired professor who drank early in the day.

"Hello, Emily! Welcome to our little hideaway!" Moving like his knees hurt, Thomas stepped off the porch. The mastiffs bounded over to their master and he flipped dog biscuits in their direction. "Everything okay, Bobby?" he asked the young man. "Did you meet our two visitors?"

"I can see 'em."

Slater approached Emily and shook her hand. "A pleasure to meet you in the flesh, Emily. So many of the people I know are just pixels on a monitor screen. And you must be Mr. Underwood. . . ."

"He's got a gun," Helen said. "More than one."

"Well, of course he does. And I'm sure those weapons make him feel better about himself." Slater smiled at me. "Let me explain what's going to happen. We're going to walk over to the bunker and meet the Turks. Then Emily will be given her flash drive with the information. And you, Mr. Underwood, will be given a downloaded statement from our official spokesman. Gregor was just about to go on a hike, but we caught him before he left the house."

"What kind of statement?"

"Gregor will reaffirm our Web site policy. We Speak for Freedom uses information freely given to us by witnesses or the participants in illegal activity. Emily changed her mind, so we're giving the files back. Is everything clear, Underwood?"

I nodded.

"Good. I realize that you're working for someone and that they don't want their secrets exposed, but there's nothing new about that. The goal of those in power is to defend and increase their power."

"Bastards . . ." Helen muttered.

"In this case, it looks like the powerful have won a temporary victory," Thomas said. "Now let's go see the Turks."

Everyone headed toward the building with the redbrick chimney. I followed them. "You have Turkish people working for you?" Emily asked.

"When the first group of helpers arrived, Helen began calling them the 'Young Turks.' That became the nickname for anyone who works for the Web site. Right now we have five people on our support team. There's a Canadian, a German, a Spaniard, a Polish woman whose family lives in Australia, and a Brazilian with a Mexican passport."

Thomas reached the woodpile and nodded at the young man. "Did you see the leaky pipe attached to the well pump, Bobby?"

"That's next on my list, Mr. Slater."

"Good. You're ten times more organized than I am."

Thomas continued walking. "After we finish our business, I want you two to stay for tea. Helen made a blueberry dessert. I've been a responsible adult for once and haven't eaten a crumb."

I was parallel to the woodpile as Bobby hammered a wedge into a chunk of wood. Then he reached beneath his shirt, pulled out a Taser, and fired it at my stomach. It felt as if my Shell had been transformed into a rigid frame, and then the shock ended and I collapsed onto the ground.

Bobby leaned over me, unzipped my jacket, and pulled the automatic from its holster. Then he patted down my legs and found the revolver. When I tried to kick him in the face, he grinned and stepped back.

"Think you're smart?" Bobby asked. "You're not smart." He pulled a handheld stun device out of his back pocket, pressed it against my neck, and gave me a second jolt of electricity. My mouth jerked open, my legs contracted, and it felt as if my Shell was cracked open and shattered into bits.

24

Bobby pulled some plastic cable ties out of his pocket and fastened my ankles and wrists together. The jolt of electricity had frozen my Shell, but now I began to recover. When I opened my eyes, I saw that everyone was looking down at me.

"Incredible. One of our plans actually worked." Thomas glanced at Emily. "I assume this is what you wanted."

"I didn't know what you were going to do."

"After our conversation, I talked to the group and Bobby came up with this idea. You told me that Mr. Underwood was carrying a gun. That meant we had to disarm him."

"Is he all right?"

Helen prodded me with the tip of her boot. "I wouldn't worry. He's a donkey that deserves every kick."

"Bobby, get the wheelchair in the front hallway," Thomas said. "We can't leave Mr. Underwood lying on the dirt for the rest of the day."

Bobby handed my revolver to Helen. He walked back to the house while Newton sniffed the top of my head, and then began panting with his lips covering his teeth. It looked as if he was smiling at me.

I took a deep breath and words came out of my mouth. "You need to give back the files or Emily is going to get killed."

Thomas shoved his hands into his pockets. "I can't return something I don't possess. Emily was worried about Internet tracking, so she never actually sent us the data. She was going to meet someone from our group in a week or so, but your presence changed the situation. We always try to protect the people who give us information."

"So where *are* the files?" Helen asked. "Are they hidden on a computer somewhere?"

"I stored them on a flash drive," Emily said. "Does anyone have scissors or a knife?"

Using Helen's pocketknife, Emily cut the lining of her shoulder bag. She pulled out a flash drive and handed the device to Thomas. "Here you go. I've been thinking about these files ever since I walked out of the bank. It's a relief to get rid of them."

Hildy barked when Bobby came out of the house with an old wheelchair. He pushed it down an asphalt pathway and stopped about ten feet away from me.

"Load him up," Thomas said. "And let's go to the bunker."

Bobby crouched down a few inches away from my feet. He grabbed my jacket with both hands and pulled me forward until I fell over his left shoulder. Using the strength of his legs, he carried me over to the wheelchair like a sack of potatoes.

"So what are we going to do with him?" Helen asked.

"Let Mr. Underwood stay with us for a short time." Thomas stood in front of the wheelchair and smiled at me. "I want you to see what we're doing here and report back to your employers. You can tell them that we're not an army of growlers and Luddites . . . just a small group of computer specialists with muddy shoes."

Feeling like a broken piece of machinery, I sat in the wheelchair with my wrists and ankles held together by the cable ties. Bobby pushed me down the path as Thomas led Emily over to the large building with the brick chimney.

"Our first computer room was in a basement office in Stockholm. Someone started calling it the 'war bunker' and we kept that term for each new location. This particular building used to be a sawmill powered by a wood-fired steam engine."

First we entered an anteroom constructed out of plywood and

sheets from a plastic ground cloth. There was a bench on one side and a row of mud-covered clogs and rubber boots. Then Thomas pushed open a sliding door and everyone followed him into the bunker.

The sawmill had been converted into a long, carpeted room with light fixtures hanging from the ceiling. The steam engine that had once powered the saw remained at one end of the room. It had pistons and gear wheels and a shiny brass boiler. The rest of the bunker resembled the workroom of a start-up software company. There was a long table surrounded by chairs, four cubicles, and a kitchen area with an espresso machine. Two large paper shredders were in the middle of the room, along with a dozen shipping boxes. It looked as if the entire operation was being packed up for an immediate departure.

A young man was working in one of the cubicles while two men and two women were shredding paper and wrapping computer equipment. The staff of We Speak for Freedom were all in their twenties. They wore jeans, ratty sweaters, or flannel shirts and looked like graduate students on a ski holiday.

"Good afternoon, everyone," Thomas said. "As you can see . . . Bobby's plan worked perfectly. This is Emily Buchanan, the young woman who contacted me. And the gentleman tied up in the wheelchair is the employee from the BDG investment bank who was trying to take back the liberated information."

Thomas handed the flash drive to a dark-haired young woman wearing an ankle-length skirt. "Lidia, open this up on the quarantine computer, then run the Ghost Killer program. For all we know, this could be a clever plan to infect our system with spyware. . . ."

Lidia took the flash drive and inserted it in the data port of a laptop computer covered with skull-and-crossbones stickers. A piece of masking tape ran across the top of the computer screen with the word QUARANTINE in black letters.

"And Emily . . . would you please explain to the group what they're supposed to be looking for?"

"Most of the data is about the black money transactions of an Indian company called the Pradhani Group. But there are three coded files that I couldn't read. A man named Jafar Desai was killed in Paris a few days ago. The coded files might explain why."

"Don't do this," I said. "The people I work for—"

"Won't be happy?" Thomas smiled. "Good. I like that possibility. That's the goal of our Web site . . . to defend the weak and challenge the powerful."

"It's not worth it."

"That's Emily's choice."

"I'm connected to what happened to Jafar and his family," Emily said. "I have to do something."

"Action requires courage," Thomas said. "Inaction only requires excuses. Bobby, please take Mr. Underwood to the cottage and wait there. I'll join you in a few minutes."

Bobby wheeled me back outside and pushed me down another pathway past a stone-lined sluice gate that fed into a pond. The concrete frame of the gate was stained and the water in the pond had a dark red color.

"What's wrong with the water?"

"Looks like blood, don't it? There's iron in the dirt around here."

Patches of shadow and light. The smell of evergreen trees. Looking up, I saw a hawk tracing a slow ellipse in the sky. The path followed the logging ditch to a one-room shack with a porch in front. The shack was set back in the forest, concealed by tall weeds and an overhanging spruce tree. It had a stone chimney and a tar-paper roof covered with dead pine needles. Bobby yanked the wheelchair up onto the porch. Hinges squeaked as he pulled back shutters and opened the door, then he pushed me into the building.

Sunlight streamed in through the windows and illuminated a single room filled with rusty bicycles with flat tires and cardboard boxes filled with junk. A worktable was in the middle of the room and was covered with strips of sheet metal, gear wheels, and a half-dozen cans of paint. Artist's paintbrushes were scattered across the table; each brush displayed a dry blob of color. At the center of the table was a wind toy: a sheet-metal silhouette of a man sitting in a chair while he held a book with two hands. A drive shaft was attached to his head.

Bobby searched the dusty room and found a wooden toolbox. He opened it up and began searching through each drawer. "Bet you think you're smart."

"I'm functional."

"Maybe that's true in the city, but you're not functioning real good today. I've seen you lookin' around, trying to figure out a way to break free. Well, that's not gonna happen."

Bobby found some more cable ties in the tool chest and used them to attach my legs to the wheelchair footplates. When the lower part of my body was secure, he fastened both of my arms to the armrests and used three ties linked together to restrain my chest and shoulders.

I heard nails clicking on the concrete floor and turned my head toward the doorway. The two dogs entered the cottage and began sniffing around, searching for food. Thump of shoes on the porch, and then the screen door squeaked open and Thomas Slater stood in front of me.

"There's water in that blue jerry can, Bobby. Pour some into those old hubcaps. I think our canine friends are thirsty."

Newton and Hildy lapped up the water, making loud slurping sounds while Thomas inspected the wheelchair. "Mr. Underwood looks very secure."

Bobby spat into the corner. "He ain't going nowhere."

"If you don't mind, I'd like to talk to him alone."

"Well, I do mind, Mr. Slater. I don't think you'll be safe with him."

"Put some more ties on if you wish, but it looks like there's more than enough." Thomas stepped forward and checked my arm restraints. "He can't even scratch himself."

"He's dangerous, Mr. Slater. Don't forget, he was carrying two handguns."

"Dangerous in *potential,* but not in *actuality.*" Thomas reached into his back pocket and pulled out a small radio transmitter. "I've got my two-way radio, Bobby. I promise to contact you right away if Mr. Underwood causes any trouble."

Bobby considered this idea for a few seconds, then nodded and opened the screen door. "I'm keeping my radio on."

"Thank you. That's a good plan."

The door slapped shut and Bobby marched back to the bunker. Thomas scratched behind Hildy's ears and then began sorting through his tools.

"This is where I make my whirligigs. Maybe you've seen some of them scattered around the compound. Helen thinks it's amusing that I've spent most of my life designing computers and software programs, but . . . up until now . . . I've never really *made* anything." He picked up a small fan. "The windmill propellers are salvaged from discarded air conditioners. The chains and sprockets come from old bicycles. Bobby sorts through the junk at the local dump and brings some of it back in his pickup." Thomas scooped up a handful of bolts and dumped them into a plastic tray. "I've decided to leave them all here when we abandon this outpost. It might be childish, but I hope they're not thrown away. Who knows? The so-called Slater Gates I invented thirty years ago are obsolete. They aren't being used by the new generation of computers. Perhaps I'll only be remembered for my whirligigs."

"You're leaving this place?"

"Yes. Definitely. Helen said that you lay down on the backseat of the car, but that's not going to help us. Now that you know our general location, a drone could find this place in a few hours. I see myself as an amiable sort of person, but a surprising amount of people want to kill me. Tonight Bobby will dump you into the trunk of a car and take you to another part of the forest. He'll leave you there, unharmed, and you'll have to find your way back to civilization. By the time you return with your associates, we'll be working at another safe location."

Thomas poured some turpentine into a glass jar and pushed in the old paintbrushes. "But you and I still have enough time for a conversation. You've sparked my curiosity, Mr. Underwood. I have a dozen questions that only you can answer."

"What kind of questions?"

"Who hired you to find Emily? Do you know their names? Did they give you written instructions?"

"I'm not going to tell you anything."

"There's no reason to be loyal to those bastards. They'd sell you out in a second."

"I'm not loyal to anyone. I do my job and get paid. We see the world in different ways. You *believe* in something."

Thomas shook his head. "I wouldn't put a label on my beliefs, and I'm definitely not a member of some political party. Nowadays true ideology has vanished, replaced by fear and fantasy. The right wing wants corporate control and a return to a past that never existed. The left wing wants government control and a future that will never exist. Both groups lose sight of the essential question: How can the individual speak and think and create freely? New ideas are the only evolutionary force that will save us from destruction."

"Say whatever you want. I'm not telling you who hired me."

"Of course, Mr. Underwood. So why don't we go outside? It's a better view."

Thomas propped the screen door open with a brick, then pushed me out onto the porch. It was late in the afternoon and the sun was touching the tops of the trees. All the colors that surrounded us— the forest ferns with their curling tips, the dead leaves lying on the wet ground, the blue sails of a whirligig windmill—looked darker, heavier, as the day fell toward night.

"This used to be a logging camp. Bobby's great-grandfather helped dig the ditch from here up to Cato Springs. Once they had the ditch, everything else was easy. They'd fell a tree, trim off the branches, roll the log into the water with a cant hook, and float the wood downhill to the catch basin."

Thomas left me alone for a few minutes and then returned with a bottle and two paper cups. "Would you like some Irish whiskey, Mr. Underwood? I know it's awkward, but I could hold a cup to your lips."

"No."

Thomas sat down on a bench, poured himself an inch of whiskey, and gazed out at the forest. "Before we came here I didn't know how to identify the different trees." He pointed his finger and began to recite. "White oak. Holly. Maple. Beech. Hardwood trees near the house. White pine and pitch pine around the bunker. I can't tell you why, but it makes me happy to know the names of all the things that grow around here. It's going to be difficult to leave. . . ."

"That's your choice, Mr. Slater."

"I agree. But you've also made some choices. Haven't you? Emily told me a little bit about what happened in New York City. You were supposed to kill her, but you refused to follow orders. So why did you say no? What was going through your mind?"

"I just did it. There doesn't have to be a reason."

"And does that choice put you in danger?"

"It's possible."

"So you rejected machine thinking and made a free choice. That means the two of us have a starting point for a larger conversation. Have you ever heard of the French philosopher René Descartes? He established an entire method of thinking based on a single premise—"

"*Cogito, ergo sum,*" I said. "But most people get it wrong. Just because something thinks, doesn't mean that it exists."

"That's right, Mr. Underwood. And this isn't just a trivial philosophical distinction. It took me years to realize that a computer would never truly be able to say *cogito, ergo sum,* although dozens of lurid Hollywood movies about robots want to leave that impression. A computer *thinks* . . . that is, it realizes it has been switched on . . . but it doesn't know it *exists.*"

"After you figured that out, you wrote 'The Decision and the Choice.'"

Thomas raised his paper cup filled with whiskey. "Here's to you, Mr. Underwood. I'm impressed that you've read my work."

"I wanted to know more about you, so I told my Shadow to find a few articles."

"'The Decision and the Choice' was my attempt to show that *thinking* does not mean *reasoning.* Our instincts, our emotions, and our moral consciousness shape the way we think."

"The article said that you designed artificial-emotion software. You were going to teach computers how to cry."

Thomas took another sip of whiskey and smiled. "The entire

project was a complete failure. Or, as Helen would say, 'a full-face fall into pig shite.' I designed programs that could imitate the human emotional response, but the machines were never really *aware* of anything. A Shadow can be programmed to say 'This makes me sad.' But it won't *feel* sad. Human beings don't think like computers. Our human consciousness is a spectrum of different kinds of thinking with different levels of intensity. Do you ever daydream, Mr. Underwood?"

"Sometimes. But I don't like it."

"And why is that?"

"When I close my eyes and see memories, it feels as if I'm wandering through a shadow land."

"I feel the same way," Thomas said. "I have high-focus thoughts when I'm solving a problem, and that gives me the illusion that I can control my thinking. But as the focus level falls, I lose control of my thoughts. This is when I can free-associate and relive memories. No machine can daydream. When they're not switched on, they're as cold as a toaster in a midnight kitchen."

"So machines can never be human."

"That's right. Not unless we alter our definition of humanity. My own life changed when I realized that fact. I wrote books and made speeches around the world, but nobody wanted to listen. They were impressed when the nubots told jokes and sold them subway cards. And the Shadows whispering in our ears were supposed to be as real as your best friend.

"Eventually, I stopped thinking about the *function* of these new machines and began to ask myself: What is their *purpose* in our society? After the mass arrests that followed the Day of Rage, I began to have 'political' opinions. The fact that the EYE system and nubots are watching us and controlling our lives gives those in power an easy way to hide their manipulations. Artificial intelligence is a concept that obscures accountability. Our problem is not machines acting like humans—it's humans acting like machines."

"Maybe we are machines," I said. "A scientist named Morris Noland told me that our minds make a decision a half second before our conscious thought."

"Yes. Of course. Benjamin Libet's experiments." Thomas reached into his shirt pocket, found two treats, and tossed them to the dogs. "But Libet also proved that even though we have the 'readiness potential' to do something, we also have the power to say no. That potential is always there, always waiting. 'No—I won't believe this. No—I won't do this. No—I refuse to go along.' Keep saying no and you can change your life."

"I had an accident several years ago, and it transformed me. I can't change that fact."

"That doesn't mean you have to work for people who want to control our thoughts and actions. What they want isn't just wrong or misguided—it's evil."

"A word like 'evil' doesn't mean anything to me. Nothing is real but the present reality."

Thomas didn't argue. He poured some more whiskey into his paper cup, swirled it around for a few seconds, and took a sip.

"Well, if you don't believe in philosophy or theology . . . then what about science? Quantum theory tells us that objects exist in a suspended state until observed, and then all possibilities collapse into one outcome. This also means that what happened in the past may not be determined until a future action occurs."

"I don't want a *theory*."

"It's a theory that's been proven by various experiments. For example, scientists have split twin photons apart and made sure that one of them would hit a monitor first. They were trying to answer a simple question: When would the first photon stop being a wave and collapse into a particle? Somehow the other photon knew what happened, as if there was no space and time separating the pair. A particle that became a wave would transform itself back into being a particle the moment its twin was observed by the experimenter."

"I've killed five men in the last three weeks. They're dead. I can't change that."

Thomas lowered the cup and stared into my eyes. "My God . . . you really did that. Didn't you? But what happens in our future can change the *meaning* of what has occurred in our past. Perhaps your decision not to hurt Emily was when your life began to move in a different direction. We're not captive to our past, Mr. Underwood. We're not doomed to a certain future. Unlike machines, we can always choose a new direction for our journey."

The dogs sensed that someone was approaching the shack. They trotted down the path, then reappeared with Emily and Helen. The two women pushed through the weeds and climbed up onto the porch.

"The Polish girl broke the code," Helen said.

Thomas raised his paper cup and toasted them. "Good. I didn't think it would be that difficult."

Emily stood beside Helen. She was watching me as if I was about to break free of the wheelchair and disappear into the forest.

"There were three special files," Helen said. "All of them provided different information. The first file was a summary of banking transactions made over a two-year period. A large amount of money was transferred from a BDG account in America to a Pradhani Group bank account in India. Then smaller amounts, in different currencies, were sent to banks in England, France, and Germany."

"So Rajat Pradhani was laundering money for someone in the United States." Thomas poured some more whiskey into his cup. "That's not surprising."

"The second file was just a collection of e-mails," Emily said. "Someone in America calling himself 'Chip Shot' was flying to Mumbai for a banking conference, but he planned to stay in India and meet someone he called 'my young friend.' Chip Shot wanted a location that was completely private, so he asked Rajat Pradhani for suggestions. After several e-mails, Rajat suggested that Chip Shot use a family houseboat that would travel through the Kerala backwaters parallel to the Arabian Sea coast. If they took certain routes, they could travel for days and never encounter another boat."

"That's also not difficult to figure out," Thomas said. "A married banker in America wanted to have a vacation with his mistress."

"No. It's much more important than that." Helen took a step forward. "The third file is a digital video that's about five minutes long, and there's a date and time stamp in the lower-left-hand corner. The cameraman is hidden in a grove of banana plants and his camera is pointed toward one of the backwater canals. A houseboat comes around a bend and slowly approaches the camera. Two men are sitting on chairs in a front deck area, under a sunscreen. When the boat passes the banana grove, the cameraman zooms in on the men. They're drinking beer and talking."

"One of the men is Alexander Serby," Emily said. "He's the head of the Brooks Danford Group. And the other man . . ."

She paused and glanced at Helen. It felt like they had just peered inside a box and didn't want to release what was still hidden.

"You'd recognize him," Helen said to Thomas. "Just about everyone knows his face. It's Danny Marchand, smoking a cigarette. Alexander Serby knew Marchand, met with him on that boat trip, and helped finance the Day of Rage."

25

Thomas sat back on the porch bench and blinked. He stayed silent and blinked again. "And you're sure this video is authentic?"

"I watched Serby give a speech at last year's holiday party," Emily said. "And everyone knows what Danny Marchand looked like."

"Go take a look at the video," Helen said. "We've already watched it four times."

"When was the laundered money sent to Europe?"

"All the transfers took place after the meeting," Emily said. "About four months after the transfers stopped, Danny Marchand and his followers bombed the schools."

"So who was the cameraman?" Thomas asked. "Sounds like he knew the boat was coming down the canal."

"It could have been one of Rajat Pradhani's employees. Pradhani wanted to know who Serby was meeting."

"And that's all we have? Is there any other evidence that connects Alexander Serby to the Day of Rage?"

"I don't know about Serby, but there have always been questions about Danny Marchand. I went online and skimmed through the report of the Presidential Commission on the Day of Rage plus the British investigation led by Lord Harwood. Marchand took fifty thousand euros from his family's trust fund, but that's not enough money to fund an attack in nine countries. It wasn't clear how Marchand paid for plane tickets, hotel rooms, and weapons."

"It's difficult to believe that Alexander Serby wanted to kill all those children."

Emily shook her head. "Do you remember what was going on during the time Serby and Marchand met on the canal boat? We had all those 'No Jobs' demonstrations, and bash mobs were vandalizing cars and breaking windows in just about every major city. They even attacked the BDG office in London."

"Serby and his friends were worried about the future," Helen said. "Maybe it wasn't their idea to bomb schools, but they needed some kind of incident that would justify mass arrests and a permanent surveillance system."

"I don't want to make an instant decision," Slater said. "Emily, stay here with Mr. Underwood. I'm going to take a look at the video."

Thomas and Helen hurried back to the bunker and the two dogs followed them. When they disappeared behind the trees, Emily began pacing back and forth, kicking up dead leaves and gravel with the tips of her boots.

"I was planning to apologize to you because you got hit by the Taser, but now I'm glad Bobby did that. Somehow . . . in some way . . . you were involved with this plan."

"That's not true."

"You're lying, Jacob. I'm sure that your boss told you why these files were important."

"She didn't say anything. I assumed that the files had information about offshore bank accounts and hidden income."

"And you just follow orders, right? Do this. Do that."

"Thomas and I just had a conversation about machines and the way people think. Everyone has the power to say no."

"But you have to *use* that power, Jacob. You can't just sit in your room and ignore the rest of the world."

The grumble of a car engine and the sound of tires splashing through a pothole passed through the forest like smoke from a distant fire. Emily spun around and looked through a gap in the trees. A white delivery van and blue pickup truck emerged from the forest and followed the driveway to the parking area. Both vehicles stopped and four men wearing identical windbreaker jackets got out. A tall man with long hair circled the truck. Lorcan Tate.

"Go into the workroom and find a knife—right *now*," I said. "Cut me free. We need to hide in the forest."

"What's going on? They look like policemen."

I recognized one other member of the group—a stocky Japanese man named Koji who had visited the training camp in North Carolina for a few days. There was a bearded man as tall as Lorcan and a young man with curly hair.

"The big man with the long hair is Lorcan Tate. He's an enforcer—like me. The other three men are also working for Miss Holquist. They're going to kill everyone here."

"How did they find this place? Did you have something to do with this?"

"No. Of course not. I'm also a target."

So far, the four men hadn't noticed us. The cottage was at the edge of the clearing, partially concealed by weeds. As Lorcan stepped forward, the front door of the main house slammed open and Bobby walked out carrying a shotgun. He raised the weapon to his shoulder, and then lowered it when Lorcan pulled a badge out of his coat pocket.

Lorcan approached the house in a slow and deliberate manner while the others remained by the van. The two men chatted for a minute or so, and then Lorcan laughed and shook Bobby's hand. "No," I whispered. "No."

Time slowed down as each small action led, in sequence, to a finite conclusion. Lorcan turned away. His right hand reached into his jacket, only to reappear clutching a handgun with a silencer. Turn. Pivot. Fire.

Blood sprayed out of Bobby's chest and he collapsed onto the porch like a bag of meat. Then Lorcan stood over the empty Shell and put a bullet into the dead man's head.

"Cut me loose," I told Emily. "We need to get out of here."

Emily stepped off the porch and ran into the forest. My Shell tried to follow her, but I was still captive, a frozen mechanism strapped to a chair. I pulled upward with my legs and arms, trying to break free. The wheelchair creaked and shivered like a living creature, but the plastic ties didn't break.

I took a deep breath and tried again. This time, the chair's left armrest moved slightly when I pushed outward. *Look up.* Koji and the young man entered the main house while Lorcan and the bearded man approached the bunker. If Emily was inside the building, she'd be killed with the others.

I pushed with my legs and twisted my entire body so that all the strength of my Shell was concentrated on my left arm. There was a cracking sound and then one of the steel tubes fastened to the armrest snapped off. I pushed even harder, concentrating on this fragile point of resistance, until the second tube snapped. Now my left arm was free.

Gripping the push rim on the outer part of the wheel, I muscled the chair forward. The screen door was still propped open and I maneuvered through this opening until I was back inside the cottage. Reaching up with my free hand, I began to search the surface of the worktable. Nuts and bolts. A cold soldering iron and a discarded fan. Near the center of the table, I found something flat and narrow with a sharp edge. It was a rusty scalpel that Thomas had turned into a shop tool.

The scalpel helped me cut the plastic ties. As each one fell away, my body felt more flexible and mobile. Finally I was free of my restraints and stood up in the middle of the dark room. My phone had been taken away from me and I had left my computer back in New York. That meant there were no Shadows to comfort me with their soothing voices.

I ran out of the cottage and was absorbed by the undergrowth at the edge of the compound. Each movement of my Shell created sounds—leaves crunching, twigs snapping. I pushed a branch away from my shoulder and it whipped back at me.

Half hidden by a spruce tree, I watched the two enforcers leave the main house. Koji spoke into a phone headset as they strolled over to the pickup. Then they pulled back a plastic tarp—revealing four red jerry cans in the back of the truck. Talking softly to each other, they pulled out the cans and placed them on the gravel. A door slammed and the bearded man returned without Lorcan. He picked up two of the jerry cans and headed back to the bunker.

An ivory-colored crescent moon glowed on the horizon. It looked like someone had taken a knife and slashed a purple canopy. Night grew in the forest; little bits of darkness were clinging to the trees. Manhattan was a grid of lines, but nothing was ordered and symmetrical in the forest. Whenever I tried to walk in a straight line, a tree blocked my way. Mud clung to my shoes and thornbushes scratched my legs.

A few steps forward. Stop. A few steps more. Finally I returned to the clearing about fifty feet away from the bunker. I circled the building and stopped when I found a back entrance. All the windows were covered on the inside and I couldn't see what was going on. I didn't have a weapon. Was Lorcan still inside?

I turned the doorknob slowly and slipped into a storage area filled with shipping boxes. Something was burning inside the building. Smoke drifted past my legs and escaped out the open doorway. The smoke had a burnt, greasy odor that appeared as a blackish-red color in my mind. It smelled as if a chunk of fat-covered meat had just been dropped into a campfire.

I entered the main room and stopped. A burning body lay in front of me. Black smoke rose up from the flesh and the remnants of the clothes. The dead man's right foot and ankle were still clean. A blue tennis shoe and a lime-green sock had survived the flames.

As I moved forward, I saw more bodies. Lorcan and his men had killed everyone in the bunker, doused the bodies with gasoline, and set them on fire. Black smoke swirled around my shoulders and I started to cough. I heard a popping sound like a string of firecrackers as sparks rose up from the burning flesh.

Searching for Emily, I wandered through the haze and discovered Helen McClatchy curled up like a sleeping child near a desk. Her clothes and hair and skin had burned away, leaving a blackened effigy of a human being. Keep moving. I found another two bodies lying next to the Polish girl, Lidia. Her legs were black and her blue skirt was now a tissue of ash that broke into bits and rose up into the air.

The fire from each body radiated a foul smell, but my Spark took control, forcing my Shell forward. Circling the conference table, I almost tripped over Thomas Slater. His forehead, nose, and eyes were still untouched, but the rest of his body was black and burning. The two dogs lay a few feet away. Hildy had been shot in the head and there was a bullet wound in the center of Newton's chest. My Spark slowed down—the world slowed down—as I knelt beside the dogs and touched Isaac's soft black ears. In my mind, he snarled and leaped forward as he tried to protect his master.

So where was Emily? I got down on my hands and knees and crawled forward. The fire from the bodies had started to spread and now the wooden floor was burning near the old boiler. Smoke surrounded me and all I could see were points of harsh red light. Since my Transformation, I had tried to stay separate from the corrupt world, but now I had fallen into a dark place.

I crawled back across the room, coughing and spitting out bits of ash. When I reached the work area, I stood up and looked around one last time. Helen's leather shoulder bag lay on the table. I reached inside and found my cell phone. As I headed for the back door, I saw that the flash drive with the stolen data was attached to the quarantine computer. I pulled the drive out and stuffed it into my pocket.

Flames rose up from the floor and touched the walls and now the light fixtures began to flicker and die. I staggered past the first body, pushed out the back door, and collapsed onto the wet ground. My Shell kept coughing and gasping for air as my lungs tried to expel the memory of what I'd just seen. For the first time since the Transformation, my Spark felt pain and longing and regret.

After a few minutes my breathing became slow and regular, and I stood back up on wobbly legs. Like a lost child, I retreated into the forest and moved to the left, away from the bunker. I stopped when

I saw Koji and the bearded man carrying jerry cans of gasoline into the main house. The young man with the curly hair finished tying a rope to Bobby's ankles and dragged him inside.

I didn't have my computer and couldn't ask Edward to suggest a plan. Hiding behind a pile of logs, I watched Lorcan drag Emily over to the truck. Her hands were tied behind her back and she was crying. Lorcan forced her to kneel in front of the headlights and grabbed a handful of hair. He was talking to her with a quiet voice and I couldn't make out the words. When she shook her head, he touched her cheek with the tip of his right forefinger. She screamed. He held her tighter, and then touched her again.

As his right hand moved upward, light was reflected off the blade of his straight razor. He was holding his weapon like an artist's paintbrush, and whenever she said no he would make a quick dabbing motion. Two lines of bright red trickled down her cheeks. It looked as if she was crying blood.

Emily shook her head and tried to get away. Once again, Lorcan touched her with the tip of the razor. More cuts. And now the lower part of her face was a mask of blood. I had heard Lorcan describe the way he could torture women for hours, but there wasn't enough time for that. The bunker was burning and the other enforcers were setting fire to the main house. He would probably cut Emily a few more times for pleasure, and then slash her throat.

I had no weapons and all four men were armed. Only one person could stop Emily from dying. Switching on the phone, I dialed Miss Holquist's number. One ring and she answered. "Yes? Hello? Hello?" For the first time in any of our conversations, she didn't sound calm and confident.

"It's Underwood."

"Good! Wonderful! We were worried about you!"

"That's not true. You sent Lorcan and three enforcers to kill me and everyone else. They've been partially successful. Thomas Slater and six other people are dead. I'm free and hiding in the forest. And Lorcan is using his razor to question Emily Buchanan."

"I swear that they weren't going to kill you. I promise that—"

"Stop talking, Miss Holquist. It's important that you *listen* to me. Lorcan set fire to the bodies, but he was moving too quickly and didn't search for the flash drive with the original data. I have the flash drive and I know all about Alexander Serby's meeting with Danny Marchand. That's a secret that's worth something."

"How much money do you want, Underwood? I could transfer the payment in a few hours."

"I want Emily Buchanan alive. I'll trade the stolen data for her life when I figure out a safe way to make the exchange."

"I can't agree to that. She's too great a security risk."

"No one will believe anything she says about Marchand. Without the video, it's just another conspiracy theory without any evidence. You know me, Miss Holquist. Unlike most Human Units, I keep my promises. Call Lorcan right away and stop this business with the razor. I'll contact you at this number when I'm back in New York City."

"Forget about Emily Buchanan!" Miss Holquist shouted, and her voice echoed slightly. I pictured her pacing back and forth in a restaurant ladies room, her heels clicking on a white tile floor. "This girl is nothing. *Less* than nothing. There's no reason for you to care about her. You don't really care about anyone. That's why I hired you."

"Yes. I know. Bosons and fermions. You explained reality."

"Right! That's right! Step back and consider what you're—"

"Call Lorcan. We'll make the exchange in the city."

I switched off the phone and remained in the shadows. Lorcan gripped Emily's hair tightly and jerked her head back, exposing her neck. He gazed down at her, enjoying this moment of power, then suddenly lowered the razor. Had he seen me? No, his phone was ringing. He reached up and switched on his headset.

Was he talking to Miss Holquist? A few seconds passed, and then he let go of Emily, pivoted around, and stared at the forest. He knew I was watching him.

I touched the flash drive in my pocket and stepped farther back into the underbrush. By now the main house was on fire. A second-floor window burst from the heat and smoke rose up into the night sky.

I had to find my way to a road, and then to the train station. When I asked Laura for directions she kept saying: "I'm searching. I'm searching. . . ." But didn't give me an answer.

Thomas Slater was right. Everyone had the power to say no. That was the true response to Descartes's statement. *Cogito, ergo*—

No. I don't believe you.

No. I won't obey you.

No.

26

Laura's voice finally returned to my phone and she guided me down the dark country roads to the Westerly train station. Nobody was watching Sean's car and I was able to drive out of the parking lot and head south on the interstate. As the sun came up, I stopped at a gas station and tried to come up with a plan. My first objective was to get enough cash to buy weapons and other supplies. I could access my overseas account at a British bank on East Forty-Seventh Street, but a withdrawal required a thumb scan and my fake fingers were back at the loft. Lorcan or one of the enforcers could already be in my building or watching the entrance. The only unknown factor was Emily. It would take some time to transport her to a secure location, and someone would have to guard her.

I parked near the Brooklyn Bridge and walked to Chinatown. All the tourists had disappeared and garbage bags from the neighborhood restaurants were piled up in the street. The early morning air was cold and damp. Steam billowed out of an orange and white pipe bolted over a manhole, and people held Styrofoam cups of tea in both hands as they hurried to their obligations. An industrial laundry was on Mott Street and I watched as workers carried out blue bundles of clean clothes and racks of dry cleaning on hangers. The men had been working all night and they looked exhausted; their drawstring pants and sleeveless undershirts hung loosely on their bodies. Perhaps they were also dead, but alive.

When I reached the end of Catherine Street, I looked for the white delivery van or the blue pickup truck. No one was sitting in a parked car or waiting on the bus bench near the intersection. I wanted to save Emily's life and that need, that desire, made me feel vulnerable. Back at the hospital, I had decided that reality was a logical sequence of events. Now I wasn't sure about that idea. Maybe everything that happened was just a larger version of Dice Night at Crawley's, but our Sparks surveyed the random incidents and imposed their own order.

I reached my building and began climbing upstairs to the loft. If Lorcan was waiting for me on the top landing, he would step out of the shadows and fire at his target. The Chinese immigrants who lived in my building avoided the authorities and they wouldn't call the police.

I unlocked the door, pushed it open, and waited. No one appeared and I enjoyed the silence of an empty room. Moving as quickly as possible, I found the cardboard box containing the fingers and stuffed it into a shoulder bag with a few bottles of Complete. A minute later I was back on the street, walking past two old ladies arguing in Chinese.

The British bank on Forty-Seventh Street opened up at eight o'clock in the morning. I bought a roll of flesh-colored surgical tape at a drugstore, taped a gummy finger to the underside of my thumb, and got in line behind the other customers. These days, many of the larger banks used nubot employees, but this branch had a human teller—a middle-aged woman with a straight line of bangs across her forehead. She looked solid and steady, attached to her chair.

"I'd like to withdraw eight thousand dollars."

"For that amount, we need double verification. Press your right thumb against the sensor, then type in your security code."

I wondered about the man who gave me his fingerprints. Was he still alive or was the warm plastic molded around a cold thumb? I pushed the finger against a sensor, flattening the plastic, and nothing happened. The teller stared at me through the Plexiglas barrier as I tried again. This time the green light appeared. After I punched in my security code, the teller's brain told her mouth to smile.

"Thank you, sir. And how would you like that amount?"

. . .

Rush-hour traffic clogged the streets as I drove uptown to St. Theodosius. This time I parked down the block and sat in the car, making sure that no one was watching the entrance. Twenty minutes
later I approached the church and pushed the buzzer for the basement apartment. Gregory opened the door a few inches and stared
at me with his pale blue eyes.

"It's not my fault."

I nodded as if I knew what he was talking about. "No one is saying that you made a mistake, Gregory."

"I told Lorcan, the big guy with the long hair, that I couldn't
guarantee results. If something didn't work . . . that's your problem."

"I'm not here to complain about anything. I've been given a new
assignment and I need some equipment."

The old man pulled open the door and allowed me to enter the
vestibule. Quickly, he snapped the lock shut as if demons were trying to break into his sanctuary. "Nobody called me. Usually your
lady friend calls me."

"I've encountered an unexpected problem."

"What kind of guns are we talking about?"

"I'd like to buy the same equipment as last time . . . a small
revolver for my ankle holster and a nine-millimeter automatic."

Gregory considered the idea for a few seconds, then nodded
and shrugged. "Okay. I can do that. But I'm adding twenty percent
to the standard price."

"Let me see the weapons first."

The old man's bedroom slippers made a scuffing sound as I followed him up a staircase. When we entered the church, candle
flames flickered in their red glass holders. The church was cold, but
the air smelled sweet and moist—like the rotting mulch in a garden.
As we circled the altar I saw that wreaths and vases of cut flowers
surrounded a coffin resting on two black sawhorses.

"Who's that?"

"Some old lady. The viewing starts at three o'clock. Mass begins
at five."

"Then what happens?"

"They take the coffin away. A few days pass, then someone else dies and they bring in another box." Gregory searched through the key ring, found the right one, and unlocked the bottom drawer behind the altar. Nine handguns were concealed beneath a priest's robe and he began sorting through the collection.

"I got two options for a revolver that would fit that ankle holster. For the larger gun, I've got a Glock thirty that's chambered for a forty-five-caliber cartridge."

"How large is it? Let me see."

Still kneeling in front of the drawer, Gregory handed me the weapon. "It holds ten rounds . . . very light and easy to carry . . . but I don't have a laser sight that fits the frame."

I pointed my new weapon at a murky painting of an angel delivering news to a monk holding a cross. "Why did you think I was here to complain?"

"Because that was the first time I ever placed a tracking chip in a handgun. Lorcan gave me the nine-millimeter automatic I sold you a couple of weeks ago. Remember?"

"That's right." I removed the magazine and made sure that the firing chamber was empty. Then I squeezed the trigger and dry fired at the angel.

"I couldn't test the chip because I don't have that kind of equipment. So I put it inside the grip and gave it back to Lorcan."

"You don't need to worry, Gregory. Everything worked perfectly."

.   .   .

Ten minutes later I walked out of the church carrying a new revolver in an ankle holster and the Glock in a plastic shopping bag. I got back into Sean's car, but I didn't start the engine.

By now Lorcan or another enforcer was inside my loft, waiting for me to return. The loft was not my home; I felt no attachment to the kitchen table or the rusty pencil machine. But at that moment I needed a quiet, open space where I could hammer a nail into the floor and revolve around it in a perfect circle.

Although Miss Holquist had lectured me about bosons and fermions, she had also made sure that she could monitor my activities. Gregory had placed tracking chips in my two handguns and I had become a little red dot moving across a GPS map. Emily was right. I was the one who led Lorcan to Thomas Slater. I was the reason why everyone was dead.

· · · · ·

Lorcan probably thought he was a wolf surrounded by a herd of sheep, but he was just another predictable Human Unit. The moment I handed over the flash drive, he would try to kill Emily. That meant I needed to figure out a way to protect her after the exchange. Sean might offer a solution to that problem, but I had to find him first. The night we met, Emily had walked to the furniture factory. That meant that she had to live somewhere nearby. I allowed my memory to see her again, drinking hot chocolate as she joked with Millicent and Sean. And what did she say when she took off her parka? *We live in a warehouse surrounded by thousands of broken machines.*

I asked Laura to search for a parts supply store within a two-mile radius of the Vickerson factory. It took only a few seconds for her to find a recycling business on Skillman Street called U-Find-It. Laura guided me across the bridge to Brooklyn and I parked outside a three-story building surrounded by a chain-link fence. There were iron rails embedded in the street, half covered with asphalt, and I wondered if the building had once been a repair shop for subway cars. I passed through the gate and followed a short driveway to a loading dock with hand trucks and cargo dollies. A sign over the open doorway read:

U-FIND-IT
EVERYTHING MECHANICAL—EXCEPT CAR PARTS
BUY AND SELL—NO DELIVERY

Two men were loading a used washing machine into a van while a growler girl with tattoos on her arms carried out three record turntables. Directly inside the entrance was an Airstream trailer with a rounded aluminum body. The trailer had been turned into a cashier's booth, and a sallow-faced man sat behind a Plexiglas window glaring at the customers.

"I'm looking for Sean."

"Walk to the back. He's in the security trailer."

The U-Find-It building was an enormous room with a forty-foot ceiling. The interior was lit by fluorescent light fixtures and divided into a grid of shelves—each aisle marked with a street sign. I turned left and walked down an aisle marked WESTSIDE DRIVE that went from the entrance to the end of the building. The massive steel shelves were twenty feet high and the shelves were filled with discarded machines and plastic bins filled with parts. Movable ladders with platforms at the top were scattered around the building so that customers could reach the machinery stored above them.

The aisle labeled FIRST STREET had water pumps, elevator cables, and the jigs and cutters for tool and die machines. Second Street had a section for nubot parts—mostly arm and leg assemblies. But there was also a bin packed with detached heads, the mechanical eyes open and staring at the wreckage around them.

A second trailer with a flat roof had been set up at the end of the building. The windows were covered on the inside with sheets of yellowed newspaper. In the cold, shadowy building, the trailer looked like a little home. A hand-lettered sign taped to the door read, THIS IS NOT A PUBLIC TOILET! PEOPLE LIVE HERE! USE THE PORTABLES OUTSIDE! I touched the doorknob and twisted it slightly. It wasn't locked—so I walked in.

Sean stood beside a table cooking a grilled-cheese sandwich in a frying pan placed on a hot plate. An unmade bed with a cartoon quilt was at one end of the room. At the other end was a desk holding three computer monitors that showed surveillance camera images of U-Find-It.

When Sean saw me, he dropped his spatula and picked up a bread knife. "Where's Emily?"

"Thomas Slater is dead. He and the rest of his team were murdered last night. The killers set fire to the bodies."

"What about Emily?"

"She was captured by a man named Lorcan. But I can trade her life for the information on the flash drive."

"I'm going to call the police."

"Don't. Emily will be killed the moment you go public with this."

Sean waved the bread knife. "I don't believe you."

I sat on the office chair and glanced at the surveillance monitors. In exchange for a rent-free home, Sean kept people from stealing machine parts. Each screen was divided into a grid so that you could see four camera images at the same time.

"Put down the knife and listen. It's your decision if you want to help me."

"Why would they kill Thomas Slater? Is some rich guy's tax fraud really that important?"

I swiveled the chair toward him. "There was a secret in the stolen files, and it had nothing to do with taxes. Alexander Serby, the head of BDG, met Danny Marchand and sent him money that was laundered through Indian banks. One of the coded files is a video of the two of them together. It looks like Serby financed the Day of Rage."

"I don't believe that."

"You and your growler friends have spent your lives coming up with conspiracy theories. Most of them are just fictions that make the craziness of the world seem logical. But what I just told you isn't a story . . . it's a fact that can cause Emily's death."

The energy that had pushed Sean through the world seemed to dribble out of him. He sighed and placed the knife on the table. "So what do we do?"

"Make the trade."

"And how do we do that?"

"When does this place close?"

"Six o'clock."

"Is there a security guard?"

"No. Just me and the cameras."

I stared at the images on the screen. An old man wearing a black overcoat was buying a mechanical clown that could blow up party balloons.

"I'll call Lorcan and tell him to bring Emily here tonight."

"And then what?"

"Once Lorcan gets the flash drive, he'll try to kill everyone in the building."

27

Around nine o'clock in the evening, Sean and I climbed onto the tar-paper roof of the U-Find-It building. On one side of the roof someone had dumped a pile of copper pipes and plumbing fixtures that had been ripped out of abandoned buildings. It looked like a giant puzzle that only angels could untangle.

"We can watch the entrance from here." Sean led me over to a low wall and we looked down at the loading dock. "So why didn't you give them an address?"

"Because Lorcan would have spent the last six hours gathering information about this building. If you have the money, you can rent surveillance drones from a company on Long Island."

"How do you know this guy? Have you worked with him?"

"After I was hired by Miss Holquist I was sent to a training school down in North Carolina. It wasn't a real school . . . just a few old buildings that used to be a hunting camp. I stayed there for three months with Lorcan and the instructors."

"What did you do at this school?"

"An Englishman who used to work for the British intelligence service was in charge of the program. Every two weeks he would bring in a new instructor who had a particular specialty. We learned how to fire different kinds of guns and disassemble them, how to conceal our actions from the EYE programs, and how to find people who were living off the grid. Toward the end of our time there, Lorcan and I had a confrontation."

"Do you think Emily is safe with him?"

"No."

"Maybe he's already killed her."

"Lorcan will obey Miss Holquist. But he'll also try to follow his own plan."

"What does he want to do?"

"If he has the time, he'll torture Emily with a knife or a razor."

Sean looked as if someone had just slapped him. "We should have called the police."

"I know these people, Sean. This is the only way to save Emily. Stay up here on the roof and you'll be safe. Do you have the flares?"

"Yeah. I'm ready." Sean reached into his canvas shoulder bag and pulled out three road flares and a cigarette lighter.

"Good. If we're on the phone and I put you on hold, it's because I'm talking to Lorcan."

I left the edge of the roof and walked over to the open hatchway. "There's one thing I don't understand," Sean said. "Why are you doing this?"

"I'm protecting Emily."

"You don't even know her."

"Sometimes I hammer a nail into the floor of my loft and then I attach a cord to the nail and walk around it in a circle. Emily is a nail and a cord for me. Thinking about her makes me feel like I'm not going to fly away and dissolve into random particles."

"You're as crazy as Lorcan."

"Just follow the plan, and don't get in my way."

I stepped through the hatchway and climbed down a metal staircase to the ground floor. All the lights were on in the building and the harsh energy from the fluorescent bulbs was reflected off the surface of the broken machinery. At the sixth aisle from the entrance, I turned and walked between the shelves. The right side of this aisle was dedicated to washing-machine parts. The left side displayed golf carts and motorized wheelchairs.

Someone had attached a toy hula girl to the dashboard of a blue golf cart. I pushed her head with my finger and her body swayed back and forth. Opening up a glove compartment, I tossed out some trash and deposited the flash drive that contained the three coded files. That would be the payment for Emily's life.

I returned to the end of the aisle and continued walking toward the trailer that contained the surveillance monitors. The U-Find-It building smelled of mold and rusty water. Everything in the building was mechanical and dead, but random sounds came from different parts of the room. I heard occasional ticking sounds and, somewhere in the distance, a scraping noise—as if two machines had come to life and decided to rub up against each other.

Sean had asked why I wanted to help Emily, and I couldn't come up with a logical reason. Human beings were simply objects in space—like a rock or a pigeon or an octagonal stop sign. But the razor that cut her cheek seemed to touch my skin as well.

I climbed the steps and entered the trailer at the end of the building. All the surveillance cameras were working, including one camera that was pointed at the entrance. I checked the monitors and made sure that no one else was in the building, then I pulled on my phone headset and called Lorcan's number.

He answered immediately. "So where am I supposed to go?"

"Are you parked on Randolph Street?"

"That's where you told me to wait."

"Let me talk to Emily."

"Why? You think she's dead?" Lorcan held up his cell phone. "Talk to your little friend," he told Emily. "Show him that you're still alive."

"Can you hear me?" I asked. "Is everything all right?"

"I'm okay." Emily's voice was drained of energy. "Just tired . . . that's all."

"So what's the address?" Lorcan asked.

"You don't need an address. Drive five blocks east to Skillman Street and turn left. You'll see a flare burning in front of a building. Get out of your car and walk inside with Emily. I'll give you instructions from there."

I put him on hold and called Sean. "See anything?"

"A white delivery van is coming down the street."

"Throw the flare and stay where you are."

I switched over to the camera pointed at the loading dock and saw a burning flare hit the driveway and roll into the street. A few seconds later, Lorcan pulled up in the van. Emily was sitting in the front passenger seat.

"A blue pickup truck just turned the corner," Sean said. "It's a block away."

A few seconds later, the pickup appeared on the monitor screen. Koji was driving and the bearded man was sitting beside him. They pulled up beside the van and Koji passed a black shoulder bag to Lorcan.

"What are we going to do?" Sean asked.

"Stay on the roof. Let me handle this." I switched over to Lorcan. "I want you and Emily to walk into the building. If anyone else is with you, then the deal is off."

"If the deal is off, then I get to kill your girlfriend."

Lorcan got out of the car with the bag slung over his shoulder. He yanked open the passenger door and pulled Emily out of the van. She had bandages on her face where Lorcan had cut her and her wrists were cuffed behind her back. Lorcan slammed the door shut, grabbed Emily's upper arm, and pulled her up the driveway. As they approached the loading dock, I could see that Lorcan was wearing a phone headset.

They climbed up the steps to the open doorway and stopped. Lorcan's head went back and forth as he evaluated the tall shelves stacked with machine parts.

"There are security cameras everywhere. I can see you and Emily and anyone else who enters this building. Do you understand?"

"Yeah. I hear you. Now what?"

I raised the microphone and used the building's speaker system. Although I was still in the trailer, I could hear my voice echo in the huge room. "Turn left and walk to the end of the shelves. You should see a little sign that says 'Westside.'"

Lorcan followed my instructions, dragging Emily with him. As they reached the beginning of an aisle, I heard Sean's voice coming from my headset. "The two men are getting out of the truck. The

Asian is carrying a handgun and a crowbar. The guy with the beard has a rifle with an ammunition clip."

I switched the microphone back on. If I made the trade fast enough, Emily and I could get out the back entrance.

"I'm watching you, Lorcan. Walk down Westside Avenue to the aisle labeled 'Sixth Street.' You'll see washing machines and golf carts."

Lorcan moved slowly, stopping at the end of each row. At Second Street, his right hand briefly slipped inside his jacket, but he didn't pull out a weapon.

"The two men are circling the building," Sean said. "But they're not going inside."

On the monitor screen, Lorcan kept pulling Emily forward. Fourth Street. Fifth Street. At Sixth Street, he paused and glanced over his shoulder.

"I'm still watching you," I said. "Now walk to the middle of the aisle and stop."

Lorcan pushed Emily in front of him and she shuffled forward. He followed after her, a few steps back, then reached out and grabbed her hair. Muttering something, he forced her to his knees, stood over her body, and shouted, "All right! We're here!"

"They've reached the building's circuit box," Sean said. "The man with the crowbar is forcing it open."

A few seconds later, the lights at the front of the building went out, and then the lights on Eastside Avenue. Sector by sector, the building was absorbed by darkness. At the last moment, Lorcan thrust his hand into the shoulder bag and grabbed some night-vision goggles. He pulled on the headgear, and then flipped the goggles down over his eyes.

Outside the building, the final set of circuit breakers were pushed down. The monitors went dead, and the lights were shut off. Now Lorcan could see—and I was blind.

"Can you hear me, Underwood? I know you can hear me!"

I stepped into the trailer's open doorway. "Yes. I hear you."

"I got the razor with me! You remember *that*, don't you? In ten seconds I'm going to start cutting Emily . . . unless you come here and face me!"

"What's going on?" Sean's voice was coming from my headset. "What's—"

I switched off the phone and tried to focus on the problem. At the training camp I had used the night-vision goggles in a variety of settings. The equipment allowed you to see in the dark—with a few crucial limitations. Feeling my way around the trailer, I found what I was looking for in Sean's toolbox, and then stumbled out of the trailer.

"One, two, three . . ."

"I'm coming, Lorcan."

"Four, five, six . . ."

Moving slowly in the dark room, I touched the shelves with my hand until I reached Seventh Street. "Almost there!" I shouted.

"Seven, eight, nine . . ."

I lit a butane lighter and held the flame beneath the tip of a road flare. A spark. And then a burst of white flame appeared in my left hand. I drew the nine-millimeter automatic with my right hand and ran down Sixth Street. The night-vision goggles couldn't process the burst of light and Lorcan was blinded for an instant. He reached up and tried to rip off the headgear, but I raised my weapon and shot him twice in the head.

Lorcan collapsed onto Emily, but she screamed and pushed the body to the floor. I dropped the flare and it continued burning as I helped her stand up. "Two men are still outside," I said. "Where's the key to the handcuffs?"

"Inside his jacket."

I knelt down and rolled Lorcan onto his back. The goggles were destroyed—shattered by one of the bullets. Trying not to get blood on my hands, I found the key and unlocked the cuffs. Then I guided Emily to the end of the aisle. "Sean is up on the roof. Climb the stairs and join him."

"Jake, be careful. Please . . ." She almost touched me, then pulled her hand back and began climbing the stairs.

Light continued to sputter from the flare next to Lorcan's body as I headed toward the front of the building. Were the men still outside? Did I need to walk out and find them? I heard voices and stepped back into the shadows as Koji and the bearded man appeared on the loading dock. The bearded man carried an assault rifle and he moved like a soldier—stopping, crouching, and looking for cover. He entered the building and went right. Koji went left, holding his automatic pistol with two hands.

I waited until the bearded man got closer, and then stepped out and fired—hitting him in the chest. Then I pivoted and ran down the aisle to Westside Avenue.

Stop. Wait. I peered around a discarded water heater and saw Koji pointing his weapon at my previous position. A laser was attached to the barrel of his automatic and the little red dot of light glided across the shelves.

In some corner of his mind, Koji was calculating the probabilities of his situation. Lorcan and the other enforcer were dead. He was alone and a man with a gun was hunting him. The laser dot began to tremble like a Spark inside a Shell. Then fear washed over Koji like a wave and he sprinted toward the exit.

I stepped out into the aisle and raised the automatic as if I was pointing my finger to emphasize a statement. The gun's firing pin struck a cartridge and the primer exploded, igniting the propellant and releasing a burst of gas that forced a bullet out of a barrel etched with spiraling grooves. This small chunk of metal flew through space like a small, precise machine until it hit Koji in the back. At that instant, the clean geometry of its movement was transformed by flesh as the bullet cut and tumbled and destroyed a human body.

28

grabbed Koji by his ankles and dragged him into the darkness, then I went back to get the other body. The bearded man was much heavier. His mouth moved as if he was talking while his head bumped across the floor. Now the two empty Shells lay next to each other like an old married couple with their eyes open and their arms touching.

I stepped away from them and switched on the phone. "It's safe now," I told Sean. "Come downstairs."

"What about the other two men?"

"They're dead. Everyone's dead."

The road flare was still burning when I returned to Lorcan. It looked as if his Spark was glowing and sputtering on the dirty floor. I leaned over the golf cart, opened up the compartment near the hula girl, and retrieved the flash drive.

It sounded like two people were tapping on a drum as Emily and Sean climbed down the metal staircase. When I returned to the entrance, I found them staring at the smeared lines of blood that disappeared down Westside Avenue.

"Where are the bodies?" Sean asked.

"They're on a side aisle, so they won't be visible from the loading dock."

Emily approached me. "What happens now?"

"It depends on what you plan to do with this. . . ." I held up the flash drive. "If you release this information, it will make a lot of powerful people angry. If you want to be safe, throw the secret away."

"I'm not throwing anything away." Emily took the flash drive and stuffed it into her pocket. "A lot of people died because Alexander Serby had a conversation with Danny Marchand. I'll send this out to a hundred different Web sites. People need to know what really happened."

"They won't believe you," Sean said. "They'll say that the bank transactions were faked and the video was created on a computer."

Emily spun around. "You put the truth out there. That's all you can do. The truth can't be destroyed. It might be ignored or hidden, but it's still there."

"Underwood is right. They'll try to kill us."

"I've made my decision, Sean."

"You've got a couple of days before they'll start looking for you," I said. "Try to get across the border to Canada, then fly to another country."

"Can we take the car?" Sean asked.

"Forget about cars. It's easy to track an object like that."

Emily nodded. "Go to the trailer and get my knapsack with the getaway gear. Hurry up. Maybe someone heard the gunshots."

Sean grabbed a flashlight from a shelf near the door. He hurried down the aisle to the trailer while Emily remained beside me. "And what about you, Jake? What are you going to do?"

"I'll figure out a plan."

"You could travel with us. Travel . . . with . . . me."

"That's not a good idea."

"We're connected, Jake. You saved my life. I know you hate to be touched, but . . ." She embraced me, her ear pressed against my chest as if she was searching for a heartbeat. I was frozen—my arms extended like a cross—then I brought my hands together and felt her body against mine.

The trailer door slammed and we heard Sean's voice. "I got the bag!"

Emily stepped away and began talking quickly. "You hide, too. Go someplace where they can't find you. When you're safe, try to contact me. I'll leave messages for you on the Dice Night bulletin board. My screen name is 'Willow.' Don't forget."

Sean reappeared, carrying a knapsack that probably contained money and fake ID cards. "Okay . . . let's go."

"Jake saved my life, Sean. He saved your life, too."

Sean turned toward me, but didn't look into my eyes. "Thanks. Take care of yourself."

He grabbed Emily's arm and they passed through the entrance together. I wanted to speak to her, but said nothing. I wanted to follow her, but didn't move. Instead, I just stood in the middle of the empty building and considered probabilities. Miss Holquist would hunt them down and kill Emily unless I changed the certainty of that equation.

.   .   .

Over on Westside Avenue, one of the dead men made a chiming sound. A few seconds later, the other corpse beeped and then Lorcan's body rang several times. I returned to Lorcan's body, searched through his jacket, and found his phone. Miss Holquist had called him, and then sent a text message:

    // What happened? Report—

Within my mind, I saw her staring at a computer screen, waiting for an answer. Using Lorcan's phone, I typed a reply.

    // The presentation went well. All three problems have been
       solved. I have reclaimed the lost information.
       Where are you?
       Lorcan

The flare had gone out, and the only light in the building came from the dead man's phone glowing in my hand. Then—

// Good work! I'm at 240 West 38 Street. 3rd floor. Come immediately with flash drive.

I left the U-Find-It building, got into Sean's car, and told Laura
to guide me to a parking lot in Midtown Manhattan. During the last
few days I had made hundreds of decisions and my Spark felt tired
and passive. It was a pleasant sensation to obey Laura like a simple
machine.

"Stay in the right lane," she told me as I guided the car up a ramp
to the Brooklyn Bridge. A dozen growlers were up on the pedestrian
walkway waving protest signs about something, and the traffic was
crawling forward.

I drove a few yards, then stopped and glanced up at my rearview
mirror. The man in the car behind me was also alone, but he looked
like he was talking to someone. It was impossible to know if he was
having a conversation with a human or a Shadow. Did it make any
difference? I wasn't sure. The silence around me had a cold blue
color and I wanted to hear a voice.

"Laura?"

"Yes, sir."

"Sing a song."

"I'm sorry, Mr. Underwood. But I didn't hear you clearly."

"You're the upgraded program, right? I want you to sing a song.
I'm sure that's one of your capabilities."

"What is the name of the song?"

"You pick one."

"What kind of song? Happy? Sad?"

"Sad."

"In English?"

"Yes. I want you to search your database and find a twentieth-
century song in English that online sources agree is sad."

I waited for several minutes, but Laura stayed quiet. She was
always immediate and efficient, and I wondered if I had just caused
a program malfunction.

"I have evaluated all the data, sir, and have created a vector with
the relevant coordinate components. With your permission, I will

sing an English language song that rated ninety-seven-point-two 'sad' on a scale of one hundred."

The tanker truck in front of me stopped again. Now I was frozen in the middle of the bridge. "Go ahead."

And Laura began to sing. It was still her voice—her clear, precise voice—but she emphasized certain words and paused at the end of each line. The song was about an Irishman who had left his country and traveled to London to find work. He was drawn to the bright lights and grand buildings of the city, but remembered his village and a young woman he once loved. Now his village had been abandoned—the walls collapsed, the fields dotted with crows. And the woman was missing or dead. All he really knew was that his past life had vanished and he could never return home.

At first, my Spark asked questions: Why didn't the singer contact the woman's family? Why couldn't he return home and rebuild the village? But when Laura began singing the song a second time, my thoughts broke free from their cage and floated away with the words.

"Should I sing the song again?" Laura asked.

"No. That's enough."

"Did I fulfill your request correctly, Mr. Underwood?"

"Yes, you did."

The traffic started moving, and I followed the traffic down an exit ramp. "We've crossed the bridge," Laura said. "Turn right on Centre Street and continue north to Lafayette."

She guided me uptown to a parking lot on West Forty-Sixth Street near Ninth Avenue. I left the key with the lot attendant and walked over to Times Square. The Broadway theaters had released their audiences and the pedestrian plaza was filled with people watching the nightly hologram show. Glowing three-dimensional figures emerged from a billboard and floated about the crowd like a collective fantasy. A hologram pirate ship sailed across the sky firing its cannon, followed by a speeding freight train and a red balloon with a basket holding Mickey Mouse. A little girl dressed up in armor stood in the air, swung a sword, and killed a fire-breathing dragon.

The tourists laughed and smiled and pointed at each hologram as I threaded my way through the crowd. I smelled hot dogs simmering in a pushcart caldron while I focused on each fragment of reality: a crushed paper cup, a cop's holstered gun, a young man selling roses held within plastic tubes.

Miss Holquist liked to rent empty office spaces in modern steel-and-glass buildings, but 240 West Thirty-Eighth Street turned out to be a shabby brick building with scuff marks on the checkerboard floor in the lobby. I stood alone, next to the elevators, and tried to figure out a plan. Then the glass doors opened with a whoosh of cold air and two couples entered laughing and chattering in Spanish. The women wore high-heeled shoes with ankle straps and tight party dresses made of shimmery cloth. The men wore loose slacks and sports coats without neckties.

The elevator doors opened. An elderly maintenance man wearing overalls waved us forward and I was swept along with the group. *"Cinco,"* said one of the women, and the elevator creaked and shivered up to the fifth floor. I stepped out with them and followed them down the hallway to a door marked BIG APPLE DANCE — STUDIOS FOR RENT. The two couples went over to a plump woman at the reception desk. She offered them a clipboard while I disappeared down a hallway.

A door was open and I saw four couples dancing a 1930s jitterbug. One of the couples stood back to back, then they locked arms and the man flipped the woman over his head. The swing music surrounded me for an instant, but I stepped back from the doorway and continued moving. Styles of music from the different rental studios—a waltz and a tango, a Broadway show tune and a salsa number—blended together into one rhythm.

An exit door was at the end of the hallway and it led to the emergency staircase. I checked both my handguns, and then hurried downstairs to the third floor. Silence. No one was dancing there. I pushed open the door, stepped into the hallway, and found the young man with the curly hair who had helped Lorcan kill the people at Slater's compound. He was sitting on a folding chair, munching a takeout sandwich. As the door behind me squeaked shut, he stared at me with a chunk of food still in his mouth.

"Have you been looking for me?" I asked, then drew my automatic and fired at the target. At close range, the bullet acted like a fist, knocking him off the chair. He died still clutching the sandwich—as if a wad of cold cuts in a French roll proved that he was still alive.

With the automatic in my right hand, I yanked open a door and stepped into a long, empty room. Fiber-optic cables slithered out of holes in a red carpet. More cables hung down from the ceiling as if the roots of a forest were growing on an upper floor.

Miss Holquist sat at a folding card table with her portfolio bag, a computer, and a Styrofoam bowl containing a dinner salad. She saw the gun in my hand and decided to ignore it.

"Good evening, Mr. Underwood. I didn't expect to see you again."

"Lorcan's dead. Everyone's dead."

"And the girl?"

"Alive."

Picking up a paper napkin, Miss Holquist wiped a spot of salad dressing off her upper lip. "It's quite remarkable that you neutralized the four people who were trying to kill you, but I shouldn't be surprised. You're my best employee, Jacob. I knew from the start that you were perfect for this kind of work."

"Were you the person who hired Danny Marchand? Was he just another employee?"

"Of course not. I didn't know the real story about the Day of Rage until the night we met Alex Serby at his office. I must admit . . . it was a brilliant plan. Only a handful of people know the truth."

"Serby killed those children."

"Don't be ridiculous. He didn't *specifically* know what was going to happen. Five years ago, our social fabric was being ripped apart and those in charge realized that we needed some sort of incident to justify the necessary changes. One of Alex's British friends told him about Danny Marchand . . . an intense young man who was upset because the Luddites had burned down a robotics research center in Frankfurt. Marchand believed that history was propelling us toward some all-knowing God computer and that anyone who opposed this idea was a lower form of life. The two of them met for the first and last time on that boat trip. Alex gave Marchand some money and explained that the only way we could guarantee the right sort of future is if we took control of the present situation. Then they went their separate ways. Alex wired more money, but didn't hear from Marchand. He was as surprised as the rest of us when the bombs started going off."

"All those people died."

"The loss of a relatively small number of people created a large benefit. Civilization is based on an ordered society. I'm sure you agree with that statement, Jacob. You like order and stability."

"There's nothing stable about my existence."

"Well, you're wrong about that." Miss Holquist waved her plastic fork. "You've been tracked and monitored ever since we learned about you. Three years ago, Morris Noland saw those computer drawings you created and called me when I was in Europe. We both thought you might be a good enforcer, so I paid for your ticket to California and your stay at the Ettinger Clinic. Noland has done that before, of course . . . sent me other job candidates. But from the start I knew you were special."

"Dr. Noland works for you?"

"It's not his main job, of course, but I pay for his vacations. Noland cleaned you up, strapped a shock bracelet on your ankle, and showed you how to function. Then we flew you back to New York and I sent you the letter."

I knew that she was telling the truth, and that made me feel weak and foolish. I began to move around the room.

"You and I are connected . . ." Miss Holquist said. "Don't you realize that? I wouldn't say that we're friends, but I've guided you ever since the motorcycle accident. I *care* about you, Jacob. I really do. And because of that, I'm going to offer you a very generous proposal. The coded files still haven't been released. Track down the girl. You probably know where she is or how to find her. If you do that, all will be forgiven. You can go back to your loft, consume your nutritional drink, and walk freely across the Brooklyn Bridge. If you want to keep working for me . . . you can. But it's not necessary."

"And if I find Emily, I'm supposed to kill her?"

"Well, of course. That's your task and my responsibility."

"No. I'm not going to obey you anymore."

I reached the wall and turned around as Miss Holquist pulled a handgun from her bag. As I raised my own weapon, she fired from a sitting position. The bullet struck the side of my left leg and I collapsed immediately. Lying flat on my back, I was conscious of my mouth opening slowly, and then I took in a breath and shifted my body around. It felt as if a fire was burning within my Shell.

Miss Holquist got up from the card table, crossed the room, and kicked the gun out of my hand. "I wasn't lying, Jacob. That really was a valid offer. Too bad you didn't accept it. I had to pick the second option."

I wanted to speak. Couldn't speak. Wanted to stand up. Couldn't do that either. The wounded leg was twisted sideways.

"You'll never find Emily."

"Of course I will. No one really disappears these days. You can pretend to escape, but the EYE system will find you . . . eventually."

The phone lying on the desk beeped and Miss Holquist's Shadow called to her, "Phone call from London."

Distracted, she turned her head and glared at the phone. "Damn. It's three o'clock in the morning there and—"

Pulling up my pants cuff, I grabbed the revolver from the ankle holster and fired twice—hitting her in the stomach and pelvis. Miss Holquist fell backward and stopped moving.

It took several minutes to roll over on my side. My arms and shoulders were functional, and I could crawl forward if I kept the weight on my right knee. When I approached Miss Holquist, I realized that she was still alive. Blood drooled out of her mouth, but she clenched her jaw as if she wanted to hold life inside her body.

"What . . . about . . . my girls?" Her voice came from a distant place.

The gray drugs had made her ageless, but now their power was melting away. As the hidden years returned, her flesh sagged, wrinkles appeared, and her body grew small and frail—like an old woman's. Then her eyes opened wide, her eyeballs turned to glass, and she stopped moving.

I stared down at her for a long time—not quite believing she was dead—then forced myself to crawl across the room. Construction workers had left a pile of steel brackets that once held air-conditioning ducts. I picked up one of them and used it like a crutch to support my shattered leg. My pants were sodden with blood and I knew that this would draw attention from the police, but I found Miss Holquist's black wool coat on the back of a chair and forced my arms into the sleeves. Then I pushed open a door and found myself on the emergency staircase.

I had experienced pain in the hospital, but it didn't touch the core within me. Pain was like a noise in the distance—like the dance music coming from the fifth floor.

But now I could feel the pain directly and it almost overpowered my Spark. Each step downward was an effort, and a groaning sound came out of my throat. When I reached the first-floor landing, I looked up and saw blood smeared on each step.

An alarm went off when I pushed open a fire door and limped down an alleyway to the street. By now the pain was so powerful, so overwhelming, that I could float on top of it—like a leaf being swept downstream. My improvised crutch clicked on the pavement as I limped and shuffled through Times Square. No one stopped me or said anything until I reached the parking lot on Forty-Sixth Street.

"You okay?" asked the parking attendant. "You want me to call an ambulance or something?"

I handed him a wad of money and turned away. "I fell down. That's all. I'm going to see a doctor."

It felt good to be sitting in the car. Clutching the steering wheel with one hand, I started the engine and drove out of the lot. When I turned onto Eighth Avenue, I activated my phone and tossed it onto the passenger seat.

"Can you hear me, Laura?"

"Yes, sir."

"Where am I?"

"In Manhattan, sir. We're traveling north on Eighth Avenue."

"Guide me to . . . to . . ."

Laura was the perfect traveling companion. She stayed silent and waited patiently. But I had no plan, no destination. Blood leaked out of me, trickled down my shattered leg, and formed a red slick on the floor of the car.

"Guide me to Marian Community Hospital in Walton, New York."

After the motorcycle accident, I had been brought to Marian Hospital, and they still had a file there attached to my past identity. Maybe a few of the nurses and doctors still remembered me as Jacob Davis.

"Drive to Ninety-Sixth Street and turn left," Laura said. "We're going to take the West Side Highway."

"Yes. That's a good plan."

I had died during my Transformation, but that was a different experience. Was I becoming a ghost? An angel? As I passed through Columbus Circle, I remembered what Monsieur Zéro had said about the angels blowing trumpets and waving swords on the Arc de Triomphe. True angels watched us and warned us and sang God's praises. They were disembodied minds unattached to our world.

.   .   .

I was driving, following the traffic around Columbus Circle and up Broadway, but it felt as if I was lying on a beach. Thoughts, like waves, washed over my body.

Remember the face of Sanjay Desai when the laser dot touched his skin. His brown eyes were solemn, not frightened, as he waited for me to make my decision.

Remember the dark gold scent from the incense burners in Saint-Sulpice. And the purple scent of the rotting flowers surrounding the coffin in St. Theodosius.

Remember the growlers smashing shopwindows on the Champs-Élysées, and the car alarms cutting the air like knives. We are not. We are not. Part of the machine.

Remember the warm, sweet taste of the chocolate served at the Vickerson factory.

Remember Emily embracing me and pressing her body against mine. And then her last look before she disappeared into the night.

I stopped at Eighty-Sixth Street. When I stared up at the red light, my Spark broke free from its prison and passed through the top of the car. Like an angel, I floated above the traffic and the concrete and those bits of life hurrying down the sidewalk.

I could have flown higher, circling the proud towers with an angel's cold purity, but my Shell saved me. As the light turned green I breathed in air and the Spark returned to my body. I was wounded and bleeding and lost and alone, but I finally wanted something—I wanted to live.

"Continue north," Laura whispered. "Continue north. . . ."

ACKNOWLEDGMENTS

I want to thank Jason Kaufman and Simon Lipskar for having faith in me.

The talented book designer Jason Booher transformed my scrawled drawings into illustrations. It was a pleasure to work with him.

I'm grateful to Glyn for his years of work on wespeakforfreedom .com. Many thanks to Ursula and Tony for their help and advice.

THE TRAVELER
Book One of the Fourth Realm Trilogy

In London, Maya, a young woman trained to fight by her powerful father, uses the latest technology to elude detection when walking past the thousands of surveillance cameras that watch the city. In New York, a secret shadow organization uses a victim's own GPS to hunt him down and kill him. In Los Angeles, Gabriel, a motorcycle messenger with a haunted past, takes pains to live "off the grid"—free of credit cards and government IDs. Welcome to the world of *The Traveler*—a world frighteningly like our own. In this compelling novel, Maya fights to save Gabriel, the only man who can stand against the forces that attempt to monitor and control society. From the back streets of Prague to the skyscrapers of Manhattan, *The Traveler* portrays an epic struggle between tyranny and freedom. Not since *1984* have readers witnessed a Big Brother so terrifying in its implications and in a story that so closely reflects our lives.

Fiction

THE DARK RIVER
Book Two of the Fourth Realm Trilogy

A fearless heroine. A tale of brother against brother. A battle for hope and freedom. Two brothers born into a race of Travelers—prophets able to journey to different realms of consciousness—have just discovered that their long-lost father may still be alive. Gabriel, who could be humanity's savior, and his guardian, Maya, want to protect him. Michael wants to destroy him and with him humanity's hope for freedom. As they race across the globe, their frantic search puts them on a collision course, and the fate of the world hangs in the balance.

Fiction

THE GOLDEN CITY

Book Three of the Fourth Realm Trilogy

A world that exists in the shadow of our own . . . the thrilling conclusion to the Fourth Realm trilogy, *The Golden City* is packed with the knife-edge tension, intriguing characters, and startling plot twists that made *The Traveler* and *The Dark River* international hits. Struggling to protect the legacy of his Traveler father, Gabriel faces troubling new questions and relentless threats. His brother, Michael, now firmly allied with the enemy, pursues his ambition to wrest power from Nathan Boone, the calculating leader of the Brethren. And Maya, the Harlequin warrior pledged to protect Gabriel at all costs, is forced to make a choice that will change her life forever. *The Golden City* is a riveting blend of high-tech thriller and fast-paced adventure, sure to delight Twelve Hawks's fans and new readers alike.

Fiction